ONE-WAY TICKET TO HELL!

Willard-Smith's whole universe was the diving ME 109 in a head-on pass, growing in his windscreen with frightening speed. He hunched forward, caressing the red button. But suddenly, either in a panic or experiencing a loss of control, the enemy pilot did the worst possible thing. He pulled back on the stick.

Shouting in triumph, Willard-Smith saw the entire Messerschmitt exposed like the belly of a trout ripe for gutting. "Here's your ticket to Mecca, or Valhalla, or wherever you're going." he muttered as he squeezed the button. At zero deflection and at close range, the sledgehammer blows of the big shells blasted chunks of aluminum into the slipstream, exposing stringers, frames, and cables.

The mortally wounded fighter shot skyward and then, as it paused in a stall, a figure plummeted from the cockpit. But the panicked pilot had jumped too soon. His parachute tangled in the remains of the tail, and as the ME streaked downward in its final dive, a waving, screaming figure trailed behind it.

"Enjoy it all the way down, you bloody bastard," Willard-Smith murmured.

TRIAL OF THE SEVENTH CARRIER

PETER ALBANO

ZEBRA BOOKS
KENSINGTON PUBLISHING CORP.

ZEBRA BOOKS

are published by

Kensington Publishing Corp.
475 Park Avenue South
New York, NY 10016

First printing: November, 1990

Printed in the United States of America

DEDICATION

For Angie Dante and Josephine Clark, who nurtured their trying little brother through the barren years. With infinite patience and enduring love, they taught him the value of compassion and understanding.

ACKNOWLEDGMENTS

The author gratefully acknowledges:

Master Mariner Donald Brandmeyer, for his generous help with the problems encountered by warships both in port and at sea;

William D. Wilkerson and Dennis D. Silver, for their advice on the characteristics of aircraft in all aspects of flight, especially in the stress of combat;

Kevin Eldridge and John Maloney, of the Planes of Fame Museum in Chino, California, who contributed invaluable information about the Rolls Royce Merlin engine and the Zero fighter;

John McCoy, of the Museum of Flying in Santa Monica, California, for offering his expertise on the Spitfire fighter;

Harvey Gray and Dave Cannalte, of the USS *Bowfin* Memorial, Pearl Harbor, Hawaii, for answering questions about the World War II fleet boat;

Mary Annis, my wife, for her infinite patience and careful reading of the manuscript; and

Robert K. Rosencrance, for lending his technical and editorial skills in the preparation of the manuscript. I am also indebted to Mr. Rosencrance for his thoughtful suggestions concerning plot and character development.

Chapter One

A slight pressure on the stick dropped the right wing of the Mitsubishi A6M2 Zero-sen, and Air Group Commander Yoshi Matsuhara stared down over his wing tip. From three thousand meters, the western Pacific was as serene and as placid as its name would imply. Here and there an occasional whitecap flecked the infinite blue with white streaks like random threads left by a careless seamstress. Fortunately, the sea was comparatively calm, easy to read when not obscured by the low-scudding clouds. However, beneath the commander and close to the water, clouds like white vaporous cotton balls paraded, casting their flat, dark shadows on the sea and blending in the distance into a solid carpet. On the northern horizon thunderheads soared arrogantly into the heavens, solid white mountaintops in the brilliant sunlight, their slopes convoluted with gray chasms and black crevices. Beneath them, solid shafts of rain screened down like curtains at a *Kabuki* theater. It was a stagy, arty scene, almost unnatural in its beauty. But Commander Yoshi Matsuhara saw no beauty, only obstructions and hindrances to his mission. Cursing, he called on the sun goddess Amaterasu o-Mi-Kami to clear the skies and help him in his search for the American submarine *Blackfin* and his friend Lieutenant Brent Ross before Colonel Moammar Kadafi's Arabs found them.

Brent Ross, the young American giant, his constant companion for the past five years, temporarily assigned to *Blackfin*, a fighter and philosopher so imbued with the spirit of *bushido* the world's news media referred to him as the "American samurai." But Amaterasu had deserted them both this day.

Searching between the clouds Matsuhara found an empty sea mocking him and cursed the gods who refused to cooperate and allow him a glimpse of *Blackfin*. The tough little sub had stalked an Arab force of two carriers, a pair of cruisers, and at least a dozen destroyers. The carriers had been the principal threat, the primary prey. The first was an old British *Majestic* class purchased from India and given the Arab name *Gefara*. The second was a new ship, the former *Principe de Asturias*, bought from Spain and renamed *Ramli al Kabir*. After *Blackfin* sank *Gefara* off Tomonuto Atoll, the enemy task force commander, lacking the stomach to engage the great carrier *Yonaga* with only one capital ship, had turned his fleet south and headed back for Tomonuto in the western Carolines or the Arab base in Surabaya in Indonesia. In any event, the enemy force had disappeared.

Blackfin's single transmission by BRT-1—a delayed transmission by a buoy left in her wake—reported heavy damage by depth charge attack. Unable to submerge, she was steaming on the surface on a northerly heading which would take her to Japan and also within easy range of Arab bases on Saipan and Tinian in the Marianas Islands. She had not been heard from in over twenty hours. Either her radios were damaged or she was maintaining radio silence. In any event, as vulnerable as she was, complete electronic shutdown was a wise decision.

Reports indicated the enemy was hunting *Blackfin*. Observers on Aguijan, a small, impregnable citadel-like island four miles south of Tinian, had reported unusual activity. At least one staffel (12 aircraft) of enemy Messerschmitt 109 fighters and "numerous" Junkers 87 Stuka dive bombers had taken off just an hour before. No doubt maddened by *Blackfin*'s destruction of their carrier, they were hunting the submarine, too. The submarine would be easy to spot if it were not for the clouds. He must find her first.

Anxiously, the commander looked for the white telltale scar of a wake, but he saw nothing, nothing at all. He was tempted to drop lower, beneath the clouds, but didn't dare. A blood-red machine had been reported as the leader of the enemy fighters. The American renegade *Oberstleutnant* (Squadron Leader) Kenneth Rosencrance flew the only red fighter in Kadafi's air force. This meant Rosencrance's *Vierter Jagerstaffel* (Fourth Fighter Squadron) was the squadron sighted by the observers on Aguijan. He knew Rosencrance and his mercenaries would fly high above the squadrons of JU 87s which were hunting *Blackfin*. The experienced fighter pilot with 22 kills, Rosencrance always sought the advantage of altitude. He would have it this day.

Matsuhara damned the clouds again. If he were attacked, he would need every meter of altitude. Actually, he was far too low now to engage Messerschmitts. Never give an ME the advantage of altitude, it could outdive anything. He pounded his padded combing in frustration.

He stabbed a finger for the twentieth time onto the chart attached to the plotting board strapped to his leg. *Blackfin*'s last position was reported at twelve degrees north, one hundred fifty-one degrees, thirty minutes east. According to his DR (dead reckoning) track, he had just passed to the north of the large red X he had marked on his chart in carrier *Yonaga*'s briefing room when he and his two wingmen had been given the latest information on the sub's position.

His wingmen. What insanity: two Englishmen flying

Seafires. He was a mallard with two albatroses dragging it down by the rudders. But ancient Admiral Fujita had insisted. Must be a sign of senility. The old admiral was over a hundred years old and still commanded with a will like the finely tempered and carefully drawn steel of Yoshi's killing blade. But his judgment was sometimes suspect, and in this case, irrational. "These are two of England's finest," the old man had insisted from his desk in *Yonaga*'s Flag Country. "The first she has sent us. There are more to come. They need experience—your expertise. Imbue them with the *Yamato damashii* (Japanese spirit) of a samurai and fearless warrior for our new emperor." And then he had added, using the honorific fourth level of speech reserved for the Mikado, "And remember, always, Emperor Akihito has proclaimed his rule as the age of *Heisei*."

"*Yamato damashii*," Matsuhara snorted to himself. These Englishmen were so phlegmatic and unperturbable he wondered how they could arouse themselves enough to "pillow" a woman. Without a doubt, the Englishwoman was the most bored female on earth. And Admiral Fujita had mentioned the age of *Heisei*—the age of "attaining peace." Yoshi laughed bitterly. "What peace?" he asked himself. With oil two hundred dollars a barrel and the Arabs buying up warships in wholesale lots, rebuilding old World War II aircraft and receiving new models from Germany, who was attaining peace? The commander laughed again. With an effort he calmed himself as a new concern entered his mind.

Straining at his six-point military harness, the flight leader twisted uncomfortably and glanced over his right elevator. He winced as he saw the Seafire F47 bounce and weave, obviously controlled by the hand of a pilot not yet totally at home with his aircraft. Pilot Officer Elwyn York, a thirty-one-year-old Cockney from London's East End, was at the controls.

Born just off Petticoat Lane in a grime-coated tenement, York proudly claimed true Cockney antecedents. When he first met the man, the Cockney had explained, "Because me Mum dropped me where you could 'ear the bells of Saint Mary-le-Bow. Them's the only Cockneys—borned that close to the ol' church."

To Yoshi, Elwyn York was an odd one indeed. Although in the old tradition of the Imperial Navy, English was the language of *Yonaga* and Matsuhara was at home with the language, he had difficulty understanding the Britisher's thick Cockney accent. Short and compact, York had a broad neck, barrel chest, and muscular arms that gave the impression of toughness, like a block of stone. Everything about him was dark—black, unruly hair that valanced over his ears and covered his forehead almost to his eyebrows, eyes the color of burned oak, skin tanned and seared by too many years in the sun. And, indeed, he had spent five years in Africa, he claimed, flying as a bush pilot. Proudly, he boasted of years at the controls of old Douglas DC-3s, Cessnas, De Havilland Caribous and Otters, Constellations, and many more. He claimed thousands of hours, flying runs in South Africa, Botswana, Rhodesia, Mozambique, Zambia, Angola, and most of the emerging nations of the continent. Yoshi suspected the experience had been military, probably bomb and supply runs for the highest bidder and not the innocuous freight and passenger flights York claimed. He had also suspected the cooling wave of *Glasnost* had put men like York out of work. His nature would take him to the hottest war, and none wad hotter than the conflict between the Arabs and the Israelis and their allies, Japan. Yet there must be some altruism in the man. Without a doubt, the Cockney had a hatred for the Arabs. If not, if he wanted a war, he could have joined Kadafi's killers for a million a year and fifty-thousand for each kill. He would only make pilot officer's pay flying for *Yonaga*.

Although Pilot Officer Elwyn York was an excellent

multi-engine pilot, he had never flown a single-engined piston fighter and had only twenty-three hours at the controls of a Seafire. He had a shocking lack of regard for authority, and his radio discipline was appalling. Matsuhara's biggest problem with York would be to keep the Cockney alive long enough to make a competent fighter pilot of him. There was an excellent chance the Englishman would kill himself long before Rosencrance and his veterans got the opportunity to dispatch him. Or perhaps he would adapt fast enough in combat to survive on his own. Some men did.

The Japanese pilot's eyes wandered over the English fighter. Adapted from its land-based variant, the Spitfire F.24, the Seafire's long, elliptical wings folded to fit carrier *Yonaga*'s nine-meter elevators. It was fitted with slinging points and a retractable arrester hook and an additional internal fuselage tank, augmented by a flush-fitting tank beneath the center fuselage and two more underwing blister tanks. The additional tankage gave the fighter a respectable range of over sixteen hundred kilometers. Overall, the British fighter was a beautiful, graceful bird; needle-nosed propeller boss, rounded hood housing its new 2550 horsepower Rolls Royce Griffon 88 engine, short bubble canopy flaring smartly into its vertical tail fin, rounded fuselage. In all, it presented a view of an aerodynamically clean aircraft with the lethal punch of four short-barreled Hispano-Suiza twenty-millimeter cannons in its wings.

Except for its black propeller boss, the Seafire was painted white, like all of *Yonaga*'s fighters, with Japanese markings on its wings and fuselage. In the tradition of the old Imperial Navy, a blue band just behind the canopy identified it as a member of *Koku Kantai* (First Air Fleet) while slightly aft of the blue band a single green stripe indicated it belonged to *Yonaga*'s air groups. The usual three-digit number on the tail identified the mission of the aircraft and the aircraft itself. It was an

12

imposing, deadly appearing machine, the consummate example of Britain's finest efforts in World War II fighter design.

But Yoshi would not trade it — or any aircraft, for that matter — for his Mitsubishi Zero-sen. With the orbiting of the Chinese deuterium-fluorine particle-beam system of twenty weapons platforms at 930 miles and three command modules in geosynchronous orbit at 22,300 miles, the age of rockets and jets had come to a flaming, shattering end in a millisecond in 1983. Now the reciprocating engine reigned supreme and the Zero had emerged as the finest of all the old resurrected World War II fighters. The Messerschmitt Bf 109 of Kadafi's air force had been a tough, redoubtable enemy, but still, *nothing* could dogfight a Zero.

Commander Yoshi Matsuhara glanced to his left. He smiled, finding a well-piloted Seafire maintaining its station precisely as if attached to the Zero's left rudder by an umbilical cord. Captain Colin Willard-Smith, thirty-four-years-old, a sixteen-year veteran of the Royal Navy, and one of the most natural pilots Yoshi had ever seen. Willard-Smith was a natural in the sense he had the innate knack of fitting his aircraft so perfectly he broke through the barrier separating man from machine and the fighter seemed to become an extension of the man himself. He knew how to push his fighter to its limit of power and acrobatics, yet never to the point of compromising control when the aircraft inevitably fought back with mushy stick and hard, balky rudder pedals and fearful vibrations. His reactions were instinctive, reflexes like lightning, a dead shot and, Yoshi suspected, an unemotional, merciless killer. In fact, Yoshi had heard the captain had three kills of Argentinian aircraft during that strange war in the Falklands in 1982. Yes, indeed, Captain Colin Willard-Smith was a welcome addition.

Captain Colin Willard-Smith eyed Commander Yoshi Matsuhara's Zero and moved his rudder pedals and control column without conscious thought, maintaining his station off the flight leader's elevator despite the light Japanese fighter's tendency to react to the wind and thermals like a feather while the Seafire, which was fifteen hundred pounds heavier, tended to plow through the invisible drifts and barriers. Tall and slender, with sandy hair and the large nose of an Anglo-Saxon aristocrat, Willard-Smith felt bulky in his fur-lined flight suit that covered his body from boots to chin. His goggles were up, his oxygen mask unsnapped and pushed to one side but still close enough so that he could speak easily into his microphone. Because pure oxygen made his throat feel raw and sore, he used his mask only when altitude gave him no choice. He disliked the goggles, too. They interfered with his peripheral vision, and without radar, only a man's eyes stood between him and a quick death.

They were within range of the Libyan bases in the Marianas, and the thought made him squirm uneasily. At a low altitude, they would be at a terrible disadvantage if spotted by a high-flying Arab patrol. "Beware of the Hun in the sun," English pilots had told themselves through two wars. The adage still remained like a genetic legacy.

Restlessly, Colin Willard-Smith moved his eyes in the quick, jerky movements of the experienced fighter pilot, side to side and then overhead, never allowing the sun or cloud formations to distract him or interrupt the rhythm of his search. He had learned long ago to depend on his peripheral vision to detect flyspecks that could develop wings and sprout machine guns and blast the unwary pilot from the sky in seconds. For some strange optical reason it was possible to spot objects as small as needle points with a quick side glance while simply staring at the same area revealed nothing at all. His neck felt stiff from the cold and continuous movement and he rubbed it briskly with a gloved palm without interrupting his search. He and Pilot Officer York were responsible for Commander Matsuhara's cover while the flight leader searched for the submarine *Blackfin*. A momentary lapse, a fleeting moment of carelessness, and they could all be dead.

He chuckled as he thought of the insane set of circumstances that had brought him to the western Pacific as a member of carrier *Yonaga*'s air groups. The son of a barrister from Barmston in Humberside, Colin Willard-Smith had joined the Royal Navy at eighteen. By age twenty-one, he had become an experienced Sea Harrier pilot. Despite the unreliable Ferranti Blue Fox multi-mode radar and armed with only two Sidewinder AIM 9L missiles, Willard-Smith grew fond of the V/STOL (vertical short takeoff and landing) Sea Harrier. It could use almost any platform to take off and land. The 21,500-pound thrust of its Rolls Royce Pegasus engine gave it a top speed of Mach 1.2, and it responded to the controls like a thoroughbred. It was capable of matching aerobatics with the best and could carry two Aden thirty-millimeter guns in wing pods in addition to the two Sidewinders.

Loaded on board the carrier *Illustrious* in May 1982 with 27 other Sea Harriers, Captain Colin Willard-Smith had piloted his fighter in the British assault on the Falkland Islands. Here he accounted for three Argentinian aircraft, a Super Etendard off Port Stanley, and two Skyhawks over Falkland Sound. But it had been a miserable little war that accomplished little and cost the Royal Navy six fine ships: *Sheffield, Ardent, Antelope, Coventry, Atlantic Conveyor,* and *Sir Galahad*. Most were easy meat for Exocet missiles. Hundreds of fine young Englishmen died, including four of his best friends who were killed when their Sea Harriers were shot down.

He would never forget 1983 and the two events that shocked and changed the world, perhaps forever. First, the impossible saga of the seventh carrier—carrier *Yonaga*. Designated as the flagship for the seven-carrier Pearl Harbor strike force in 1941, the one-thousand-foot warship had been frozen-in in a secret cove on Siberia's Chukchi Peninsula two months before the attack. Breaking free after forty-two years of icy entrapment, the great carrier, manned by aging, maddened samurai led by the indomitable Admiral Fujita, had stormed south from the Bering Sea and destroyed the carrier *Peleliu* and sunk the battleship *New Jersey* in Pearl Harbor. Then the return to Japan and the crew learned the impossible had happened: Japan had surrendered nearly four decades before.

Then the second cataclysmic event occurred the day *Yonaga* anchored in Tokyo Bay. Captain Colin Willard-Smith had been flying at thirty-three thousand feet with his two wingmen just south of Portsmouth on a routine training mission when the orbiting Chinese particle beam system malfunctioned. He would never forget the great flash that lit the heavens with an atomic glare, the laser beams like sheet lightning that struck all three fighters simultaneously. His wingmen were killed instantly as their fuel exploded while he was more fortunate, his engine burning and vibrating its way right off of its mountings. Luckily he had had time to eject just before his tanks exploded. From that day forward, not one jet, not one rocket had flown.

Willard-Smith liked his Seafire, which had been completely rebuilt by Vickers. Certainly it was an antique, with a top speed of less than one-half that of his Sea Harrier. But it was a pleasingly simple aircraft, with only seventeen instruments to read and no high-tech electronics equipment to malfunction. With this generation of aircraft, you could see the man you killed or he could see you as he pressed his own red button. Death was delivered from close range, sometimes under a hundred yards, not impersonally from over the horizon by radar and computer-guided missiles that implacably hunted down invisible targets. There was the anticipation here of the hunt for like creatures of like intelligence. He smiled, thinking of the ducks he had shot in the marshy fens of Northumberland. But the birds he hunted now were armed with machine guns and cannons and could shoot back.

He scanned his instruments. All was well, but he had edged up a hair on the flight leader. Easing the throttle with a touch like a feather, he watched his rev-counter drop slightly, to 2,000 rpms. Grunting with approval, he noted his manifold pressure holding steady at thirty inches, airspeed 180 knots, oil pressure 80 pounds, coolant temperature 102 degrees Celsius. And now he was on station precisely where he belonged.

But not Pilot Officer Elwyn York. The poor Cockney was dragging low and wide to the right. He could be a liability, would be easy meat for any experienced enemy pilot. York was a likable young man with a Cockney accent thicker than Yorkshire pudding. He felt that someday York would be a fine fighter pilot, but not yet. It was still too soon. Willard-Smith hoped for an uneventful patrol.

He turned his head sharply, glanced over his shoulders and into his rearview mirrors. Nothing, not even a sea bird. He felt relieved. He glanced at the Zero. The air group commander flew the only Mitsubishi that was not painted in the standard pattern of white fuselage and black cowling of *Yonaga*'s Zeros. Instead, Commander Yoshi Matsuhara's Zero was distinctive, with red cowling and green hood.

Captain Colin Willard-Smith had learned much of Commander Yoshi Matsuhara during his two months of training on board the carrier *Yonaga*. The commander was probably the finest fighter pilot he had ever met and an enigma that defied time and understanding. First, the man was over sixty-years-old, yet his hair was as black as

17

newly mined coal, his face unlined, with intelligent eyes that were bright and alert. This astonishing resistance to aging had been evident in all Japanese holdouts Willard-Smith had met. Especially in old Admiral Fujita. Matsuhara's old crew chief, Chief Teruhiko Yoshitomi, had put it succinctly one day in *Yonaga*'s hangar deck. "Without tobacco, sake, and women for forty-two years, of course, we are still young!" Then the old chief had cackled, spraying spittle like a broken garden hose.

Ironically, Matsuhara was an American. He had been born in Los Angeles but raised in the Japanese tradition of bushido by his father, who had been a gardener and trashman. He entered Japan's equivalent to the Royal Naval College, Eta Jima, when only fifteen and was flying with the first squadron of Zeros in China by 1940. This remarkable squadron shot down 99 Chinese aircraft in less than a year while losing only two of their own antiaircraft fire. Then Matsuhara's transfer to *Yonaga* and the long entrapment on the Arctic Circle. The breakout, attack on Pearl Harbor, and return to Tokyo.

Immediately, the orbiting Chinese laser system turned the world upside down. With their rockets and jets nothing but useless, rusting junk, United States and Russia found their hegemony broken. Their fleets, dependent on high-tech controlled rockets and cruise missiles, were rendered practically impotent. Second-rate powers such as Greece, India, Brazil, Chile, and dozens of others, armed with hundreds of World War II ships, emerged as new powers. *Glasnost* became a mockery and as foolish a word as *detente*. Terrorism ran wild. Awash in oil money and wearing a new cloak of arrogance, Colonel Moammar Kadafi stormed onto the world stage in a leading role as unifier and leader of the Arab *jihad* (holy war) against Israel and all infidels—especially Israel's new ally Japan. The oil embargo by OPEC followed, and massed Arab armies attacked Israel and Japanese hostages were murdered by the hundreds.

Commander Yoshi Matsuhara led *Yonaga*'s air groups when the great ship charged into the Mediterranean and smashed Kadafi's land-based air power and saved Israel. More battles followed in the Southwest Pacific, over Korea and the Yellow Sea. With the usual mind-set of the Arab, not one defeat, one insult, one slight had been forgotten by Kadafi. The war raged on, feeding and growing on Arab hatred and Japanese pride. It seemed to have a life of its own, and men like Matsuhara and Kenneth Rosencrance were its lifeblood. In fact, it was said Commander Matsuhara now boasted over thirty Arab aircraft added to his kills.

Now all Englishmen had a score to settle with Moammar Kadafi, too. In an insane attempt to corner the world market on oil, Arab submarines had torpedoed eleven oil-pumping platforms in the North Sea, killing over a thousand men. Then an enraged Margaret Thatcher foolishly dispatched a carrier force to the Mediterranean where *Illustrious* and *Hermes* were lost along with most of their aircraft. A dozen of Willard-Smith's best friends died. It was then he decided it was time for revenge. He resigned his commission and joined *Yonaga*'s air groups as a special employee of the Japanese National Parks Service, the carrier's ludicrous cover forced on Fujita by the Diet. By coincidence, he and Pilot Officer Elwyn York had joined on the same day. He had heard York's brother had been killed on one of the oil rigs.

Matsuhara's voice in his earphones interrupted his thoughts. "Edo Flight, this is Edo Leader. Sighted a wake at two o'clock. Am investigating. Edo One and Edo Two remain in top cover."

Pulling his mask close and securing it over his mouth, Willard-Smith acknowledged, "Edo Leader, this is Edo Two. Remain in top cover." Dropping his right wing, the Englishman stared down hard to the northwest through a large break in the clouds. To the north and west he saw a white streak in the sea like a hyphen ending in a blue-green dot plodding on a northerly heading. It most certainly looked like a submarine. Perhaps it was one of Kadafi's old *Whiskeys* or *Zulus*. They were known to be operating in the area and would look like *Blackfin* from the air. Then he heard York repeat Matsuhara's command.

Quickly Matsuhara's voice came back, using *Yonaga*'s code name, "Iceman," and reporting the sighting to the carrier. Then, with the grace only shown by the Mitsubishi A6M2, the Japanese fighter whipped into a half roll and split-essed into a dive, cowling pointed toward the strange vessel.

Driven by her four powerful Fairbanks-Morse diesels, *Blackfin* bulled her way through an unusually large swell like a pregnant whale. Challenged by the heaving deck, Lieutenant Brent Ross clung to the windscreen shielding the bridge and cursed as a hail of spray struck him in the face like handful of frozen pellets. Six-feet-four and weighing a trim, muscular 220 pounds, the young lieutenant called on all the power in his arms and legs to keep his balance behind the twin wooden grips of the fifty-caliber Browning Mark 2 machine gun as *Blackfin* crashed through the blue wall and rolled down into the inevitable trough that followed.

At battle surface, the upper works of the submarine were crowded: two lookouts high on their platform on the periscope shears and two more in the small enclosed bridge platform; five members of the stubby five-inch, twenty-five caliber dual-purpose cannon aft of the bridge huddling forward of their weapon under the "cigarette deck," a small platform extending back from the bridge; six men manning a pair of twenty-millimeter Orlikons on the cigarette deck; four more men ready behind a pair of fifty-caliber machine guns in the bridge enclosure itself.

Here Brent Ross and his loader, Gunner's Mate Third Class Humphrey Bowman, manned the port machine gun while Cryptologist Third Class Tony "Crog" Romero manned the starboard fifty with his loader, Yeoman Third Class Yuiji Ichioka. Adding to the crowded conditions were Quartermaster Second Class Harold Sturgis gripping the helm and Seaman First Class Tatsunori Hara at the annunciators. So big he seemed like a crowd himself, the captain, Lieutenant Reginald Williams, stood between Sturgis and Hara just behind the huge pair of binoculars secured to the TBT (Target Bearing Transmitter,) a waterproof instrument that automatically transmitted target bearings to the attack team in the conning tower under his feet.

Brent had learned to appreciate *Blackfin* despite her antique design. Her ten torpedo tubes gave her a deadly sting, and her thin cylindrical pressure hull was surprisingly durable. Built by the Electric Boat Company at Groton, Connecticut, in 1942, *Blackfin* was of the *Gato* Class, arguably the best fleet boat of World War II. Small by modern standards, she was only three hundred twelve feet long with a beam of twenty-seven feet. She displaced one thousand five hundred twenty-six tons surfaced, two thousand twenty-four tons submerged. Her four new six-thousand horsepower Fairbanks-Morse engines could drive her on the surface at twenty-six knots while submerged her battery could push her up to nine knots.

But she was a wounded boat, a speared fish punished by six-hundred-pound depth charges. With the tops of a dozen cells of her battery cracked and leaking chlorine gas, a bilge pump knocked completely off its foundation, two compressors disabled, and three sea valves ruptured, *Blackfin* could not submerge. Damage Control was repairing the cells by drawing hot soldering irons across the cracks, melting the mastic and resealing the cracks. The sea valves were being torn down and either repaired or replaced. But there was nothing that could be done about the bilge pump and the pair of compressors. Heavy equipment in a yard would be required to lift and reset the units. And the pressure hull had an ominous bulge between frames forty-six and forty-seven just abaft the five-inch gun. It had not leaked, but the threat of collapse was there. Brent knew Williams did not dare submerge the boat. *Blackfin* was locked on the surface and forced to steam the shortest possible course for Yokosuka—a course that had taken her within easy range of Arab bases in the Marianas. And her radios, ESM (Electronic Support Measures), and ECM (Electronic Counter Measures) gear were out and they had used their last BRT-1 buoy. In a very real sense, the boat was blind and deaf and mute.

The two-day hail of perhaps hundreds of depth charges had taken its toll of the crew, too. Every man was fatigued, nerves worn to a hard, ragged edge. Two fights had broken out in the engine room. In the last, one machinist's mate had almost killed another with a wrench. Both men were on report and would be court-martialed when they reached Japan.

Brent sighed as the waves calmed, and his nerves unwound slightly with the flattening sea. He patted the breech of the machine gun and ran his fingers over the huge belted bullets all the way to the ammunition box. Caressing the big slugs gave him a feeling of confidence and helped calm him. He chuckled to himself at the incongruously gay effect of the color coding: blue for armor piercing, red for ball, and yellow for tracer. Ordinarily, an enlisted man would be the gunner. However, during shakedown outside New York, Brent had proved himself the best marksman on the ship. Consequently, he had been assigned to the port fifty. This pleased Brent. His unerring accuracy was well known. In fact, during the past five years, while serving on *Yonaga,* he had shot down a Douglas DC-3 and two Messer-

22

schmitt 109s while riding as the tail gunner in a Nakajima B5N torpedo bomber. He had a knack for quickly analyzing and solving the perplexing multidimensional problems of aerial gunnery and anticipating his enemy's moves. He also knew he had been very lucky.

He glanced at Lieutenant Reginald Williams' broad back and thick neck. Williams was a Negro, so black his skin appeared blue whenever the sun broke through and reflected from it. Sweeping the horizon with his binoculars, Williams turned to port. Brent stared at the rugged profile. The cheek was strong and regal, his forehead deep and intelligent, his nose flattened as if he had been pounded in too many street fights. And indeed, raised in south-central Los Angeles, Williams had had more than his share of back alley brawls. He had been All City Player of the Year in high school and an All American linebacker at the University of Southern California when Brent had achieved the same honor at the Academy as a fullback. They had never met on the field, and Williams had taunted Brent, claiming he could have taught Brent something about defense. Despite their having shared mortal dangers together, Brent had not been able to shed a distrust, a dislike for his vaporish captain. Someday he would find the time and place to force the big man into making good his boasts.

And there was another reason to despise the big black. The sub's original captain had been Admiral Mark Allen, who had been Brent's lifetime friend and mentor. When Admiral Allen died of a stroke and massive heart attack while under depth charge attack off Tomonuto Atoll, Williams, then the executive officer, took command. Immediately, he had ordered the admiral's lungs pumped full of air and then had his body fired out of a torpedo tube along with bits of wreckage. Certainly, as a military expedient, the decision was correct. Wreckage, a body, and hundreds of gallons of oil had convinced the pair of stalking Arab destroyers that the submarine had indeed been sunk. This ruse had led to the successful attack on the *Gefara*. Yet the imperious, uncaring attitude, the arrogance and cold enigmatic smile that turned Williams' thick lips at the corners as if he had found some private amusement in Brent's agony, grated on the young lieutenant. No, Brent Ross would not forget. There were things to be settled between them. If they survived.

"Captain," came up from the conning tower. It was the voice of Electronics Warfare Technician Matthew Dante. "I've got the ESM working, sir."

"Well done, Dante. Any readings?" Williams asked, leaning over the hatch.

"Two powerful transmitters with signature characteristics of land-based radar, but I don't have them in my threat library. Big, sir. Each at least fifty-five-hundred megahertz. On the bearings of Saipan and Tinian."

"Are they ranging us?"

"Negative, sir. Too long a range. The curvature of the earth is sending their search right over us."

"Good. Good. Anything else. Ships? Aircraft?"

"Negative, sir. The usual UHF and VHF ship to ship garbage bouncing off the ionosphere on the other side of the pond and a few faint radar pulses from the Marshalls and Gilberts and the eastern Carolines and that's it."

"What about our IFF (Identification Friend or Foe)?"

"Sorry, Sir. Still out."

"Damn," Williams spat, punching the steel wind screen so hard it rang like a bell. "Stay with it Dante and keep a close watch."

"Aye, aye, sir."

"Aircraft! Aircraft! Bearing two-four-zero, elevation fifty!" a lookout shouted from his platform on the periscope shears.

Every head turned, the five-inch gun crew leaped to their weapon, and every machine gun on the port side swung to the port quarter. Unlocking his weapon, Brent swung the perfectly balanced sixty-five-pound machine gun to the left and bent his knees as he elevated the muzzle and pushed a small lever on the breech from "Safe" to "Fire." Carefully, he grasped the handles and placed both thumbs on the rodlike trigger. From the corner of his eye he could see Gunner's Mate Third Class Humphrey Bowman reach down into the ready box and unfasten the top on another ammunition box.

"All guns that bear, stand by to open fire on aircraft closing on our port quarter!" Williams shouted.

Brent found the diving aircraft and centered it in his ring sight. Radial engine, white wings, and two more white aircraft circling above it. White, the color of Japanese fighters. But the aircraft circling above were not Zero-sens. They were unlike any fighters he had ever seen. Was this an Arab trick? Then the lieutenant saw a flash of orange and green as the diving aircraft flattened its dive. "Yoshi! Yoshi Matsuhara!" Brent shouted.

"Yoshi what?" Williams countered.

"Friendly aircraft, Captain," Brent said.

"It's not a question of identity, Mister Ross," Williams said, staring through his glasses. "Only range."

"It's a Zero! My God, man. Are you blind?" Brent heard Bowman gasp, and every man on the bridge turned, wide-eyed.

"Belay that crap, Mister Ross!" Williams bellowed. "You know I can't allow any aircraft to make a run on this ship. I don't give a goddamn if Jesus Christ is at the controls."

Brent locked the machine gun in place and waved at the sky frantically. "But they're friendly fighters! That's Yoshi Matsuhara's paint job." There was desperation in his voice.

"He'll be the late Yoshi Matsuhara if he gets any closer," Williams rumbled. Brent whirled on the captain, crouching, muscles bunched. Williams faced him, glaring. Every man stared at the pair with disbelief. Their captain and executive officer were about to come to blows. The impossibility of the situation was written on every face.

As if he had heard the threat, the pilot of the diving fighter pulled up, well out of range of the machine guns but not the five-inch. He was obviously showing his markings—big red circles outlined in black on his wings and fuselage.

"Permission to open fire," the gun captain, Chief Gunner's Mate Phil Robinson, shouted.

"No!" Brent screamed.

"Very well, Mister Ross," Williams said in a sudden change of mood, voice almost placating and condescending. "You're right. You're right." And then to Robinson, "Negative! He has Japanese markings. Secure your weapon." He stared at Brent out of the corner of his eye. There was obvious concern in the intense black eyes. There was also fatigue. He knew Brent, too, was worn out, his nerves drawn taut as a bowstring. None of them were acting normally.

Brent wondered at his actions, his words. He had lost control with his captain in front of enlisted men. This was unforgivable. Militarily, he knew Williams had been correct. Yet the thought of sacrificing his best friend to military expediency had been intolerable. He knew Williams was trying to restore the situation. He sighed and choked back the sour gorge that had burned the back of his throat. He studied the fighter through his glasses.

Every man watched as the Zero banked toward the ship and began a shallow dive. The canopy was open and the pilot was waving. The engine backfired, and a small puff of black smoke like a punctuation mark was left in its slipstream. "He's throttling down, Captain," Brent shouted.

"Very well," Williams said. "Machine gunners! Put your weapons on safe and stop tracking," the captain added.

Now low on the water and very close, the lithe fighter

came up on the stern of the sub, passing to port with the grace of a gliding gull. Brent's eyes feasted on the beautiful bird. It was like finding an old friend. The red cowling covering the powerful new Sakae engine, the muzzles of the two twenty-millimeter cannons protruding from the wings, the channels in the orange hood for the 7.7-millimeter slugs of the two synchronized machine guns, the graceful rounded wings and tail surfaces, the long tapering fuselage painted a gleaming white that glared in the sunlight like Alpine snow, high canopy which was open, making the pilot clearly visible. He was smiling and waving, and his goggles were up. There was a white band wrapped around his head.

Brent felt the last of his anger melt, and for the first time in weeks he felt a surge of relief and happiness. It was Yoshi Matsuhara. There was no doubt about that. Dropping his binoculars to his waist and waving frantically, Brent shouted, "Banzai! Banzai!" He was joined by Crog Romero's loader, Yeoman Third Class Yuiji Ichioka, and the man at the annunciators, Seaman First Class Tatsunori Hara, who shouted their own Banzais!" The Americans stared at Brent and the two Japanese curiously.

"What in hell was that about?" Williams asked, calmly and with the quiet authority of the officer in command.

Brent acknowledged his captain's change in demeanor with the respect expected of a subordinate. However, he could not completely shield his distaste for the man. "An old Japanese greeting," Ross said curtly.

Williams' chuckle could not wash away the lingering tensions. "Yeah. Like a cheer after a touchdown."

Humphrey Bowman stabbed a finger at the fighter, which had banked sharply and had begun a run down their starboard side. "He's wearing a white bandana around his head," he said, turning to Yuiji Ichioka, who stood behind him next to the starboard's Browning's ready box.

27

Ichioka stared stoically, "That's not a bandana."

"What is it, Yuji?"

They all stared as the beautiful fighter swooped even lower and dropped its starboard wing, passing only a few feet from the submarine's starboard side. After the bark of the big radial engine subsided, the Japanese answered. "It's his *hachimachi* headband. It shows his determination to die for the Emperor."

There was a long silence as all hands watched the Zero begin to turn again, several miles astern. "You still believe in that stuff?" Bowman asked. Williams stirred restlessly but remained silent.

"We still have those traditions, our code of bushido," Ichioka said.

The usually taciturn Seaman First Class Tatsunori Hara turned from the annunciators and said to Bowman, "All good Japanese are raised in the tradition of bushido. Know the *Hagakure,* respect the emperor . . ."

"Belay the bullshit," Williams snapped. "We still have a war to fight. All hands will observe bridge silence." Bowman turned away: the Japanese hunched over stiffly and appeared crestfallen.

"Captain!" a lookout, Seaman Max Orlin, shouted from his perch on the port side of the shears. "He's really taking off." Orlin waved at the Zero.

With its Sakae screaming at full power, the white fighter was rocketing skyward in a near vertical climb. Brent squinted into the sky in confusion. Orlin cleared his confusion.

"Aircraft, bearing two-two-zero. Elevation thirty-five," the young seaman shouted from the shears. The voice was suddenly high, nervous, and frightened.

Every head swung and binoculars came up in unison as if choreographed. Brent flicked his focusing knob and found them. A dozen needle-nosed aircraft with fixed landing gear. He knew they were JU 87 Stuka dive bombers before he saw their Libyan markings. They were in trouble. Serious trouble.

When Commander Yoshi Matsuhara heard Captain Colin Willard-Smith's cooly modulated voice reporting, "Stukas! Many Stukas bearing two-six-zero, altitude twenty-two-hundred meters, range twelve kilometers," he was just turning to make another run past the submarine. It had been a joyful moment. He had seen Brent Ross. Clearly, the big bulk of his friend had been visible waving from the bridge of the *Blackfin*.

Immediately, Matsuhara put the big American out of his mind. His hands moved in a blur, palming the throttle into overboost, enriching his mixture by pushing forward on the black lever attached to the throttle quadrant, pulling back hard on the stick, slamming the canopy shut, locking it and snapping on his oxygen mask. A flick of his thumb flipped the safety cover off the red firing button on his control column. As the blue line of the horizon plummeted beneath his cowling and the fighter rocketed upward, his windscreen filled with a sky that had cleared with the suddenness peculiar to latitudes neighboring the Tropic of Cancer. Then he saw them, a swarm of specks on the far western horizon. Even at this long range, he could see the unmistakable gull wings and spatted wheels of the Junkers dive bomber. They were in their usual inverted V. The formation was straggling and sloppy. Must be Arab pilots. The mercenaries flew much tighter formations.

Yoshi spat an oath. He was in the worst possible position to intercept . . . low, out of range, easily visible to the enemy. But York and Willard-Smith were in an ideal position. Yoshi's oaths turned to grunts of satisfaction. Side by side and from above the two Seafires were curving toward the intruders.

The commander spoke into his microphone, "Edo Two and Three this is Edo Leader. Intercept! Intercept!" He heard acknowledgments from his two wingmen. Then watching the white needle of his altimeter chase around the dial, clicking off hectometers like seconds, he cursed and pounded the instrument. "Izanagi and Izanami," he pleaded, naming the gods who created the Japanese Islands, "Faster faster!" he shouted, in an agony of frustration.

He heard Captain Colin Willard-Smith's crisp, cultured voice as calm as a man ordering sushi. The man could move from English units to metric and back to English with amazing agility. "Edo Three, this is Edo Two. Form up two hundred yards off my starboard wing. We'll boff the last two blighters. Take the one on the right. Chop, chop, old boy."

York's metallic voice touched with a wry edge of irony came back without a hint of fear or even nervousness. "Roger, your lordship. I'll scrag the last sod on the right."

Yoshi nodded in approval. Willard-Smith knew what he was doing, and York certainly sounded confident for a new man. By attacking the last two aircraft, the Seafires would avoid most of the fire from the enemy's gunners. Perhaps he had underestimated his two new wingmen. He toggled the radio to the carrier frequency. "Iceman, this is Edo Leader."

"Edo Leader, this is Iceman. Go ahead."

"Iceman, submarine sighted is *Blackfin*. Many enemy dive bombers approaching from the west. Coordinates the same. Am engaging. Request fighter support."

"Roger, Edo One. Six sections enroute. Any enemy fighters?"

Yoshi searched the sky frantically. He saw nothing but the two thunderheads on the northern horizon tapering and blending into a high cirrus "mackereled" sky which had drifted south like a thick lace curtain. There could be enemy fighters above the cirrus. They must be somewhere. Surely the enemy would not send his bombers

30

into an attack without escorts. But Arabs could be bold beyond belief or as cowardly as whipped curs. They were completely unpredictable. He shifted his search to the enemy bombers, which were above him and to the west and closing fast, and the two British fighters curving into shallow dives as they began their first run.

"Negative. No enemy fighters," Yoshi said.

The next transmission froze Yoshi's blood. "Edo One. Many enemy fighters closing your coordinates high and northwest of you. We are monitoring their fighter frequency."

After acknowledging, the commander made a quick sweep of the sky, and sighed with momentary relief when the search failed to reveal any enemy fighters. But he knew they could pour down through the cover at any moment. He prayed for at least enough time for one pass before the Messerschmitts arrived.

Now he was close to the approaching bombers. He could see an awesome 500-kilogram bomb slung beneath the fuselage of each plane on a crutch and four 50-kilogram bombs racked under their wings. Suddenly, tracers leaped from the rear-guns of the last half dozen Junkers. White fireflies whipped upward, converging on the two diving British fighters like a snow storm. But the Englishmen ignored the deadly hail and continued their dives, holding their fire for point-blank shots. They were in range, and as the Japanese watched, the two Seafires slashed down on the two trailing bombers like sharks following a blood scent. Flashing red gouts of flame, their twenty-millimeter cannons thumped out rounds, leaving brown puffs pockmarking the sky behind them.

Yoshi shouted "Banzai!" as a Stuka lost a wing and flipped over into an impossibly tight roll and tumbled crazily toward the sea. Another, trailing a thick ribbon of black smoke, dropped out of the formation and corkscrewed into a near vertical plunge. The Englishmen were good. "Banzai! Banzai!" he shouted. Licking his suddenly parched lips with the tip of his tongue, his thumb closed over the red button as the belly of the leading JU 87 filled the first ring of his range finder.

The flight commander heard Willard-Smith exult, "Tally bloody ho!"

Then Elwyn York, "I boffed 'im, the bloody whoreson!"

The Seafires plunged through the formation and began to pull out for a second pass. The bombers plodded on, ignoring their losses. Almost casually, the survivors changed formation, stacking up in an oblique line which always preceded an attack. Abruptly, Yoshi saw the Stukas' hinged slatlike air brakes drop below their outer wings and the formation slowed as the pilots set their propellers at full course. They were preparing to dive. They were very brave for Arabs. They would press home their attack despite the fighters. The three fighters could not destroy them all and they knew it. Some would get through to *Blackfin*. The leading JU 87 filled the second ring of Yoshi's range finder, and his thumb restlessly caressed the red button. "Not yet. Not yet," he told himself. "One more ring." Out of the corner of his eye he could see the Seafires pulling out of their dives and curving up for their second pass.

Still climbing in full overboost, the Mitsubishi began to vibrate its objections. Apprehensively, Commander Matsuhara eyed his instruments. The needle of the tachometer was pushing toward the red line at 2800 rpms, manifold pressure 105 centimeters of boost, cylinder head temperature an alarming 255 degrees Celsius, and the needle was flirting with the red line at 260. He could burn out his engine. But he had no choice. He left the throttle in full overboost. Hunched over his controls, he bit down hard on his lower lip until there was a salty taste in his mouth. The first Stuka grew in his range finder and, at last, filled all three rings.

Hanging on his propeller with the fighter threatening

to stall and shaking like a sapling in a monsoon, he punched the red button. The tremendous recoil of the two Orlikons and two 7.7 millimeter machine guns slowed the fighter even more and it actually seemed to stop in midair, defying the laws of physics, gravity, and aerodynamics. Yoshi was convinced he was hanging in the sky in the grasp of some benevolent sky *kami*. Firing from below and at one-quarter deflection ahead and at a range of only one hundred meters, the Japanese could not miss. With a warm rush of near ecstasy, Yoshi saw his shells and bullets blast and chew the JU's belly. Huge chunks of aluminum skin were blasted and ripped from the bottom of the bomber as if some maddened invisible giant were attacking the airframe with an ax, exposing the bottom keel and "U" stringers, frames, and control runs. For one horrifying moment, he realized his stream could set off the bombs, detonating an explosion that could destroy killer and killed. Then his fighter made its own decision.

With insufficient airspeed and lift lost, the Zero dropped off onto its port wing and began to twist into its notoriously tight spin. Pushing the stick forward, and balancing with a touch of rudder, Matsuhara turned with the torque of the great engine, regaining speed and control. With air rushing over his airfoils again, he eased the spin into a spiral and pulled back on the stick.

Glancing skyward, he shouted "Banzai!" as he saw the leading Stuka with a dead man at the controls turn and fall into in own final spinning death plunge. His shouts were interrupted by Willard-Smith's voice, "Many fighters to the northwest, high. Diving."

Then Pilot Officer Elwyn York's voice. There was unbelievable confidence in the timbre, "More bloody fighters to the nor'east, comin' on like a pack o' whores sniffin' a quid."

Bottoming out, Yoshi swiveled his head frantically at the two sightings. With a blood-red Messerschmitt leading, twelve enemy fighters were pouring out of the high cirrus cover just where he had expected them. He felt a cold reptile twist in his guts. Captain Kenneth Rosencrance and his Fourth Fighter Squadron. The butcher was back. However, to the northeast, four sections of three Zeros were closing at a tremendous speed. Yoshi felt his heart leap with joy.

The bombers were still doggedly holding to their run while squadrons of fighters converged on the same tiny spot in the Pacific where the catalyst of it all, the prized *Blackfin,* plodded slowly below. This was how battles developed. Unexpected. Unplanned. A sudden tactical situation that could initially involve a few and then more and more until a grand strategic encounter developed where ships, planes, and men were squandered like pawns by drunken chess players. There was even potential for a major carrier confrontation here. Perhaps a surface action. Thousands could die for the life of the single old wounded submarine plodding along so innocuously far below. That is if the Arabs had the stomach for it and would bring their carrier battle group north. Yoshi knew Admiral Fujita would not hesitate to stack all the chips and roll the dice.

A new voice filled his earphones. He recognized the voice of Lieutenant Todoa Shigamitsu, a young veteran of the Self Defense Force and superb pilot. "Edo Leader, this is Ronin Leader. Have you in sight. With your permission, I will intercept enemy fighters."

"Roger Ronin Leader. Engage enemy fighters. I will continue to engage enemy bombers. Out."

Matsuhara's mind worked with the speed and precision of a computer. With a little luck, Shigamitsu's Zeros would intercept Rosencrance somewhere to the north and above the bombers. But only a fool could expect the Japanese to stop all of the ME 109s. After all, the Fourth Fighter Squadron was composed of hand-picked mercenaries: Germans, Russians, Americans, and at least one

Japanese renegade Yoshi had heard about. They were the best. Not one Arab was included. He looked to his right and then to his left. York and Willard-Smith were climbing with him.

Keying his microphone, Yoshi spoke, "Edo Flight, this is Edo Leader. Continue to engage bombers. Individual combat. Banzai!"

"Roger, Edo Leader," Willard-Smith's voice oozed back. "And 'Banzai' to you, old boy."

"Roger, guv'nor," York said, suddenly keying into the frequency. "Let's bugger the lot."

The three fighters zoomed upward.

"All guns that bear, stand by to open fire!" Williams shouted. Lieutenant Brent Ross already had the lead JU 87 in his sights. However, the plane was far too high. He muttered a few choice obscenities under his breath. They would be forced to wait until the enemy delivered his attack. Wait until the bombs were already dropping before they had a shot — if then. He gritted and ground his teeth in frustration.

To the north, two dozen Japanese and Libyan fighters were locked in a tumbling, blazing battle. Already two fighters had flamed and plunged into the sea. A single white parachute was drifting slowly downward. Almost directly above, Commander Yoshi Matsuhara and his two strange companions, which had been identified as British Seafires, had shot down three of the bombers and were climbing desperately in an attempt to bag more. But the trio could not stop all the bombers. That was obvious. Hell would be raining from the sky soon.

The young gunner was shocked by Williams' command. "Five-inch, commence firing. Commence! Commence!"

Before Brent could say a word, Crog shouted, "Our fighters, Captain?"

"They'll have to take their chances and they know it."

Brent choked back his own objections. Williams was right again and he knew it. In fact, if he were in command, he would give the same order.

The five-inch gun was specially plated and lubricated to withstand repeated immersions. However, the incursions of salt water made the mounting of an automatic loading machine impossible. Manually loaded, it could fire only about ten rounds a minute with a maximum range of 8,000 yards. Without radar fire-control and with fuse settings called out by Chief Gunner's Mate Robinson, who was using a pair of range-finding binoculars, it would be highly inaccurate. But it might frighten the bomber pilots. Perhaps spoil their accuracy. And perhaps destroy a bomber or a friendly fighter.

Elevated to almost fifty degrees and pointed to port, the muzzle of the cannon was almost even with Brent's head. There was a flash, a sharp explosion that struck the young lieutenant's eardrums like the end of a whip. Every man rolled with the blast like a fighter taking a punch. There were groans, and hands flew to ears. The staggering concussion sent the bearing ring flying off of the gyro repeater and a log book, pencil, and parallel rules were catapulted off of the small chart table mounted in a corner of the bridge. "Jesus Christ," Brent heard Bowman moan. There was a faint smell of cordite, but most of the smoke was blown aft and over the stern.

Brent watched as a brown smear of smoke burst high above like a malignant tumor in the blue sky. "Five hundred feet low, and, Christ, a half-mile to the right. My God man, what are you shooting at, Shanghai?" Williams roared, dropping his glasses to his waist.

There was a clatter of brass on steel as two men manhandled a sixty-five-pound cartridge to the breech and rammed it home. Then the shouted commands of the gun captain. The pointer and trainer cranked their wheels furiously and then Brent heard a chorus of, "On target.

On target."

Again the cannon spat its yellow tongue and the groans came as the blast lashed the bridge crew. Another brown puff, this time above the bombers and to the left.

"Jesus, man," Williams stormed, staring through his binoculars. "A thousand feet high and a quarter-mile to the left." He punched the wind screen. "Rapid fire, but try not to sink us. On the other hand, those enemy pilots might laugh so much they might not be able to hit us."

Brent wondered at Williams' words. Doom was closing in above, yet the man could actually joke. He felt a new respect for the big black.

Matsuhara and his wingmen were ripping through the long line of bombers from ahead, curving in from below and the side, making desperate passes that brought them under fire from both the pilots' two fixed 7.92-millimeter machine guns and at the same time drew fire from some of the twin machine guns mounted in the rear cockpits. Tracers glowed, smoked, and crossed in mad patterns as if an insane spider were hurling a web across the sky. The leading bomber burst into flame and then tumbled across the sky in wild gyrations like a demented moth that had dared a candle's flame once too often. A Seafire blasted the landing gear from another, shattered the cockpit, and the big Junkers curved toward the sea manned by dead men. But the seven survivors plodded on with a determination that froze Brent's blood.

Then a new fear struck him. Three ME 109s had broken through the dogfight high to the north and were streaking downward and toward Matsuhara's fight with the bombers. Matsuhara's section would be forced to disengage the bombers and defend themselves. And that was precisely what they were doing, abandoning the attack on the bombers, pulling up hard and climbing to meet the three plunging Messerschmitts. Brent narrowed his eyes and stared above, a jolt of hate flowing through his veins and charging his entire being. A red Messerschmitt was leading. *Oberstleutnant* Kenneth Rosencrance. And one of his wingmen was flying a black fighter with garish white stripes. Captain Wolfgang "Zebra" Vatz. Rosencrance and Vatz, the enemy's two most cold-blooded killers. Brent prayed for Yoshi.

Abruptly, his attention was diverted to the preservation of his own life. The first JU 87 had peeled off into its dive. Instead of diving in the usual stream, the remaining six began to circle above, watching and waiting for their own turns. Either they were inexperienced or so supremely confident they were using *Blackfin* for target practice. Or maybe the wild firing of the five-inch had disconcerted them. In any event, they had made a mistake. The submarine's AA guns could concentrate on one target at a time with time to reload and regroup between attacks.

"All ahead flank!" Williams screamed. "Right full rudder! Secondary armament commence firing when in range!"

Brent felt the boat surge as the four Fairbanks-Morse diesels were throttled to full power, delivering 24,000 horsepower to the twin bronze screws. At the same time he felt himself pushed to port as Quartermaster Sturgis cranked the wheel and *Blackfin* turned sharply to starboard.

"Twenty-six knots, four hundred sixty revolutions," a tight, nervous voice shouted up the hatch from the conning tower.

"Very well," Williams yelled down the hatch.

The five-inch barked again and again, but the rounds were hopelessly wide and poorly fused. Brent was on his own, could open fire at his own discretion. But the big plane was still too high—too high for even the Orlikons. He watched fascinated as the plunging Stuka grew in his ring sight—the big Jumo 211 engine blasting its power out of six exhaust ports on each side of the hood, the graceful gull wing and the clumsy fixed landing gear, the high canopy and the pilot's goggled head behind his sight, the big air brakes like boards stretched beneath the outer wings, and the huge bomb slung beneath the fuselage on its trapeze-like crutch.

The bomber had steepened its dive to about eighty-five-degrees, which was the favorite bomb release angle. "Six thousand feet, five thousand five hundred feet," Brent heard Williams chant as he studied the Junkers. Abruptly, the captain turned to Quartermaster Sturgis. "Rudder amidships, steady on zero-nine-zero."

"Rudder amidships. Steady on zero-nine-zero, sir," Sturgis repeated.

Suddenly the boat was enveloped by a sound like a hundred tortured banshees. Brent had heard the frightening sound many times before. There was a chorus of, "What's that noise?" "For Christ's sake, what's that?"

"Don't let it bother you," Brent shouted. "They have sirens on their landing gear. The Arabs call them 'Trombones of Jericho.' They're supposed to scare us."

"Shit. I don't need no more scarin'," Bowman said.

At that moment the twenty-millimeter guns began to fire and at the same time Brent saw the 500-kilogram bomb suddenly swing far below the Stuka's fuselage on its crutch and hurled clear of the propeller like a shiny black marble flung by a slingshot. Four smaller bombs were released at the same time.

Like all men under dive-bombing attack, Brent felt the bombs were headed directly for him, would actually land on his head. His stomach became a cement mixer and he could taste the ham sandwich he had had for lunch trying to spasm its way up through his throat. His flesh was icy, and tiny insects with frozen feet were racing up his spine. He had never known such fear, such horror. But the men could not know this, could not suspect. He was an officer. Must set an example. Grunting, he choked back the curdled, acid taste that fouled his mouth, squared his shoulders, clenched his teeth, and skinned his lips back in a rictus of determination. The black, finned missiles were growing and shrieking as they plunged downward. But Brent kept his whole attention, his whole being concentrated on the target.

In a hail of twenty-millimeter tracers, the pilot pulled back hard on his stick. But his momentum was carrying the plane very low. The Stuka's wingspan became a diameter of Brent's ring sight, and part of the underside of the bomber's fuselage was visible as well as the dive flattened. Leading the bomber like a hunter shooting game birds, he pressed the trigger.

His Browning and Crog's starboard fifty stuttered to life simultaneously. The belt jerked and raced through the breech, and the ejector sent a stream of brass cartridges clattering into the canvas bag. He saw his tracers blast the big air-scoop and radiator from the bottom of the aircraft, and immediately a white stream of glycol shot into the slipstream. As the pilot pulled up and careened to port, black smoke trailed him like a dirty string in the sky. Brent heard some men cheer.

The cheering was stopped by a cataclysmic explosion to port. The 500-kilogram bomb ripped a blue-green tower from the sea not more than fifty feet from the port side, the flash of the high explosives snuffed out immediately by the water. There were hums and whines and clattering ricochets as shrapnel tore the sea and sailed over the bridge. Not all missed. There was a scream from periscope shears, and the port lookout, Seaman Max Orlin, doubled over, nearly cut in half by a piece of bomb casing the size of a stewing pot. Blood, torn intestines, and gore rained on the bridge and on every man. Then the lookout's eviscerated body tumbled from his platform, bounced off the deck, and rolled off the pressure hull and into the sea. A bloody streak smeared the submarine's wake.

The starboard lookout in the shears began to howl, "Max! Max! My God, Max!"

"Shut up and get back to your watch," Williams yelled. The howling stopped.

Brent did not have time to wipe the blood from his face or even feel the anguish and horror of the moment. The second bomber had dropped off into its dive while the others continued to circle. He heard Bowman whimper, and his loader dropped a box of ammunition. "God damn it! Shut up and stand by to load," Brent shouted.

"Sorry, sir." The loader picked up the box and came erect.

While the Orlikons yammered and the cannon roared, the second plane's dive steepened and the shrieking began. "Left full rudder!" Williams screamed.

Again the wings of the Stuka filled Brent's ring sight. His thumbs stiffened on the trigger.

"Edo flight! Form up! Form up!" Commander Yoshi Matsuhara's voice squawked in Captain Colin Willard-Smith's earphones. "Follow my lead. Intercept and then individual combat!"

Both wingmen acknowledged. The command was not really necessary. One pass as a unit, and then it would be every man for himself in the wildest kind of bloody barroom brawl where the stakes were life or death. Willard-Smith and York were closing in fast on the Zero's elevators as the flight commander pointed his cowling at the three diving Messerschmitts. *Blackfin* would be on its own until they disposed of the mortal threat thundering down from above.

No doubt about it, Rosencrance was leading with Captain Wolfgang Vatz's zebra-striped fighter on his left side with the usual solid black Messerschmitt of every other member of the Fourth Fighter Squadron covering his right. And at least a dozen more ME 109s were pouring in from the west, while an equal number of Zeros streaked in from the north and east. This battle was developing into one of the greatest dogfights of the five-year war. Not since the storied Mediterranean engagement of 1984 had there been so many fighters locked in combat. Already the toll had been heavy. An ME was burning and streaking toward the sea like a meteor, a Zero had exploded, and another ME had lost most of a wing and was disintegrating as it tumbled downward. Two parachutes descended slowly toward the sea.

With the Rolls Royce Griffon screaming in war emergency power, Willard-Smith was pushed back into his seat by acceleration and gravity. Anxiously, the Englishman glanced at his instruments. The oil and coolant temperature readings were crowding their red lines at 105 and 121 Celsius. Passing 2850, the rev-counter, too, was approaching the danger area while the manifold pressure gauge showed 67 inches of boost, which was about all the engine could take. But even in this climb, the airspeed indicator showed 360 knots. Fast, but barely enough to keep his station off Matsuhara's tail.

This would be a head-on pass, the enemy fighters diving, Edo Section climbing. Moving the stick slightly, Willard-Smith brought the reticle of his electric reflector sight to the right-hand Messerschmitt. It was completely black, but now he noticed it had a white propeller boss. The boss became his bull's-eye. The diving trio was still far out of range, but with a combined closing speed of almost a thousand knots, they would be in range in a less than a minute. His right hand gripped the loop at the top of the control column, and his thumb moved to the firing button.

The fighter circuit was filled with the frantic voices of aerial combat, but they did not distract him. "Ronin Green. Take your section higher! Higher! Upsun. We need top cover."

"Roger Ronin Leader. Climbing to nine thousand meters."

"Kudo! One on your tail. Five o'clock. Break left!"

"Breaking left, Shigamitsu."

"Shigamitsu. They got Ikeda. He's burning."

"Watch your own backside, Okumura. Two MEs closing fast. Are you blind?"

"See them. Give me some help, Watanabe. Tell me when to break."

"Okumura, I have the one on the right. In the name of the gods, turn! Break left now! Now!"

"Breaking left, Watanabe."

"No! No! Okumura. Don't dive! You can't dive with them!"

"Shigamitsu, this is Kudo. I sent the *yatsu* (bum) straight to his hell, prebaked in his own stew."

"This is Watanabe. Okumura has joined his ancestors."

"Ronin Flight, this is Ronin Leader. Many enemy fighters high and to the west. Ronin Green, where are you?"

"Intercepting. But there is a full squadron up here, Ronin Leader."

"Ronin Flight. Disengage! Climb! Climb! They cannot climb with us."

Shigamitsu was taking his sections up to meet the new threat. He was gaining altitude, a fighter pilot's most prized possession. His fighters had shot down three or four of the Fourth Fighter Squadron but had lost three or more of their own. However, help had arrived. Perhaps fifteen more Zeros were streaking across the sky to help Shigamitsu intercept the new squadron of enemy fighters.

Willard-Smith ignored it all. His whole universe was the diving ME 109, growing in his windscreen with frightening speed. He was thankful for his ninety-millimeter armorglass windscreen, but knew it could not stop a twenty-millimeter shell. In a millisecond his mind reviewed everything he knew about the Messerschmitt: level flight speed of 360 knots; extremely good climb and dive speeds, could out-dive both the Seafire and the Zero, direct fuel injection which functioned without missing a beat in negative-g maneuvers, rugged construction but a little weak in the wing roots, two wing-mounted Mauser twenty-millimeter cannons and two cowling mounted Borsig 7.9-millimeter machine guns. He must look for its limitations: heavy ailerons at high speeds and, also, elevators hard to move at combat speeds; no rudder trimmer which made long flights extremely tiring; prone to high-speed stalls and it had a wide turn radius.

He hunched forward, caressing the red button. A head-on pass canceled out most advantages and disadvantages except armament. Here he had the advantage. Without moving his eyes from the reflector sight, he picked up Commander Matsuhara's Zero creeping ahead. The new Sakae 42 was pulling the light fighter ahead of the Seafires. And Rosencrance's red machine was far ahead of his diving companions.

Both Rosencrance and Matsuhara opened fire simultaneously. Bright orange and yellow fire motes flickered from hits on both aircraft. Rosencrance turned to his left slightly. Matsuhara turned with him. They were hub to hub, firing and closing at an incredible speed. It appeared Matsuhara was determined to ram the *Oberstleutnant*.

Willard-Smith stiffened and his eyes widened as the wings and hood of the black ME 109 blossomed with the deep red of roses in full bloom. Tracers streaked toward him and dropped off. "Too far, amateur." He brought his nose up slightly to bring the black machine into the lighted orange circle. At last, the wings of the black machine stretched far enough to touch the circle like a chord and the reticle was on the boss. He whispered as he squeezed the button, "Here's your ticket to Mecca or Valhalla or wherever you're going, you bloody bastard." The recoil of the four Hispano-Suiza cannons shook the airframe like an old building in an earthquake, knocking open the flare-gun locker and raising dust in the cramped cockpit. Willard-Smith felt his teeth chatter, but he was not sure it was from the recoil. In the corner of his eye he saw Matsuhara and Rosencrance pass each other, Rosencrance pulling up at the last instant. They had both apparently missed delivering mortal damage to each other.

But he was too close to miss and so was the enemy. A trip hammer began to drum on the Seafire's right wing, and holes appeared in the aluminum magically. But the Englishman was scoring, too. His heavier armament told immediately. A shell blew off the ME's port exhaust manifold fairing strip and ripped the ejector exhaust. Then the port cowling fastener was blown loose and the cowling ripped and bent up into the gale like a piece of paper and smashed into the armored windshield frame, bounded over the cockpit taking the RDF loop and antenna mast with it. Passing the tail, it ripped the top from the rudder and vertical tailplane.

Either in a panic or experiencing a loss of control, the enemy pilot did the worst possible thing. He pulled back on the stick. Shouting in triumph, Willard-Smith saw the entire bottom of the Messerschmitt exposed like the belly of a trout ripe for gutting. At zero deflection and at close range the big shells blasted chunks of aluminum into the slipstream, exposing stringers, frames, cables. The sledgehammer blows marched to the tail, blowing off the tail wheel and then the port elevator and the rudder.

With a complete loss of control, the fighter shot skyward, revolving like a mortally wounded gladiator trying to prolong his life by refusing to leave his feet. At the moment the fighter stalled, a figure plummeted from the cockpit, the leader from his parachute trailing. But the panicked pilot had jumped too soon. His parachute tangled in the jagged remains of the tail, and as the ME streaked over into its final dive, a waving, screaming figure trailed it. "Enjoy it all the way down, you bloody bugger," Willard-Smith muttered.

He continued to pull back on the stick, reaching for the sky and the treasure of altitude. He watched Matsuhara's Zero snap into a tight loop and half-roll and roar into a dive after Rosencrance. But the canny American was miles to the north and west, taking advantage of the Messerschmitt's tremendous diving ability. The *Oberstleutnant* knew he could not turn with a Zero. At least a mile to the right, Willard-Smith saw York's Seafire continuing to climb with him, while far below and trailing Rosencrance, Vatz's ME 109 flattened its dive only a few feet above the sea. The striped fighter was hopelessly out of range and curving to the west. Vatz, too, had no stomach for a dogfight with a more maneuverable enemy.

The black ME with its pilot trapped in his parachute shrouds twisted into the sea far below while to the north and west a half dozen ribbons of black smoke spelled out the epitaphs of immolated fighters. More parachutes were drifting toward the sea. To the north, Willard-Smith saw a flock of JU 87s circling in a single line over *Blackfin* like vultures. Then, in his earphones, he heard Matsuhara's voice. "Edo flight, this is Edo Leader. *Blackfin* bearing zero-zero-zero. Engage bombers! Follow my lead."

Willard-Smith's acknowledgment was followed quickly by York's.

The English captain pulled back on the stick, kicked left rudder, and then pushed the control column forward, split-essing into a near vertical dive. With his stomach pushed down hard by centrifugal force and his bladder suddenly feeling very full, he watched the sky revolve, and then the blue line of the horizon shot up. Abruptly his windshield was filled with the vast expanse of the Pacific and the pressure on his stomach and bladder eased. A little right rudder balanced by a touch of elevator and aileron turned him toward the bombers. Gradually the

46

tail of the Zero worked into his gunsight. His left foot moved slightly, ruddering him to his position on the leader's left while York crept up on the right. Far ahead and below he could see the JUs casually circling over their target. Suddenly, the leader peeled off into a dive. They would arrive at the bomb line late—too late.

Cursing, Willard-Smith pounded the instrument panel. Another bomber was streaking for *Blackfin*. It must be hell down there. Hell!

The third bomber had waited until the second had released its bombs before dropping out of the circle and diving on *Blackfin*. Obviously upset by the vicious, accurate antiaircraft machine guns, the second Junkers had veered at the last instant and its bombs did nothing more than kill a thousand fish a good three hundred yards off the submarine's starboard quarter. Despite the pilot's maneuver, a twenty-millimeter shell had smashed the oil intake and cooler of the big plane and Brent had shot off the JU's left wheel. With bits of wreckage tearing off into the slipstream and with the big Jumo engine vomiting black smoke like a lung-shot animal blowing blood, the Stuka clawed for altitude. It was followed by the cheers, jeers and waved fists of *Blackfin*'s gun crews.

But the third bomber pilot was made of tougher stuff. Trombones screaming, he put his spinner right on the submarine's bridge. The cannon spat its flames and roared its challenge, its shells screeching past the diving bomber, but, this time, exploding amongst the four remaining bombers high above. Although none was destroyed, the ring was broken and the big planes wheeled in confusion like a covey of terrified quail scattered by a hunter's shotgun.

With the gun crews cheers echoing in his ears and Williams yelling, "Kill the motherfuckers!" Brent felt an inexplicable calm grip him as he watched the bomber grow

47

in his sight. Bowman had loaded another full box of ammunition and he had found the first two bombers highly vulnerable. Now he realized they must drop into range if they wished to attain killing accuracy. He had had hits on both of the first two. He licked his lips. Felt a warm primal heat down low. The same heat he had felt the last time he had made love to Dale McIntyre. Strange. No, it was insane how the sexy woman could come back at a moment like this. Where was his early fear? The terror? How could sex and killing walk through a man's mind hand-in-hand? He was confused. Combat could fan all of a man's emotions and power them like nothing else. And sometimes, in a queer way, it compressed his entire life and ran it past him kaleidoscopically like a broken projector. *The drowning swimmer syndrome,* he snorted to himself.

"Fighters! Three fighters! Japanese! Bearing one-nine-five, elevation angle thirty. Closing on the bombers."

Out of the corner of his eye, Brent could see the white fighters bolting down in a perfect V on the four high-flying bombers, which had reestablished their ragged circle. Matsuhara was back. He knew his friend would return. But there was no time for distraction, no time even to cheer. He had taken his deep breath and was holding it in his lungs — a ritual he had learned as a youth when hunting game birds in the woods of New England with his father. "Hold your breath, keep both eyes open, and squeeze the trigger steadily but gently," his father had drummed into his head on a hundred hunts.

The shiny black bombs dropped and the terror, the horror, returned. Mesmerized by the projectiles, Brent felt the flush of deep warmth vanish, replaced by ice water that seemed to drop through his bowels. His emotions had come full circle — fear to courage and back to fear again. Hands trembling, heart beating so hard he could feel the blood pounding in his temples, he sighted on the Junkers. He expected it to begin its pullout, but instead

48

the pilot continued his dive. Bright red began to wink just outside the breaks in the gull wing, and it screamed down only a few feet from the swarm of falling bombs. They were being strafed. Incredible. The JU could die in the explosion of its own bombs. The pilot must be a fanatic, or insane. The twenties blasted to life and Brent pressed the trigger. Shaking from the recoil and balancing the weapon against the submarine's roll by counteracting with the powerful muscles of his thighs, back, and arms, he kept the big spinner in the center of his sights. The smell of cordite hit his senses like an elixir.

Seven-point-nine-two-millimeter slugs struck the steel deck with clangs and pings, ricocheting with high whines and sharp buzzing sounds, as if a hive of nasty insects had been unearthed by a plow. Struck on the front and top of his helmet by at least four slugs, Chief Gunner's Mate Phil Robinson was hurled to the deck, helmet flying, the gray-yellow contents of his skull scattering across the deck in a slimy mass. The one remaining lookout on the shears clutched his chest and then, screaming through a gout of blood, toppled over his safety rail with the roll of the boat. He tumbled into the sea like a child's rag doll. More blood rained on the bridge crew. Brent groaned aloud and cursed into the roar of his gun.

"Left full rudder!" Williams shrieked. "Kill him! Kill him!" The boat heeled into a sharp turn.

The bombs screamed down. They would impact in seconds. They were so close, the big cylinder and its four smaller companions seemed to diverge and each became a distinct canister of doom, finned, fused, ready to blow *Blackfin* to oblivion. It was like a nightmare where you run and run but you are sliding in grease and a hideous monster gains on you, comes closer and closer until you gag on its foul breath. Then it bares its fangs and reaches out with claws like razors.

Brent shook the paralyzing images from his brain, ignored the bombs, fought back. He would kill his killers.

Chaplets of tracers like strings of burning beads converged on the Junkers. Bits and chunks of skin were blasted from the leading edge of the wing. Bright yellow flashes blinked on and off like Christmas lights, and the right dive brake and aileron were blown off by twenty-millimeter strikes. Immediately the plane veered to the left, giving Brent a clear shot at the right side of the cockpit. His big rounds blew out the rear canopy and decapitated the gunner. He wanted the pilot. Cursing, he adjusted his stream with a hard, even tug on the right handle. More bullets smashed the canopy and shot out the armorglass windscreen with the pilot's face dissolving in the blizzard of shattered glass. With two headless men in the cockpit, the big bomber half-rolled to its left and smashed into the sea with a violence rarely seen by any man.

At that instant, the bombs struck just off the the starboard bow. The 500-kilogram bomb sent an enormous cliff of water soaring majestically into the sky so close the boat leaped from the sea like a harpooned whale. Ringing and booming, a sound like a great temple gong reverberated through every strake and frame in the boat. The concussion knocked Humphrey Bowman and Yuiji Ichioka from their feet. Ichioka slid across the deck, his helmet striking the binnacle post so hard the impact sounded like a sledgehammer striking a pot. He rolled to the side, groaning. Brent staggered and grabbed the windscreen while Bowman was knocked across the ready box. There were screams of pain and fear.

Then the tower collapsed into spreading rings of ripples, green water, and spray drenching every man. Holding the fifty-caliber with one hand, Crog Romero reached down and pulled the groggy Ichioka to his feet with the other.

"Steady up on two-seven-five!" Williams shouted, big fists firmly gripping the windscreen as the submarine bounced and wallowed in the tortured sea. He glanced at

Hara, who was still on his feet but stunned. "All ahead one-third." The Japanese pulled the levers of his annunciator stiffly, like an automaton. The engines slowed. Williams shouted down the hatch, "Communications! Damage report!"

"Communications, aye! I have Damage Control on line. Nothing yet, sir," a frightened voice came back.

"Very well. Hurry it up."

"Speed eight, one-hundred-eighty-revolution, sir," Hara said in a flat voice.

"They're all coming!" the starboard bridge lookout shouted.

Williams threw a glance skyward. He had no choice. "Fuck the damage. All ahead flank!"

"All ahead flank, sir." Hara pushed the levers all the way to the last stop. The rhythm of the four diesels picked up and the boat surged. They were not down by the head yet. Brent sighed with relief. Maybe their battered pressure hull had withstood the shock. Certainly the explosion of the 500-kilogram bomb had been more devastating than any depth charge they had taken. His neck was sore. The concussion had jerked his head so hard, his helmet had come up off his skull and then been snapped down by his chin strap. That had never happened before in the many battles he had fought.

Williams shouted down the hatch, "God damn it. Where's that damage report? I want a report from the forward torpedo room and battery room immediately."

Pushing his helmet back, Brent stared skyward and shook the numbness from his brain. A sharp pang brought his hand to his neck, and he rubbed it mechanically. Another bomber had peeled off, and the three remaining had stopped circling and were in a line behind it like impatient commuters waiting to board a train. And, indeed, they had a very good reason to be impatient. Matsuhara and his two Seafires were streaking down on them like lances hurled by a vengeful deity. The JUs had

51

wasted time in their leisurely attack and now the price would be paid. Another Stuka fell off into its dive at precisely the moment Matsuhara and his wingmen opened fire.

The next moments were a continuation of the mad nightmare for Brent Ross. Two diving bombers, fighters ripping into the two left in the depleted circle, a Seafire plunging desperately after the last diving Stuka, the explosion of the cannon, the deafening chatter of the machine guns, the smell of cordite, the vibration of the Browning that jarred his teeth and strained the muscles of his arms and shoulders, the terrible pain that shot downward from his neck. And the ring sight and his target, Williams shouting commands to the helmsman, desperately trying to throw off the enemy pilot's aim. Kill or be killed. Another wild, inexplicable swing in emotions. Terror or a killing frenzy. He knew not what it was. Perhaps a mixture of both. It made no difference to the enemy. They were coming after him en masse this time.

Just before the lead Stuka reached the bomb release point, it vanished in a blinding explosion like a nova blossoming in a millisecond of glory. Releasing the trigger and blinking out the afterimages flashing from his retinas, Brent stared in amazement. A huge circle of sky above was filled with flying wreckage, roiling smoke, flashing reds and oranges of burning vaporized clouds of fuel and showers of aluminum that actually burned in a smoking rain like a beast with ten thousand tentacles. Big chunks dropped too: the engine crashing a hundred yards ahead of the boat, a spatted wheel bouncing off the stern. And small bits of hot aluminum rained down, but most missed *Blackfin*.

Brent heard the trombones before he saw the next bomber. Now he felt thankful for the noisemaker. He brought his ring sight to the precise center of the point where the Stuka had exploded. The Junkers plunged through the smoke. Instantly the machine guns yammered out their welcome. Brent's eyes widened with new fear and dismay. A Seafire was close on the tail of the bomber. Both were firmly locked into the cascade of tracers. The pilot of the Seafire was firing. Both aircraft were close — very close.

Caught by twenty-millimeter shells from behind, and ripped by twenties and fifty-caliber slugs from the submarine, the Stuka came apart at precisely the moment its pilot released his bombs. It was not more than a hundred yards above the bridge and slightly to starboard. First its right wing broke away at the fillet in a welter of torn skin, broken spars, and stringers, spilling its entrails — a ganglia of broken wires, color-coded control wires, broken fuel lines, and spraying red hydraulic fluid from broken piping like a slashed carotid artery. Then its engine vibrated from shot-out mounts and pulled the big plane to the side. It tumbled crazily around its one remaining wing and then it too broke loose. The fuselage plummeted downward into the sea as if it had been suddenly turned to cast iron and the bombs burst harmlessly off *Blackfin*'s starboard beam. There were cheers and then the cheers turned to groans. The Seafire was in trouble. They had hit it, too.

Engine smoking and trailing a thin white mist of glycol, the British fighter pulled from its dive and curved off to the west, gradually gaining altitude. "He's had it," Williams said grimly. "Keep a sharp lookout. If he bails out or ditches, we'll pick him up."

"They got 'em. Got 'em both, Captain," a bridge lookout shouted, pointing overhead.

The men began to cheer. Matsuhara and the pilot of the second Seafire had scored. One of the two remaining Stukas was spinning into the sea, its engine burning like a blowtorch. The other Stuka was diving, trailing smoke. As Brent watched, the big bomber flattened its dive just a few feet above the water. "He's going to ditch," Brent observed.

"If our fighter doesn't kill him," Williams said, gesturing at the second Seafire that was circling above the doomed bomber.

Slowly the big bomber settled, catching first a low swell with its tail wheel and left elevator, bouncing high and then dropping down again. This time it came down flat, the pilot trying desperately to keep his wheels from catching the sea and flipping him over. In a burst of blue water and white spray, the bomber plopped into the sea, dragging its tail and then dropping on its belly. It bobbed up and down and immediately began to settle. Two figures were seen scrambling out of the cockpit. The Seafire circled once more and then pulled into a sharp climb, pointing its nose toward Matsuhara's waiting Zero and the dogfight that still raged on the far horizon.

Williams turned to Tatsunori Hara, "All ahead standard." And then to Harold Sturgis, "Left standard rudder, steady up on the downed plane."

"Are we going to pick them up or kill them, Captain?" Brent asked casually.

"What would you suggest?"

Brent did not hesitate. He spoke through the heat in his guts, his chest, his heart: "Kill 'em." Shocked faces turned toward the young lieutenant.

Williams pondered for a moment. "Now I know why they call you 'the American samurai.'"

Brent stiffened, not sure if he had been insulted or complemented. Before he could answer, a shout turned his head. "The Seafire's back. It's ditching. Fine off the starboard quarter."

Every man turned, watched and prayed as the damaged British fighter glided low over the sea, close aboard the starboard side. With his landing gear retracted, the pilot's problem was simpler than that that had faced the pilot of the JU 87. Slipping and skidding across the surface like a thrown rock, the wings of the sleek fighter sent up two enormous sheets of water as it tore through the surface at at least eighty knots. It bounced high, slapped the water, bounced again, and then was caught by the grasp of the sea and wrestled to a stop in a geyser of white spray and blue water. Immediately a figure threw out a dinghy, stepped gingerly to a wing, and slipped into the raft.

"Made It. Made it," Williams said with obvious relief. He turned to Sturgis. "Belay my last order. We'll pick up our own first. Can you track him?"

"Aye, aye, sir. I can track him."

"Very well. Call out your course once you steady up on him."

"Aye, aye, sir. Call out my course."

"Sir," a voice came up from the conning tower. "Damage control reports the intake valve on our number one main ballast tank is ruptured and we're taking on seawater. The chief engineer says we can hold even with the pump."

"Tell him to jury-rig the number two pump. It can be crossed over."

"He is, sir."

"Very well."

Sturgis said to Williams, "Steady on zero-four-seven, sir."

"Well done, Quartermaster. Hold her there." Williams turned aft. "Five-inch gun crew," he shouted. "Stand by to pick up survivors." The men left their weapon. Stepping gingerly around their dead gun captain, they began to unpack lines and life preservers from a locker under the cigarette deck. The captain announced to the bridge crew, "We'll pick up our own first, then we'll take care of the enemy." He waved to the port bow, where two men were visible floating in an inflatable dinghy and faced Brent. Then, with his face as inscrutable as a sealed book, he said softly, "I'll keep your suggestion in mind, Mister Ross—yes indeed."

Nodding, Brent glanced at his ammunition belt. Only

a single round showed. He pulled back hard on the wooden grip of the cocking handle and ejected the last three rounds. Quickly, Bowman removed the empty box and dropped it into a corner of the ready box. Then, with Brent helping, he lifted a fresh box containing 110 rounds up to the breech and snapped it into place. Brent flipped up the top cover of the machine gun's breech. "Load one!" Brent ordered.

Bowman passed the brass tag loader of the belt through the block. "One loaded," he said.

Brent pulled back the handle on the side of the block and let the powerful spring drive the first round home, the gib at the top of the extractor gripping the cartridge. "Load two!" Brent snapped. Bowman jerked the brass tag leader, and Brent pulled back on the handle and let it fly back again. The first round shot smoothly into the breech. Then the lieutenant raised up and peered into the breech to assure himself the belt was seated properly, slammed down hard on the cover, engaging the two spring-loaded locks. "Loaded and cocked," he said, glancing at his loader out of the corner of his eye. He locked the weapon into a vertical position and watched curiously as they closed on the downed pilot of the Seafire. He raised his binoculars.

Bobbing in his tiny yellow life raft, the man was dressed in a brown flying suit, and a helmet with goggles up. With white skin, large nose, and big round eyes, he was definitely not Japanese. He was waving at the submarine and smiling. "Sure as hell not a Japanese," he heard Williams mutter. The captain turned to Hara. "All ahead slow."

"All ahead slow, sir." The rhythm of the big diesels dropped.

Williams glanced at the gyro repeater. "Left to zero-four-five, helmsman. We'll come alongside starboard side to."

"Left to zero-four-five, starboard side to, sir."

"Very well." Williams pulled a loud hailer from its brackets on the windscreen and raised it to his lips. Turning to the stern, he shouted at the five-inch gun crew which was standing just aft of the cannon with buoys, life preservers, and lines. "Starboard side to!"

A young sailor, Boatswain's Mate Second Class Hitoshi Motoshima, who was the senior surviving petty officer, shouted, his hands cupped around his mouth, "Starboard side to, sir."

The floating pilot was just a few yards ahead and off the starboard bow. "All stop." Despite the stopped engines, the submarine continued, its great momentum carrying it forward.

"All back one-third."

Brent felt the vibrations come through the grating as the screws fought almost sixteen hundred tons of inertia. Instinctively he steadied his weapon. Now the pilot was very close and off the starboard beam. Motoshima began to whirl the "monkey's fist" at the end of a line over his head. With a quick, expert flip of his wrist, he released the line and the lead weighted "fist" carried over the raft and the line actually dropped over the pilot's shoulder. The pilot grabbed the line and began to pull himself in.

"All stop!" The boat wallowed in the gentle swell, its idling diesels alternately burbling under water and then firing blue smoke and spumes of eggwhite spray into the air as the seas first covered the exhausts and then fell away with the submarine's roll. Quickly the pilot was pulled in, and in a moment Boatswain's Mate Motoshima, secured to a stanchion by a life line, pulled the tall, thin pilot aboard. The flier steadied himself by gripping a lifeline and then, helped by the boatswain's mate, walked toward the bridge, grinning.

"Lend a hand," Williams said to Bowman.

The loader reached down and pulled on the pilot's flying jacket as he mounted the ladder slowly to the bridge. The captain extended his hand and had to actually look up to find the lanky airman's eyes. Tall, slender, and hawk-nosed, with high cheek bones with hollows beneath them, the man had a narrow but square, strong chin. His most impressive feature was his eyes. Wide and blue, they had the look of a one who could recite Shakespeare, Shelley, or Keats or kill with equal aplomb. Over all, he bore a striking resemblance to Basil Rathbone playing Sherlock Holmes in an early B movie.

Williams said to the newcomer, "Welcome aboard. I'm Lieutenant Reginald Williams. I'm the captain of this boat."

The pilot smiled enigmatically, and looked around the bridge at the crew, which stared back curiously, as if they were studying an alien from outer space. Grasping the captain's hand, he spoke in a cultured voice made hard by a nasal twang, as if his nose were stuffed with hollow iron beads. "Captain Colin Willard-Smith here." He dropped the captain's hand and glanced around at the twenty-millimeter guns and then at the Brownings. His eyes came to rest on Brent Ross. "I say, old chaps—your shooting was a bit of all right." He studied the blood on the lieutenant's helmet and life jacket, but said nothing.

Brent stared back. "Didn't mean to knock you down, Captain." And then with a wry smile, he added, "Not really cricket, was it?"

Willard-Smith laughed. "Quite so. But I was hard on that JU's arse." He looked around and then returned to Williams. "You chaps put up quite a lot of flak. Upon my word, amazing accuracy. Shot out my oil tank and coolant lines."

"Sorry, Captain," Williams said. He stared over the port beam where the two enemy airmen drifted in their raft. After a quick sight through the bearing ring, he said, "All ahead slow, left standard rudder. Steady up on one-nine-zero."

Brent unlocked the fifty-caliber and began to bring it to bear on the two men in the raft. Every man on the bridge stared at him and at Williams. Willard-Smith caught on quickly. "I say, chaps. You're not . . ."

Williams interrupted him, "We're going to pick them up, Captain." And then to Brent, "Secure the fifty, Mister Ross."

"Aye aye, Sir," Brent said, locking the weapon into place.

Williams glanced at the sky, forward, aft and then shouted down the hatch into the conning tower, "Plot! Have you been able to keep your DR track?"

The voice of Navigator Lieutenant Charlie Cadenbach came back, "Plot aye. We have, sir. I've been reading your course and speed changes from my repeaters. But you know I could be miles off. I need to shoot sun lines—run up my noon sight. Request permission to come to the bridge."

"Negative! You'll have to wait until we secure from battle surface. We'll be stopping in a hundred yards to pick up a couple of fliers. Then I want your best course back to Yokosuka."

There was a short silence interrupted only by the roar of the diesels and the sloshing sounds of water running down the hull and out the scuppers and drains. Then Cadenbach's reply came up through the hatch, "I suggest three-five-zero, Captain." There was disappointment in his voice.

Williams returned to the pilot, "If you drop down that hatch," he gestured to the hatch to the conning tower, "Lieutenant Cadenbach will direct you to the wardroom. You'll find hot coffee and sandwiches there." He waved around the bridge grimly where coagulating blood still oozed down the steel windscreen as if it had been flung from the brush of a madman. "We've had casualties. I can't spare a man."

The Englishman pursed his lips and then tightened his jaw. "With your permission, Captain, I'll remain here. I have excellent eyes." He gestured at the gore-splattered

59

periscope shears and the windscreen. "I can stand duty as a lookout."

"You're up to it? After all, we just shot you down."

The Englishman drew himself up and spoke with astonishing quiescence. "Quite fit, thank you. Been shot down before. Almost bought the farm in the Falklands. This bit was quite easy. Didn't even get wet."

Williams smiled. "Very well. Keep an eye on the sky. Our radar is out." Williams glanced off the port side where the two enemy flyers stared back from their raft. "All stop. Prepare to pick up survivors." The five-inch-gun crew moved to the rail.

Willard-Smith waved a hand to the northwest, where a great dogfight had sprawled across most of the western horizon. "They're jolly well having a go at it up there. Must be the biggest show since the Battle of Britain." He spoke to Williams. "Captain, aren't you going to try to pick up more survivors?"

"I wish I could." Williams gestured at the two enemy pilots, who were now only a few feet off the port quarter. "After we pick them up, we've got to head for the yards. We're badly damaged. Taking on water in one of our main ballast tanks and leaking chlorine. And there could be more Stukas around. Another near miss could deep-six us." He shook his head with resignation. "Admiral Fujita may send some destroyers. But it's risky — very risky. Saipan and Tinian are just too close."

Brent stared up at the sky. It looked as if at least a hundred aircraft were trying to destroy each other. The fight had drifted quite low, and individual aircraft were easy to see. There was smoke in the sky like twisted black pillars, and several parachutes drifted slowly toward the sea. He raised his glasses and almost chortled with joy as he found a Zero with a red cowling and green hood. It was climbing over the fight with a Seafire hard on its rudder. He fingered the Browning and muttered to himself, "Yoshi Matsuhara, may your kamis be riding with you this day."

"Survivors aboard," was the shout from the stern.

"Very well. All ahead standard. Come right to three-five-zero."

Slowly, *Blackfin* picked up speed and curved toward the north.

Commander Yoshi Matsuhara cursed. Rosencrance and Vatz, flying in tandem, were a thousand meters beneath him and perhaps twenty kilometers to the north. Rosencrance had lost one wingman and so had he. Willard-Smith was gone, perhaps dead. His last transmission still rang in the flight leader's ears. "Sorry, old chaps," the Englishman had said as if he were excusing himself from a table ladened with tea and crumpets. "I've caught one. Got to ditch straight away."

"Hit the silk!" York's anguished voice had countered.

"Sorry, old man. Beastly luck. My chute's been shot out. Got to take the old girl for a swim. Best of luck and all that. Cheerio." Then Willard-Smith's radio went dead.

"Tenno Jimmu," Yoshi implored, calling on the spirit of Japan's first emperor. "Look out for him, sacred one. He is a good man." He needed the skillful Englishman. He had fought with rare verve, panache, and audacity. In fact, even the new fighter pilot, Pilot Officer Elwyn York, had adapted miraculously as soon as the firing began. Some men were like that. The Cockney, too, had put on an amazing performance. He had already shot down two Junkers and damaged an ME 109. Yoshi needed more pilots like these.

Climbing to 8,000 meters on a big semicircular swing far to the southwest, Yoshi dropped his starboard wing to give himself a view of the fighting below. It was the single biggest air battle he had ever seen. Admiral Fujita had committed at least four squadrons of *Yonaga*'s fighter group to the fight. He wanted *Blackfin* and would sacrifice almost anything and anyone to save her. It was more than just the submarine, more than just hunger for victory, more than the obsession to destroy his enemy. It was his attachment to Brent Ross . . . Yoshi was sure of it. He had long ago suspected the big, brilliant, brawling American had become the old admiral's surrogate son—a replacement for Kazuo, his boy, who had been incinerated at Hiroshima in 1945.

The fighter circuit was filled with frantic shouts of triumph and fear. "Break left Shizuyo! Now! Now!"

"Breaking left. Your radio sounds awful, Arii."

"Shigamitsu! Where are you? It's Arii."

"Below you, Arii. Stopped one with my engine. Losing oil pressure. You are in charge. Banzai!"

Yoshi's eyes were caught by a burning Zero curving up in its death agony. A heart-wrenching plea came through the earphones, "Bail out, Noritaka. In the name of the gods, bail out!" But the Zero fell off into its final plunge with a closed canopy.

"Above you! Above you, Mizumoto. Two of them at five o'clock."

"See them, Tokita. Stay with me."

"I have the one on the left!"

"Turning, Tokita."

"No! No! Dive! Dive, Mizumoto!"

There was a gigantic explosion below and to the north. A Zero and an ME 109 had collided head-on. Yoshi punched his instrument panel. It was the young NAP (Naval Air Pilot) Masaichi Mizumoto. He had stormed through the gates of the Yasakuni Shrine in a spectacular blaze of glory—a heroic demise that had burnished his karma and ensured that his spirit would dwell for eternity with the countless heroes awaiting them all at the sacred Yasakuni Shrine. "Banzai!"

Stomach churning, the flight leader ignored the carnage and fought the overpowering urge to plunge into the battle. He had one quest. A single quarry to hunt.

Finally Matsuhara saw what he had been looking for: a flash of red below and black-and-white zebra stripes. Rosencrance and Vatz. Unlike all other participants in the sprawling brawl, these two were flying in perfect syncronization, Rosencrance leading, Vatz behind and off his port side. As usual, Rosencrance was looking for an easy kill and had found it. Just as Yoshi's eyes came into focus on the pair, Rosencrance blasted a crippled Zero out of the sky almost casually with a short burst. The perfectly aimed shells and bullets struck the fighter's fuselage tank, and the small plane vanished in a single Vesuvian blast. "New self-sealing tanks! That isn't supposed to happen!" Yoshi anguished. But Rosencrance was already banking toward another smoking Mitsubishi fleeing toward the northeast, away from the fight.

Without conscious thought, and broiling with hate and anger, the Japanese pilot punched the engine into overboost, pulled back hard on the stick, and then pushed the control column hard to the left, half-rolling into a dive. A quick glance told him Pilot Officer Elwyn York had anticipated the maneuver and was holding his position. Yoshi spoke into his microphone, "Edo Three, this is Edo Leader. Stay with me on my first pass on the red Messerschmitt. Then individual combat."

"Right, guv'nor. I've got the black arsehole!" And then York's hate, too, boiled through the earphones, "The bloody butchers."

Accelerating in near vertical dives, the pair flashed past a smoking ME 109 just as it rolled and a body dropped out. Quickly a parachute popped opened. Yoshi felt the Zero-sen begin to vibrate. Anxiously he stole a look at his instruments; tachometer crowding the red line at 2,800 rpms, 107 centimeters of manifold pressure, cylinder head temperature still a tolerable 200 degrees Celsius. And the white airspeed needle chased around the clock faster and faster — 320, 360, 360 — the white needle overtaking the slower red danger indicator.

The vibrations increased until the aircraft was gripped with fearful shaking, like an old man dying of fever. Both hands could not hold it still. The muscles of Matsuhara's arms and shoulders began to ache. His airframe was in jeopardy, but he had no choice. Rosencrance was hard on the tail of the smoking Mitsubishi and was almost in range. It was Shigamitsu. He could see the single red stripe of the section leader on the Zero-sen's rudder. The American renegade had a perfect killing angle — astern and above the tail. Flame leaped from his guns.

With the airspeed indicator showing 410 knots, Yoshi pulled back on the control column. At this tremendous speed he stood a good chance of overtaking his enemy before Rosencrance could kill Shigamitsu. He also stood a good chance of losing consciousness or his wings or both. He braced his feet and pulled back on the column with both hands with all the strength he could muster. He thought the stick would break off in his hands like a piece of bamboo. As the dive flattened, the g-forces went to work. He could feel his cheeks sag, his eyes water, and tears run down his cheeks, his mouth as dry as the Gobi. His head became a rock that bent his neck and forced him deep into his parachute pack until he thought his spine would crack. Then the heavy, dull aching pain in his stomach began, the dampness in his crotch as his bladder dribbled, and he feared for his bowels. Now his worst fears were realized. As the airframe shook and trembled, bouncing him about in his seat against the restraints, the wings began to flap as if they were trying to break off. The weight of the huge new Sakae 42 engine persisted on its trajectory toward the earth and had increased his wing loading far beyond design specifications. But the little machine held together, flattened out behind Rosencrance and Vatz, just where the commander wanted to be.

However, very swiftly, Commander Yoshi Matsuhara's body lost its battle with gravity and inertia. With centrifugal force draining the blood from his head, his peripheral vision was first to go, leaving him with the peculiar sensation of looking down a tunnel. Then the universe clouded and darkened as if misty gray lenses had been drawn across his eyes. He was on the very edge of unconsciousness. He slipped into the darkness and knew not when or for how long before the twilight of consciousness crept back. Groggily, he shook his head, tightened his stomach muscles, and breathed in short, explosive gasps, screaming "Amaterasu!" over and over again to relieve the pressure. Then, with blood pumping back into his brain, his vision cleared like a slowly opening curtain. The Zero was standing on its starboard wing and was on the brink of a stall. Hastily he brought it back under control. The amazing York was still with him.

He was too late. Shigamitsu's Zero was a roaring torch, twisting into the sea, leaving thick black smoke like a streamer of black silk behind. Lieutenant Todoa Shigamitsu was drifting above it under the glaring white canopy of his parachute. Casually the two Messerschmitts banked toward the parachutist. Shigamitsu saw death coming and raised his pistol in a last futile, defiant gesture. Yoshi screamed "No!" as the red fighter fired. Shigamitsu jerked as if he were shocked by great jolts of electricity and then sagged in the embrace of death.

His vision still shadowed by the g-forces, Yoshi felt a ravening beast break loose in his guts. Shrieking with tears on his cheeks and his judgment clouded by rage and the lack of blood in his brain, he fired. At six hundred meters and with the ME filling only two rings in his range finder, the full deflection shot missed. Immediately the two enemy machines looped and half-rolled in a perfect Immelmann, a quick, smart maneuver that took Yoshi by surprise. They must have heard a warning on their radios. Abruptly his vision cleared and his sensibilities returned. Wiping his cheeks and nose with the back

65

of his glove, he cursed his poor judgment and amateurish performance. "MEs are not supposed to turn that short—that fast," he muttered deep in his chest. A glance in his mirror told him York was still on station off his starboard elevator. He felt a new wave of confidence. Hunching forward, he brought the red machine into his range finder. *Revenge! Revenge! The samurai's most precious commodity.* He *must* have it at any cost.

Rosencrance had kicked left rudder brutally in an attempt to bring his armament to bear on the peril bolting down from above. From one-quarter ahead, both Matsuhara and York opened fire. But the canny American had anticipated the attack and kicked opposite rudder, winging over and away from the tracers with Vatz still maintaining his station 300 meters from his leader. It was precise, professional flying, as if the two men had but one mind. Yoshi saw the bright flashes of strikes as his stream caught the red ME's fuselage far back near the tail. However, both of the enemy aircraft showed no disabling damage. In fact, Yoshi's dive had carried him below the MEs, which were now climbing and turning to come about for their own pass.

Kicking rudder and pulling back on the stick, Yoshi rolled toward the enemy so tightly he felt the juddering that warned of a high-speed stall. Cursing, he eased off, and Rosencrance had his opening. Flame flickered on the leading edges of the ME's wings and from the cowling. It was a short but accurate burst. Yoshi felt the stick and rudder pedals vibrate as slugs tore into his tail. With the danger of stalling gone, he jinked below his enemy's guns and then just as quickly fooled his enemy by curving up and toward the Messerschmitt instead of rolling away into the dive Rosencrance had every right to expect. "Never dogfight a Zero-sen, you cowardly butcher!" he screamed.

The ME finally filled the required three rings. The cross hairs were on the cockpit. Now barreling down on each other nearly head-on, both pilots fired together. Gunfire winked bright red, tracers glowed and left white trails, tying the two machines together with a deadly gossamer web. The commander felt the fighter jerk and shudder, and then there was a loud bang as a piece of aluminum was blasted from his port wing and more jolts as bullets ripped his fuselage. But he was scoring. Bright fire motes blossomed on the enemy's hood and fuselage, but the cockpit was still intact. Now the enemy's propeller boss filled his windscreen. He would ram his despised enemy and avenge the dead Shigamitsu, who was drifting far below. Exit this world and enter the next in a blaze of glory, like Mizumoto. Sacrificing his life for the Emperor would assure him of entry into the Yasakuni Shrine. Masaichi Mizumoto, Todoa Shigamitsu, his one love, the beautiful Kimio Urshazawa, and dozens of others awaited him. The best company in the realm of the gods for eternity. He skinned his lips back, clenched his perfect white teeth in a grimace of determination.

Rosencrance read his mind. Frantically, he horsed back on his stick and banked sharply to port. Yoshi countered with stick and rudder. But his port wing dropped too much, and the fighter slewed down and to the left. He was out of trim. The wing had taken too much punishment. It was serving as an air trap.

With only a few meters to spare, they passed each other like two smoking projectiles fired from duelists' pistols, Rosencrance slightly above and to the right of Matsuhara. Yoshi saw the canopy and Rosencrance's leering smile as he flashed past, and then the Mitsubishi rocked and wallowed in the ME's turbulent wake. He had scored no hits on the cockpit and missed his second attempt to ram. The butcher was still alive. "Amaterasu!" he screamed. "Where are you? He should be dead! Dead!"

A glance in his rearview mirror told him Rosencrance and Vatz were not turning for another pass. Instead they were diving to the south and west in the ME 109's favorite evasive tactic. Rosencrance must be damaged. He killed like a wild animal, but he never abandoned a fight. Maybe he was wounded or out of ammunition. Certainly the Zero-sen's ammunition tanks were nearly empty and fuel was low.

Miraculously, the skies were suddenly empty. Every aircraft except York's and the two fleeing MEs, which were rapidly dwindling on the horizon, had vanished. It was an astonishing phenomenon he had experienced many times before. At one moment the heavens would be filled with tumbling, snarling aircraft shooting each other to pieces; in the next they would vanish as if swept from the sky by the broom of a bored god. Incredible, but he and Pilot Officer Elwyn York owned the sky. And *Blackfin* was nowhere to be seen. Maybe she had been sunk and Brent Ross had been killed, too. Yoshi sighed and choked back a sour taste that suddenly filled his mouth. Many good men had died this day. He glanced upward. "Please spare Brent Ross," he pleaded.

There was something wrong with his controls and thoughts of self-immolation were suddenly banished from his mind. A dead man could avenge nothing. The left rudder pedal was very heavy, and the drag pulling to the left had increased. The hole in his wing was gulping air, and the skin of the wing was bulging with the pressure. He could see his main spar, hydraulic lines, and control runs. Frantically he throttled back to 1,700 rpms and left his propeller in fine pitch. Then he cranked his trim wheel and felt the pressure on the left rudder pedal ease as the change in trim compensated for some of the drag. He gently tried his ailerons and rudder and found the response sluggish but firm. Glancing over his shoulder, he saw York still holding station. He was apparently undamaged except for some rents in his fuselage and tail. He was a good man . . . a very good man.

The young Englishman throttled up and pulled alongside. He drew a finger across his throat in the universal sign of low fuel levels. Yoshi nodded his understanding. The Cockney's radio must have been shot out. In fact, he could see a half-dozen holes just forward of the pilot's seat. He verified by calling out, "Edo Three," three times on his radio. Only the hiss of the carrier wave answered his call, and glancing at his wingman he saw York raise both hands and shrug in a gesture of helplessness. He had seen Yoshi speak into his microphone and understood there had been a radio check. Yoshi stabbed a finger to the north and mouthed, "Home! Home!" York bobbed his head up and down and smiled.

Carefully, Commander Yoshi Matsuhara banked the Zero, compensating for the drag with right aileron and elevator. There was a familiar seething, burning deep in the pit of his stomach. Anger and frustration was corroding his guts like boiling acid. Rosencrance had made his kills and escaped him again. The butcher was still loose. At fifty thousand dollars a kill, the American renegade had probably made one hundred fifty thousand dollars for his afternoon's work. And something else frightening had become apparent: the Arabs had a much more formidable base in the Marianas than he had suspected. Counting the bombers, perhaps seventy enemy aircraft had been in the air. Maybe more.

He clenched his jaw so tight his teeth ached. *Yonaga* and all of Japan could be open to attack by long-range aircraft. He sighed deeply, trying to rid himself of the vision of Shigamitsu's death and the terrible tension that turned his muscles to steel, his blood to ice. Sighing explosively, he relaxed his back and neck, but not his grip on the control column or the pressure on the rudder pedals. He watched the horizon swing slowly beneath his cowling and stared at the card of his magnetic compass. And then his eyes moved to the chart strapped to his knee for *Yonaga*'s point option data. "Zero-four-zero," he said to himself. "That should be our course if she has not changed hers and if," he threw a glance skyward, "the gods smile on us."

He centered his controls as the compass settled on the desired course and sagged back in his seat. He must conserve fuel. He thinned his mixture and throttled back to 1350 rpms, releasing the lever when the engine's backfires told him it would take no more. His airspeed indicator showed 140 knots. It would have to do. He glanced at York, who had followed his lead dutifully and then threw one last look to the southwest horizon. Rosencrance and Vatz had vanished.

Slowly the two fighters droned through the empty sky toward the cold mists on the far horizon.

Chapter Two

Seated alone at the single table in *Blackfin*'s tiny wardroom, Brent Ross toyed with his coffee mug with fingers
as numb as his mind. His ears still rang from the gunfire, and there was a dull ache in his neck. Slowly and
deliberately he rubbed the big corded muscles, but his
mind was elsewhere. They had just buried Chief Gunner's Mate Philip Robinson and the captain had said a
memorial for the two dead lookouts, Max Orlin and Bob
"Tuck" Tucker, at the end of the chief's services. All three
were together now for eternity in the 6,000 fathoms of
the Marianas deep. Brent shuddered. It was very cold
down there, and with a complete absence of light, the
creatures that lived there were blind. He looked up from
his coffee as if something in the familiar room could distract him, take his mind off of the visions of the dead
men, the blood splattered bridge, the gore on his helmet,
life jacket, and binoculars that he had washed off with
the frantic motions of a man trying to rub out reminders
of his own mortality. That could be the worst part of funerals — the reminder that yours was yet to come.

There was no relief, no solace in the small room. He
was alone, terribly alone, in one of the most crowded
places devised by man. His eyes wandered restlessly over
the opposite bulkhead where a small refrigerator was
built in under a stainless-steel drainboard and sink and a
high rack of steel cupboards; he gazed at the forward
bulkhead, where a compact desk, counter, and slotted

box holding thumb-worn magazines and paperback novels were crammed into a minute space the officers sarcastically referred to as "rest and recreation areas."

Brent sniffed and wrinkled his nose in distaste. "Chlorine," he muttered to himself. Despite repairs made to the damaged cells of the battery and the efforts of the ship's ventilation system that was operating at full capacity, Brent could still smell a faint odor of the gas. And other evidence of *Blackfin*'s wounds came up through his feet and the seat of his pants. Although he could not hear Number One and Number Two ballast pumps over the rumbles of the diesels and the hiss and clatter of the ventilating system, he could feel the vibrations of the two machines as they attempted to stay ahead of the water entering the Number One ballast tank through the damaged sea valve. With the sixth sense of all men who serve for long, lonely months at sea, Brent was more than just intimately acquainted with his ship. He was as much a part of it as a blood cell is a bit of a human body, and the boat was much more a part of him than any woman could ever be—or had ever been.

He had known many women, explored every hidden part of their bodies, knew how to fondle and tantalize with just the right touch in just the right places. Pamela Ward, Sarah Aranson, Mayumi Hachiya, Kathryn Suzuki, Dale McIntyre; he had orchestrated all of their passions like a conductor coaxing the utmost from an orchestra. But none of them had ever really become part of him or he part of them even when locked in the most intimate acts of love.

Blackfin was different. The old fleet boat had become the ultimate courtesan, a tyrannical, demanding mistress. But more than that, he was bound to her as he had never been bound to anyone or anything: a bondage of a human to a machine that no longer was a machine but a vital, viable creature made of metal. He smiled at his irrational thoughts. But there was truth there. Why was

72

it always *she* or *her*—the feminine? He knew when speed was changed by the variations in the pulse of the four main engines; when a new course was cut by the slightest alteration in roll and pitch patterns. These changes would jar him awake like no change in a woman's mood ever had. He would lie rigid in his bunk, wide-eyed for a moment until he was convinced there was no problem, no threat. He would live or die with her. No one could argue with that.

All men who fight at sea carry an atavistic dread of entrapment in a sinking hull. A submarine can hold particular horrors unique to the species. Even when surfaced, a submarine is on the edge of negative buoyancy, with most of her pressure hull below the waterline. Submerged, the pitiless, cruel sea has an enormous advantage. A depth charge exploding within fourteen-feet can crush the hull like an eggshell. And a special kind of death awaits the submariner. Death does not come by drowning. In fact, drowning would be a pleasant alternative. The truth known to all who fight in the depths is that pressure inside the boat is instantly compressed to many atmospheres and the air super-heats to hundreds of degrees. Bulkheads are ripped out before the onslaught of seawater under hundreds of tons of pressure. Steel fittings and shattered bulkheads pepper the declining spaces like hails of bullets and shrapnel. Lungs roasted and bodies riddled by flying steel, it is instant death for every man.

Cursing, the young lieutenant tried to shake himself free from moribund thoughts. He had fought well, hit every JU that had come within range. Crog and the two gunners on the Orlikons had scored, too. They were all picked men, known for their accuracy. Then his spirits dropped again. Yoshi Matsuhara had fought Rosencrance. He had caught glimpses of them trying to kill each other, sometimes so high they left condensed vapor trails in crazy patterns. There was no way to know if his

73

dearest friend was still alive. Maybe he had entered the Yasakuni Shrine through Neptune's Gate. The mixed metaphors of the two mythologies gave Brent's fatigued, distressed mind no trouble. He was a man of two worlds and was too preoccupied with death, anyway.

He had seen many aviators die this day. The chief, Max Orlin and Bob Tucker had been joined by many more who had fallen from the skies. They were all down there now, suspended in the depths, attracting the creatures that fed on the flesh of the dead. But not Phil Robinson. Wrapped in canvas and weighted with two five-inch shells, the chief would find the bottom. And they would not have him, at least for a long while, and then they would find nothing but bones. *Great triumph*, Brent thought bitterly.

He was angry with Williams. The prisoners should have been killed. An Arab and a German, both were as feisty and belligerent as wet roosters. Strangely, they blamed each other for their misfortune. The German, a big, heavy man who seemed quite elderly for a flier, was the pilot of the bomber—the only pilot who had not been an Arab. *"Hauptmann* (Captain) Conrad Schachter, *Sechste Bombardement Geschwader* (Sixth Bombardment Squadron)," he had announced, as he was pulled to the bridge, dripping wet. And then, glaring at his Arab gunner, he spat in surprisingly good English, "This *dummkopf* bedouin goatherd is my gunner. He could not hit the side of a mosque with a fist full of camel shit from one meter or we would not be here."

The Arab was a short, dark man with the narrow, shifty eyes of a hawk and a nose to match. His most prominent aspect was a great drooping mustache which obviously served as a warrant to his masculinity. "I am Feldwebel (Sergeant) Haj Abu al Sahdi," he said, palming some beads he had pulled from a pocket. And then staring balefully at Schachter, his contempt for rank became obvious. "This son of a donkey could not drop a

74

ton of shit into the Pacific Ocean if he jumped in with it! He could not fly a kite in a *khamsin.*" His eyes narrowed and his mustache contorted in a terrible leer and he spat, "Your mother's cunt was an oasis for camels, you toothless dog!"

Roaring like a prodded bull, the German had leaped for the Arab's throat. It took the entire bridge gang to pull them apart. Then, with the help of four members of the conning tower crew, Williams had them dragged below. Now they were chained to stanchions in the forward torpedo room a safe distance apart. The German had been furious at the indignity of being confined in enlisted men's country. He became even more obnoxious. "I am a *hauptmann*—a captain, you *arschlochs* (assholes,") he shouted pompously. "I demand quarters in the wardroom!" Everyone ignored him.

There was the sound behind Brent of a curtain being drawn open and a young, tall rail of a man, Navigator Charlie Cadenbach, entered. With a sharp-chiseled nose, narrow face, sunken cheeks and the slight stoop to his shoulders so common to gaunt men, Lieutenant Junior Grade Cadenbach exuded an air of weakness completely inconsistent with his strength of character and boundless energy. But his energy was elsewhere at this moment. With a sigh, he sank on the bench across the table from Brent. "I'd give my left nut for an SINS (Inertial Navigation System.) But I finally got my sun lines and ran up my noon sight." And then sarcastically, "Got my fix, by God, just the way Christopher Columbus used to do it. Only four miles east of our DR track." The young officer drummed the table with four bony fingers and stared at Brent's unexpressive face—a rigid face that seemed fixed in concrete. He tried again, "Good shooting, Lieutenant. You guys up there were uncanny. You saved us. I hear you hit every plane. Unbelievable. That kind of gunnery is damned near impossible."

Brent was nodding and mumbling his thanks when the

swinging doors in the aft bulkhead opened and Mess Management Specialist Pablo Fortuno entered from the galley. He was carrying a pitcher of coffee and a tray with two thick sandwiches. Short with the large lips and wide, flat nose typical of the Kanakas of the South Pacific, his hair was coal-black and his swarthy skin pockmarked, giving evidence of the variety of poxes that had bedeviled and decimated his people since the arrival of the white man.

Brent was not hungry and had not ordered a sandwich. But the crafty Pablo sometimes knew more about his officers than the officers knew about themselves. He handed Cadenbach a steaming mug of coffee and refilled Brent's. Then he placed the sandwiches between the men and left. Brent was suddenly ravenous. He picked up a ham sandwich and savored the taste of the meat and the mayonnaise. Lettuce, tomatoes and other fresh vegetables had vanished five weeks into their patrol. Now, virtually everything they ate came out of cans or sealed containers, even ice cream. He began to feel strength flow into his muscles and his spirits rose. He sipped his coffee and said, "I haven't seen the English pilot lately."

Cadenbach nodded, obviously pleased his executive officer had come to life. "The skipper gave him Admiral Allen's cabin. He had some chow, a shot of Williams' own private Haig and Haig Pinch and hit the sack."

For the first time, a smile toyed with the corners of Brent's lips. "I think he saved our butts. That Kraut would've laid his egg right down the hatch if Willard-Smith hadn't been on his ass." Brent drummed his temple in mock frustration and switched to German, "I mean on his *arschloch*."

Cadenbach smiled and became very British, "Right-oh, old boy." They both chuckled. He sipped his coffee and became serious. "Mister Ross, we've been briefed on the enemy over and over, but no one ever mentioned their use of German designations for their air force instead of

Arabic — squadrons, rank, rate. They assign Arab names to their ships, don't they? Why refer to their squadrons in German? Even the Arab gunner did it. He called himself a *Feldwebel,* too, instead of 'sergeant.' There aren't that many Germans working for Kadafi. Schachter claims he was the only German pilot in the JU squadron."

Brent cleared his mouth of the rest of his sandwich and washed the remnants down with coffee before answering. "At first most of his mercenaries were Germans. They used their own nomenclature and the names stuck. And, don't forget, most of their combat aircraft are still German."

"But, now, their force is truly international. He's hired mercenaries from all over the world."

"Right, Charlie."

The navigator rubbed the short whiskers on his chin with his thumb and forefinger, obviously pleased with the opportunity to talk privately with his usually reclusive, taciturn executive officer. Rarely did a man find an opportunity like this on a submarine. They had privacy, except for Pablo Fortuno, who was probably eavesdropping. Brent was a veteran and admired by the entire crew, a man who had fought the Arabs for six years and knew them better than anyone on board. "Why don't they use more Arab pilots?" Cadenbach asked, eager to keep the momentum of the conversation rolling. He was not disappointed.

Brent's eyes took on a new lustre as he warmed to the topic. Talking to the navigator had helped pull him from the trough. The hatred and repugnance he felt for the enemy made him suddenly garrulous as bitter thoughts crowded his mind, queuing up like impatient commuters waiting to articulate their way through a metro's door. Words poured out of him as if each were a brick in a barrier, walling off the terrible depression for a moment, at least. "It's simple. Consider this, over two — hundred-million Arabs can't whip four million Israelis. And why?" He did not wait for an answer. "You've got to understand the Arab. He can't take discipline and he's completely irrational. You just saw their bombing attack on us. The Kraut was the best of the lot. Their attack was slipshod and poorly coordinated. They came too low, gave us a shot they shouldn't have given us. It's typical of them. Arab armies lack organization, cohesiveness and the will to fight as a unit. Why else does Israel exist?"

The navigator pondered the rhetorical question and then surprised Brent with a singular insight. "You know a lot about them—more than you should know from just fighting them. You've been to the Middle East, haven't you."

Straightening, Brent made a temple of his fingers and then locked them into a single fist. "You're very perceptive, Navigator," he said. "In fact, when I was fourteen my father was assigned as a naval attaché to the ambassador in Cairo. For two years his duties took us all over the Middle East from Iran to Morocco." He sighed and drummed the table with his locked fists. "It was an education—a real education you can't get in a classroom or a briefing."

Cadenbach nodded and pushed on, "You said their armies were undisciplined—like a rabble."

"Right. *Rabble* is a good word."

"But there was Jordan's Arab Legion. Glubb Pasha was a fine general. They were good—pushed the Israelis back into Jerusalem back in '48 and '49."

Brent nodded approval of Cadenbach's knowledge. "You've studied your history, Navigator. They were a good outfit. But they were British trained and British led. And don't forget, Glubb Pasha was actually an Englishman named John Bagot Glubb. When he and his officers left, the legion collapsed." Brent felt an old anger begin to mount as cruel memories flashed from the dark recesses. "You know I've fought them since 1983. Do you know what started this whole thing with Kadafi?"

"One of *Yonaga*'s fighters tangled with a Libyan DC-3."

"Right. It was over Tokyo Bay. I saw the whole thing. The transport intruded into *Yonaga*'s air space after repeated warnings. Commander Matsuhara shot out one of its engines."

"He didn't destroy it, Mister Ross."

"That's correct. And there were no casualties."

"But I know all of this didn't grow out of that one trivial incident."

"But that was how it started. It was an insult, and Arabs never forget." Brent dug his fingers into a dull pain that persisted at the base of his skull. The pressure brought immediate relief. "Of course, there's the small matter of world domination, the oil embargo, the killing of hostages." The hand dropped to the table and the fingers began to war with the steel top in a series of taps. "But basically, yes, it all started with that one incident over six years ago." The fingers became a fist that pounded down on the table with a loud clang. "They'll go after you any way they can."

"What do you mean?"

"Have you ever heard of Hasan ibn-al-Sabbah?"

"The 'old man of the mountains.' Founded the assassins in Persia—maybe a thousand years ago." Cadenbach's face took on a grim cast. "They still operate, Mister Ross."

"Correct, Charlie. Call themselves 'Sabbah.' They're fanatically loyal to Kadafi. Their preferred attack is with the knife, but they'll use anything from AK 47s to plastique. They like to catch their victim unawares and stab him in the back. Do you know I've fought them with pistols, fists, boards, knives, even a wrench—in alleys, parking lots, a park, the dining room of the Imperial Hotel, the UN?" He stabbed a finger directly at Cadenbach's face, stopping only inches from the navigator's sharp nose. "And know this, you're a prime candidate, too." The hand dropped to the table with a thump.

Cadenbach eyed the fatigued, flushed face as if he were seeing his executive officer for the first time; as if he had opened a long locked closet and discovered things inside he preferred not to see. He muttered, "I've heard of them—heard of the things they can do."

Brent stared over the navigator at the far bulkhead and was at another place at another time. "They murdered Yoshi Matsuhara's fiancée in Ueno Park." The voice suddenly filled with irony, "From ambush, of course. An AK 47. Six slugs in the chest." He slapped the table so hard the steel top rang from the force of the blow and the mugs clattered. Steadying his mug, the young navigator looked up in alarm as Brent raced on, "What else can you expect from the Arabs? All they've known is tyrants and assassination. In a way, they're all Sabbah. For centuries their leaders have manipulated them ruthlessly, used them for the dirty work while they wallowed in luxury. And Islam just adds more bars to the prison. It's a dry, barren religion as dry and barren as the land they grow up in. And it's fatalistic, strips them of what little optimism and ambition they might have. Hatred and vengeance is all they live for—the only things that give meaning to their miserable lives and keep in mind, they are quite ready to die attacking. Eternal paradise awaits the soul of the assassin, you know. After all, Islam promises this."

Cadenbach shifted uncomfortably and they both sat quietly, the only sounds intruding were the usual ship's sounds of blowers and engines. The young navigator broke the silence. "I know, Mister Ross. But there must be some scruples, some honor!"

Brent laughed, a hollow sound completely devoid of humor. "Oh, the Arab has his honor, his 'face,' and can feel shame. An honorable man will boast of his brave exploits and bore you to death with his lies. And his 'face' is skin deep. He wears it with his honor on his sleeve and then will betray his mother for a pile of camel dung for his fire."

"But you said he knows shame?"

"Shame comes from coming in second in a deal. You feel shame when you don't lie convincingly enough to cheat your best friend—your brother, father. Or, a man feels shame if he must work at a menial job to survive." He raised a finger and shook it for emphasis. "Keep this in mind, Charlie, shame never comes from crime, but only in the betrayal of their twisted code of duty. Then a man finds shame and maybe a knife in the back in a dark alley."

"They've had great writers, mathematicians, physicians, Mister Ross."

"A thousand years ago. But today they're so full of envy and hatred toward us, their literature is filled with self-hatred and loathing for everything we stand for."

"There is nothing redeeming about them, Mister Ross?"

"Absolutely nothing."

Cadenbach squirmed uneasily. "Then people like this can never accept defeat."

"Right. That's why they've been at war with Israel since 1948. They can't accept the dishonor of defeat, and they'll kill any Arab who even suggests compromise. Remember what happened to Anwar Sadat?"

"Then it will never end for us." There was finality in the voice.

Brent nodded grimly. "You have a point, Navigator."

Cadenbach fell silent and shifted his body uneasily, his mind leaving the Arabs and finding another troubling thought. His entree was puzzling, "The talks in Geneva between the United States and Russia?"

"What about them?"

"Do you think we can we trust them—can we trust the

Russians to withhold their latest weapons from the Arabs?"

Brent stared at his mug. "That's the agreement. But only because they're afraid of ours. And don't forget, technology is the only thing the United States and Russia can hold over the rest of the world now."

Cadenbach shifted his eyes away from Brent's, as if he were afraid the executive officer might find something there he preferred to keep hidden. "You think homing torpedoes and their new RBU 6000 depth-charge launcher will remain out?" he asked, staring at the table.

Equipped with active and passive homing devices and a wire, the Russian 533 torpedo could hunt and track a maneuvering submarine to its doom, while the RBU 6000 was a fearsome mortar that fired six 300-millimeter charges weighing 400 pounds each, six-thousand meters ahead of the attacking vessel. With automatic reloading, it was an awesome killer of submarines, especially diesel-electric boats. Brent could understand the young officer's nervousness. Every man in the crew had been worried about these new weapons despite promises from Geneva, Moscow, and Washington that they would never be handed to the Arabs.

Brent spoke reassuringly. "Why, of course. There's no chance they'll be used. They wouldn't dare use the RBU and guidance systems for torpedoes. They know damned well the US Navy would turn their latest stuff over to the Japanese and all of their allies. We've complied and so have they. It's a balance of fear and distrust just like the nuclear balance that scares the piss out of everyone, and that no one will upset. And never forget, Russians don't trust Arabs either, Charlie. During the Six-Day War, the Egyptians ran so fast, they left behind whole SAM (surface-to-air missiles) batteries complete with radar control and hundreds of the latest Russian tanks and artillery. The Russians have never forgotten or forgiven."

Cadenbach nodded but did not look up. "I know. I

know, sir . . ."

Before he could continue, the conversation was interrupted by a speaker mounted in the maze of pipes and conduits overhead. "Mister Ross, Chief Engineer Dunlap requests you lay aft to the aft torpedo room," it squawked metallically. Brent muttered an oath under his breath. He was beginning to enjoy the conversation. The bright young Cadenbach had taken his mind from the trap of its own morbid jungle. He suspected the navigator had done this deliberately, maybe even conspired with Pablo Fortuno. They were fine men. He glanced at the brass clock mounted over the entrance, which showed 1320 hours. "Got to hurry—got to see what wild hair is bugging Dunlap and relieve the watch at fourteen hundred." He tossed off the rest of his coffee and rose.

"See you around, sir," Cadenbach smiled.

"I'll be around. Might run into you again, Navigator. It's a small world."

"It's a small, small world," the young junior lieutenant said as he began to hum the melody from the famous Disneyland ride.

Brent was smiling as he stepped into the passageway. Walking aft, he passed through the Chief Petty Officer's stateroom, where only a single chief, Chief Electrician's Mate Momoo Kenkyusha, sat at the small table, sipping tea and wolfing down a sandwich—the ship's supply of sushi had long since been exhausted. As all other Japanese members of the crew—thirty-one out of sixty-seven officers and men—Kenkyusha was a veteran of Japan's Self Defense Force and an experienced submariner. Short, round, and middle-aged, the chief was bleary-eyed, and his round face was deeply etched with lines of fatigue. There were only four chiefs on board, each an expert in his field, and since the vicious depth charging, they more than any other other members of the crew had been thrown into the breech to repair *Blackfin*'s wounds.

The chief began to come to his feet, but Brent waved

him back. The lieutenant felt a pang of guilt as he thought of the long, casual conversation he had just had with the navigator. "Good shooting, sir," the chief said in the perfect English mastered by every Japanese member of the crew. "Heard you hit every one of the *dorobos* (gangsters)."

Brent smiled his thanks and stepped over the high coaming of a doorway in a watertight bulkhead to enter the control room. Unlike the chief's quarters, this room was crowded, and the smell of diesel oil and unwashed bodies endemic to diesel boats was heavy and oppressive. Thankfully, the odor of chlorine was no longer detectable. Walking aft, Brent passed the "Christmas Tree," which was the heart of the diving station. The panel known as the Christmas Tree was a huge board covered with gauges and green and red lights that gave the board its name and indicated whether various openings in the pressure hull were closed or open. At the moment, the board glowed a mix of red and green; red for the open main induction valve, exhaust ports, conning tower hatch, and ventilation intakes, all of which Brent expected to see for surface running. However, a red light indicating an open sea valve in the Number One ballast tank burned ominously. Green should be there, and every man knew it.

The executive officer passed men who sat or stood before engine room controls, fuel gauges, rows of voltmeters, ammeters, shaft-revolution indicators, mazes of valves, cranks, levers. Polished brass gleamed everywhere even in the hushed red glow of battle lamps. It was an entirely different world from the computerized control room of the SSBN (nuclear ballistics submarine) *George K. Polk* Brent had served on when fresh out of the Academy. He passed the two large wheels of the diving planes, still manned despite the boat's inability to submerge. Two men slumped on their stools before the line-wrapped and varnished wheels, and the diving officer, a young, slight boyish ensign named Herbert Battle, leaned against the bulkhead next to the depth indicator, which was calibrated from zero to six hundred feet. No further calibrations were necessary, because at depths exceeding six hundred feet, the sea would crush the boat's welded hull like crackers in an angry man's fist.

Battle came erect, and his brown eyes caught Brent's. "Good shooting, sir." Then the dozen other men in the tiny room turned and shouted their congratulations.

Brent felt a sudden rush of warmth that a man can feel only when he is obviously admired and respected by the men he commands. "Thank you, thank you," he muttered thickly, walking quickly to the entrance to the combination radio room and crypto-center. As communications officer, he had direct responsibility for the equipment and men in this division. He paused and looked inside.

The two men occupying the small compartment had the boat's two radios dismantled and spread on a small bench. One of the men was the starboard fifty-caliber gunner, Radioman Second Class Tony "Crog" Romero. He was dismantling a power-supply unit with a long, slender screwdriver and a pair of needle-nosed pliers. Squat, dark, and barrel-chested, he had muscular arms that were so long his huge hands hung almost to his knees. With a wide, narrow forehead trapped between a shock of bushy black hair and heavy eyebrows that met just over the bridge of his flat nose, he had a physique and unusual countenance that had earned him the sobriquet of "Crog," an acronym for Cro-Magnon. Fortunately, Romero's disposition was as sweet as his appearance was fearsome, and he accepted his nickname with good spirits. Brent liked the young radioman. He had a bright mind and knew his equipment.

The other man was Cryptologic Technician First Class Don Simpson. Tall, slender, and fair, Simpson contrasted sharply with his companion. He, too, was intelligent and highly competent. But at the moment, he was also obviously frustrated by the damaged equipment. He spoke to Brent who leaned into the room. "Not working yet, Mister Ross." He gestured toward the control room. "Only the ESM, sir."

"Hang in there, boys," Brent said, resuming his hurried walk aft. "I'll be back."

"Roger, sir," Simpson said. He smiled. "And great shooting!"

"Thank you," Brent said, stepping through the hatch in another watertight bulkhead. He had not trusted his voice enough to call attention to the other gunners who had delivered such devastating fire on the diving bombers. But he had been the most accurate. The men knew this and so did he.

He passed by the minute 6-by-11-foot crew's galley in three long strides and entered the crew's mess, which was the single largest living space in the boat. Built on top of the aft battery compartment, it contained four tables with eight benches. Thirty-six men lived in this part of the submarine. Eleven crewmen sat around the tables: four Americans playing poker, four Japanese hunched over a game of *go,* three men reading. No one smoked. In fact, the "smoking lamp" had been out since the depth-charging.

Brent was surprised by the size of the group. He had expected most off-duty men to be in their bunks. But obviously the depth-charging, dive-bombing attacks and the grisly deaths of three shipmates and their funerals had left them all distraught with nerves drawn to a razor's edge. Obviously most of the men were no more capable of sleep than their executive officer.

Brent shouted "As you were!" before anyone could rise. But a machinist's mate came to his feet anyway, and the others followed. Again, Brent heard the chorus of "Great shooting, sir." "You saved our butts, Mister Ross." And again Brent did not trust his voice. Just managing to mumble his thanks he hurried through the sleeping area, where the chain-suspended bunks had been pulled against the sides of the hull and secured away from the center line of the ship. Stepping high, he passed through the next watertight door into the forward engine room.

Holding onto a steel rail, he began to walk a narrow catwalk that ran the length of the compartment between two powerful Fairbanks-Morse diesel engines. The noise was overwhelming. What had been a muffled bark of exhausts on the bridge and a rumbling vibration in other parts of the boat was a blasting roar in the confines of the small compartment. Combining with the sounds of the combustion were the clatter of valves and lifters, and the whir of gears. Below the catwalk and geared to the engines were two 1,100 Elliot generators which added their high-pitched whines to the cacophony. When needed, their power could be shunted to the 252 cells of the battery. However, the forward and aft storage batteries were already fully charged and the two generators were feeding their full power to the two main motors, which were driving the shafts; these in turn drove the bronze screws.

There were three men in the engine room gang. Chief Machinist's Mate Hisao Fukumoto was standing to the port side, studying a panel of gauges and instruments while two third-class enginemen were checking oil levels and inspecting pressure gauges mounted on small panels above the sixteen-cylinder engines. All three men carried rags tucked into their pockets. The engine room gleamed like an operating room. There was no dirt, no grime, no splattered oil. A man could eat a meal off the floor plates.

The gang came to attention, and Brent shouted "At ease! As you were!" and waved. He knew they could not hear him but that they understood clearly. The chief returned to his panel, and the two ratings stepped aside as the executive officer passed. Brent stepped through a hatch and entered the aft engine room.

The second engine room seemed like a duplicate of the first. Three men were on duty, and the same noise overwhelmed Brent's ability to hear. But there was a difference. There was still another sound detectable to Brent's trained and experienced ears. Beneath the rumble of diesels and the whine of the Elliot generators Brent could hear the high barking roar and hum of an auxiliary diesel generator set below the catwalk. With Number One and Number Two Main Pumps fully occupied with the water leaking into Number One Main Ballast Tank, the auxiliary diesel-generator was operating at capacity, running the boat's auxiliary pumps and compressors, maintaining the boat's trim. Nodding and smiling to the crew, Brent Ross hurried through the compartment and slammed the door behind him. Mercifully, most of the assault on his ears died with the closed hatch. He was in the maneuvering room, a small compartment almost directly over the main motors.

A rating stood before the control stand, a large panel with rows of indicators, volt meters, ammeters, and massive switches. Here current was shunted between generators, batteries, and motors to change speed or shift the power source from engines to batteries. Beneath the panel was a pair of annunciators for remote control of the engines in the event the other three became casualties. Brent narrowed his eyes grimly. The very last of the last resorts. The rating snapped to attention, and Brent nodded and stepped through a doorway that opened into the aft torpedo room.

The torpedo room was a jungle of congestion that made most of the rest of the submarine appear spacious and uncluttered in comparison. Built above the shafts and propellers, this was a place where one could always feel the vibrations of the drive-trains more than in any other part of the boat. And the compartment did not impress with the perfect roundness of other parts of the hull. Instead, it tapered sharply toward the stern and its four new Mark 68 torpedo tubes.

Set in vertical banks of two, the solid brass doors of all four torpedo tubes were closed. Twenty-one inches in diameter, they glistened with polished brass and were surrounded with mazes of pipes, fittings, springs, levers, and switches. A firing panel with four red glass windows and four switches was mounted between the two banks of tubes.

Secured to both sides in pairs, one above the other, were four nineteen-foot-long Mark 48 torpedoes. Shorn of its wire and its active and passive homing systems, the Mark 48 could deliver its 600 pounds of explosives only in the old-fashioned unguided mode of World War II. But its maximum speed of 55 knots and range of 28 miles made it superior to every torpedo in the world—including the Russian 533. The men grumbled about the restrictions, but the Arab 533s and entire arsenal of ASW (antisubmarine warfare) weapons were as unguided as thrown rocks. If not, *Blackfin* would have been killed long ago in its first encounter with enemy destroyers.

Bunks were fitted above the lethal fish. *What, a bedmate?* Brent thought, viewing the arrangement.

There were eight men in the room. All were huddled around Number Ten tube—the lower torpedo tube on the ship's port side—and all were torpedo men except for Chief Engineer, Senior Lieutenant Brooks Dunlap. About thirty years old, Dunlap had yellowish hair streaked with platinum. His most striking features were his eyes, light blue speckled with green. In the reddish glow of battle lamps, they could take on the strange aspect of purple marbles veined with silver. Dunlap turned and came erect. Before any of the others could move, Brent said, "As you were."

Dunlap's fatigue was emphasized by the grease that had been ground into the creases around his eyes and fell off from the corners of his mouth, leaving black lines. His tans were filthy, and his rolled-up sleeves revealed forearms streaked with grease and dirt. He waved at the tube, "The outer door's been jammed open."

Brent nodded. He knew the jamming of the heavy bronze muzzle door was not serious damage as long as the inner door to the tube was secure. And it certainly appeared secure. But there was water on the floor plates, and he could hear a hiss. Dunlap gestured to a stream of water jetting from a valve beneath the torpedo tube. "Goddamned sea valve is ruptured, too."

"The bilge pumps can take care of that," Brent said, feeling annoyance that he had been summoned for a minor matter—certainly minor when compared to the damage to Number One Main Ballast Tank. He could have been informed over the ship's PA system. Dunlap was surely capable of handling this situation. He stabbed a finger aft at a jumble of pipes and fittings. "Anyway, there's a cut-off valve further up the line. Why don't you secure it?"

Dunlap bit his lower lip and released his breath in a sign of weariness. "We will, sir . . . as soon as we track every leak, find all the damage."

"Is that all?" Brent asked impatiently.

"No, sir," Dunlap answered, reading his executive officer's irritation perfectly. He gestured forward to the maneuvering room. "The real problem is up there." He led Brent forward into the small room and stopped in front of the control stand. The rating stood aside. The chief engineer gestured at the bank of switches and said, "Somewhere our main wiring is ruptured, and I haven't been able to track it."

"What are you trying to tell me?"

"We can't switch to electric drive. Even if we can fix the Number One Ballast Tank, I can't give you power submerged."

Brent nodded understanding. Now, more than before,

90

they were bound to the surface. They were completely dependent on their diesels and could not use their electric drive until the break was found and repaired. "I'll report it to the captain." He ran his eyes over the tired face. "You have some men on it?"

Dunlap nodded. "I've got six electricians on it now, Mister Ross. But the damage is somewhere beneath the aft battery room in the bilges, probably about where the hull was damaged between frames forty-six and forty-seven. There's still some gas down there, and the repair party must wear respirators. It's a son-of-a-bitch, sir." He rubbed his jaw thoughtfully. "I'd guess the blasts broke the insulation, and now, with the leaks and more water in the bilges, the whole system has shorted out."

The full implications of the situation struck home, and Brent felt a familiar icy creature crawling up his spine. He nodded and said, "Christ. We're lucky it didn't short out at four hundred feet. We'd still be down there." He grabbed the engineer's shoulder in a reassuring gesture. "We're stuck on the surface, anyway, Lieutenant. At the moment it doesn't affect our sea-keeping efficiency."

"I know, sir. That's why I didn't call the captain. He has enough problems just keeping this tub afloat."

Brent nodded agreement. "I've got to relieve him now on the bridge. I'll give him your report."

"Thank you, Mister Ross."

Brent turned and began to retrace his steps forward. He was halted by Dunlap's voice as he reached the door to the aft engine room. "Great shooting, Mister Ross. You guys up there saved our ass."

Mumbling his thanks, Brent stepped through the doorway. Quickly he retraced his steps until he reached the control room. Here, Electronics Warfare Technician Matthew Dante, a bright young petty officer with black hair, wide brown eyes, and a pleasant, friendly face, stopped him. The best ESM technician Brent had ever known, the young petty officer was seated before a unit with the US

Navy designation of WLR-8. On line with a powerful Sylvania computer, the WLR-8 could automatically acquire and isolate signals, measure direction of arrival, frequency, modulation, and pulse width. All this information could be fed into the computer's threat library for identification. It was like having a spy on every ship tracking them.

Dante gestured at the waterfall display stretching across his screen. "Just picked up a big unit."

"Ranging us?"

"Not yet, Mister Ross. But he will. According to my library, it's DD (destroyer) Number One. Our friend Captain Fite. He's bearing zero-three-seven true, steaming course two-one-seven, range one-one-zero. With our low silhouette and coat of RAM (radar absorbent material) he'll have a hard time picking us up."

"But he will, and if he's an Arab, we could be dead."

Dante's voice became mechanical as if he, too, were part of the machine. "He's searching with a pencil beam with an azimuth width of one-point-five degrees and elevation width of one-point-two degrees, frequency ten gigahertz. His antenna is one-hundred-eight feet above the waterline, with a rotation rate of sixteen rpms . . ."

"Very well. Very well," Brent said impatiently. "You're sure its DD One."

"Absolutely, sir. It's his signature, all right." He patted the computer. "This baby's no pussy. It never tells a lie."

Brent could not help but grin at Dante's sharp wit and bright, cheerful face. "Very well. I'll report it to the captain immediately," he said, patting the young technician's back.

Quickly, he walked forward through the control room and entered the passageway that ran the length of "officer country." He could feel gloom and tension begin to ease and slough away as if a suit of chain mail had been stripped from his body. Warm memories began to crowd in. *Captain John "Slugger" Fite* ran through his mind.

He could see the big, bearlike escort commander with white hair like a snow cap, and a broad, strong face. He was the bravest man Brent had ever known. Twice—once in the Mediterranean and again in the Southwest Pacific—Fite had saved a damaged *Yonaga* by leading his Fletcher Class destroyers in suicidal torpedo runs on enemy cruisers and destroyers. He had lost five ships in the two attacks and nearly been killed himself. But he was back: unstoppable, invulnerable, motivated by hate only death could quench. His only son had been assigned to the American ambassador in Damascus as an interpreter. He had been kidnapped by terrorists in 1981 and held for ransom. When the ransom was paid, his body had been dumped on a garbage heap in the outskirts of the city. He had been skinned alive, penis slashed from his body and in the Arab tradition, stuffed into his mouth. Fite could not kill enough. With men like Slugger Fite on your side, it was hard to lose a war.

Brent Ross entered his small cabin, pulled a double-knit turtleneck sweater over his head, shrugged into his fur-lined foul weather jacket, squared his hat low over his forehead, and stepped back out into the passageway, zipping up the jacket. In a moment he was back in the control room at the foot of the ladder. He bounded up the ladder and into the conning tower.

A cylindrical compartment sixteen feet long and eight feet in diameter, it was actually a small pressure hull mounted on top of the main pressure hull and separated by a watertight hatch. This tiny compartment was the nerve center of the boat. Here were two periscopes—a wide-angled night periscope and the narrow, six-power magnification attack periscope—helm, depth and pressure gauges, engine room controls, speed indicator, revolution counters, telephone circuit board, sonar, radar, TDC (Torpedo Data Computer), torpedo firing keys. Crowded in this tiny tank, the attack team plotted and maneuvered until *Blackfin* was in position to fire her torpedoes. At this moment, except for the captain and executive officer at the periscope, the conning tower was fully manned. Brent smiled. This was the only place in the boat that was more congested than the aft torpedo room.

There were six men in the conning tower, and as one they turned and greeted their executive officer. Brent faced the only officer in the room, Ensign Robert Owen, who was the JOD (Junior Officer of the Deck). He was standing in front of the TDC. Heavy-set, with a small paunch despite the deterioration of the ship's food supply, the young ensign wore his usual warm, friendly smile as if God was in his heaven and all was right with *Blackfin*. Owen seemed to read Brent's mind. He gestured at the computer. "Damned rugged machine, sir. I've checked it out and it still works."

Brent stood in front of the TDC and ran his eyes over it. It was the heart, the brain of the entire attack system. The TDC was his responsibility and he was not satisfied. He glanced at his watch. He was still early for his watch. Hurriedly he threw a switch, and instantly the small room was filled with the sounds of the TDC's small motors coming up to speed. He ran his eyes over the four-foot-tall machine, which was divided into two panels. The top panel was black, with twelve circular dials highlighted with white letters and calibrations. Each was labeled with the information necessary to kill: Target Speed, Target Length, Target, Own Ship, Relative Target Bearing, Own Course, Time. In the upper right-hand corner was an elliptical Distance-to-Track indicator which had a grid face. Here a red solution light in the form of an F would glare when all data had been digested and torpedo depth, running speeds, and firing angles automatically transmitted to the torpedo tubes. At that moment the doom of a ship's crew was sealed.

Brent reached to the lower panel where there were eight cranks arranged in two rows of four. He cranked in a problem and watched the indicators and dials turn as they registered the information. He nodded his approval.

"Not quite like the high-tech glamor stuff on the new SSBNs, Mister Ross," Owen said. "But it works."

"The *Gefara* can testify to that," Brent said. Everyone in the compartment laughed.

Brent switched off the TDC and then turned to a stubby Japanese petty officer, Radioman Second Class Goroku Kumanao. Fortyish, with thinning black hair, Goroku had spent eight years in the Merchant Marine and ten in the Self Defense Force. Intelligent and resourceful, he learned quickly, digesting US Navy manuals as if English were his first language instead of his second. At the moment he had the computer unit of the SPS-10, D-band, surface and air-search radar spread on a small pull-down table mounted against the bulkhead next to the sonar. Brent peered down at the dismantled computer. "How's it coming, Kumanao?" he asked. "Was the hard disc damaged?"

The Japanese stabbed the point of a tool as thin and fine as a scalpel at a board that had obviously been seared by a short circuit. "The hard disc is fine, sir, but the force of the depth-charging caused a short circuit here," he moved the tool like a pointer, "shorting out the parallel ports."

"What about the serial ports," Brent said, staring at the board. "And the software? No correction there?"

Kumanao moved the tool slightly, obviously surprised by his officer's depth of knowledge. He shook his head. "Our software is not very forgiving. So this unit requires two serial ports." He tapped a tiny ceramic device with the end of the tool. "I'm trying to reconfigure the ports by flipping these switches."

"Will it work? What does the manual say?"

The Japanese shrugged and turned up his hands. "The manual is nonsense."

"What do you mean?"

Goroku thumped a thick volume on a shelf above the computer. "This board was manufactured in Singapore by, ah—as my American shipmates would say, built by spastic cretins—and the manual was written in their own brand of Japanese-English sprinkled with Chinese. Only the man who wrote these hieroglyphics could understand it." He tapped the table top in frustration. "We need a new board, Mister Ross. I can tell you that."

"Do we have them?"

The technician shook his head. "Negative, sir."

"Damn," Brent said. "Next time we'll back up all of our units—everything."

"Good idea, sir. We need a complete set of spares." A slow smile spread across the broad face like spilled oil. "And good shooting, Mister Ross." There was a chorus of approval from the other men in the compartment.

Quickly Brent grasped the ladder. Voicing thanks under his breath, he climbed up to the bridge. There were ten men on the bridge instead of the usual six to be found for ordinary steaming watches: Lieutenant Reginald Williams, who had the deck; a helmsman who manned the annunciators, too; port and starboard lookouts in the bridge enclosure; two more lookouts on their platforms on the periscope shears; and four men manning the two twenty-millimeter Orlikons on the cigarette deck. Williams glanced at his watch and smiled. "You're early, XO," he said, using the familiar term that only the captain exercised when addressing the executive officer.

Brent choked back his dislike for the man. Williams was obviously trying to mend fences. Brent responded with forced jocularity. "Got lonely down there, Captain. No one to talk to." They both laughed. Then Brent informed the captain of the jammed torpedo tube muzzle door, the leaking valve, the break in the power cables, the loss of electric drive, and Dante's detection of John "Slugger" Fite's radar signal.

Williams nodded gravely as he digested this information. He pounded the windscreen. "God damn it, I'd like to have those motors on line. But it doesn't change anything—at least for the moment. No telling what can happen between here and Tokyo Bay, though." He sniffed and tugged on his broad nose with a thumb and forefinger. "And this Captain Fite is the escort commander?"

"Yes, sir."

"What's the cruising speed of a Fletcher Class can?"

"Knowing Fite, he's probably pushing her at twenty-four knots." The executive officer smiled. "Some of his officers call him, 'Full-Ahead Fite.'"

"Guy's got a lot of nicknames."

"He's very unusual, Captain."

Narrowing his eyes, Williams tapped the windscreen. "If he maintains his course and is making twenty-four knots, we should sight him in about four hours, XO—near the end of your watch."

"That's what I figure."

The speaker came to life. "ESM to Bridge."

Williams keyed the speaker. "Bridge aye."

"Target at zero-three-seven has locked on us. Range nine-seven-miles. My library identifies the vessel as Destroyer Number One of carrier *Yonaga*'s escort. Commanding officer is Captain John Fite."

"What is his closing speed?"

"Closing speed is twenty-four-knots, Captain."

"Very well." Williams turned to Brent with new respect in his eyes. "You know these people pretty well, XO."

"I've steamed with Captain Fite for six years, Captain."

Williams looked off into the distance at a hump of clouds on the northwestern horizon—the only trace of clouds in the great eggshell blue vault of the sky. It was a magnificent day, a light and fickle breeze scratching dark patches on the surface of the rolling deep blue sea. "You know, Brent," he said almost wistfully, "who could ever believe this?"

"What do you mean?"

"I mean this." He waved the length of the boat. "A World War Two fleet boat manned by a crew of Japanese and Americans and commanded by a—a black man."

"It works, Captain." Brent was glad Williams had avoided the word *nigger.* Williams had thrown the word at Brent in the past in a fit of anger. Again Brent's mind went back to the time when they had first met and shared a small room in New York City. The big black man had been drinking too much, becoming belligerent and argumentative, spicing his polemics with *nigger* repeatedly as he shouted at Brent, expounding on everything from football to race relations. It was the heated exchange over football that had almost led to violence. It was a childish argument fueled by liquor, Williams contending he could have "fed you gopher shit and dirt and turf," while Brent was equally vehement, claiming, "I would've left cleat marks up your ass." The evening had left a bad taste in both of their mouths, and the bitter exchange had ripened into a mutual, cordial loathing that was held just beneath the surface on both sides. "And the men work together very well," Brent added.

Williams nodded and smiled. "I have the best fuckin' crew in the world."

For a moment, Brent felt the animosity fade. "I agree there, Captain. If they weren't the best, we'd have been in Davey Jones locker long ago."

Abruptly Williams became all business. Staring at Brent with his black, bloodshot eyes, he raced through the usual duty officer's monologue. Brent was already familiar with most of the facts, but naval tradition and regulations required the formal transfer of information with the change in watch. "Steaming on zero-three-zero, speed sixteen. All four main engines on line, turning at three-two-zero revolutions. Wind Force Two from the northwest, moderate swell running from the same direction. Radios, IFF, and radar are out. Sonar is operable.

Recognition lights are rigged." He gestured to the twenty-four-inch signaling searchlight mounted on a small platform at the rear of the bridge. " 'Bridge to bridge' and FM-ten are still out. So Fite will challenge with flashing light. When he challenges with *Alpha, Alpha,* the response is *Zulu, Oscar* and then identify the ship."

"Zulu, Oscar," Brent repeated. "Understood, sir."

Williams rubbed the bridge of his broad nose in a tired gesture. "I'll be on the bridge by the time he's hulled-down, anyway. But keep your signalman on the ball. I don't want to be blown out of the water by our own escort commander."

Brent felt a pang of resentment at the words which were more of a lecture than the usual sing-song phrases of an officer being relieved. However, he managed a respectful, "Aye aye, sir."

Williams continued, "We're shipping maybe seventy tons of seawater in Number One Ballast Tank, but the pumps are holding it even. I won't counterflood with Number Two Main Ballast Tank because I don't want to lower our bow anymore. Instead, I'm trimming with Numbers Two and Four trim tanks. Your JOD is Ensign Battle. He's at the diving station, and he's on the ball." He waved aft. "The twenty-millimeters are our ready guns, and the fifties are loaded and set on safe. If we go to GQ (general quarters), the lookouts can man them until relieved. Any questions?"

"Sunset? Change of course?"

"I'll check with Cadenbach and give you time of sunset on the PA. I don't anticipate a change in course on your watch, but I'll let you know after the navigator's evening sights." He gestured to a small speaker mounted on the front of the wind screen between the helm and annunciators. "The bridge speaker's working again. Saves a lot of yelling down that hatch." He stabbed a finger downward. "If we take any seas, close the hatch and latch it."

Brent felt more irritation. What had been mentioned

was SOP (standard operating procedure). Only in diving or in emergencies were the hatches dogged watertight, and then only by order of the captain or diving officer. The command had been unnecessary, but Brent managed a businesslike "Aye aye, sir. I won't dog it unless you order it or in extreme emergency."

"That is correct, XO."

"I relieve the watch, Captain."

"Very well."

The speaker came to life with Crog's voice, "Bridge!"

"Bridge, aye," Williams said, leaning over the small box.

"Our IFF is working, sir."

"Well done. Four-oh," Williams said, his voice filled with relief. He turned to Brent, "That'll help, XO. Our own forces will know us now."

"Yes, sir. Good news, Captain."

There was a clatter of sea boots on steel rungs, and enlisted men streamed up from the conning tower to relieve the men on duty. In a moment, Williams had vanished down the hatch with his section. As Brent Ross stepped close to the wind screen and stared over the bow, Seaman First Class Jay Overstreet took over the helm and annunciators. Two new lookouts took their positions on the bridge while two more scrambled up the short ladders to their platforms on the periscope shears. Four more men settled behind the pair of Orlikons. Everyone wore heavy foul weather jackets and had binoculars hanging around his neck. Immediately the four lookouts began to search their sectors. Brent warned all hands about the oncoming destroyer, although he knew they were all quite aware of the intruder. The mysterious ship's "telegraph" was by far the fastest and most efficient communications system on earth.

He turned to the port lookout, Signalman Second Class Todd Doran, who was the signalman of the watch, and explained the challenge and response. A small, fair youngster with the flaps of his cap hanging loose, Doran appeared almost buried in his foul weather gear. Doran repeated the signals and returned to his sector, his eyes to his binoculars. Brent was quite capable of sending and receiving flashing light. However, as OD (officer of the deck), his was an overall tactical and ship-handling responsibility and he could not lose himself in such small details. Brent brought his binoculars to his eyes.

With a heavy bow, *Blackfin* rode sluggishly, her knifelike prow smashing instead of slashing into the small seas, sending spray and green water rippling the length of the superstructure above her pressure hull. Larger swells raced the length of the deck, crashing against the bridge structure, sending water and spray geysering upward in jets and sheets to rain down on the bridge crew. Occasionally quartered, she rolled ponderously, exposing her pressure hull. The rolls sent water pouring through the rows of open ports perforating most of the submarine's 312-foot length, which allowed quick drainage on the surface and rapid flooding when submerging. When beneath the surface, the exhaust ports rumbled and sent their gases to explode on the surface in great bubbles, while their opposite numbers exposed to the air, barked their power in staccato blasts of blue smoke and white spray. Sluicing along both sides, her bow waves sent water churning through the ports and drains, straining water like a great baleen whale skimming crustaceans and making that hissing, burbling sound peculiar to submarines. Astern, her rolling wake widened in a wedgelike scar all the way to the southern horizon.

Suddenly a large swell swept the boat, crashing against the conning tower and sending a sheet of water shooting as high as the lookout platforms on the periscope shears. There were shouts of anger and surprise in the conning tower as water poured down the hatch. Brent slammed the heavy bronze hatch down and latched it. He keyed the speaker. "Captain!"

"Captain, aye," came back immediately.

"Permission to rig out bow planes, sir. We just took blue water over the bridge and the swells are increasing."

"We'll lose speed, Mister Ross."

"I know, sir. But if we're forced under, we have no electric power." The prospect was chilling and every man on the bridge turned toward the executive officer. The force of fear was palpable.

"Very well, XO. I'll give the order immediately. You decide on the angle."

Within seconds, there were two thumps as the bow planes were rigged out like elephant ears from their flush slots in the hull. Brent studied the bow and shouted into the speaker, "Diving station!"

The voice of the diving officer, Ensign Herbert Battle came back, "Diving station, aye."

"Up four-degrees on the bow planes."

"Up four-degrees on the bow planes, Mister Ross."

Immediately the bows were lifted almost to normal steaming depth. At the same time, the beat of the diesels slowed as they felt the additional load.

Brent sighed with relief as *Blackfin* lifted herself to a more seaworthy attitude. She was not steaming in a fully surfaced condition and would not with the damaged ballast tank, but her decks were free of all but the largest seas. He snapped open the safety latch of the hatch and stepped aside as the large coiled counterbalancing springs flung the hatch cover open, banging it against the side of the bridge and latching itself open with a loud, clanging thud. There were some grumbles from below as water dripped in.

Returning to the windscreen, he gripped it with both hands. The small cloud on the horizon had now reared up in an ominous mushroom. A thunderstorm. So quick to strike in these latitudes. He could see flashes of internal lightning and the entire area under the cloud was obscured by rain so thick it appeared like a solid lead sheet.

Incongruously, the slanting rays of the sun caught the rain and playfully sent colorful rainbows arcing gaily up to the clouds.

The storm was to their north and to the west, off their track at the moment. But It was a clear and present danger and was responsible for the seas which were now taking the boat on the port bow in endless rows. If they were caught in the heart of the storm, the damaged tank could flood and the boat would be driven beneath the seas. Without electric power, she would be doomed. It would be a slow and horrible death.

Brent gripped the windscreen with both hands and stared into the distance, scanning the sharp line of demarcation between sea and sky. Despite the storm, despite the damage to the boat, despite his boorish captain, he felt sudden contentment. Captain John "Slugger" Fite was over the horizon. And *Yonaga* was there, too. Soon he would see his old friends — his comrades-in-arms of so many years and so many bloody battles. And the living anachronism, Admiral Fujita, awaited him. The brilliant tactician, incomparable seaman, the walking encyclopedia of the knowledge of the ages whose inquiring mind had found challenge in all areas of human endeavor. They were all there over the horizon — those who were still alive.

Nothing can bring the realities of life and death home like the sea. Here a man challenges an element that is forever hostile even when in its most docile moods. Man does not belong here. He must fight a host of elements and sometimes other men and here he often dies with rare violence and horror. Yet, the irresistible fascination has lured men for millennia. Brent Ross was no different.

For nearly two hours the watch was uneventful. With bridge silence in force, there was no chatter, the only breaks coming when the quartermaster took his hourly readings of the barometer, thermometer, clouds, and sky conditions and entered them on his log sheets. Fortunately, the storm began to break up and move in fragments along the western horizon, its outriders a row of line squalls that paraded like skirmishers to the south, each a complete, tiny storm dropping rain like funnels of pearl dust into the sea while brilliant sunlight streamed all around. With the danger diminishing, Brent felt relaxation begin to creep through his tense muscles, and the last vestige of his depression fled with the wind.

Dale McIntyre came back—returned with the jarring reality known only to bored men who stand long, lonely watches at sea, week after week, month after month. She had visited him and tortured him many times on this patrol: on watch, in his bunk. They were back on her brass bed in her Manhattan apartment and she was nude as she always was in his fantasies and usually was in his presence. Her magnificent sculpted body was so real he felt he could reach out and touch her; the rounded breasts with areolas like rosebuds, tiny trim waist, hips and buttocks that would have challenged Goya. He could feel her hot flesh like fine silk under his hands, smell the perfume she always wore behind her ears and in other places far more private. Gripping the windscreen fiercely, he closed his eyes as he actually felt her pelvis grind against him, eyes slitted, mouth wide with passion.

"Range to DD-One three-seven-miles, bearing unchanged at zero-three-seven true," came through the speaker. Dale fled.

"Very well," Brent said, far more curtly than he had intended. He shook his head completely free of his reveries. Fite was very close and on a course of interception. Friends and safety were just over the horizon. For the first time in months, he was aware of the beauty that can be found only by men who travel the seas. The young lieutenant fixed his eyes on the sky above Fite's bearing. Here the far horizon glared blue as polished aquamarine while below the small ripples serrating the surface of the sea diffused the sun, reflecting it like chips of newly mined mica. Only at sea could a man find such beauty. But it could be misleading, as devious as a diseased harlot.

The swells rolled past and spray tingled his cheeks. He filled his lungs with pure, clean air and tasted the salt spray on his lips. The cold wind brushed his nose, tingled his cheeks. After the horror of the depth-charging and the prospect of a hideous death that had appeared so imminent, the breath of the cool wind seemed sweet against his face, his neck, his hands and an elixir in his lungs—a tonic that wiped away the smell of vomit, excrement, rancid oil, and fear that had fouled the bowels of the ship. The breeze whispered in his ears soothingly and coiled about his body like a friendly comforter. For an instant it seemed divine, caressing and assuaging, and he stood rooted to the deck in a perfect, timeless joy and harmony. *I'm alive, and young and strong,* ran through his mind.

After a battle he always reveled in life, savoring his own survival made more salient by the deaths of so many of his enemies and so many dear to him. The carnage always left him wondering how many more times he could challenge the black phantom and best him. Inevitably, when the last shots were fired, he would chant to himself, "It's over and I'm alive." He knew now that the sea, like nothing else, brought these thoughts home to the men who fought on and beneath her.

The last hour of the watch seemed far shorter than each of the first three. The storm moved off further to the west, which was its predicted track, and the swells moved with it, gradually diminishing in size. The sun was low on the horizon, and its still strong rays filled the circular vault above with an intense blue glare. Periodically Dante gave reports on the approaching destroyer. Finally, with DD-One only twenty miles to the north, Captain Reginald Williams came to the bridge. "He's bearing zero-three-seven true, zero-one-zero relative, range nine-

105

teen," he said to Brent Ross, raising his binoculars.

"Yes, sir. We should sight his mainmast soon." Brent turned his head upward to the periscope shears, the useless radar antenna, and the lookouts. "Keep a sharp watch, there, men."

"Aye aye, sir," the lookouts chorused, leaning into their glasses.

Williams spoke into the speaker, "ESM! I want a report." He rubbed his chin thoughtfully. He had not shaved for days, and the fingers actually flicked the stiff bristles like a brush.

Dante's voice called the bridge. Williams leaned over the speaker, and Brent could hear the tension and confusion in the young technician's voice, "Target at zero-three-seven has gone to thirty-two-knots, Captain."

"Any change in course?"

"Negative, sir. He's still steaming two-one-seven."

"Very well." Williams scratched his cheek and stared off at the horizon on the bearing. He turned to Brent. "That's his flank speed, XO?"

"That is correct, Captain."

"That doesn't make sense."

Brent was gripped with a premonition, a feeling of disquiet and unease. Things were not as they should be. It was an intangible thing, another sense a man develops after surviving innumerable battles. "I suggest battle surface, Captain," Brent offered quietly.

"You're right, XO." Williams shouted down the hatch. "Communications. Sound the alarm. Battle surface!"

Immediately, the alarm sent its "Bong! Bong!" ringing through the boat. There were the sounds of sea boots thumping on steel floor plates and on ladder rungs. Within minutes the battle-surface crew manned its weapons and most watertight hatches in the hull were slammed shut and dogged down. Brent jammed on his steel helmet, unlocked the Browning, and swung it from side to side as Gunner's Mate Bowman unlatched the ready box. Crog did the same with the fifty-caliber mounted on the starboard side of the bridge. There was a clatter of steel on steel as the five-inch gun crew rammed a round into the breech. Williams took his position as OD at the front of the bridge and locked his range-finding binoculars into the TBT while the most experienced helmsman, Quartermaster Second Class Harold Sturgis, took over the helm and annunciators. The casualties and damage to the boat had forced Williams to assign the regular man at the annunciators, Seaman First Class Tatsunori Hara, to one of the damage control parties. Two new lookouts scampered up onto their perch on the periscope shears.

The usual reports flooded up through the speaker. "Forward torpedo room manned and ready, maneuvering room manned and ready, control room manned and ready, forward engine room manned and ready . . ." The disembodied voices droned on one after the other as they had so many times in the past. Finally, with Ensign Robert Owen's report from the conning tower, the ship was primed and as ready as she could ever be for battle. But Chief Dunlap had reported the electric motors still off line despite the frantic efforts of his crew. Williams bashed a fist against the steel screen and cursed.

A new voice came up through the hatch. "I say, up there. Permission to come up on the bridge, if you please, Captain." It was Captain Colin Willard-Smith. "I must say I've got the bugger-all to do down here, Captain, and it's getting on my wick. I've got bloody-good eyes, sir. Can't you use me up there?"

Williams' face twitched, and for a moment Brent thought the big man would smile. "Permission granted," he said gruffly.

Willard-Smith, dressed in Admiral Allen's foul weather gear and with a pair of binoculars hanging at his waist, pulled himself up through the hatch. "Bloody decent of you, Captain," he said, coming erect.

Williams waved at the horizon. "There's a can bearing down on us like a whore after a John on Broadway on Saturday night."

"*John,* sir," the Englishman said in obvious confusion. "You mean a harlot after a mark?"

Brent and Reginald both chuckled while the enlisted men held their silence with an effort. "Coming like a demon out of Westminster, Captain Willard-Smith," Brent added.

"Quite right, old boy," the pilot chuckled, moving to the rear of the bridge and bringing his binoculars up. "Dash it all," he said almost immediately. He turned to the captain. "You said our intruder was off there." He waved airily off the starboard bow. "Then what's that out there at ten o'clock?" He caught himself and lapsed into Royal Navy terminology in an effort to be nautical, "I mean red sixty."

"Red sixty?"

Brent turned so quickly, his helmet flopped and the soreness came back into his neck. "He means three-hundred-degrees relative, Captain."

"That's jolly well right, old boy."

A shout from the shears. "Destroyer bearing three-zero-zero, range eleven."

A half-dozen pairs of binoculars came up and Brent found it: still hulled down but charging over the curvature of the earth were the upper works of a destroyer. It was emerging from a squall which it had obviously been using for cover. It had probably been hiding in the storm for hours. Brent came up on his toes and suddenly felt a deadly tension scrape along his spine like a gapped knife. "It's an Arab, Captain."

"How can you be so sure?"

"It's a *Gearing* that's been through FRAM (fleet rehabilitation and modernization) conversion. One five-inch gun house removed forward, fourteen feet added amidships for bunkerage. You can't miss them and we don't have any. Our escorts are all *Fletchers*."

"Five-inch! Commence tracking target bearing three-zero-zero. All weapons stand by to engage." Williams turned to Brent, "He must've been sneaking up on us with all of his electronics gear shut down."

"I don't think so, Captain."

"What do you mean?"

Brent waved off at the still unseen friendly contact. "I think he's been tracking Captain Fite. Probably been on lifeguard duty and was informed by one of his reconnaissance aircraft of Fite's can closing on the combat area. Fite's probably on the same duty and he's looking for us, too. The Arabs think we're sunk. And with our RAM and being so low in the water, we're hard to track. He's trying to surprise Fite."

"He can't. Fite must have him on his radar, XO."

"He's an Arab. They're completely unpredictable. Fite picked him up when he came out of the storm and that's why he went to thirty-two knots."

"Our IFF?"

"The Arab probably couldn't pick it up. It's frequency jumps and transmits in millisecond bursts."

"Right. Right, XO." Williams thumped his head with a closed fist and spoke to himself in obvious exasperation, "What's wrong with me? I'm forgetting everything."

They were interrupted by a shout from the shears, "Vessel bearing zero-one-zero, range twelve."

Brent swung his glasses. "A fighting top, Captain. It's a *Fletcher*. One of ours, all right."

Williams shouted down the hatch. "We'll run on course zero-one-zero. There's a hostile vessel bearing off our port bow at three-zero-zero. I'll begin giving you bearings on the TBT in a moment. Mister Owen, crank it into the TDC. Both torpedo rooms are to stand by." He shouted into the speaker, "Chief Dunlap!"

"Dunlap aye."

"Give me all the speed you can without sinking us."

"Maybe twenty-knots, sir."

"The main shaft bearings?"

"They're cool, Captain."

"Well, thank God for that." Williams turned to Sturgis. "All ahead two-thirds."

"All ahead two-thirds, sir." There was a clang of bells as the quartermaster pushed the two annunciators forward. Immediately the rhythm of the engines increased and the boat began to slam into the small swell. A sea ran the length of the deck and soaked the five-inch gun crew. "Up three degrees on the bow planes," Williams shouted into the speaker. The bow came up slightly and the seas sloshed along the boat's sides.

A shout came up from the conning tower. "Captain, the pitometer reads twenty knots, rev counter shows four-hundred-ten-revolutions on both shafts."

"Very well."

A shout from the shears: "She's opened fire!"

There were flashes and twin puffs of brown smoke on the bow of the Arab. There was a rustle, and canvas ripped overhead as air rushed in to fill the vacuums left by two fifty-five-pound shells. Twin towers of water shot skyward a hundred yards beyond the submarine. "Jesus Christ, he has us in range already," Williams shouted at Sturgis. "Right full rudder. Steady up on those splashes. We'll chase salvos." He glanced at the bearing repeater. "Steady up on zero-nine-eight."

Sturgis repeated the command, glancing at his rudder-angle indicator.

Willard-Smith spoke to Brent. "We have five-inch, too, Mister Ross. Why don't we fire?"

Brent shook his head grimly. "Out of our range. We have a hand-loaded five-inch, twenty-five-caliber gun." He stabbed a finger at the enemy, who was now clearly in view and almost over the horizon. "He has four five-inch, thirty-eight-caliber machine-loaded cannons. We can fire about ten rounds a minute, and he can put out

110

over twenty-rounds per gun, per minute. He can out shoot us and outrange us. His next salvo will be short. He should try to bracket us, and then he'll turn to bring his full armament to bear and commence rapid fire."

"That's over a hundred rounds a minute."

"That's right."

The Englishman popped his lips and tightened his jaw. "I say, a bit of a sticky wicket, wouldn't you say, old boy?"

There was a flash, more smoke, and a screech that faded quickly. Two green towers of water shot up fifty yards off the port quarter and well astern. "Short! Short!" someone shouted.

"We're bracketed," Brent said.

"Our knickers are in the bloody twist," Willard-Smith mumbled.

"Steady on zero-nine-eight, sir," Sturgis said.

Owen's voice: "TBT reading, Captain?"

"Not yet. Just watch your goddamned instruments, Mister Owen."

Shouts of "On target! On target" came from the pointer and trainer perched on their bicycle seats on the five-inch mount.

"In range, Captain," the gun captain shouted.

"Commence firing! Commence! Commence! Rapid fire! I don't give a shit where the stuff lands. We won't go down like pussies."

Flame leaped from the short tube, and a thunderclap struck the bridge as the cannon fired. Everyone rocked and groaned. Immediately there was the smell of cordite and excited shouts as another round was pulled from the ammunition scuttle and rammed into the breech. A column of water erupted short and to the left of the *Gearing*. Brent could hear the gun captain: "Up two degrees, right eighty yards, deflection three-zero."

Again the gun fired and the size of the target increased. "He's turning to starboard, Captain," Brent

111

shouted: "Giving us his beam."

"Our can is ranging, sir!"

The gray *Fletcher*, now off *Blackfin*'s port beam, had heaved over the horizon, the turmoil of her bow wave a white bone in her teeth. Brent always marveled at the graceful, flush-decked beauty and grace of the class. A big number 1 was painted on her bow which slashed through the seas, hurling up sheets of blue water and spray as she ripped the sea at flank speed. Her two forward mounts were vomiting flame. More splashes appeared around the Arab. Most were short. Strangely, the enemy captain seemed to ignore the *Fletcher*. Instead, he seemed intent on *Blackfin*. His main battery went to rapid fire and the shells began to rain down.

Staring through his binoculars, Brent thought he was looking into the inferno of hell itself. The guns fired so fast, the destroyer appeared to be on fire. Brown smoke trailed her in clouds and the shells swarmed in, moaning, hissing, sighing, and ripping. The tortured sea was flung up in curtains, but most were short. Fite had forced the enemy to turn much sooner than he had intended. At best, a submarine offers very little freeboard and at long range is a terrible target. The Arab was trying to sink *Blackfin* with the sheer volume of his fire.

"Why doesn't he try to boff our friend?" Willard-Smith shouted into Brent's ear.

"Now he knows who we are. He's an Arab. I would guess he's out to get vengeance for *Gefara*."

"Stupid. Stupid."

Williams shouted at Sturgis, "Right full rudder. Steady up on two-six-five." And down the hatch, "Mister Owen, stand by the TBT repeater. I'll start giving you bearings as soon as we steady up on two-six-five. But be ready for quick course changes. I'll want a hundred-percent spread on the fish."

Brent was stunned by the maneuver. Williams was actually coming about to close the range on the *Gearing*.

112

This would take them into easy range of the enemy guns, but would bring all six forward tubes to bear. They would be sunk long before they reached the optimum torpedo range of twelve hundred yards or less. The captain must have a long shot in mind. A hundred-percent spread meant one at the bow, four amidships and the last at the stern. No fish aimed ahead or astern of the target. This was an ideal cluster for a long shot that might turn the Arab, upset his gunnery, and make him an easy mark for Fite. Williams had guts. Most skippers would run to the protection of their own destroyer. That was what logic and discretion dictated. But logic and discretion won far fewer victories than daring and bold, unexpected tactics. *"We won't die like pussies,"* Williams had said. Obviously he had meant it.

"Open outer doors, tubes one through six," Williams shouted down the hatch.

"Captain," Brent said, leaning close. "I would suggest you're opening the doors too soon, sir. At twenty-knots we can flood our torpedoes."

Williams nodded and cursed and then shouted, "Belay that order, Mister Owen. Outer doors are to remain closed."

Blackfin had heeled halfway through her turn when the first shell hit. It was clearly visible and Brent saw it coming. It was a defective round with perhaps a broken copper firing band. Or it might have been fired from a barrel with worn rifling. In any event, it fell short and flat instead of plunging. It skipped across the water, tumbling like a great blue bottle. Fascinated, every man on the bridge watched as death ricocheted and whipped toward them, end over end, kicking up water and leaving a trail of spreading ripples, dappled with spray and droplets.

It came over the starboard quarter and struck the base of the cannon. Every man ducked instinctively. There was a flash like an enormous photographer's bulb, a concussion that knocked Bowman from his feet and staggered Brent. Screams and shouts of anger, rage, fear, and agony dinned in his ears. Shrapnel clanged against the three-eighths-inch steel sides of the windscreen and whined off the periscope shears, and wreckage and pieces of steel and men rained and splattered.

Shaking his head to clear the patches of darkness, Brent found Williams and Sturgis both down and the helm swinging wildly. Brent shouted down the hatch, "Steady on two-six-five, God damn it. Mind your helm. We have casualties up here. You're supposed to back up the helm down there. What the fuck's wrong with you? We've taken one up here. Corpsmen to the bridge. We have many casualties."

"Aye, aye, sir. Yes, sir," came from the frightened voices of a half-dozen men in the conning tower.

Williams was flat on his back at Brent's feet, helmet askew, blood covering his forehead and streaking his shirt. The five-inch had been blown from its mount and hung precariously over the starboard side, held by only one deck bolt, swinging from side to side with the roll of the boat. Four of the crew had been blown over the side while the other two had been smashed against the bottom of the cigarette deck and back of the bridge like crushed insects. All four members of the two Orlikon crews were down and the guns wrecked. Brent could hear screams and keening sounds like those an animal makes when it is mortally injured. One of the lookouts on the shears had vanished while the other hung over the rail like a bloody mattress, blood streaming from a chest ripped down to his lungs. White ribs protruded like broken sticks. One of his legs had been blown off at the knee. Crog and his loader, Yeoman Yuiji Ichioka, were standing along with Willard-Smith, who leaned against the windscreen. All appeared dazed but unhurt. Both bridge lookouts and Humphrey Bowman crouched low in the corners of the bridge, staring at Brent with wide, frightened eyes.

"Back to your stations," Brent roared, mustering all the command he could find in his voice. The two lookouts and the gunner's mate came to their feet and returned to their watch with their binoculars to their eyes.

Owen's voice: "There's blood down here, sir. It's coming through the vents."

Brent knew one of the five-inch-gun crew must be hemorrhaging into the main induction valve. There was nothing he could do about it. Now the boat was actually bleeding.

"Change in course?" Owen shouted up from his station at the TDC.

Looking around at the charnel house, Brent felt a familiar consuming heat flare like a volcano deep in his guts and spread through his veins like lava. *Revenge! Vengeance!* flared in his mind. Caution, fear, reason were all consumed by the primeval lust to kill. He was hungry for blood—the blood of those who had done this to his ship, his shipmates. He would kill them or be killed trying. "No change! We're going to kill the son-of-a-bitch," Brent roared. "Tracking party stay on the ball."

Suddenly Hospital Corpsman Chisato Yasuda and two seaman strikers were on the bridge. Each had a kit slung over his shoulder. One of the strikers rushed aft to the cigarette deck while the other remained with Yasuda. "Clean up the main induction valve after you take care of the wounded," Brent shouted after the man running aft.

Sturgis struggled to his feet and returned to the helm no more than dazed by the concussion. But Williams was unconscious. With the help of the men in the conning tower, the big bulk of the captain was lowered through the hatch, no longer a man Brent disliked so intently, but now a wounded ally.

There were more sharp fluting sounds like great insects passing close to their heads, and water rained down on the bridge, more shells roaring in close aboard. But the fire was slackening. Fite was turning toward *Blackfin*, drawing off the Arab's fire and uncovering his entire broadside of five five-inch guns; one more than the *Gearing*. Now the enemy was in trouble, a five-inch shell hitting amidships and blowing a forty-millimeter quadruple-mount over the side. Two more hits started a fire amidships and a hole was blown in the forward funnel.

Brent took the OD station next to Sturgis. "You okay, Quartermaster?"

"Yes, sir. Four-oh," the young petty officer said, gripping the wheel firmly. And then, as if to reassure his officer, "Course two-six-five, speed twenty."

A man with chest and neck wounds and another with his left arm missing were lowered through the hatch by Yasuda, Crog, and Willard-Smith. "The rest are dead," Yasuda said. Brent glanced over his shoulder at the horror hanging from the periscope shears. Blood was still streaming from the corpse in dribbles and gouts like strawberry jelly.

Yasuda read his glance. "Should I send a man up after him?"

Brent shook his head. "Too dangerous. Later. Tend to the living." The orderly and his two assistants vanished down the hatch. He turned to Willard-Smith. "We'll need you more than ever, Captain. We're shorthanded. I can't take men from other battle stations or strip the damage control party."

"I'm quite fit and ready for your orders."

"Can you fire that fifty-caliber?" Brent gestured at the port Browning machine gun.

"Quite. We're well acquainted, Mister Ross."

"Very well. I may need you. Stand by."

The Englishman ran a hand over the breech and patted the ammunition box. Gunner's Mate Bowman lowered his binoculars and said, "Full load, sir. One hundred ten rounds." Willard-Smith nodded and raised his

116

binoculars.

Brent leaned against the windscreen and looked about quickly, analyzing the situation. The Arab was steaming across his bow from starboard to port at a high speed and almost directly south. He was burning, but both mounts were firing. Both of his quintuple mount torpedo tubes had been swung out. Fite was charging down on *Blackfin*'s starboard side, and if every captain held his course, DD-1 would pass astern of them while the *Gearing* crossed their bow. They would actually be caught between two destroyers trying to kill each other. His jaw tightened with his resolve. He'd hold course, take his chances, do anything to get a shot. The Arab would be distracted and his chances looked better.

He yelled in the speaker: "Torpedo surface. Tracking team stand by for first observation." He glanced at a chart hanging from the windscreen and shouted into the speaker, "Height of mast one hundred twenty feet." Then he stared into his binoculars. The *Gearing* was split in the middle, the left half above the right half. Thumbing the dial of the range finder, he brought the halves together, forming a coherent whole. He spoke into the speaker, "Bearing mark!"

Owen's voice came back as he read the repeater, "Bearing zero-two-three."

Brent read the range scale on the binoculars, "Range mark, eight-eight-double-zero," he called out. He made an educated guess, the only alternative he had without radar. "Target course, one-five-five, angle on the bow port zero-four-two." The target was on a southeasterly heading and forty-two-degrees from heading directly at *Blackfin*.

Owen repeated the data and then shouted "Set," which meant the information had been fed into the TDC.

"Distance to track?" Brent said into the speaker, asking for the distance from the submarine to the target's projected track.

117

"Five-one-zero-zero, sir," Owen answered. "Suggest you change course to two-four-five. This will give us an approach angle of eighty-degrees starboard on the target. And I suggest you reduce speed."

"Very well. Left to two-four-five," Brent ordered. Sturgis put over the helm. Brent continued, "But negative on the speed change. We'd never get in a shot and we'd be too good a target ourselves."

The data was terrible, and Brent knew they had little chance of hitting the enemy at this range unless the enemy captain changed course or slowed.

But the tide of battle was turning. There was an explosion near the stern and the Arab began to lose speed. All of his fire was now directed at the *Fletcher*, which was directly astern of the submarine. Hundreds of shells from both ships ripped and hissed through the atmosphere above and Brent felt he was in some invisible tunnel of death. But *Blackfin* continued to close on the target, almost ignored by the two combatants.

Brent took another observation and the distance to track was down to 4,710 yards. Still too far, and the *Gearing*'s speed made it almost an impossible target to hit. His course remained unchanged.

Fite took two hits astern and Number Five gun house fell silent, swinging idly with the roll of the ship. He began to slow. But the Arab was being punished cruelly. His forward mount took a direct hit, and one gun was blown over the side while the other pointed uselessly at the sky. At least four shells hit the superstructure, destroying the pilothouse and blowing the director into the sea. Two more hits on the bow and she began to list and her bows dipped low as she took water. Her speed dropped dramatically down to perhaps ten knots. Yet her aft mount was still firing, though without director control the rounds were poorly aimed. Brent relayed the new target speed into the speaker.

Owen answered, indicating the computer had absorbed

the information, "Change made. Ready light."

Brent exulted as he stared through the binoculars. He shouted another observation and this time the range was down to four thousand three hundred yards, distance to track three thousand two hundred. He wanted to close to twelve hundred yards, but the Arab could train his twin five-inch guns on *Blackfin*. At this range, even average gunners should be able to hit the submarine over open sights.

It was time to open outer doors. "All ahead one-third."

"All ahead one-third." The bells rang and the boat slowed. "Speed eight, one-six-oh revs, sir."

"Set depths all six fish eight feet, speed forty-five. Fire at six-second intervals in normal order. Open outer doors," Brent ordered.

The voice of Seaman Burt Nelson, the talker in the conning tower, came through the speaker: "Forward room reports all torpedo tube doors open. Tubes are flooded. Torpedoes are set for eight feet, speed forty-five."

"Captain!" Signalman Todd Doran shouted. "Our can's turning away."

A glance aft uncoiled an icy snake in Brent's chest. Fite was hurt and obviously out of control. His steering gear appeared to be damaged, and DD-One was swinging erratically. His shells began to spray the ocean around the Arab wildly instead of being tightly bunched. At that moment, the *Gearing*'s gun house swung toward *Blackfin* and the muzzles depressed. Now it was kill or be killed.

Brent shouted to the attack team: "My next observation will be a shooting observation. I'll want a one-hundred-fifty-percent spread." Brent knew with his enemy's slow speed and broadside for a target, this spread would be most effective; one ahead, four at the hull, and one astern. With a little luck, he should get at least two hits. One should sink the damaged *Gearing*, which seemed unable to turn or increase speed. Her bridge had been destroyed, and she seemed out of control. She should turn. Compound *Blackfin*'s firing scheme. Most of her officers were probably dead, and she was plodding along as if her rudder was jammed in one position. But the five-inch shells began to drop around *Blackfin*. The fire was wild, rounds tearing over, falling short, others bracketing to both sides. There were some brave men in that lone gun house, and now they recognized the menace of the submarine's torpedoes.

Brent stared into the binoculars, "Bearing mark!"

"Zero-one-zero," Owen said.

Brent carefully adjusted the focusing knob. "Angle on the bow zero-eight-zero, range two-thousand-seven-hundred." The destroyer's full port side was his target and *Blackfin* was on a track perpendicular to the target. This was the ideal setup all submarine commanders work for and dream about.

Owen's voice: "Torpedo run two-thousand-one-hundred — I have a solution light, Mister Ross."

Brent almost shouted with joy, realizing a red F was glowing on the face of the TDC. Speed was of the essence because the target was crossing *Blackfin*'s bow from starboard to port and out of optimum firing position and his shells were sending up towers of green water all around.

"Fire one!" Brent shouted. He glanced at the big sweep hand of his wristwatch and then down the hatch at Ensign Frederick Hasse, the torpedo officer. Stiffly, the young officer reached up to the firing panel where six red lights glowed. He pulled the switch beneath the first window and pushed the round brass plate of the firing key with the palm of his hand. At the same time he started a stopwatch that he held in his other hand. It was his duty to start the watch when he heard the command "Fire" and to mark the dial and case with a pencil when he heard each torpedo explosion. In effect, he was the official timer and his data would supply the exact range

120

between the submarine and its target—if *Blackfin*'s torpedoes scored. In this way the entire attack plan and execution could be checked.

Blackfin jolted as if she had been struck by a whale, the huge compressed air blast driving the torpedo from the tube. Accelerating to forty-five knots, it swooshed away in a cloud of bubbles with a twenty-four-degree left gyro angle steering it on a collision course with the target.

"One fired electrically," the talker, Seaman Burt Nelson, shouted.

"Torpedo run forty-eight seconds," Owen said, staring at the TDC.

Hasse switched the selector switch to the Number 2 tube and waited for the six-second interval, staring at his stopwatch. He fired the second torpedo, jolting the submarine again. Then the last four torpedoes were fired and a steel-like tension filled the boat. Two shells exploded close aboard the starboard side, the submarine shuddering while shrapnel whined and ricocheted off the hull.

It was time to put distance between themselves and the enemy. "All ahead two-thirds. Left full rudder," Brent said to Harold Sturgis. "Steady up on zero-three-zero." He shouted the change in course and speed to the attack team. And then to Ensign Owen, "Have the aft torpedo room stand by all tubes."

"Number Ten is out of commission."

"Damn! That's right!" Brent groaned, slapping the windscreen. He glanced at his watch and cursed. Number One had missed. A few seconds later, he agonized again. Number Two had missed.

Then a huge explosion amidships lifted the *Gearing* from the sea. Before she could settle and wallow in her spreading agony, another colossal blast in almost the same spot broke her keel, heaving her up in an inverted V. Either her torpedoes or a magazine exploded, flinging her aft mast, AA director, gun tubs, a stack, and dozens of men high into the sky on the tip of a giant yellow tongue of flame. Brent stared in awe as plates, deck-houses, and twisted wreckage weighing hundreds of tons were flung casually in a great circle like wood splinters in a gale, pockmarking the sea as they rained down in a half-mile radius.

Every man on *Blackfin*, from the battery-room crews to the bridge, cheered at the top of his lungs. Crog jumped up and down, pounding Brent's back and nearly knocking the executive officer into the windscreen. Shouting, "Good show! Good show!" Colin Willard-Smith added his palm to Crog's. Brent cheered and laughed and gripped Sturgis's neck and shook the young quartermaster playfully. Brent saw the concussion coming, rippling across the sea like the breeze before a tsunami. "Brace yourselves!" he shouted.

The hot wind ripped past and the breeze waffled in Brent's ear and then was gone. He turned to Sturgis. "Right standard rudder, all ahead one-third, steady up on the wreck." Brent relayed the information to the attack team and ordered the aft torpedo room secured.

Slowly the submarine came about and Sturgis carefully steadied the bow on the center of the cataclysm. The destroyer was sinking in two distinct parts: just the very tips of her bow and stern projecting above the surface. Burning oil was spreading through the usual "dust on the sea" found after every catastrophe: planks and timbers; barrels; wooden furniture; casks; rafts, whole and in pieces; and men . . . always men. Swimming away from the burning oil frantically. Some had already lost the race and Brent could see them gulping in the flames, roasting their lungs, and trying to leap from the sea in their agony. Fortunately their screams could not be heard. A huge black pall of oily smoke began to stretch like a shroud overhead.

Brent felt a deep warmth spread like a hot hunger

much like the anticipation he had known in Dale McIntyre's bedroom. He stared at the destruction he had wrought and licked his lips. He felt giddy. Snickering, he murmured to himself, "Eat fire, you pricks."

"Sir," a lookout shouted. "Captain Fite's astern of us at two-zero-zero."

Brent threw a glance over his shoulder. He sighed with relief. *DD-One* was off their port quarter, gaining and obviously under control. The fires were out, and although the Number Five gun house was still smoking, no other damage was apparent except for a slight list to port and a blackened, burned area amidships between the stacks.

Now they were very close to the scene of the sinking. Survivors were everywhere. Some swimming, others clinging to wreckage and still others, more fortunate, sitting on large pieces of floating wreckage. One group of six had found a raft and were furiously paddling it away from the burning oil and toward the submarine.

"All ahead slow." Brent said to Sturgis. Immediately, the rhythm of the big engines slackened and the submarine began to roll and wallow, her speed dropping to only four knots. "Do you have steerageway, helmsman?"

"Aye, sir. But a little sluggish."

"Very well." Brent said to Willard-Smith and Crog, "Stand by the fifties."

Motionless, the two men looked at each other and then at Brent. "Stand by for what, old boy?" Willard-Smith asked, his voice uncharacteristically hard and suspicious.

Brent waved impatiently. "To open fire—to exterminate those vermin."

For the first time, the Englishman's face showed emotion. "I say, old man. That's not sporting."

Brent felt the blade of anger in his guts burn cold and sting sharp, and blood rushed to his face and pounded in his temples. Rage exploded from his lips. "I don't give a

123

shit *what* you think. I said stand by to open fire." He turned to Sturgis. "All stop."

"All stop, sir." The rolling and pitching increased.

Willard-Smith drew himself up. His face was as implacable as stone. "Respectfully," he said with no respect in his voice. "I refuse to be a part of bloody murder. Must I remind you, sir, I am not part of your command."

Brent whirled on Crog, the last vestige of his control slipping. He stabbed a finger at the raft which had been paddled only a hundred yards from their starboard side. "Radioman Romero, open fire. Kill them," he snarled.

Torn between the admiration and respect he felt for his officer and the repugnance of the order, Tony "Crog" Romero was in a turmoil. It was there on his face for all to see, his massive jaw working and his lips a pallid slash. "Under protest, sir," he managed gutturally.

"Protest all you fuckin' well like. I command you to open fire."

Willard-Smith, Humphrey Bowman, and Crog's loader, Yuiji Ichioka, stared at the big gunner. Signalman Todd Doran and the other lookout, Ben Hollister, gazed in shocked awe. Crog took a deep breath and spat his words out as if they were poisoned and he were purging his mouth. "I can't be a party to murder. I refuse, Mister Ross."

A silence as deep and icy as the hush at the polar cap gripped the bridge. Brent growled deep in his throat like a predator about to leap. A madness was on him; no fear, no doubts, not even conscious thought. Pushing Crog aside, he swung the machine gun down onto the raft. He could see them over the sights: six men staring at the submarine hopefully.

Raising up on his toes, he brought the muzzle down and centered the sights on the raft. Anticipating the roll of the submarine, he leveled the barrel and held it steady like a gyro. At a hundred-yards, it was almost impossible

124

to miss even from the rolling platform. Just before he pressed the trigger, he felt a familiar hollow hunger in his guts, the almost sexual ache in his loins as if a naked woman were opening for him.

The machine gun leaped joyfully in his hands, the metallic link belt racing up from the magazine to be devoured by the breech. Splashes as tall as small saplings leaped from the sea, tracers, ball and AP rounds ripping the raft and tearing into the men. The great bullets pulverized flesh and smashed bone, tearing off limbs, ripping open torsos, and decapitating one man as he jumped over the side. The men leaped, whirled, and tumbled into the sea. Brent kept on firing short bursts at two heads that bobbed near the wreckage of the raft, not stopping until he had split them both open like shattered melons. A great red splotch began to spread.

"Bully for you, old boy," Willard-Smith scoffed. "Good show. I'll put you in for the Victoria Cross."

Filled with blood lust and growling like an animal, Brent whirled on the Englishman, fists balled. His heart was a trip-hammer and he could feel the pounding in his throat. "Sir!" Crog shouted, stepping forward. "You can't . . ."

Signalman Todd Doran's voice interrupted. "*DD-One*'s calling us, Mister Ross." He leaped up onto the signaling platform and turned on the light.

"Give him a K (go-ahead,)" Brent said through rigid jaws. He glared at the Englishman, who returned his stare without giving quarter.

"Stand by to write, Hollister," Doran said to the lookout. Hollister pulled a pad and pencil from his pocket.

Doran began to read the destroyer's flashing light, opening his shutters for a short flash to acknowledge receipt for each group. " 'Well done. You saved my ass. I will escort you to Tokyo Bay. Greetings to Lieutenant Ross. Is he in good health'?"

Brent felt the heat of fury begin to drain away and

control return as he pictured the big, burly Captain John "Slugger" Fite standing next to his signalman and dictating each word. He heard Doran roger the transmission and then the signalman turned expectantly to Brent Ross. Brent said, "Thank him and tell him Brent Ross is in good health but Admiral Allen is dead and we have many casualties and serious damage to the boat." He rubbed his chin. "And tell him thanks for saving our ass and we will follow in his wake after . . ." He fixed Willard-Smith with cold eyes, "after we clean up the garbage in the water."

While the light clattered, Brent returned to the front of the bridge. The submarine was wallowing and drifting to the south. "All ahead slow, steady on two-seven-zero," he ordered so that his voice was heard in the speaker and by the helmsman at the same time. Sturgis acknowledged the command and rang up the order to the engine room on the annunciators. Slowly the boat picked up speed and turned her bow to the west. Immediately the roll and pitch slackened. Brent returned to the machine gun.

Doran reported Fite's transmission to Brent: " 'My regrets for Admiral Allen. Cease fire. Cut a course for Tokyo Bay. I will tend to the survivors.' "

Brent grunted angrily and glared at Crog and Willard-Smith, who stared back at him unflinchingly. "Give him a 'Wilco' and AR (end transmission.)"

While Doran worked the light, Brent shouted his commands. "Right standard rudder, steady up on three-three-zero. All ahead two-thirds." The rhythm of the engines picked up and the boat swung in a big arc to the west and then north until Sturgis met the swing and finally said, "Steady on three-three-zero, sir."

"Pitometer reading sixteen knots, three-hundred-twenty revs, sir," came up from Nelson in the conning tower.

"Very well," Brent answered. And then down into the speaker, "Navigator, cut me a course for Tokyo Bay."

Cadenbach's voice squawked back. He was obviously

looking at his gyro repeater. "I would suggest you maintain course three-three-zero until I take my evening sights, sir. I've got to bring my DR track up to date. We must be miles off our last estimated position."

Brent glanced at the low sun which was balancing like a red ball on the string of the horizon. It would be less than an hour before the fix. "Very well," he said.

There was a clatter on the ladder and Lieutenant Reginald Williams pulled himself up through the hatch. A bloody bandage was wrapped around his head, and he gripped the windscreen, unsteady on wobbly legs. With anger clouding his face like the shadow of a squall darkening the sea, he glared at Brent with eyes as black as the bottom of a grave. All eyes were riveted on the two officers. "The stink of death woke me. Blood sprayed through my vent," Williams hissed. He stabbed a finger within inches of Brent's face. "You sank the can," he spat.

"That is correct."

"And you expect a 'well done' for this?"

"I expect nothing."

"And you shot survivors in the water."

Brent's voice was calm. "That is correct."

"Correct my ass. Not in my command."

"May I remind you, Captain—with you disabled, I *was* in command."

"You don't remind me of shit, mister. Those were helpless men."

Brent felt the heat begin to rise again. "They were terrorists. They're animals to be exterminated. That's all they are."

Williams spoke as if he had not heard. He waved at the butchered lookout, hanging from the shears. "Flying your pennant, Mister Ross?" he said, voice stinging like dry ice. "How appropriate."

"I won't take that," Brent snarled. He eyed his captain's injury and relaxed his fists. "When you're well we

127

have a few things to settle."

"I agreed long ago, 'American samurai.' We'll do it privately." He turned to Crog and Yuiji Ichioka and his voice was suddenly thick: "Bring him down." He stabbed a finger at the corpse. "He deserves better than that." The two men moved quickly to the ladder.

Williams shifted his eyes back to Brent, but before he could speak, he was interrupted by gunfire. Hollister screamed, "They're killing them!"

Everyone looked back over the stern. Fite was steaming through the wreckage at a high speed, machine guns firing, blasting men off wreckage and shooting swimmers. Then six great explosions blasted hundreds of tons of water and spray into the sky like great blue-white cliffs as six-hundred-pound depth charges set for thirty feet ripped the sea.

"Salt water enemas, you pricks!" Brent shouted gleefully, waving a fist.

Williams stared at Brent with disbelief. "My God . . . is that 'tending to the survivors'? What kind of war is this? What kind of war is it where you shoot helpless men in the water, bust their intestines with depth charges?"

Willard-Smith, Humphrey Bowman, Todd Doran, Ben Hollister and Williams stared hard at Brent's face. The lieutenant answered quietly, "The only kind of war they know. They made the rules. No Geneva Conventions, no humanity, no gentlemen in this war." He gesticulated wildly at the carnage. "This is the only kind of war they know."

"The only kind of war?" Williams repeated.

"Yes. You should ask Captain Fite about his son, Captain. Maybe then you'd understand."

There was silence on the bridge as *Blackfin* steamed into the gathering gloom.

Chapter Three

Luckily, the first part of *Blackfin*'s 1,000-mile voyage to Tokyo Bay was made in mild weather with only the scend of the flat North Pacific swells pushing in unchecked from across the width of the ocean. The five-inch gun was secured with cables on the centerline of the boat. The short in the electric cables was found exactly where Lieutenant Brooks Dunlap had predicted, and electric drive was restored. However, Number One Ballast Tank continued to leak, and the sounds of pumps were heard day and night. Speed was held down to sixteen knots, the boat finding the way a trifle smoother in the wake of *DD-1*, which steamed five hundred yards ahead of her.

The captain remained in his bunk for most of the first day. His long and vicious head wound had laid the skin open to the bone from just above the right eye to a point behind his ear. Sixty-seven sutures were required to close the gash, leaving the captain unsteady on his legs and with a shattering headache. Corpsman Chisato Yasuda was forced to administer a strong sedative. Brent conducted services for the dead at dawn.

Although Brent stood over five canvas-wrapped bodies, he said services for nine men — four members of the five-inch gun crew had been blown over the side. Three of the dead were Japanese and, to the surprise of the seven men standing at attention by his sides, he mouthed both Christian and Buddhist prayers from memory. For the Christians he called on Psalms 107:23, 24, and 25, which traditionally consign "Those who go down to the sea in ships," to their graves in the deep. Then, quotes from the Four Noble Truths from the Sermon of Benares were the last rites for the Buddhists. There was no time for eulogies, and after the prayers, the bodies were quickly consigned to the deep. Four Christian crewmen remained to recite the Twenty-Third Psalm together.

That afternoon Reginald Williams revived and began to wander around the boat like a lost spirit. But he was still capable of exercising command and wanted all hands to know this. He had little to say to Brent Ross, only those words required by command and discussions of problems which demanded the attention of the executive officer. The implacable black visage remained free of emotion, but Brent could see hostility and acrimony lurking in the eyes as if small lamps backlighted the gleaming pupils. Strange how he seemed to collide with this man on every major issue from football to the treatment of prisoners.

Fite had not killed all the prisoners. He had picked up four men who had paddled a raft to the periphery of the massacre. Brent could not understand why Fite relented. Perhaps he wanted some prisoners for interrogation. But Arabs knew little, and they rarely divulged useful information. Limited by a lifetime of tribal and village feuds, they had little knowledge of naval tactics and utterly no concept of global strategy. Sometimes, however, with some persuasion, they could provide information on their own units and on the strength of others. But they seemed incapable of relating pieces to the mosaic of the whole. Or maybe they were clever. Certainly, as the most treacherous people on earth, they all shared the common characteristic of duplicity. Killing them was the best decision.

With thirteen dead and three wounded, *Blackfin* was terribly short-handed. Restricted to the surface, there were enough men to steam her, but not to fight her. Captain Colin Willard-Smith became part of the ship's company. He actually asked to be assigned as a gunner-lookout in Brent's section. This pleased Brent. Despite their bitter disagreement, he liked the Englishman and was pleased with his company. He found Willard-Smith reciprocated. Both men wanted to put the heat of their clash behind them, and the pair had long conversations in the wardroom when off duty. The killing of the four men on the raft was never mentioned. Instead, they talked of the usual things lonely men at sea talk about: home, girl friends, their favorite cities—London, Liverpool, Paris, Southhampton, New York, Los Angeles—nightclubs, pubs—and of course, food and good liquor.

Less than two days out of Tokyo Bay, the first PBM Mariner picked them up. Fite had detected the aircraft and its IFF on his radar and ECM, relaying the information to *Blackfin* by flashing light. When the graceful gull-winged flying boat finally droned over the horizon, it dropped down cautiously and made a big circular reconnaissance of the two vessels, well out of AA range. The bridge crew waved and cheered, and a half-dozen off-duty men crowded onto the bridge and the wet main deck aft, where they were all soaked. So much hell had fallen from the skies, but now an ally, a friend, had found them. The cheers became frantic as the big plane finally dropped down almost wave-high and thundered over the submarine, barely clearing the periscope shears, her two huge Pratt and Whitney Double Wasp radial engines deafening everyone and shaking the entire bridge structure with their power. The lookouts on their platform actually ducked, which brought raucous laughter from those beneath them.

There was more joy when Radioman Second Class

131

Goroku Kumano repaired the SPS-10, unshielding the boat's eyes. Now Brent could look at the revolving antenna behind the shears and feel confident the unseen beam was searching both sea and sky in an eighty-mile radius. The radios remained out, apparently damaged beyond repair. Then, just one day out of Tokyo Bay, the storm struck.

It was not a severe storm for these latitudes and at first did not threaten with particularly fierce winds. In fact, the barometer never did drop beneath 1002 millibars. However, in *Blackfin's* damaged condition and with its low freeboard, any storm was a menace. It struck during Brent's afternoon watch.

First a dark, mountainous shape humped up over the northern horizon where most North Pacific storms are born. Then solid droves of puffy clouds stormed over the horizon and swirled and raced to the south like terrified wildebeest fleeing the lion of the wind, dark gray on their undersides, brilliant white where the afternoon sun caught their peaks. Quickly the low clouds scurried above *Blackfin,* filling the void to the south. The seas became leaden rollers that swelled and peaked frothily, rushing down on the submarine relentlessly in infinite rows that stretched from horizon to horizon.

With the sun turned into a Satanic red low on the horizon, the light faded and changed, turning a sickly greenish-yellow hue like the shine of decay on a corpse. The strange light caused the clouds overhead to glow with a malevolent jaundiced yellow. Staring at the phenomenon, Brent felt an icy dread grip his soul. "Satan's Beacon"—the harbinger of doom—came to mind. It was everywhere, filling the voids of shadows like liquid. And it came from all directions: from the heavens, the clouds, from every atom of air, the steel of the submarine, filling every corner of the bridge, bathing the boat, turning flesh the color of days-old corruption. Mariners of all races, of all persuasions, knew it and feared it. He looked around at the other men, wondering if they, too, were gripped by superstitious dread. Their faces told him they were. Even Captain Colin Willard-Smith appeared awed by the preternatural glow, pivoting his head, his pilot's eyes apprehensive and puzzled.

Brent knew the fear was foolish and irrational. He had been to sea for too many years and knew better. He assured himself the eerie light was nothing more than the rays of the sun low on the western horizon slanting into the cloud peaks and reflecting downward and at the same time streaking in from below to color the streaming clouds and their vaporous trails with beams of filtered light. But somehow he could not rationalize away this malignant phenomenon that was part of the mariner's lore, the fearsome stygian light that lured a doomed ship inexorably to its fate.

Fortunately, the weird light faded with the sun and the mood went with it. "In for a bit of a blow," Willard-Smith said, staring at the clouds while pulling the hood of his parka over his head and securing it with its drawstring. Every man in the bridge force emulated the Englishman.

The wind increasingly mourned about them and then the rain crashed down in torrents, obscuring vision beyond an arc of a few hundred yards. Now the destroyer was visible only in intermittent glimpses. Abruptly the wind backed into the north and the pattern of the rollers changed, taking *Blackfin* on her starboard bow. Born in latitude seventy, the gusts were icy with Arctic cold, ripping the breaths from the men in ribbons of steam and splattering the rain on their faces with the sting of frozen sand.

Still heavy in the bow, the submarine was unable to woo the swells; instead she warred with them, trying to crush them and churn them under, and failing in her attempts. All ships have elasticity built into their hulls, but a submarine is a rigid steel tube built for the depths.

133

Seas crested against *Blackfin*'s unyielding hull and swept the length of the weather deck, battering the bridge and rolling the boat brutally from side to side. Brent called the lookouts down from the shears and latched the hatch cover to the conning tower.

Clothed in heavy foul-weather gear, Reginald Williams came to the bridge. Brent reported course and speed to the captain. Williams nodded and clung to the windscreen, a dull look that bordered on incomprehension in his eyes. He clutched his head suddenly with a single huge palm and rocked from side to side. "Bitchin' headache—a real bitchin' headache. The goddamnedest hangover I've ever had," the captain said. At that moment, Brent realized the blow to his captain's head had done more damage than he had at first suspected. Williams had the look of a man with a concussion.

Brent gesticulated to the north. "We're taking the seas on our starboard bow, sir," he shouted into the roaring wind. "I suggest we change course to zero-zero-zero. Put our bows into her."

Williams nodded his agreement and Brent gave the order to Seaman Tatsunori Hara, who was manning the wheel and annunciators. Hara put the helm over, and immediately the violent rocking diminished. But the pitching and the assault of the seas on the boat's hull and exposed decks did not. Doran informed *DD-1* of the course change by flashing light. Then, Fite, too, changed course and the violent rolling of the narrow-beamed destroyer lessened.

The swells mounted and seas swept in and crashed against the bridge like battering rams. Solid water impacted the superstructure with the force of great boulders, the entire structure shaking with the force of the attack, groaning, popping, and whimpering. The periscope shears snapped hard fore-and-aft and beam-to-beam against their stays—clanging, banging, and vibrating like green saplings all the way down into their wells in the control room. Alarmed, Brent shouted into the speaker, "Anemometer reading?"

Cadenbach's voice came back, "Force nine, sir."

Brent's mind digested the information quickly. Force nine on the Beaufort Scale indicated a strong gale, winds up to 54 miles an hour, a much stronger gale than he had expected. True, it was far below the maximum at force twelve and wind speeds of over 130 miles an hour, but still very dangerous.

"Captain," Brent said, close to Williams' ear. "We have fifty-mile-an-hour winds. This beating must be hard on the damage between frames forty-six and forty-seven and the sea valve in Number One Ballast Tank could let go. I suggest we reduce speed to eight knots. It would be easier on our hull, and we would still have good steerage way."

Williams indicated agreement with a nod and said, "Good idea, XO. Give the order." He rubbed his head gently. "I'm not thinking."

Blackfin reduced speed, and the change was relayed to Fite, who brought his own speed down. The reduction in speed inflicted greater punishment on the tall, narrow vessel, but any other option might prove fatal to the submarine. The two vessels wallowed and plunged ahead, the heavy submarine battering and shouldering her way through the crests and dropping ponderously into the troughs like a pregnant beast. These were the terrifying moments — the moments when the seas loomed above the submarine like majestic liquid mountains ready to avalanche down and smother the tiny vessel in the sheer weight of thousands of tons of water. But the gallant boat always managed to struggle up the slopes, screws straining against the tide, wind, and gravity, and churn through ridges and crests with angry bursts of water and spray.

There was terror here, yet Brent felt himself filled with a perverse feeling of joy, a realization that at the moment

135

he was pitted against one of nature's most awesome on-slaughts and he was prevailing in an arena where survival was victory. It was like fighting enemy depth charges, aircraft and artillery. Like all men who have fought other men at sea and grappled with the vagaries of the sea it-self, Brent Ross lived life to the fullest when challenging death.

"Captain," he yelled into the wind. "I suggest full up on the bow planes."

Williams stared into Brent's eyes. There was no ani-mosity there, only the look of a confused man looking to another in his struggle to survive. "They could be car-ried off, XO."

"I know, sir. But we have no choice." He gestured at the combers.

"Very well."

Brent gave the order.

"Bridge!" came up from the conning tower. It was Ra-dioman Goroku Kumano. "I'm getting a lot of electrical interference from the storm—sea clutter and ghosts are jamming the radar scope."

"Damn!" Williams said. "Can you track the de-stroyer?"

"Yes, sir."

"Good. We just lost him in a squall."

Seaman Burt Nelson's voice in the speaker: "Captain. Lieutenant Dunlap requests your presence in the maneu-vering room."

Williams grasped his head and rocked with pain. "Very well," he managed.

Alarmed, Brent and Willard-Smith gripped the cap-tain's arms and helped him into the hatch. Hands reached up from the conning tower to guide the captain down the ladder. He looked up into Brent's eyes. "Some-times I hate your guts, XO. But you're the best god-damned seaman I've ever known. I hate to ask any man to do this, but stay on the bridge until this storm blows over." He pulled the wooden toggle and slammed the cover shut before Brent could respond.

"Daresay, that man's a real gamecock. He's bought it and doesn't know it. He should be in his bunk," Willard-Smith shouted. "But he jolly well he confidence in you, old boy—and so do I." He clapped Brent on the shoulders and returned to his post next to the port Browning.

Brent felt a deep warmth spread as if he had just chuga-lugged four ounces of Haig & Haig. His peers respected him, admired him. And then the warmth was replaced by a shudder. Williams had actually placed all their lives in his hands. He took his station next to Hara and steadied himself with a firm grip on the windscreen.

Burt Nelson's voice scratched in the speaker: "Bridge, Hauptmann Conrad Schachter and Feldwebel Haj Abu al Sahdi are very ill. They've vomited all over the mess hall. Hauptmann Schachter demands to be released and allowed to come to the bridge for some fresh air. He said something about the Geneva convention. . . ."

Brent shouted into the speaker: "Tell Hauptmann I'll give him some fresh air—compressed air when I blow his ass out of a torpedo tube. Tell him that's the 'Brent Ross convention.'" Even in the howling wind, Brent could hear the laughter in the conning tower as Nelson acknowledged the order. There were no more complaints from the prisoners.

For an hour they continued on the same heading. The watch changed and Hara was replaced by Seaman First Class Jay Overstreet. But Willard-Smith remained. The force of the wind did not increase, but it did not abate, either. With all the stars blotted out by the storm, the world was filled with a blackness broken only by the dull red glow of the compass repeater in front of Overstreet. The seas would cause the boat to pitch and yaw, however, the experienced helmsman always met each roll and inevitable yaw with opposite rudder, holding the battered submarine to her course with remarkable accuracy.

Occasionally the wind faded and Brent's hopes rose; but every time they would be banished by a particularly brutal gust that howled in like a ravening beast, whipping the top off the sea and hurling thick white curtains of spray and saltwater into his face and flooding the bridge. Then the boat would struggle up, water streaming from her scuppers and drains, and the process would be repeated.

It could have been at 2100 hundred hours—Brent's fatigued mind had lost track of time—that the storm provided a spectacular electrical display. Passing under the heart of the storm, a thunderhead that could have reached as high as sixty thousand feet, they were suddenly bathed by eye-searing bolts of jagged lightning followed by shattering cannonades of thunder. Here, in the great vaporous tower, racing, spinning air generated hundreds of thousands of volts of electrical energy.

Willard-Smith circled a hand overhead and then stabbed a finger straight up. "A thunderhead," he screamed into Brent's ear. "Could be the heart of this storm—the end of the bloody thing."

"I hope you're right, old boy," Brent shouted back.

Captain Colin Willard-Smith was right. Within thirty minutes the wind began to diminish and another half-hour brought stars to the northern horizon. The sea began to calm, and the severe rolling and pitching was reduced.

"I say, good egg," Brent quipped in a sudden jovial mood, "you were bloody well right."

Willard-Smith roared with laughter. "Thanks awfully . . . ah," he groped for a phrase he had heard in the enlisted men's mess. "I mean, you're *fuckin' A,* chum."

Their laughter was interrupted by Williams' voice in the speaker. "Bridge!"

"Bridge aye."

"Mister Cadenbach recommends we return to our base course of three-three-zero. Do you agree?"

Brent glanced overhead. Now stars were visible in the entire northern hemisphere of the sky. "Looks good, Captain."

"Make the request by flashing light."

"Aye aye, sir."

The message was sent, and then both ships came left on a heading for Tokyo Bay.

Chapter Four

The next morning at dawn the radar picked up the first traces of Japan. The islands of Mikura Jima, Miyake Jima, Nii Shima, To Shima, and Ō Shima, lying in a straight line like an arrow pointing toward home for the homesick sailor, glowed brightly on the scope. And the clear morning sky glowed as if all of nature were welcoming the Japanese members of *Blackfin*'s crew home. There was palpable air of expectancy, of suppressed joy in the boat. Brent could feel it.

Aircraft swept over. Another PBM followed an hour later by a great graceful PBY that snooped and stared. Then a section of three Zeros roared over the horizon wave high and circled close aboard both vessels. With their canopies back, the pilots waved and the bridge watch waved back. Both Brent and Colin Willard-Smith were bitterly disappointed that Matsuhara's fighter was not among them.

By ten hundred hours they had left the first of the islands to port, clearly visible only six miles away. Now the radar traced Point Iro Zaki to the east and Nojima Zaki to the west and the shorelines on both sides leading to the huge harbor. Their bows were pointed directly into the center of the channel of the still unseen Tokyo Bay. By noon they made their landfall and passed the sea buoy. Entering the narrows, which the Japanese called

Uraga Suido, it was all visible: the Izu Hanto Peninsula to the west, the Bōsō Hanto Peninsula to the east, the sweeping coastline of Kanagawawa to port, the rugged green beauty of the tree-covered hills of Bōsō Hanto looming closer and closer to the starboard side. *DD-One* continued to plod five hundred yards ahead.

Williams came to the bridge, but did not take the con himself. This he left to Brent with the comment, "You've steamed these waters for years. Take her in, XO." Although the tone was cursory and the eyes still glassy, Brent thought he heard a glimmer of respect in the cold voice. Despite his antipathy for the man, Brent knew Williams was a good captain. He was courageous and intelligent and had never allowed personal feelings to interfere with the efficiency and safety of his command. Brent could not help but feel his own respect for the big man grow. He was obviously hurt, his head wrapped and that pained look still dulling his eyes. But he was much steadier on his feet.

Fite's light began to flash, and Signalman Second Class Todd Doran began to mouth the words to the writer, Ben Hollister. Immediately, it became obvious Captain Fite was relaying a radio message. " 'Com *Yonaga* (Commanding Officer Carrier *Yonaga*) to *Blackfin*. Proceed submarine base Yokosuka to Berth Four, Pier Three. Commanding officer and executive officer report immediately to Com *Yonaga*. Well done.' "

Williams said to Doran: "Tell him we have three seriously wounded and severe damage to the boat and we have Captain Colin Willard-Smith aboard and two prisoners."

There was a clatter as the venetian blind-like shutters were worked furiously by Doran's right hand flipping the handle of the light. Brent smiled. Even the fastest signalmen were capable of transmitting and receiving only about fifteen words a minute. Doran was pushing the limit while Williams twitched impatiently. Finally Doran "Rogered" and turned to the captain, ignoring his writer. "He says to bring the Englishman and the two prisoners with you to *Yonaga*. An ambulance will be waiting at the dock. *Blackfin* will be dry-docked as soon as one becomes available."

"Damn! We need a dry dock now. Tell him we will need a high-capacity pump on the dock—one large enough to handle the water in Number One Ballast Tank. If our pumps give out, *Blackfin* will sink. We need to be dry-docked immediately."

More clattering of the light and then there was an uneasy pause as Fite was obviously relaying the information by radio to *Yonaga*. Then the light on the destroyer began to speak again. Doran's voice: "Dry dock will be made available tomorrow. Two pumps will be waiting on the dock."

Williams nodded and said, "Very well. Give him a 'Wilco.' "

Doran returned to the light and then spoke to his captain, "He gave me an 'AR'—end transmission, sir."

"Very well."

Nelson's voice from the conning tower: "We've crossed the hundred-fathom line, Captain."

"Very well." Williams turned to Brent, "We're low in the water—drawing nearly seventeen feet forward. Any problem?"

"Negative, sir." He gestured at the straits, which were growing narrower. "Good water all the way in. No problem, sir."

"Very well, XO—ah, I mean 'Pilot'—it's your ball game."

A light flashed again from the destroyer. "Proceed independently," Doran said.

"Very well." Brent peered through the bearing ring's gunsight, read the repeater, and turned to Quartermaster Overstreet, "Right to zero-two-seven, all ahead one-third."

Overstreet brought the helm over slightly, and a ringing of bells slowed the engines. "Keep her in the center of the channel, fifty yards to the left of the red buoys, Quartermaster."

"I understand, sir."

Brent shouted down the hatch, "Fathometer?"

"Ten fathoms under the keel, sir," came from Seaman Tak Ishinishi, who was manning the steering and engine room controls in the conning tower.

"Let me know if she shoals less than six."

"Less than six, sir."

A new voice came from the conning tower. It was Chief Electrician's Mate Momoo Kenkyusha. "Four off-duty men request permission to come up on deck, sir."

Williams chuckled. They all knew the Japanese members of the crew were hungry for a glimpse of their homeland. Williams bent over the hatch and grabbed his head and said, "All off-duty men wishing to come on deck may come topside." He glanced forward where the bow still rode low in the water. "But you may get your feet wet."

Chief Kenkyusha, Yeoman Yuiji Ichioka, Seaman Tatsunori Hara, and old, tough Chief Torpedoman Masayori Fujiwara all raced up the ladder, bowed, and saluted the captain and hurried forward, ignoring the occasional rivulet of water that sloshed over their boots. They stood in a tight group, laughing, pointing, and pounding each other on the back. They were alive when by all rights they should have been dead, they were home when they had many times given up all hope of ever seeing their beautiful islands again. Their joy was unbounded, and Brent felt it.

They crept toward the narrowest part of the channel between Uraga Point and the Bōsō Hanto Peninsula. A few houses were visible, but most of the land was covered with lush stands of pine, firs, beech, ash, and oak. Thick foliage rioting with blooms grew in barricades between the trees. The beauty, joy of seeing solid earth again, penetrated every man's soul and warmed his heart. Brent was filled with thoughts of this strange land that had been his home for the past six years.

Here, a man was not admired for his consistencies, but, instead, his manhood was measured by the number of contradictions he could hold and still keep his balance. The young American had learned to live with paradoxes everywhere: guests kept their hats on but removed their shoes; wine was heated; fish was eaten raw, even the *fugu*, which could be fatal; bathers scrubbed themselves clean before entering a bath; mourners wore white; an emperor who was the one-hundred-twenty-fourth descendant of the immortal god Amaterasu-O-Mi-Kami had just proved his immortality by dying; one was ushered into the world with Shinto rites and exited with the chants of a Buddhist priest; the most literate nation on earth was shackled with a maddening non-alphabetical language, based on two thousand Kanji characters that could have almost as many meanings as readers.

And the women came back. Here he had met Sarah Aranson, the Israeli Intelligence agent. They had burned in each other's passion from her apartment in the *Shinjuku-hu* to her place in Tel Aviv. Then there was Mayumi Hachiya, young, virginal, with ethereal beauty as delicate as bridal lace and as passionate as a rutting animal in heat. He had met CIA agent Dale McIntyre on *Yonaga*—Dale McIntyre, who was so worried about the "big four-oh" which had loomed only a year away. "Too old for you, Brent," she had said as she led him into her bedroom for a series of sexual adventures and acrobatics he had never believed possible in his wildest fantasies.

And then there had been the traitor and enemy agent, Kathryn Suzuki. He always thought of her as the "black widow." After one wild sexual fling with him in Hawaii, she had tried to kill him twice—the first by leading him into an assassin's ambush, and the second when she charged a truck loaded with plastique down on the great graving dock at Yokosuka, where a damaged *Yonaga* rested on her blocks. Flat on her back after a machine gun had wrecked the truck, she had stared up at Brent.

Brent would never forget the moment—the exquisite moment when the Otsu bucked in his hand and the small round, purple hole appeared precisely in the middle of Kathryn's forehead. There was the usual jerking of limbs and twitching as brains gouted out of the huge exit wound in the back of her skull left by the seven-millimeter slug and then she was still. She had never left his mind. In an inexplicable way, he still yearned for her despite the fact her death had been earned a hundred times over and his actions had been highly praised by his shipmates, especially Admiral Fujita.

As they cleared Uraga Point, the vast expanse of Tokyo Bay became visible. The binoculars of every man on the bridge came up in unison. Yokohama, Japan's greatest seaport, stretched in an ugly urban smear along miles of the northwestern coastline. Kawasaki could be seen further north, but the great urban sprawl of Tokyo was still invisible over the far horizon. Revolting in its contrast with the pristine blue sky above was the vast metropolis's filthy air, which hung like an obscene brown blanket over the entire northern horizon. But in the far distance, the snow-capped pinnacle of Mount Fujiyama still poked its head defiantly through the noxious brown layers.

Shifting his glasses to the west, Brent could see the city of Yokosuka and its great naval base only five miles off their port beam. Fite had already made his turn. Sighting through the bearing repeater ring, he said to Overstreet, "Left standard rudder. Steady up on two-eight-one."

The command was repeated, and the submarine came about slowly to her new heading. Electronics Warfare Technician Matthew Dante's voice came up the hatch from the SPS-10. "I have a lot of clutter on the radar scope, sir. But it looks like many small craft are headed this way."

Brent had been searching the forest of cranes, radar antennas, and upper works for the massive superstructure of *Yonaga*. He had just found the single great stack

145

and bridge when Dante's report pulled his glasses down to the bay. He saw them, dozens of gaily decorated boats plowing through the small chop toward the two vessels.

Williams turned toward Brent, beaming. "A welcoming committee, XO. They're happy to see us." He was obviously feeling much better and was in high spirits.

"Yes, sir. Most of them. As Admiral Fujita would say, 'They would love anyone who would keep gas in the tanks of their Hondas.' "

"Cynical old man, isn't he?"

"A wise old man, Captain."

Williams rubbed his chin. "You said 'most of them.' What did you mean?"

Brent waved at the approaching boats. "Some could be *Rengo Sekigun.*"

Williams, Willard-Smith, and Overstreet stared at the executive officer. But the two Japanese lookouts exchanged a knowing look.

Brent continued: "The Japanese Red Army."

Williams nodded. "Terrorists, of course."

"They're quite capable of loading a boat with plastique and ramming us just as that Arab terrorist did in Lebanon when two hundred forty-one of our marines were killed in their barracks at the Beirut Airport."

"What would you suggest, Mister Ross? Should we machine-gun the lot of them?" Every eye turned to Brent.

Brent was taken aback. An amalgam of anger and resentment creased his face with hard, down-turning lines and shadowed his eyes. It boiled from his lips, "That was uncalled for!"

"I'll decide that, XO." And then, with forced contriteness, "I didn't mean to offend."

Shaking with anger, Brent grunted acknowledgment of the weak apology and held his tongue with an effort. The apology had been so bland, it had hardly been expiatory at all. A burning cauldron churned in his stomach. In a short time he would be off the submarine and back on board *Yonaga* and rid of Williams. He must control his temper; not do something foolish—something that could end his career. Williams had almost goaded him into intemperate acts in the past. He would not be baited. He would bide his time and catch the big black alone, someday, and then settle everything between them. After all, they were of equal rank.

Willard-Smith's voice broke through the turmoil swirling in Brent's brain. "By Jove, our escort's tracking the boats with his secondaries."

Brent glassed the approaching flotilla. They were very close. In fact, some had already passed *DD-One*. Staring through his glasses, Williams came erect with a start. "You're right. Fite's tracking those boats with his twenties and forties."

Turning his thick lower lip under, he clamped down hard on it with his perfect white teeth. His Adam's apple worked up and down furiously. He spat into the speaker, "Battle surface! Man the fifties! Cryptologist Crog Romero, Yeoman Yuiji Ichioka, Gunner's Mate Humphrey Bowman—to the bridge on the double! Man collision stations. Close all watertight doors and dog them except for the conning tower hatch. And I want the two Thompsons on the bridge."

Within seconds, Brent and Crog manned the fifties with their loaders, Humphrey Bowman and Yuiji Ichioka, standing by the ready boxes. Quartermaster Sturgis replaced Overstreet at the helm, and the seaman disappeared into the conning tower. Two old-fashioned Thompson 45-caliber submachine guns were passed up through the confusion as the four Japanese who had been standing on the foredeck dropped down the hatch. Each of the cumbersome weapons had a fifty-round drum magazine. Williams kept a Thompson and handed the other to Willard-Smith. "You wind it up like this," Williams said, turning a key on the drum. "Until you hear nine clicks. Puts spring tension on the rounds." He flipped a small lever on the breech to "Safe" and pulled back hard on the cocking handle, driving a round into the firing chamber.

Willard-Smith followed the captain's example. "I'll be buggered," the Englishman mused, turning the key. "Winds up just like a bloody toy. That's a bit of all right."

"Watch it when you fire," Brent cautioned, with a controlled, steady voice. "It pulls up real hard on a long burst. Squeeze off short bursts." He managed a weak joke, "Even Al Capone had trouble with the damned thing." Two American lookouts laughed nervously.

Brent said to Williams in a formal, military timbre, "Captain, I suggest we have the fire-and-rescue team on deck—unlimber a fire hose."

"Good idea, XO." Williams shouted the command, and three men rushed up through the hatch and ran forward to a locker attached to the front of the bridge. Within seconds, a large fire hose was pulled out from its reel and two men held the nozzle firmly. The leader of the group, Chief Torpedoman Masayori Fujiwara, looked toward the bridge for instructions.

"Check pressure!"

The hose thickened and writhed like a live reptile, and a fierce stream shot out over the side at least thirty yards.

"Secure." The streaking water died off, and Williams said, "Hit any boat that comes into range!"

"Aye aye, sir.

"Radar! Range to the nearest small boat?"

"Two hundred fifty yards, sir."

"Very well." The captain checked his safety on his Thompson and then slung it over his shoulder. "None of them are making a move on the DD."

Brent said, "If there are any *Rengo Sekigun,* they'll want *Blackfin.* By now the whole world knows we destroyed *Gefara* and put down one of their cans."

"What are the chances?"

"Very remote, but you can never tell—never predict

148

what a terrorist will do."

"Yes. Of course. We won't risk our boat."

Now the first of at least a score of boats decorated with gay ribbons and balloons and colored paper lanterns were sweeping down on the bow. Most were crowded with screaming people waving streamers of colorful paper banners. Williams leaned over the windscreen. "Chief, Fujiwara! Turn on the hose and spray it in an arc ahead of us and to the beams. Let 'em know they can't come in close."

The chief cranked the handle on the brass nozzle, and the stream shot in a forty-yard arc from beam to beam. The small boats parted and swung to the sides. Brent and Crog brought the muzzles of the Brownings down. Seeing this, the wildly cheering men and women crowding the boats lost most of their enthusiasm. They began to circle, most moving out to about a hundred yards. The occupants continued to wave, however, the cheering almost ceased.

With the boats circling, the two warships steamed in slowly toward the great naval base. "Seems okay," Williams said, almost to himself. Fite's speed dropped suddenly. "All ahead slow," Williams said to Sturgis.

"Speed four, sir," Sturgis said.

Before Williams could answer, a lookout shouted, "One's coming in at two-seven-zero."

"Fire hose!"

Chief Fujiwara pulled the hose to the port side and let loose the stream. The boat, a powerful speedboat with an inboard motor, dug its stern into the water and leaped forward in unbelievable acceleration. There were two men in the cockpit, and one appeared to be armed with an automatic rifle.

"Right full rudder. All ahead flank and keep her in a circle!" Overstreet whirled the helm over hard and rang up the command on the annunciators. But it would take time—too much time to bring the heavy boat up to speed. And there was no chance *Blackfin* could outmaneuver a speed boat.

"If the stream doesn't stop them, open fire!" Williams screamed.

"Might be too late, Captain!" Brent warned, bringing the boat into his sights. Already he was forced to come up on his toes to bring the muzzle down enough to line the target up in his sights. Willard-Smith snapped off his safety and stood next to Brent, his Thompson leveled. Williams, too, crowded to the port side, weapon ready. The boat reached the edge of the stream, not deviating from its course.

"Commence firing!"

The roar of the Browning and the two submachine guns deafened everyone, the windscreen vibrating with the blasts. Acrid smoke rolled up and hung in a brown cloud in the heavy air of the bay. Hundreds of bullets ripped the water and smashed into the boat. But the two men had disappeared. Brent guessed behind a sheet of armor plate. They could even have a periscope. He kept the trigger down, spraying the front of the boat and try- ing to punch holes in at the waterline. However, the craft was built of plastic, did not shatter and splinter like wooden boats. Forty yards, thirty yards it charged into the storm of bullets. Suddenly it swerved and began to slow, its bow dipping low as it scooped up water. Then the blast came.

The bow vanished in a bright orange flash that shook the bridge and hurled water, wreckage, and spray in a wide ring. Plastique had been packed into the bow—not a big charge like the five-hundred-kilogram bombs dropped by the Stukas, but big enough to blow a hole in the damaged *Blackfin*'s pressure hull and sink her.

Brent looked around anxiously. A few fragments of wreckage had hit the superstructure but all hands seemed unscathed, including the fire party and the lookouts on the shears. Everyone straightened and peered at the shat- tered boat where the water still boiled and debris contin- ued to rain in a wide circle.

Explosives can do strange things. Indeed, the bow and entire front of the boat had vanished, but the rear half from the cockpit aft had shot back as if propelled by a rocket charge and actually appeared intact as it slowly sank. A head bobbed up through the wreckage and an arm made a weak attempt to swim. One man with a life jacket. The other man had vanished.

"Course, sir?" Sturgis shouted.

Williams, leaning over the windscreen with his Thompson raised, seemed not to hear. He brought up the weapon and squeezed off a long burst, holding the bucking weapon down with his powerful arms. The great tumbling slugs struck with uncanny accuracy and devastating effect. The head jerked in a thicket of splashes, pieces of bone and gray brains exploding from the skull and scattering across the blue water. Finally, the firing pin struck on an empty chamber. Slowly he lowered the weapon, breathing like a man who had just run a hard ten-kilometer race. The black eyes were the pitiless, fierce eyes of a predator. Everyone stared in amazement.

Sturgis caught Brent's attention and gestured to the repeater, which was clicking off the degrees like seconds as the boat continued to circle and gain speed.

"Captain," Brent said in alarm, "we're going in circles."

"What? What?" Williams stared into Brent's eyes. The glassy look was back. He seemed not to understand. "They tried to kill my ship," he pleaded, as if he were trying to convince a tribunal.

There was an awkward silent moment. "We know, sir," Brent said softly. He circled a single finger over his head and repeated, "We're going in circles, sir."

Williams looked at the dead man, whose head had been shot off down to the jaw. Only his lower teeth, tongue, and one ear remained, surrounded by the shattered bone of his skull like a jagged, bloody bowl. His throat had been punctured and a jugular still spurted blood, a red stain spreading in a widening circle. A laconic smile twisted the captain's lips into a frightening leer. "Going in circles. Yes, indeed, we're going in circles, aren't we. Round and round we go . . ." He began to laugh, a frightening, humorless sound.

The captain seemed to be losing his grip on reality, his ability to command. As executive officer, Brent was empowered, actually compelled, by naval regulations to take command if the commanding officer was incapacitated. "Sir!" Brent persisted for the last time. "Your orders, Captain." He gesticulated anxiously at a covey of boats fleeing the bows of the rampaging submarine. "We'll ram them!"

Williams shook his head like a man awakening from a bad dream. "You have the con, XO, and take her in."

"Aye aye, sir." Brent spoke to Sturgis, "All ahead slow, left full rudder. Steady on . . ." He sighted through the bearing ring. "Steady up on two-seven-seven." The quartermaster rang up the command on the annunciators and put the helm over. Brent eyed the captain who was leaning against the windscreen. "May I suggest, Captain, that you get some rest. I'll call Corpsman Yasuda . . ."

"Negative!" Williams retorted hotly. "I'm okay—okay. Just follow my orders—con the boat." He turned to Bowman and spoke with authority as if to show everyone his composure had returned and he was still in command of himself. "Put on a full box of ammo and stand by the port fifty." And then to Willard-Smith, "Stand by, we'll remain at General Quarters." He shouted down the hatch. "Four more drums for the Thompsons." Then he leaned over the screen and spoke to Chief Fujiwara on the foredeck, "Keep the hose manned. Your orders are unchanged."

"Aye aye, sir," the chief torpedoman said.

Sturgis said to Brent Ross, "Steady on two-seven-seven, sir."

"Pitometer?"

"Speed four, Mister Ross."

"Speed over the bottom?"

152

"Three-point-five, sir."

"Very well. There's very little set. Steady as she goes." And then into the speaker, "Station the Special Sea Detail!" Within seconds, a dozen men clambered up the ladder and joined the fire-hose party on the deck. The four mooring lines were broken out from their lockers.

Slowly *Blackfin* cleared the end of the first pier and entered the channel that ran between two rows of berths. First built by the Imperial Navy and then expanded and improved by the occupying Americans, Yokosuka was a vast installation. Shops and warehouses, some still housed in the old semicircular quonset huts of World War II, lined the shore. Cranes like arthritic old birds crouched over a pair of *Fletcher*-class destroyers, a half-dozen supply ships, a depot ship, and swarms of lighters. *DD-One* already had her lines over and was mooring at Berth Five.

Brent could see huge "4" painted on a warehouse and on the pier in white. An ambulance was parked next to the warehouse, and four white-jacketed attendants were standing next to the vehicle. Two large pumps had just been unloaded from a truck, a crane still hulking above them. With the cables from the crane still attached, yard workmen were already scurrying about, hooking up wires and hoses to the pumps. A black Mercedes staff car and a large van with barred windows were parked close to the edge of the pier. Big and burly, a half-dozen seaman guards with slung Arisakas stood in a group watching the submarine.

And indeed, hundreds of pairs of curious eyes were focused on the damaged submarine. Workmen stood on the buildings and the docks and crews came to the rails of their ships to stare in amazement at the low-riding submarine with the blasted, blackened foredeck and wrecked guns. As they passed the depot ship and two *Fletchers,* crews dressed in blues lined the weather decks at quarters and saluted smartly. Then a roar of thousands of voices shouting *"Banzai!"* turned Brent's head.

The crew of *Yonaga* was drawn up in solid rows of blue on the edge of her flight deck while hundreds of others crowded her upper works. Again and again they shouted *"Banzai!"* and waved their hats. Brent's throat suddenly thickened and the deep blue of his eyes glistened with a layer of moisture.

Technically, the crew of *Blackfin* should have been called to quarters. However, short-handed and with the special sea detail posted, Williams was incapable of mustering enough men on deck to answer the honor. Instead, the captain turned and saluted smartly at each vessel as the cheers rolled in and the deck force waved their hats and shouted their greetings.

"Bowman!" Williams shouted hoarsely. "Stand by the gaff."

Quickly the gunner's mate dropped down the ladder and took his station aft, loosening the lines to the ensign. Then one after the other the depot ship and the three warships dipped their colors.

"Dip colors!" Williams yelled back over his shoulder.

Working the halyards, Bowman dipped the battle ensign four times. Cheers rolled and echoed back and forth, most resounding from the gargantuan bulk of *Yonaga* like a great sounding board.

Lieutenant Brent Ross was jarred from his euphoria by the voice of Lieutenant Reginald Williams. "I'll take the con, XO."

Brent stared at the captain. Although the lines of fatigue that framed his mouth were deeply chiseled, the black eyes were steady. Calmness and composure showed on the massive face. No doubt Williams felt compelled to show the crew and the thousands watching he had his senses and the best start would be to dock *Blackfin*.

"Aye aye, sir. We're coming alongside starboard side too. Speed slow ahead both main engines. I suggest we rig in the bow planes."

"Very well." Williams said into the speaker, "Diving station! Mister Battle, rig in the bow planes." Slowly the

154

steel pinions rotated ninety degrees and thudded into their recesses. The captain looked around. Not a single small boat was in the restricted waters of the naval base. He shouted into the speaker, "Secure from collision stations, secure from battle surface." And then to Sturgis after glancing at the dock and the repeater, "Right to two-eight-zero—steady as she goes." And then down to the deck crew standing by with lines, "Stand by to moor starboard-side-to."

"Starboard-side-to!" Boatswain's Mate Hitoshi Motoshima shouted back.

The dock was very close. "Dead slow ahead all engines!" Williams said.

Then as the distance to the dock narrowed even more and the bow swung in, "All stop!"

Momentum kept the boat moving through the water slowly. Motoshima whirled a monkey's fist over his head and a line whipped over to the dock, where a seaman grabbed it and pulled the mooring line ashore and wrapped it around a cleat.

"Number two spring line secure, sir!" Motoshima shouted.

"Very well. Port engine back one-third." Then quickly two more lines were over and *Blackfin* was warped smartly into her berth, the stern line put over last to keep the slack free of the screws. "All stop!" The vibrations ceased and all lines made fast. "Light-off Auxiliary Engine Number One!"

Brooks Dunlap's voice came back through the speaker, "Auxiliary Engine Number on line."

"Very well. Secure the main engines."

The throbbing rumbles and blasting exhausts of the two big Fairbanks-Morse engines ceased abruptly. The silence was eerie. It struck with physical force, a cool salve that refreshed battered eardrums and soothed taut nerves. *Blackfin* was at rest at last.

Exhaling his tensions with a loud sigh, Brent sagged against the windscreen and moved his eyes hungrily over

155

the great carrier across the channel. He had a full, warm feeling as if he were seeing his home after a long absence. Pride stirred and the old sense of value achieved swelled, the feeling of spiritual and physical exhaustion sloughing away. Even his anger with Williams faded. In six years of serving on *Yonaga,* he had never been able to truly appreciate the carrier's size. On the high seas there are no comparisons to be made except for sea, sky, and a distant escort. But here she dwarfed everything. Here she was gargantuan. And she was beautiful.

Her battleship antecedents had given her a low flight deck that swept back elegantly in a straight line for almost a fifth of a mile. Pyramiding upward gracefully like a great gray Fujisan, her superstructure was layered with the flight control bridge, flag bridge, and navigation bridge, and topped by her optical gun-director station. All were of molded steel and glittered with armored glass. Scaffolding had been erected on the giddy heights; the men working there and other crewmen still staring down at the submarine were as small as insects.

Her mast was a tripod, topped with more range finders, AA-guns, radar antennas, and signal flag halyards. In typical Japanese style, her single huge stack tilted outboard slightly. It was cluttered with four searchlight platforms and rows of life rafts. Attached to the back of the stack was the aft mast with its battle gaff where the ensign was flown when at sea. Her flight deck was lined with galleries where triple-mount 25-millimeter machine guns and five-inch dual-purpose cannons pointed toward the sky like a young forest. Everything, ships, warehouses, water towers, and office buildings were dwarfed by the behemoth. She was splendid, majestic, and powerful, and the fact that she could obey the will of one man defied credibility.

Brent knew her intimately. For six years Admiral Fujita had pored over her blueprints with him, explaining her unique design and incredibly complex construction. Led by Yoshi Matsuhara, he had studied her from directors to keel, from bulbous bow to graceful cruiser stern, not missing one of her 1176 compartments. He knew her better than *Blackfin,* better than anyone or anything he had ever known. Her history and the secrets of her construction had been pounded into his brains during hours of study and discussions with Fujita, Matsuhara and a dozen other senior officers.

The fourth of the *Yamato* class of superbattleships, she was the largest and most powerful. The first two hulls became battleships *Yamato* and *Musashi.* Displacing 64,000 tons and armed with nine 18.1-inch guns, both were sunk by aircraft. *Shinano,* the third hull, was converted into a 71,890-ton aircraft carrier. She was sunk by submarine *Archer-Fish.* All of the class were 853 feet long and were powered by twelve Kanpon boilers driving four geared turbines at 27 knots. But not *Yonaga.*

Admiral Hiroshi Fujita conceived, planned, and supervised her conversion. He brought in an old friend and Japan's greatest naval architect, Vice Admiral Keiji Fukuda, as a consultant. The pair lengthened *Yonaga* to 1,050 feet and equipped her with sixteen Kanpon boilers, driving her four geared turbines with 200,000-shaft horsepower and raising her flank speed to 32 knots. They retained the large torpedo blisters below the waterline and her main deck already armored with from four to eight inches of tapering steel became her hangar deck. When the flight deck was built on top of the hangar deck, Fujita had it layered with 3.75 inches of steel, reinforced by a layer of .75-inch steel 33 inches beneath it. Box beams were sandwiched between the two layers and the space filled with concrete, sawdust, and latex. The two admirals calculated it was capable of withstanding the impact of 1,000-pound bombs. The rectangular flight deck was gigantic. One thousand by 130 feet, it had an area of almost 15,000 square yards (over three acres) and was punctured by two large elevators, one forward and one aft.

To enhance its watertight integrity, Fujita had Fukuda

design a longitudinal bulkhead that ran from bow to stern and from the third deck to the keel. In addition, a steel box Fujita called the "citadel" was installed to protect the very heart of the ship. Made of 8-inch steel plate, it extended from frames 70 to 185 and from beam to beam. It housed essential equipment: boilers, engines, steering equipment, electronic and communication gear, and the magazines. Fujita even added additional fuel tanks that gave the carrier a cruising range of 10,000 miles. When he and Fukuda planned the aviation fuel tanks, they surrounded them with armor and circumferential tanks filled with seawater for added protection. The weight of the steel installed for defensive purposes alone totaled 19,600 tons—more than the tonnage of a heavy cruiser. In all, fully loaded, *Yonaga* displaced 84,000 tons. She was even larger than the largest American nuclear carrier, the USS *Nimitz,* which displaced 82,000 tons and was commissioned thirty-six years after *Yonaga.*

Brent's reminiscences were broken by Williams' shouted command to Boatswain's Mate Motoshima, "Bring aboard the shore power, phone, and water lines." Into the speaker, "Corpsman Chisato Yasuda, prepare the wounded for transfer ashore immediately. Lieutenant Dunlap, report to the bridge on the double. Prepare to jury-rig shore pumps to Main Ballast Tank Number One." Then straightening, he waved at the carrier and said to Brent, "Get your gear, XO. We have a date with the boss."

Chapter Five

Crossing the accommodation ladder onto a small section of *Yonaga*'s third deck, which served as the quarterdeck, Brent was filled with an ineffable joy, a feeling of euphoria a man knows when he finally returns home after a long, perilous journey. And Commander Yoshi Matsuhara was alive. Immediately after securing the Special Sea Detail, Brent and Captain Willard-Smith had stood anxiously over Todd Doran as the signalman flashed inquiries in the form of greetings to *Yonaga*'s signal bridge. Both Matsuhara and Pilot Officer Elwyn York answered the greetings with calls of, "Welcome home."

Now with two seaman guards leading, the group from *Blackfin* crossed the gangway that led to the heart of the monstrous carrier. Crewmen standing on scaffolding and chipping paint and rust turned from their work to shout *"Banzai!"* Others leaned precariously from the gun galleries high above on the flight deck to add their own cries of *"Banzai!"*

Williams, his hat squared precariously on top of his bandaged head, led the group, saluting and nodding carefully. Brent walked close behind his captain, followed by the Englishman and two wounded on stretchers. Prodded by four seaman guards, the two prisoners came last. Hauptmann Schachter muttered oaths constantly at his guards, sometimes shouting obscenities in German. *"Verfluchte scheisse"* ("damn shit") was his favorite appellation for the most aggressive guard, a big chief boatswain's mate who periodically rammed the butt of his Arisaka into the German's ample buttocks when the fat pilot lagged. But the German was filled with a venomous hatred that could not be squelched. *"Banzai! Banzai!"* Schachter jeered, waving a single finger at the cheering Japanese. A particularly vicious blow from the rifle butt knocked the wind from the German and silenced him temporarily. Feldwebel Haj Abu al Sahdi looked around like a frightened cur and held his tongue.

Stepping onto the quarterdecks, the officers first saluted the stern where the battle ensign flew and then saluted the junior officer of the deck, a young, eager-eyed junior lieutenant named Asaichi Kubo whom Brent had met just before he had been detached to *Blackfin*. Kubo had been an ensign then. "Welcome aboard, sir. Welcome aboard," the young lieutenant said, saluting and greeting each officer in turn. He stared long and curiously at Williams' black skin as the captain of *Blackfin* was introduced. Brent smiled, realizing most of the Japanese had never seen a Negro before. This was going to be interesting.

Lieutenant Kubo turned to a rating standing at attention next to a table with the log. Just above the table were a half-dozen bulkhead-mounted phones and rows of switches. "Yeoman, inform the admiral that the party from *Blackfin* has reported aboard and as per his orders, and are on their way to Flag Plot." The rating threw a switch and spoke into a phone.

Williams gestured to the wounded. "Sick bay," he said, the urgent timbre of his voice indicating more of an order than a request.

Kubo pointed up the passageway and shouted an order. The stretcher bearers hurried past with their burdens. Staring at the prisoners, Kubo said to Williams, "The admiral wishes to see the prisoners. They are to be taken to

Flag Plot." Then, condescending to superior rank, "With your permission, Lieutenant."

"Very well," Williams said, gesturing to the guards. "Flag Plot."

Passing Williams, Schachter spat, "Blackamoor *scheisse.*"

"Up yours, asshole," Williams retorted, cracking the German's buttocks with the toe of a boot.

The pilot squealed in pain and shouted more obscenities as he was pushed and prodded down the passageway. Hunching over, as if he were trying to withdraw into himself and not be noticed, Haj Abu al Sahdi scurried past.

Brent quipped, "Great soccer-style kick, Mister Williams — a real sidewinder." Everyone laughed.

Then there were shouts in the passageway and the sounds of boots pounding on steel. Yoshi Matsuhara and Elwyn York rushed up. The air-group commander grabbed Brent's hand and pounded him on the back at the same time. *"Banzai!* Great work! Well done. Thanks to the gods, you are back. I was sure you had entered the gates of Yasakuni, Brent-san. . . ."

Brent muttered his own greetings through a tight throat, unable to take his eyes from his friend's face. The man's defiance of time was astonishing. His coal-black hair glistened as if lacquered, his black eyes glowed with vigor and vitality, and only a few incipient wrinkles that fanned downward from the corners of his eyes hinted at his six decades. Although the pilot was at least five inches shorter than Brent, his shoulders were broad, his chest full, and his waist small: the physique of the trained athlete, a man addicted to weights and long runs on the vast flight deck.

"I'da bet a quid to a pinch of dung you 'ad bought it, Capt'n," Elwyn York said, gripping Willard-Smith's hand. "Good show, Guv'nor."

"Quite right, old boy. Thought I'd bought the whole bloody farm, too," Willard-Smith replied. "And a good

161

show yourselves—both you chaps."

Brent introduced the two pilots to Reginald Williams. Lieutenant Kubo interrupted, "Please, gentlemen. The admiral and his staff are waiting, and as you well know, the admiral is not a patient man." He gestured forward. "Please take the elevator."

Flag Plot was located in the aft part of the flag bridge next to Admiral Fujita's cabin. It was the largest room in "Flag Country." Long and narrow, it was dominated by a highly polished oak table that ran its length and appeared massive in the narrow confines of the room. A dozen chairs surrounded the table. Next to the door a rating manned communications gear. Overhead two blowers and a speaker were mounted in the usual maze of conduits and cables. A dozen lightbulbs shining from their fixtures like wire cages lighted the room. At the far end a picture of Emperor Akihito had replaced the equestrian of a young Emperor Hirohito that had hung in the same place for over forty years. To the right of the picture a small paulownia wood shrine was attached to the bulkhead. Filled with icons, talismans, and holy relics of both Shinto and Buddhist origins from the shrines at Minatogawa, Kochi, and Yasakuni, it looked much like a small log cabin with one wall removed to show rows of shiny metal markers. Charts covered most of the remaining space on the bulkheads. The room was a place for plotting, scheming, arguing, praying, and hopefully, wise decisions.

There were seven men in the room, their dress blues contrasting with the tans worn by the submariners. All were on their feet. None saluted because following the tradition of England's Royal Navy, the Japanese Imperial Navy had considered this area "below decks," and the crew of *Yonaga* still observed the customs of the long-dead Imperial Navy. However, standing rigidly, they bowed and shouted *"Banzai!"* over and over as Reginald

Williams, Brent Ross, Colin Willard-Smith, and Pilot Officer Elwyn York entered. Ordinarily Pilot Officer York's low rank would have excluded him, but his presence had been commanded by the admiral. Brent guessed Admiral Fujita wished to honor the young Cockney. He needed more flyers like his Englishmen; that was obvious.

Brent stared down the length of the table at the tiny figure at the far end. More than a foot and a half shorter than Brent, Admiral Fujita had a body deeply eroded by time, leaving only sagging and folded skin, stringy sinew, and brittle bones. However, the ancient sailor's diminutive size belied his great strength of character, the steely resolve of command that had hardened his spine like the fine-tempered steel of his sword. No one was sure of his age, but Brent knew he had seen more than a century. Sea, wind, and sun had hardened the skin of his face like saddle leather while the years had ravaged it with long furrows and creases that crossed-hatched his face like a latticework. Notwithstanding, the black eyes were alert, and pierced everyone and everything with a perceptiveness that bordered on the supernatural.

However, Fujita was no mystic. Indeed, he was the most pragmatic man Brent had ever known. He had an uncanny awareness of other men's motives and how they could be levered to suit his own purposes. He exercised absolute power, yet his Oriental sense of self-irony focused a wary, testing eye on himself, searching for his own failings which apparently did not exist. Never would a man like this succumb to the vanity and corruption of power.

He was the consummate commander, fitting all the requisites proscribed in Brent's classes at the Naval Academy. With his determination and the sharing of mortal dangers with his men, he projected the heroic style of Alexander the Great. Ulysses S. Grant, too, came to mind, riding into battle with a cigar clenched in his teeth. Fujita's planning was intricate and exhausting in its detail, equal to that of the Duke of Wellington and Field Marshal Bernard L. Montgomery. Both leaders had been meticulous planners; Wellington carefully crafted tactics defeating Napoleon at Waterloo, Montgomery declawing the "Desert Fox" Rommel at El Alamein after months of careful planning. Fujita was all of them and more.

Instinctively, Fujita showed a mastery of the imperatives of command, his men knowing he understood them and cared for them. He had a numinous knack for defining tactical and strategic problems precisely and conveying to each man what was expected of him and why. Every man from watertender to squadron commander was convinced he would be rewarded if he fought well, punished if he failed, especially if Fujita believed *Yonaga* had been dishonored by cowardice.

In battle the old admiral intuitively sensed the most propitious moment to attack, committing his air groups and escorts like a master chess player who had access to his opponent's mind and could checkmate the best-planned strategies. And he always commanded from the exposed flag bridge during the most intense bombing and torpedo attacks. In fact, once, caught by enemy cruisers in the Mediterranean and under heavy bombardment from big guns, the old man had refused to take his command into the safety of the conning tower and the protection of its foot-thick steel. No, indeed, if the peril was there, the tiny old mariner defied the fates with the men he had sent out to fight and often die.

As an aide to Admiral Mark Allen, Brent Ross had debriefed Admiral Fujita in 1983. He knew the old man's antecedents and personal history better than anyone alive except the admiral himself. He had it all on tape.

Admiral Hiroshi Fujita's tenure in the Japanese Navy had endured longer than the life expectancy of most men. The son of Seiko Fujita, who had been a professor of mathematics at Nagoya University, Hiroshi Fujita was born in Sekigahara, a suburb of Nagoya. He had one sibling, an older brother, Hachiro. A proud family deeply rooted in samurai tradition, the Fujitas had a centuries-old tradition of service to the emperor—a lineage extending back to the Heian period and the establishment of the Tokugawa shogunate in 1600. Honoring their samurai roots, Hachiro joined the army and Hiroshi entered Japan's naval academy at Eta Jima. Both were sixteen years old when they enlisted.

On February 10, 1904, war broke out with Russia, and Hachiro was killed in a fruitless assault on the Russian works at Mukden. Hiroshi's mother, Akemi, was shattered. Hiroshi gained a measure of revenge in the Korean Straits in the massacre of the Russian Fleet that would forever be known as the Battle of Tsushima. Here, as fire control officer of the after turret of the battleship *Mikasa,* Lieutenant Hiroshi Fujita had the satisfaction of finding the enemy in the cross-hairs of his range finder and of personally firing the two twelve-inch guns. He killed hundreds. His joy was unbounded as he reveled in the samurai's most valuable commodity, revenge—the classic revenge of the fabled Forty-Seven Ronin.

Because the Imperial Navy was modeled after the British Navy and the language of the fleet English, hundreds of officers were sent to English and American universities for advanced studies. In 1919 Fujita enrolled in the University of Southern California, where he distinguished himself in graduate studies in the English Department. He was deeply impressed by America. He agreed with his friend Isoroku Yamamoto, who was a student at Harvard and would one day command the fleet in the war against America, that the United States showed the latent power of a sleeping giant.

In the early twenties, Commander Hiroshi Fujita attended the Kasumigaura Air Training School, where he earned his flyer's patch. He was over forty years old. A month after his assignment as Air Operations Officer to the new carrier *Akagi,* he married Akiko Minokama. They established their home in Hiroshima, where the carrier was based. Their first son, Kazuo, was born in 1926, their second, Makoto, in 1928.

The decade of the thirties found Fujita and Yamamoto viewing the army's growing ambitions in China with alarm. After the Kwangtung Army seized Manchuria, the Russian bear growled its disapproval and bared its claws in bloody clashes along a 2100-mile front that sent the Kwangtung's best divisions reeling. Eighteen thousand Japanese troops were killed. It was obvious to Fujita and Yamamoto that a war with the inexhaustible manpower of both China and Russia was unwinnable. Expansion was possible only to the south, where the raw materials of Malaya and the priceless oil fields of Sumatra and Java in the Dutch East Indies beckoned irresistibly.

By the middle of the decade, Fujita had risen to the rank of rear admiral and was on the staff of Isoroku Yamamoto, a full admiral. Then the murders began; the army openly assassinated politicians who opposed expansionism in China. It culminated in 1936 in the *Koda-ha* action when the First Infantry Division rebelled and murdered some of the nation's most prominent politicians. By pure chance, the prime minister escaped. Although the mutiny was suppressed and the leaders executed, the army emerged with control of the cabinet. The march toward war accelerated.

The war with China accelerated, and Japanese divisions bogged down in the Chinese quagmire of numbers just as Fujita had expected. Demanding Japanese withdrawal from China, the Americans, British, and Dutch imposed sanctions, the most crippling of which were the embargoes on scrap iron and oil. Japan produced a mere dribble of oil and had only an eighteen-month supply in storage. It was submission or war. Submission was surrender, and surrender was unthinkable to the samurai. War became inevitable.

The Naval General Staff sent word to Admiral Yamamoto to draw up plans for a sneak carrier attack on the American fleet based at Pearl Harbor. It was to be patterned after the devastating British attack on the Italian fleet at Taranto in November of 1940 when twelve antique Swordfish torpedo bombers launched from the carrier *Illustrious* sank the Italian battleship *Cavour* and damaged battleships *Littorio* and *Caio Duilio*. Yamamoto was opposed, considered a war with America national suicide. Fujita agreed. However, the consummate professional Admiral Yamamoto assigned his most competent planners—Admiral Hiroshi Fujita, Captain Kameto Kurashima, and Commander Minoru Genda—to the task.

In November of 1941 Admiral Hiroshi Fujita stood rigidly as Akiko and his two sons, Kazuo and Makoto, bowed, clapped, and implored the gods to smile on husband and father. *Yonaga* was waiting for him in the roadstead off Hiroshima. His last remembrance of his family was a picture in his mind's eye of his wife, flanked by the boys, waving as he entered his staff car. They would all be vaporized in 1945.

Yoshi Matsuhara was the first to point out to Brent that Kazuo Fujita was a giant for a Japanese: six feet tall and weighing perhaps 180 pounds. "You remind the admiral of his son, I'm sure of it. I met the boy in 1940, just after I was assigned to *Yonaga*. I knew him well. Your size, build, mannerisms, your walk, even the way you speak and your awful temper are just like Kazuo's. Mark me, Brent-san, you've taken Kazuo's place with him, and he does not even know this himself." Brent had only shrugged skeptically.

Brent was jarred back to the present by the admiral's voice. "Welcome gentlemen," Admiral Fujita said in a low voice that rasped with age yet carried with it the unmistakable timbre of authority. He focused his remarkable eyes on Brent Ross. "Before introductions are made—before any reports and business are discussed—I wish to say I regret the loss of Admiral Mark Allen, who has added his life to the sum of life as all men do. He was a brilliant tactician and is a irreplaceable loss to all of us." He turned to the shrine and clapped twice to attract the attention of the gods. Brent Ross along with every Japanese in the room also clapped.

"Oh, Ninigi," Fujita said, calling on a powerful Shinto god who was Amaterasu's grandson and the founder of the Imperial Dynasty, "honor the *kokoro* (heart and spirit) of our fallen comrade, who challenged his enemies with a constantly believing heart and fought with the *Yamato damashii* of a samurai. We call on you to help our honored Admiral Mark Allen find the peace and contentment in whatever paradise or nirvana he seeks."

He paused, the room filled with the ship sounds of blowers and auxiliary engines. Inevitably he lapsed into the Buddhist chant which was de rigueur for services for the dead. "Oh Blessed One, if our honored one seeks nirvana, aid his search to find the beatitude that transcends suffering, karma, and samsara, and relieve his spirit of all consciousness—the illusions of desire, imagination, memory, and the past, and help him find that cosmic state which is beyond our knowledge, the measure of our words, our rhetoric, our polemics. If this is the existence he seeks, point the way with the Four Noble Truths, shorn of the ignorance and anxiety of science, paradigms, religions." He paused, his eyes finding Brent Ross. "If you would like to say a few words in the Christian tradition, Mister Ross, I feel the admiral's soul would respond best to that religion—would be most at home." The tone was reverent and the expression sincere, despite the absurdity of the entire ceremony.

"Of course, sir," Brent said, softly. He could understand Fujita's thinking. To his Asian mind, the greater the number of religions exhorting the transmigration of Allen's soul, the greater his chances of spending infinity in some state of nirvana, paradise or whatever reward might await him. Fujita's Asian mind saw no conflicts, no paradoxes whatsoever.

But not Williams, York, and Willard-Smith. The trio stared in wide-eyed wonder as Fujita reached under the table and drew a Bible from a small drawer. None could believe the proceedings, but they remained silent, faces as impassive and inscrutable as those of the Asians surrounding them. The Bible was passed down the table to Brent.

Brent thumbed through the book until he reached Admiral Allen's favorite verses. He looked up. "Admiral Allen favored John, Chapter Fourteen, verses two through six. I heard him use them over our Christian dead twice. Once in the Mediterranean and again in the southern Pacific, after we sank the three carriers and two cruisers off Indonesia and—and took heavy casualties."

Everyone stared at the young lieutenant as he choked back a swelling that suddenly filled his throat. It came back hard; his oldest friend, the man who had helped raise him, the man who had promoted his career with NIS (Naval Intelligence Service) and brought him to *Yonaga* as a green ensign . . . now these words were for him as he knew Mark Allen would have wanted. Brent read as everyone dropped his eyes reverentially: "In my father's house are many mansions . . ." his voice was unusually deep but as true as a plumb-line. ". . . I go to prepare a place for you." Slowly he read through the tender verses, ending with, "Jesus saith unto him, I am the way, the truth, and the life: no man cometh unto the Father but by me." He closed the Bible and stood silently, eyes cast down in an arena of silence.

After a long moment, Fujita's voice broke it: "Gentlemen, please seat yourselves." Every chair was occupied with officers rigidly seated in descending order of rank from Admiral Fujita at the head to the last officer, Pilot Officer Elwyn York at the far end. Now the curious stares began as heads turned toward Lieutenant Reginald Williams. Brent knew Admiral Fujita had seen Negroes in America. However, most of the Japanese in the room had never seen a Negro before. Some of the narrowed eyes and curled lips gave him a feeling of unease. He knew Williams' pyrotechnic temper would tolerate no slight, no masked affront. The big black was always on guard, sniffing out the scent of prejudice. Brent sensed trouble brewing. He knew Japanese history and prejudices well.

An island people who had lived in virtual isolation for thousands of years, the Japanese had very little exposure to cultural differences for most of their history, developing a sense of uniqueness that encouraged feelings from indifference to outright hostility toward foreigners. Over the millennia, in-breeding produced virtually a single, pure race in Japan—the type of racial purity to which Adolph Hitler aspired, but which in fact had been made a macabre joke by the European melting pot. And compared to the mixed races of the West, Japanese *did* look alike with their black hair, yellow skin, and similar facial features. In this homogenous society, strangers stood out, and Brent had discovered immediately that the Japanese were not immune to xenophobia and stereotyping.

At first he had heard "round-eyed barbarian," "filth-eater," and many more epithets hurled his way. In 1984 he had nearly killed Lieutenant Nobutake Konoye on the hangar deck after being called a "white-faced, water-eyed Yankee pig." After the fight, the insults were whispered behind his back and out of earshot. Only over the years, fighting shoulder-to-shoulder with the *Yonaga*'s samurai and demonstrating his great physical strength, bravery, and uncanny eye, had he broken free from the harsh racial feelings and earned the sobriquet "American samurai." Despite his acceptance, his exalted station with his Japanese comrades-in-arms, he knew intolerance was still virulently alive all over Japan.

Looking at Reginald Williams' black skin, he cast back in his mind to an experience he had in a restaurant he had visited only once in Tokyo's Ebisu district. The restaurant called itself *Chibi Kuro Sambo*—Japanese for "Little Black Sambo." He had been looking for American cuisine, but was not prepared for what he found. On entering, he was shocked by a decor loaded with dozens of comical black dolls, waitresses with their hair set in the style of African dreadlocks and wearing red gingham smocks. The menu boasted "little black fried chicken" and "little black potatoes." One look at the place had filled him with revulsion, and he'd left. Brent visualized Reginald Williams entering *Chibi Kiuro Sambo*. Mayhem! The big man would run amuck, and there would be many smashed dolls.

He had witnessed one violent racial incident on a suburban train. A dark-skinned Pakistani had been deliberately pushed by a group of rowdies into a corner with shouts of *"Songokul"* (Monkey!") Only Brent's and Yoshi Matsuhara's intervention prevented possible serious injury to the man. "Just like America forty years ago," he had said to Yoshi as they'd left the train.

Racial bigotry could be found even in the highest political offices. No one could forget former Prime Minister Yasuhiro Nakasone's remark, "America has a low intelligence level because of its black and Hispanic minorities."

Even members of Japan's ethnic Korean minority often felt the barbs of prejudice. Descendants of forced laborers brought to Japan during the colonial period, they still faced discrimination in employment and marriage. But the dark-skinned—some were actually black—Pakistanis suffered the most. Immigrating by the tens of thousands, they flocked to the unskilled jobs that were so plentiful before the orbiting of the Chinese laser system. Immediately there were rumors that the newcomers were dirty, did not remove their underwear when entering baths, had skin diseases, and stole prolifically. They become societal pariahs almost overnight.

A gesture from Admiral Fujita cut through Brent's thoughts. He was about to address Reginald Williams. There was no tension, no prejudice apparent on the admiral's face, which was usually unreadable anyway. But he spoke matter-of-factly, exactly the way he spoke to any of his officers. "You are Lieutenant Reginald Williams, the captain of *Blackfin*." It was a statement of fact, not a question.

"Correct, sir."

"You sank *Gefara* and the Arab destroyer *Tubaru.*"

"I didn't know the name of the DD, sir." He turned to Brent. "In all honesty, sir, Lieutenant Brent Ross was our attack officer during both attacks. Also, his superb seamanship brought us through a storm when we were heavily damaged and could not submerge."

"You are wounded, Lieutenant."

"A scratch, sir."

Brent found new respect crowding out the dislike he felt for the man. Williams had taken none of the glory for himself. He had been candid to the point of self-deprecation. Brent spoke up. "Lieutenant Williams is not entirely honest, Admiral." There were murmurs and the turning of heads. "He suffered a severe wound to the head and a concussion when we were hit by a five-inch shell. He resumed command when he regained consciousness despite terrible pain and the fact he has sixty-seven stitches holding his head together."

"Hear! Hear!" Captain Colin Willard-Smith said in a loud voice.

"Gentlemen, gentlemen," Fujita said, raising his hands, his voice filled with rare good humor. "Well done. Well done. Your actions saved *Yonaga* from a major engagement with two carriers. We would have been outnumbered. You saved many lives and, perhaps Japan. Well done."

The room resounded with shouts of *"Banzai!"* Brent breathed easier. Every man in the room seemed to respect the big black. But then, at that moment, a challenge of Williams would be a challenge of the admiral. No one was that foolish.

"It was expensive, sir," Williams said. "We had thirteen dead and two badly wounded, and the boat is severely damaged."

Fujita nodded. "And you, Lieutenant, you need medical attention. I'll send for an orderly."

Williams shook his head. "I would like to remain for the meeting."

"You are certain?"

"Yes."

"Very well. At the end of the meeting I will send for medical personnel. We have the finest facility in Japan—perhaps the world."

"Thank you, Admiral."

"When can *Blackfin* be returned to service? We need her, you know. All of the Self-Defense Force's submarines were destroyed in the Arab air raid a year ago or," his face soured as if he had bitten into something distasteful, "or their traitorous, mutinous crews scuttled them like frightened women."

Williams rubbed his bandage gingerly. "It's hard to say, Admiral. I know we have damage to our pressure hull, and one of our main ballast tanks is leaking. Most of our electronics gear was damaged." The rubbing continued. "I can give you a better estimate after we go into dry dock, but at this moment, given efficient yard workmen, at least four weeks—maybe more."

"We have the best technicians in the world. She will be ready for sea in three weeks."

"I hope so, sir."

"We shall see." Fujita introduced his staff, giving a brief history of each. Most were quite old. To Brent, most of the faces were familiar, but two were strangers to him. On the Admiral's right sat his ancient scribe, Commander Hakuseki Katsube. The old man appeared as withered and vital as a mummy, and his back hooked forward in a permanent arthritic bend. He could turn his head only slightly to either side, looking down the table with the corner of one eye like a cyclops staring through a shiny black marble. He had the disconcerting habit of giggling to himself and sometimes drooling into his work. Because both he and the admiral rejected modern recorders, the old scribe hunched over a pad and gripped a brush in a gnarled hand. He had already filled two sheets with ideograms.

The admiral introduced his executive officer, Captain Mitake Arai, who had been promoted from commander during Brent's absence. A distinguished destroyer skipper of World War II, he had sunk cruiser *Northhampton* off Guadalcanal with a brace of Type 93 *Long Lance* torpedoes. Still tall and ramrod straight, despite his age, which Brent guessed at near seventy, he was a sober, highly respected officer.

The next officer was a stranger. He was Takuya Iwata, the new commander of the dive-bombing squadrons. A full commander whose youth contrasted sharply with Fujita's, Arai's, and Katsube's great age, he replaced Commander Kazuoshi Muira, who had been killed by Rosencrance and Vatz while on a reconnaissance mission off the Marianas Islands. Muira and his gunner had been shot to pieces while floating helplessly on their raft.

Iwata stood while the admiral described his background. He was huge for a Japanese, over six feet tall and easily 200 pounds. His skin was clear and unlined, and his eyes intense and very black. He stared first at Brent and then at Williams. Brent detected a baleful glimmer, especially when he stared at Williams. He had an interesting background. He had spent fourteen years in the Self-Defense Force flying fighters. When the Chinese laser system was orbited, he switched to anything that would fly, including old North American AT-6s, DC-3s, Cessnas, and even an old Zero that had been exhumed from a museum at Osaka. He resigned his commission in 1984 and applied for duty with Admiral Fujita. He had had a long wait.

In his youth, he had been a fanatical disciple of the late Yukio Mishima, a poet and novelist whom the admiral admired and whom Brent held in contempt. An ultra right-wing nationalist who lamented the loss of glory that vanished with Japan's defeat in World War II, Mishima had been appalled by the irreverence the younger generations showed toward the Mikado. He exhorted a return to the strength and glories of the past. Born too late to fight in the war, he waged his warfare in his writings, where he fought on behalf of romantic passion, the sea, the Emperor, the old values. Finally frustrated beyond reason, Mishima had committed a spectacular *seppuku* in the offices of the Self-Defense Force. Hundreds of his followers and spectators had looked on in awe as the great man slit his stomach in traditional style.

Brent had found again and again in Mishima's writings the desire to reclaim a regal, glorious aura lost amid the smug, complacent materialism of postwar Japan. Even the exquisite style could not hide the fact Mishima was a political writer on a mission to reconsecrate a homeland on which might once again shine a sun "speckled with golden dust." But this dust was blood to Brent, and he always felt the corpse that had been put to rest in 1945 should be allowed to lie undisturbed. But not commander Takuya Iwata. Brent could see the ominous glint, a latent malevolence in his eyes. Like his idol Mishima, Iwata had been born twenty years too late. In Nazi Germany he would have worn a brown shirt.

"Your report?" Fujita said to Iwata.

Glancing at a small notebook, Iwata spoke in a deep, powerful voice strident enough to fill the hangar deck. "When enemy fighters ambushed Commander Muira, you all know we lost five more Aichi D-Three-As." He shifted his stare to Commander Yoshi Matsuhara. "They have not been replaced. Five more are badly damaged, and we are suffering from a lack of spare parts. Consequently, I can put only forty dive bombers in the air."

Air Group Commander Yoshi Matsuhara said, "I have constant liaison with Aichi and Nakajima. New airframes and engines are on the way. It takes time to tool up. The old machine tools had to be rebuilt . . ."

"I can't attack the enemy with promises, Commander Matsuhara," Iwata said, a slight mocking smile turning his lips.

Yoshi came out of his chair, back knotted steel, eyes

flaring. Everyone stared, including Admiral Fujita, who, true to his nature, refrained from interfering. The old man's reluctance to intercede in clashes of his subordinates confused Brent. Sometimes Brent felt Fujita allowed the disputes to flower and burn because of the long entrapment in Sano Wan. There, they were imprisoned together, and it was inevitable that many disputes broke out. Perhaps, then, it was better to allow the belligerence to run its course and die of its own weight in the exposure, like airing out a festering wound. But the crew of *Yonaga* was samurai: proud, intransigent, vindictive, followers of the vengeful tradition of the Forty-Seven Ronin. More times than not, they did not allow arguments to fade in the fresh air of exposure. Indeed, Yoshi had told Brent that at least twenty men had been killed in duels with swords and *wakizashis* (nine-inch knives) in the Shrine of Infinite Salvation, a combination shrine, temple, and mausoleum in a corner of the hangar deck. Brent's own father, Ted "Trigger" Ross, had killed two men there in hand-to-hand combat while Fujita and a hundred officers looked on.

Brent studied Fujita's face as the old man stared at Matsuhara and Iwata. The flat visage, usually as placid as a stone temple Buddha, showed a glimmer of pleasure. Brent was convinced the old man derived an arcane sense of gratification from the inevitable clashes that occurred between his subordinates. Perhaps the maddening sexual frustration they had suffered for forty-two years exploded in these murderous encounters, providing a strange, twisted release. In any event, Fujita made no attempt to halt the exchange.

Yoshi leaned forward on his fists, which were balled and braced on the table top. He was surprisingly controlled. "I ask no one to take any risks that I would not take myself." Iwata stared at Yoshi with eyes as cold and glazed as burnished stone. "My fighter strength has been reduced by seven, and my squadrons must await new aircraft and spare parts, too. I cannot fly promises either."

176

Commander Takuya Iwata leaned forward. The two officers were of equal rank, but Yoshi Matsuhara was vastly superior in seniority. Iwata's attitude was actually that of superiority. He mocked Yoshi with a voice that singed: "Perhaps the great ace from China can no longer cope with his responsibilities. Perhaps his age . . ."

"I will not listen to this. Watch your mouth, Commander," Yoshi interrupted with a voice that slashed.

The dive bomber commander seemed not to hear. "I requested the replacements the day I reported aboard, over six weeks ago. I have received nothing." He stabbed a finger at Matsuhara, "I repeat, if you cannot execute . . ."

Yoshi slammed a big, flat palm down on the table with a sharp report. "Enough!" he shouted, coming to his feet. "If you wish to settle this privately—in the Shrine of Infinite Salvation . . ."

Fujita interrupted, surprising Brent and every Japanese officer in the room. "Gentlemen," he said. "I cannot argue with your resolution of his problem. However, we are short not only of aircraft, but of pilots, too. I forbid any solution to be found in the Shrine of Infinite Salvation until I feel we have the strength in personnel to accept the loss of one or perhaps both of you." He patted a leatherbound copy of the *Hagakure* (Under the Leaves, the handbook of bushido, and the Bible of the samurai). It was always on the table, and he quoted it: "To die without reaching one's aim is to die a dog's death." He stabbed a bent finger like a crooked dagger first at Iwata and then at Matsuhara. "Your aim is to defeat Japan's enemies."

Yoshi stared at the volume and said, "Respectfully, sir, the *Hagakure* also teaches, 'Meditation on inevitable death should be performed daily. The samurai should welcome being ripped apart by arrows, rifles, spears and swords, being carried away by surging waves, being thrown into the midst of a great fire . . .' "

"I know," Fujita said, waving the volume impatiently.

177

"Meditate all you like. But remember, you have also been taught, 'There is a time to live, and a time to die.' I, your commanding officer, have decided this is not your time to die." He gestured at both men, "If you are *shini-gurai* (crazy to die,) I am sure our Arab friends will be happy to accommodate you. Now, please find your seats, your tempers, and your silence, gentlemen." Glaring balefully at each other, the two antagonists dropped slowly into their chairs.

The next three officers introduced were familiar to Brent. The first, Gunnery Officer Commander No-bomitsu Atsumi, was a "plank owner" (original member of the crew). He, like so many of the holdouts, had shown an astonishing disregard for time. His full head of hair was a glossy black, his face showing only a few creases that would have been a compliment to a man twenty years his junior. He stood with an erect, military bearing and gave his report. "All 25-millimeter mounts are operational, and the same is true with our 127-milli-meter guns. All magazines are full." He moved his eyes to the executive officer, Captain Mitake Arai. "However, twenty-two of my machine-gun barrels are so worn my gunners could do better throwing rice balls at enemy planes. I have the same problem with thirteen cannon barrels. The rifling is almost gone. We could just as well be firing mortars. We will be fortunate if our shells do not seed our own decks."

Arai and Fujita exchanged a glance. The executive of-ficer squirmed uncomfortably before speaking to the problem. "I have the same problem the air group com-mander has. Nakajima and Mitsubishi are both slow in making replacements. All of the machine tools of the ar-maments industry were destroyed over forty years ago when General Douglas MacArthur ruled Japan." He sighed. "It will take time."

"How much time?" Fujita demanded.

"Another month—perhaps six weeks, sir."

The admiral turned his thin lips under. "The Arabs

may not be that generous with time."

"I know, Admiral."

Fujita ran a finger over the *Hagakure* and again quoted it directly without opening it. "If I do not know the way to defeat my enemy, I will find the way to defeat myself."

Captain Arai flushed. "I request permission to visit the Nakajima works tomorrow."

Fujita's eyes were cold. "I am not giving you permission, Captain, I am giving you an order. You are to expedite delivery at Nakajima, Aichi, and Mitsubishi, and you are to leave when this meeting is concluded."

"Aye aye, Admiral."

The admiral turned his attention to the chief engineer, Lieutenant Tatsuya Yoshida. Another "plank owner," Yoshida was one of the oldest members of the staff and he had aged dramatically since Brent had last seen him. In his eighth decade, he showed the years; he was bent and gray, with a stiff, shuffling walk. He spoke in a voice so high, the timbre reminded Brent of the ludicrous falsetto used by American rock singers. "Boilers four, seven, ten, and eleven are down for descaling. Evaporators one and two are down and must be repiped," he said without glancing at any notes. "Also, a main bearing in Number Two generator has burned out." He glanced at the executive officer. "There are no replacements available on board or on the beach, so we must machine it in our own shops. It will take us at least four days to put it back in working order."

The boilers and evaporators that are down for repairs?" Fujita asked. "When will they be on line?"

"A week, Admiral."

"The other boilers?"

"Three hundred pounds of steam in all of them, sir. I can give you give you seven hundred fifty. Fuel tanks are topped off. We can put to sea at a moment's notice."

"Very well." The admiral gestured to the second stranger in the room. "This is our new torpedo bomber com-

179

mander, Lieutenant Joji Kai." A short, roly-poly man with white hair and a beatific smile that seemed permanently frozen to his face like a mardi gras mask, Kai broke the traditional mold of the stoic, inscrutable samurai. His cherubic nose, round face, and multiple chins appeared layered with a glistening patina, as if freshly oiled. Brent chuckled to himself. If the Japanese had believed in Santa Claus, all Lieutenant Joji Kai needed to play the part was a white beard. Either he was perpetually amused by secret jokes or he was so frightened he hid behind a mask of good humor—the refuge of so many frightened, cowardly men. However, Kai was no coward.

Pushing his chair away from the table to give his ample waistline clearance, the little torpedo squadron commander stood. "Put three 'oles in 'is gut and a bloke could roll-a-roll-a-ball a penny a pitch, guv'nor," Brent heard Elwyn York whisper into Colin Willard-Smith's ear. Brent chuckled.

"Lieutenant Kai reported aboard just yesterday," Fujita said. "He replaces Commander Shusaku Endo, who was relieved of his command two weeks ago."

Brent remembered the bombastic Endo. He had disliked Endo the first moment he had seen him. The bad blood had been instant and deep and mutual, a fierce smouldering chemical reaction between them. A swaggering braggart, Endo had been just as belligerent and aggressive toward Admiral Allen and Brent as Iwata had just been to Matsuhara. However, his courage had been "all in his mouth," his nerves melting while leading an attack against four enemy *Gearings* off the Marianas. He had dropped his torpedo at an impossibly long range and veered off. All twelve Nakajima B5Ns of the squadrons missed their targets, and four were shot down by enemy fighters. Fujita sacked him immediately. It was rumored Endo had committed *seppuku*. Brent doubted that the big commander could find the mettle.

"I have known Lieutenant Joji Kai's family since I was

a boy," Fujita said, attempting to smile his tiny cracked smile at the new torpedo bomber commander. And then the expected, the common thread that wove through all of the admiral's selections. "The Kais are a fine samurai family. Eight of Lieutenant Kai's ancestors fought for Lord Ishinaka and Lord Tomonishi, who ruled Takaoka in the fifteenth century." He shifted his eyes to Brent, Reginald, Elwyn, and Colin, explaining in an aside, "Japan was feudal then." The four Westerners nodded understanding. Fujita returned to the entire staff, his voice filled with respect. "For their years of loyalty Lieutenant Kai's ancestors were rewarded with large rice payments and tracts of good farmland. In fact, one of the lords gave one of his faithful retainers, Baron Kusuyuki Kai, a new surname—*Kunitomi.*" Again a glance at Brent, Reginald, Elwyn and Colin. "A rare honor in that time, indeed. *Kunitomi* means *land of wealth.*" Joji Kai held his chin up and beamed proudly.

Fujita continued, "Lieutenant Kai has had a distinguished career. In 1945 when he was only sixteen he enlisted in the Special Attack Corps." The Americans and the Englishmen jerked their eyes from Kai to each other in confusion. There was a murmur amongst the Japanese, then shouts of *"Banzai!"* and cries of *"Tenno heika banzai!"* ("Long live the Emperor!") Even the old scribe Hakuseki Katsube looked up, wiped his chin, and croaked *"Banzai"* in a spray of spittle. Fujita restored order with a raised hand and moved on. "After completing his training at Nobeaka, he was assigned to the Second Wing . . ."

"Your pardon, sir," Brent said, interrupting. "The Special Attack Corps was a suicide outfit—the *Kamikazes!*"

"That is correct, Lieutenant Ross. The *Divine Wind*—named after the wind that destroyed the fleet of the Mongol invaders in the eleventh century." More cries of *"Banzai!"* and *"Tenno heika banzai!"*

"Well, ah, sir, how many missions did he fly?" Brent shouted through the noise.

181

Again Fujita raised a tiny hand and brought it down in a sharp motion, the shouts ceasing as if chopped off by a meat ax. "Why, one—of course." Kai nodded and beamed, face brightening as if lighted by a bulb hidden behind his forehead.

Captain Colin Willard-Smith offered, "With all respect, Admiral, Lieutenant Joji Kai bought a one-way ticket to blighty."

Fujita nodded grimly. "Lieutenant Kai was most unfortunate. He was flying a Zero-sen with a five-hundred-kilogram bomb in an attack on the American fleet off Okinawa. He was diving on an American carrier when he was hit, his controls shot away. He crashed in the surf off Naha and was knocked unconscious."

"The bomb?"

"More bad luck. It was a dud. He was denied his bid to die for the Mikado." Fujita raised his hands to stop the shouting before it could start. "He was pulled from the wreckage and spent the remainder of the war in an American prisoner-of-war camp."

Kai spoke, an irritating, grating sound one might hear if he were trying to listen to the efforts of a drunken flutist. Many of his words were mangled as if he were a foreigner having trouble with a new language. "They told me I missed the carrier *Bon Homme Richard* by only twenty meters," he said. His eyes moved over the older Japanese, and the line of his jaw altered. The perennial smile vanished. "As you can understand, the news was devastating." Old heads nodded. "They had to tie my hands. Keep me in a straight-jacket." He squared his narrow shoulders with new pride. "I tried to kill myself four times. Even bit my tongue." More shouts of *"Banzai!"*

Now Brent understood the mutilated diction. Apparently the man had succeeded in biting off part of his tongue; he was almost incapable of pronouncing "t." And Brent pondered the man's stability. Perhaps Admiral Fujita had made a mistake. Errors in judgment were rare. In fact, Endo had been the Admiral's first poor choice. Uneasily, Brent told himself Fujita had made his second.

Kai gave his report in his ruptured diction. Everyone was impressed by how much Kai had learned about his command in only one day. "I am down to only forty-one operational Nakajima B-Five-Ns," he sputtered. "But I have three flyable aircraft that I must use for spare parts." He looked at Yoshi Matsuhara. "I am pleased to see all aircraft are equipped with the new Sakae Forty-Two, 2000-horsepower engine. I test flew one of my aircraft this morning and found it was capable of 260 knots fully loaded—20 knots over designed speed."

After Iwata's abrasive attitude, Kai's demeanor was a refreshing change. Yoshi spoke to the torpedo bomber leader. "All of our aircraft are equipped with the new engine. Within a month, Nakajima will have the new Sakae Forty-Three engine in mass production. It has water-methanol injection and develops 3200 horsepower." There was an excited babble.

Fujita asked, "Can the Zero-sen take such a power plant? It was originally designed for a 950-horsepower engine."

Yoshi shrugged. "We have reinforced our main wing spars, wing fillets, control cables and surfaces, and engine mounts. I believe it can, although the torque will be greatly increased. I will test fly the first fighter equipped with the Sakae Forty-Three myself."

"You may leave your wings with *Susano* (the impetuous god of the storm clouds)."

"I know, Admiral."

"When can I expect replacement aircraft?" Kai asked.

"Nakajima, Aichi, and Mitsubishi have promised replacements by the end of the month," Yoshi Matsuhara said. He turned to the Englishmen. "Two more Seafires will be unloaded tomorrow. They're at the dock now."

"Good show," Captain Colin Willard-Smith exulted.

Matsuhara continued, "We will continue with our training at Tokyo International Airport and Tsuchiura.

About one-third of our pilots are young and green or have experience in jets only and have never flown aircraft with reciprocating engines before." He looked at Commander Iwata and then Lieutenant Kai. "I expect to see both of you squadron commanders at Tokyo International tomorrow morning at 0800 hours. We must accelerate our training." Both officers nodded compliance.

All heads turned as an officer entered the room. He was carrying an attache case. To his surprise, Brent recognized Colonel Irving Bernstein of Israeli Intelligence. Dressed in his usual desert fatigues of Israeli infantry, the colonel was a small, wiry man with gray-white hair and a small, pointed beard that hyphenated his chin like a white spade. His skin was darkly tanned by years of exposure to the fierce desert sun of the Middle East. Webs of lighter lines coursed downward from his bright, intelligent eyes, carved there by age and the deep set of suffering. Although the man was slight of build, his knotted neck, breadth of shoulders, and assured walk hinted at reserves of strength and endurance. His most distinguishing feature was the six-figure blue tattoo on his right forearm. "Auschwitz, Class of '45," he would tell anyone foolish enough to inquire.

He had been assigned to *Yonaga* on liaison since 1984, when the carrier had made her sortie into the Mediterranean to relieve the Arab pressure on Israel, and he remained on board when *Yonaga* had been attacked by bombers off the Cape Verde Islands and torpedoed and nearly sunk southeast of Hawaii. By this time a vital member of her intelligence staff, he was ship's company during the ferocious, bloody battles off Indonesia, in the South China Sea and the Korean Straits. He had been detached for a special mission to the UN seven months earlier and sent to New York on the same aircraft with Brent Ross and the Japanese detachment assigned to *Blackfin*. After the disastrous meeting at the UN with the Arab delegation, he had been recalled to Tel Aviv for a special briefing. However, before leaving, he had visited

Blackfin at her Hudson River berth and met the entire crew. He was highly respected for his incisive intelligence, strength of character, and sophisticated wit, which reminded Brent of the writer Budd Schulberg. Brent and Reginald Williams came to their feet. Both were surprised and delighted to see the Israeli. They shook hands vigorously before the colonel found his chair next to Brent.

Before Brent could ply Bernstein with questions, Admiral Fujita explained, "Colonel Bernstein reported back aboard three weeks ago. Captain Marshall Katz was recalled by Israeli Intelligence and Lieutenant Joseph Carrino by NIS when he came aboard."

Brent was shocked. "No replacement for Carrino, sir?"

The admiral shook his head. "A replacement was assigned before Carrino left. He was to report yesterday, but bad weather on the West Coast of the United States has delayed flights. He should be here any time. He is an admiral—an old comrade of Admiral Allen's. His name is Whitehead, Rear Admiral Byron Whitehead."

"Whitehead?" Brent repeated in surprise.

"You know him?"

"Why, yes, Admiral. He and Mark Allen were my father's best friends. They were in the same class at the Academy and served together during World War II—ah, the Greater East Asia War and in NIS. He was on Admiral Mark Mitscher's staff in Task Force Fifty-Eight, was in over a dozen carrier battles, holds the Navy Cross and the Purple Heart. Admiral Whitehead is an expert on intelligence and carrier warfare." Brent carried the description no further. He found no reason to upset the superstitious Japanese with the admiral's sobriquets, "Deep Six" and "Sinker"—names attached to Whitehead when he was sunk on *Lexington, Yorktown, Hornet, Wasp,* and *Princeton.* He had heard his father and Mark Allen joke that Whitehead had spent more time on survivor's leave than he had at sea. It was also said that near the end of the war, dozens of officers would request

185

transfer whenever Byron Whitehead was assigned to a ship.

"Good. Good," Admiral Fujita said, obviously pleased by Brent's remarks, despite the painful memories reference to the war brought to the Japanese. He tapped a dossier on the table before him. "I notice he served on a great variety of carriers, Mister Ross."

Brent gulped, "True, sir."

"Five were sunk." The old Japanese exchanged smiles of pleasure.

Brent cursed himself. Nothing! The old man missed absolutely nothing. "Ah, he suffered a bit of bad luck, sir." There was an anxious rumble of voices.

"Obviously," Admiral Fujita said. "The sea *kamis* turned their backs on him on five occasions."

"But he planned the attack that sank *Yamato*," Brent said eagerly before thinking. He almost bit his own tongue. The Japanese were very sensitive about the destruction of *Yonaga*'s sister ship *Yamato*—the name-ship of the class. The smiles vanished, replaced by an exchange of hard looks.

Fujita found the topic unsettling. Turning a wrinkled lower lip under like a sliver of weathered driftwood, he gestured to Irving Bernstein and moved on to a new topic. "Your report, Colonel. You have the latest on Arab carriers, troop strength, and LRAs (long range aircraft) in the Marianas?"

Everyone was worried about the bases in the Marianas. From there, LRAs could range Japan and, with luck, find *Yonaga* at her berth. Six Zeros of the CAP (combat air patrol) were kept in the air constantly over the carrier, while six more fighters were on ready alert at Tokyo International Airport.

Coming to his feet, Bernstein pulled some documents from his attaché case and studied them for a moment. He spoke in a low, level voice without accent, but with a surprising timbre and resonance. "I have reports from both Israeli Intelligence and the CIA." He began with the worst possible news. "The enemy's new carrier, the *Al Kufra,* was sighted yesterday by an American submarine at 1340 hours in the Indian Ocean at latitude 3 degrees, 23 minutes north, longitude 82 degrees, 20 minutes east. She was on an easterly heading and escorted by three Gearings . . .

"*Al Kufra?* New enemy carrier?" Brent interrupted in astonishment.

Bernstein's voice was grim. "You and Lieutenants Kai and Williams haven't been briefed. Sorry." His voice was heavy. "She's an *Essex.*" He stared at Lieutenant Joji Kai and said, "She's your old friend, Lieutenant Kai."

"My old friend?"

The Israeli nodded grimly, "Yes. *Al Kufra*'s the old *Bon Homme Richard.*"

Kai came to his feet, eyes wide, tongue darting over his thick lips, chins quivering. "A second chance." He raised his eyes prayerfully, "This time, this time Amaterasu-O-Mi-Kami . . ."

He was interrupted by Reginald Williams, "An old *Essex?* The *Bon Homme Richard?*" Williams exclaimed. "How did the Arabs ever get their hands on her?"

Bernstein exchanged a grim look with Admiral Fujita. "*Glasnost.*"

"*Glasnost!*" Williams, Kai, and Brent Ross chorused.

"She was laid up at Bremerton and . . ."

Brent interrupted: "The *Oriskany* was there, too. And there are more of them—the *Lexington,* the *Coral Sea.* They're used for training."

"Correct," Bernstein said.

"And the *Intrepid,*" Williams added. "She's a museum ship. She was moored near *Blackfin* in the Hudson River."

"These are powerful, fast ships, the best American carriers of the war," Brent Ross offered. "You said *glasnost.* How in the world could *glasnost* put such a weapon in the hands of our enemies?"

"By simple logic and gross stupidity," Bernstein remonstrated, voice seething with anger and frustration. He focused his brown eyes on Brent Ross, "You know there are continuing negotiations in Geneva between the Russians and the Americans."

"Of course, this has been going on for years. This is where they speak piously of disarmament and decide what weapons we and the Arabs can use to kill each other." There were nods and bitter words.

"It was decided over a year ago by the negotiators of both powers that as a gesture of good will, units of the reserve fleets would be scrapped."

"Yes, I remember. The *Bon Homme Richard* was stricken from the lists."

"Of course," Bernstein said. "Fourteen months ago she was sold for scrap to India. She was to be towed to Bombay. However, it was claimed by the Indian government both tug and tow were lost in the Bay of Bengal during a great storm."

"But it was a lie."

"Yes, Mister Ross. She was secretly sold to the Arabs for a promise of unlimited cheap oil and refitted at Midras. That's an Indian port on the Bay of Bengal. She was sighted for the first time only six weeks ago steaming west to the Red Sea to pick up her air groups. As far as we know, she is in her classic original World War II configuration."

"This has been a closely guarded secret," Williams said.

"Of course," Bernstein agreed. "The Arabs fooled us completely. They know we keep a close watch on Alexandria, Benghazi, Tripoli, Tunis, Oran, and Casablanca. We noticed intensive exercises with torpedo and dive bombers in the Mediterranean but never put these exercises together with an American carrier reported lost in a storm in the Bay of Bengal. It's been kept out of the media and, obviously, the Arabs know how to keep their secrets."

Fujita broke in, a little frown of worry creasing the

brown furrowed parchment of his forehead, and shadows were in his eyes. "Colonel Bernstein, you said she was in her original Greater East Asian War configuration?"

"Right, sir."

"Then do you have her specifications?"

The Israeli pulled a document from a pile of printouts. "Yes, Admiral. One of our agents transmitted the data this morning. I just decoded it." He sighed. *"Al Kufra* is formidable. Displacement over 37,000 tons, depending on load . . ."

"Aircraft? Aircraft, Colonel!" Iwata shouted.

Bernstein waved him off like an irritating fly. "Length 271 meters . . ." He glanced at the Americans and the Englishmen and then a conversion table, "Ah, 890 feet, beam 30.78 meters or 101 feet, draught 9.44 meters, or 31 feet."

Iwata twisted in frustration. "Aircraft! Aircraft!"

Bernstein stared at his notes as if the big leader of the dive-bombing squadrons did not exist. *"Al Kufra* is powered with four shaft Westinghouse geared turbines, developing 150,000-shaft horsepower, flank speed 32.2 knots. Armament twelve five-inch dual purpose cannons, sixty-eight 40-millimeter guns, seventy-two 20-millimeter Orlikons. Her range at twenty knots is 27,360 kilometers, which converts to 17,000 miles." He looked up into Iwata's smouldering eyes. Bernstein smiled, "She can operate from 90 to 108 aircraft."

"Does she have her full complement of aircraft?" Fujita asked.

"Our operatives report she carries 36 Messerschmitt 109s, thirty-three Junkers, 87 dive-bombers, and 32 North American AT-6s converted to torpedo bombers."

AT-6s!" Yoshi Matsuhara said in a rapid voice. "Why, they're nothing but old advanced trainers, slow, lightly armed, not maneuverable."

"They will have their fighter escorts," Fujita said. And then to the Israeli, *"Al Kufra* was headed for the Straits of Malacca, Colonel?"

"She was reported on that heading, Admiral."

The old admiral tugged on a single white hair dangling from his chin. He came out of his chair slowly, straightening one vertebrae at a time, as if he were unlimbering an old, rusty anchor chain. He moved to a chart on the bulkhead behind him and picked up a pointer. Tracing the chart with a rubber tip, he said almost to himself, "If they are ready for combat operations, they will steam the straits, but our agents in Singapore will sight them here." He stabbed the chart at the southeast end of the Straits of Malacca. "And we will know immediately. They will enter the Java Sea here, steam east around the southern tip of Borneo, and then turn north into the Makassar Straits. I would expect them to fuel at Balikpapan on the east coast of Borneo and then steam north to the Celebes Sea." The pointer traced northward toward the Philippine Islands. "Then a turn east and a run well south of Mindanao and into the Philippine Sea. Then east to the Caroline Islands and Tomonuto Atoll."

Fujita thumped the point on Tomonuto Atoll several times while he stared thoughtfully. "It would not be to our advantage to advertise her existence." He turned to the staff and waved a hand disdainfully. "There are weak, sniveling cowards with the spines of women in the Diet who would pounce on the opportunity to surrender, cower at Kadafi's feet, lick his boots, and trade their souls for oil for their Hondas. No! Only the officers in this room know of her existence." There were nods and a rumble of approval.

"But, sir," Brent said. "The whole world knows their carrier *Ramli al Kabir* is based at Tomonuto with two cruisers and escorts. Add *Ramli al Kabir*'s air groups to *Al Kunfra*'s and they outnumber us."

"True," Fujita said. "They have always outnumbered us, but never outfought us." There were shouts of *"Banzai!"* that drowned out Brent.

Williams broke through to Fujita. "Then we must add India to the list of our enemies."

190

Fujita placed his hand on the *Hagakure,* looked at the Americans, and spoke with force. "The samurai cares not for the size of his enemies' forces, only the number he can kill before he himself is dispatched to his ancestors." There were more shouts of *"Banzai!"*

Fujita continued speaking to Williams, "One must not underestimate the power of blackmail by oil. In a very real sense, most of the world is arrayed against us." He returned to Colonel Bernstein, "You have information on the Arab bases in the Marianas?"

Bernstein shuffled some papers. "Yes, Admiral." He looked around the room. "As most of you know, the Arabs occupied Saipan and Tinian six months ago—the Fifth Special Combat Battalion landing on Saipan, and the Seventh Parachute Brigade occupying Tinian. Our agents on Aguijan, which is only five kilometers from Tinian, report numerous reinforcements. Intelligence reports the Ninth parachute Brigade to Saipan and the Twenty-Second Regimental Combat team reinforcing Tinian. They've been digging in—rebuilding old Japanese bunkers."

"But they are only Arabs," Commander Takuya Iwata sneered.

Bernstein nodded grimly. "But well led and superbly trained. Easily compare with Jordan's old Arab Legion. We've already fought some of these units in the Sinai."

Iwata persisted, "You said 'well led'?"

"Yes. All officers down to company commanders are German, Russian and, ah . . ." He sighed, "And American."

Williams squirmed uncomfortably, and Brent stared at the table, muttering curses under his breath.

Fujita said, "There are renegades of all nationalities. No one nation has a monopoly on scoundrels. And all of you remember, bullets are not aware of national origins. We will kill them all."

"Banzai!" and *"Tenno heika banzai!"* resounded from the steel bulkheads. The old scribe Hakuseki Katsube

staggered to his feet, waved a fist, and slid to the floor like a sack of broken bamboo. Chief Engineer Yoshida and Dive Bomber Commander Iwata picked him up and jammed him down into his chair. His head thumped forward onto the table, but he continued to screech *"Banzai!"* and drool into his notes.

Fujita restored order and spoke to Bernstein, "Enemy aircraft strength in the Marianas?"

"Perhaps four squadrons of ME 109s operating out of the old strip at Isley Field. And two more using the old bomber strips on Tinian. But they took heavy casualties during the recent fighting. We estimate their effective fighter strength as under 30 aircraft."

"Long-range aircraft?"

"A half-dozen Lockheed Super Constellations based on Tinian."

"They can range us easily," Brent said. "But they were designed as transports, not bombers."

Bernstein sighed and tapped his temple in frustration. "They've been converted."

"That's almost impossible," Yoshi Matsuhara asserted. "Why, their control channels run right through the bottom of the fuselage."

"I know," Bernstein said. "But they have some of the best technicians in the world. In fact, a few of the mechanics worked on the original Constellations." His face became very grim. "They've solved the problem. They have their bomb bays and can carry a payload of five tons of bombs. Gentlemen, we've got to face the fact that the enemy possesses a LRA that can attack us from land bases at any time."

The room became a tomb. Fujita broke the ephemeral silence. "They would not dare to attack without fighter escort. Our CAP would cut them to pieces. And those Messerschmitts do not have the range for such a long flight. The enemy would be forced to commit his carriers. That is precisely what we want."

"Banzai! Banzai!"

Commander Yoshi Matsuhara came to his feet. "Too soon. Too soon, Admiral. Our pilots are only half-trained, and we do not have our full complement of aircraft. If they attack now . . ." He shrugged and turned his palms up.

Fujita turned to Bernstein. "Does Israeli intelligence feel the enemy is ready to attack?"

Bernstein tapped the table with a single finger. "They have suffered casualties to their escorts, and their carrier *Ramli al Kabir* at Tomonuto lost heavily in fighters during her last sortie. The CIA could help, but Carrino—"

He was interrupted by a knock. Fujita nodded and the rating manning the communications gear opened the door. CIA Agent Dale McIntyre walked in carrying a small valise.

Brent jolted erect like a careless electrician who had touched a live wire. No one had warned him that Dale McIntyre was in Japan. The last time he talked to her by phone in New York, she had told him she was on her way to Washington, DC for permanent assignment at CIA headquarters. When *Blackfin* steamed out of New York Harbor, he felt he had lost her forever. But here she was, in Japan, on board *Yonaga*. Impossible, a dream come true.

And how he had dreamed of her on those interminably lonely watches on *Blackfin!* How many times had he relived those ecstatic nights in her Manhattan apartment? How many times had memories of lost moments without the sensation of hot, yielding flesh brought torture instead of pleasure? He had tried to put her out of his mind, but her hungry open mouth, elegantly coltish body, and the feel of her long limbs enclosing him, trapping him in their crucifix, had intruded into his consciousness despite his efforts to banish her. Time and again he had felt his stomach turn empty and sick as his mind carried him back to those nights when their lovemaking propelled them both to heights of sensuous pleasure that crashed through all restraints, becoming a kind of sexual madness. How many times had he seen that perfect body in his reveries, thrashing, hips thrusting wildly to meet his assault? The gasps, the groans . . . the moans that gradually intensified to explosive shrieks of insensate pleasure. The collapse, his suddenly dead weight pressing her into the mattress, the sweet kisses and muttered promises all lovers exchange at this moment. Inevitably, reality would gradually creep back on the cacophonous waves of Manhattan's deathless roar. Then dawn would come, and *Blackfin* waited at the dock.

Now he was in the same room with her. If he raised his hand, he could almost touch her. He clenched his teeth to shield the turmoil he felt deep in his guts as his eyes roamed her. Despite visualizing her many times in his fantasies, he realized now he had forgotten just how attractive and sensuous she really was. She was wearing a black business suit with the ruffled lace collar of her blouse accenting the tan of her long, slender neck. Obviously tailored, the suit snugged up to her large breasts, trimmed in at her tiny waist, and flowed out sinuously over her full, sculpted hips and buttocks. With her skirt cut just below the knees, her well-shaped legs were well displayed and made more spectacular by glistening hose. She took only a few strides into the room before stopping, her striking green eyes finding Brent and then jumping to Admiral Fujita.

Strange, how her face, which was not classic by any means, could be so appealing. Certainly, her thin nose appeared sharp, lips too small, chin cut off abruptly as if fashioned by a wood carver impatient to finish the job. But her hair was magnificent, long, of burnished gold, and with platinum streaks which appeared brushed in by Renoir. As usual, it was knotted and wound up into a chignon. Brent knew she was forty years old, but only a few incipient creases in the smooth, tanned flesh at the corners of her eyes hinted at the four decades. To the deprived men, she was sex personified. Brent wanted her here, now, in front of God and everyone. And so did every other man in the room, except, of course, Admiral Fujita.

Brent remembered the first time Fujita had met Dale—the terrible scene when his nineteenth-century Japanese chauvinism collided with the liberated twentieth-century woman. She had prevailed then, but only because she carried information from the CIA vital to the survival of *Yonaga*.

Brent, Reginald Williams, Colin Willard-Smith, and Elwyn York came to their feet. The Japanese remained seated, but every eye was focused on the woman.

Fujita's little jaw twitched, and a thumb and forefinger found the single white hair dangling from his chin. "Miss McIntyre," he said in a carefully modulated voice. "You have information for us from the CIA?" The timbre was surprisingly cordial, not warm, but certainly not cold. He gestured to a chair which the communications rating had pushed to the table between Reginald Williams and Brent Ross.

Dale nodded to the admiral and smiled at Brent Ross, Reginald Williams, and Colonel Irving Bernstein. "Good to see you again, gentlemen." The three men rose, nodded, and muttered pleasantries before dropping back into their chairs.

Although Dale had already met Scribe Katsube, Chief Engineer Yoshida, Executive Officer Arai, and Gunnery Officer Atsumi, Fujita introduced all the members of his staff as if she were meeting them for the first time. Each man stood and twitched self-consciously like a schoolboy. No one bowed. Brent was sure the old man had forgotten just who the woman had met.

Dale did not seat herself. Instead, she opened her valise and removed some documents. She looked up. "I have some information for you," she said. She gestured to a chart mounted on a bulkhead to Fujita's side. He nodded assent. She walked to the chart with every eye fixed on her. Some of the old Japanese in the room had not touched a woman in over forty years. Brent saw actual pain on some wrinkled faces. Old scribe Hakuseki Katsube propped his sharp chin on a bony palm and stared wide-eyed as the hips swayed past him, eyes moving from right to left like two big black marbles rolling free in their sockets.

Dale picked up a pointer and glanced at a small notebook she held in one hand. "I have the latest intelligence for you from the CIA." She stabbed the chart. "As you know, since the Chinese laser system destroyed all reconnaissance satellites and grounded our AWACs, intelligence gathering has been very difficult. We have a few piston-engined AWAC aircraft now, but most of our information on Russian and Arab movements is reported by our *SSNs* (nuclear attack submarines) and *SSBNs* (nuclear ballistic missile submarines.) *Los Angeles* is on station here," she moved the pointer, "at the western entrance of the Malacca Straits, *Phoenix* is south of the Philippines in the Celebes Sea, *Providence* is off Vladivostok, *Norfolk* is on station in the Coral Sea just south of the southern tip of New Guinea and, just one week ago, *Dallas* took station off Tomonuto." She made a big circle which encompassed most of the southwestern Pacific with the tip of the pointer. "No Arab force can enter this arena without being spotted, and all sightings will be reported to you."

"That is not enough!" Iwata shouted angrily. "We are fighting your war." His flaring black eyes moved vehemently from Dale to Brent and Reginald and back to Dale. "You give us barely enough oil to keep Japan alive, equip us with inferior weapons, and then expect us to die for you."

Brent saw Fujita's eyes glint with new interest, like a fire fanned by a breeze. The woman was about to be tested—put in her place. Brent knew the old man would not interfere.

The woman's eyes bored into the dive bomber commander like lasers. Her reaction shocked every man in

196

the room except Brent. "We ask you to do nothing for us. You volunteered for this duty as I have for mine." She slammed the pointer down hard on the table. It cracked like a whip, and everyone jerked back. "With the oil embargo the United States is hard put to just keep her allies supplied. We are on strict rationing, and you still get all of our Alaskan production." She stabbed a finger at Brent and Reginald. "Americans are dying for you."

"We Japanese do most of it, and less would die if we had better equipment," Iwata insisted.

"Then the Russians could equip their Arab lackeys in the same way." She placed her hands on the table and leaned over it toward Iwata, the movement hiking the back of her skirt up above her knees. Her lower hips and sculpted buttocks showed through the tight-fitting skirt, and her curvaceous legs glistened like polished ivory. Heads turned and eyes ogled wildly. Katsube wiped his chin. "I'm sorry, gentlemen, this is the best we can do. Take it or leave it," she said. She straightened and began to stuff her documents back into her valise. Katsube groaned.

Fujita raised both hands in a gesture of frustration, realizing he had entered the exchange too late. Serious damage had been done. "Miss McIntyre," he said, glaring at Commander Takuya Iwata. "Please continue."

Dale paused, looked up at the old sailor, and then turned her eyes to Iwata. "I'm sorry, Admiral," she said, deep in her throat. She held Iwata with her eyes, which were chips of green ice, and pointed a finger at him like a dagger. "I'll take no more crap from him." She continued gathering papers.

There was a startled exchange among the Japanese. They had never seen a woman like this, heard such words fall from female lips, experienced such petulance and strength. Commander Takuya Iwata's face became the color of sunset, and Brent snickered into his palm.

Fujita turned his tiny lips under and gestured to the

197

chart. "Please, Miss McIntyre. We need the intelligence. The fate of our nation, of your nation, is in the balance." His eyes roamed over his entire staff, finally settling on Iwata. "There will be no further outbursts."

Brent could not believe his ears. The old man was pleading with a woman, treating her as an equal. But *Yonaga*'s very existence could depend on what the CIA knew — what this woman knew — and *Yonaga* was everything.

The woman sighed, stopped stuffing papers, and looked up. "That's a guarantee?"

The old man swallowed hard, as if his Adam's apple were his pride and he was choking on it. "A guarantee," he managed. He pointed at the chart.

Dale tapped the table with her small knuckles. She had won, and every man knew it. "All right, sir. We'll give it another try." She returned to the chart and thumped the Western Carolines with the pointer. Her voice was surprisingly composed as if she were describing her apartment, a sunset, or a landscape, or ordering dinner. "Carrier *Ramli al Kabir* is anchored here with cruisers *Babur* and *Umar Farooz,* an oiler, three depot ships, and three *Gearings.*"

"Only three escorts?"

"Yes admiral. *Blackfin* sank one and either your aircraft damaged three more or they broke down. In any event, they are being repaired at Surabaya." There was an excited rumble.

Fujita spoke thoughtfully. "Then they would be insane to put to sea without adequate escorts." He stared at Dale. "Any estimate when repairs will be completed on the destroyers?"

The woman narrowed her eyes thoughtfully. "Perhaps six weeks. Our agents reported one DD under tow. But keep in mind, their *Essex,* the *Al Kufra,* is making for the Straits of Malacca with three escorts."

"Not enough." Everyone nodded. "When the battle group puts to sea, they must leave at least two destroyers to cover the two entrances to the atoll. They need the three destroyers at Surabaya before they can attack." He looked down the table at his air group commander. "Commander Matsuhara, the gods have given us a period of grace."

"Yes, sir," Matsuhara said. "In six weeks we should have our air groups up to full strength."

Admiral Fujita struggled to his feet. "Then we shall deal with these vermin who would threaten our sacred land." He gesticulated at the chart behind Dale McIntyre. "We will make a feint at the Marianas, pull them out of Tomonuto, and destroy them all!"

Cries of *"Banzai!"* and *"Tenno heika banzai!"* filled the room. Brent joined in, and Dale stared at him mouth agape, eyes wide.

Fujita glanced at a bulkhead-mounted brass clock and quieted the uproar. "It is late, gentlemen and . . ." he glanced at Dale, "lady." He stared at his men. "There is much to do before we are ready for sea." He faced the shrine and clapped twice. Every officer stood. Again, Brent clapped with the Japanese. Dale, the Englishmen and Williams gaped at him curiously. Fujita spoke softly, mixing both Shintoism and Buddhism, "Oh Blessed One, let us meet our enemy recklessly like those already dead and follow Hachiman San (god of war) with constantly believing hearts. Let us strengthen our karmas on the field of battle, and if we are fortunate enough to yield up our spirits in service to the Son of Heaven, let us find permanent reality in nirvana. The Blessed One reminds us there are non-born, non-caused. If there were not, there would be no refuge for us, that which is born, becomes, is created, is caused, dies on the field, and seeks nirvana." He lowered his eyes, staring the length of the table with eyes like glazed black buttons. "Let us keep forever in our hearts our immortal Emperor Akihito's declaration that his reign shall be that of *Heisei*—'the age of attaining peace'—a peace we shall find for him in an ocean of our enemy's blood." Lines of satisfaction creased the flesh of the corners of his mouth. "This meeting is closed," he announced.

"Banzai! Tenno heika banzai!"

"Sir! Sir," Dale McIntyre shouted through the din. "I haven't finished my report."

Fujita silenced the men with a wave. "I know, Miss McIntyre. You will remain."

"And sir," Brent said, "Mister Williams and I have a detailed report for you on the condition of *Blackfin.*"

"Of course. Of course.".

Brent continued, "And our two prisoners are out in the passageway . . ."

"Two prisoners?" The old admiral appeared confused. Brent saw the same confusion he had noticed before. Age had taken a toll. Fujita's memory was slipping.

"Yes, Admiral. You ordered . . ."

"Oh, yes. I will interrogate them later. Put them in irons in the brig." He gestured to the door. "Return to your duties."

The officers filed silently from the room.

Chapter Six

The atmosphere in Admiral Fujita's cabin was formal yet far more relaxed than that Brent had felt in Flag Plot. It was the second-largest room in Flag Country, only slightly smaller than Flag Plot. The old admiral walked stiffly to his polished teakwood desk and gestured for Brent, Dale, Yoshi Matsuhara, and Reginald Williams to seat themselves. Williams had insisted that he was strong enough to attend, and after Brent had assured the admiral he would conduct Williams to the sick bay personally, the old admiral had relented.

Looking around, Brent felt a warm feeling of nostalgia fulfilled as his eyes ran over the familiar surroundings. Behind the admiral hanging on the bulkhead was a large portrait of Emperor Akihito in mufti. In fact, there was no hint of militarism in the serene likeness. A Shinto-Hindu shrine similar to that in Flag Plot hung next to the portrait. Low bookcases jammed with hundreds of books were bolted to each bulkhead while charts were attached to the spaces above them. A door in the aft bulkhead led to the admiral's sleeping quarters, while another opposite led to the cabin of a long-dead flag officer. This large room had been converted into the admiral's library.

Here there were thousands of books dealing with World War II. The remarkable old man had studied and digested the information stored in each one. Many times Brent had seen him astonish officers with his knowledge of the Great Conflict. At times, an awed Brent had regarded Fujita as a "walking encyclopedia."

Sighing, the old man seated himself at the desk that glistened like a highly polished mirror. The top was remarkably clean and neatly arranged, a stack of bound reports occupying a corner next to a two-tiered basket marked "Incoming" and "Outgoing," a pad, pen, and brush in a polished ebony box in the center, and three telephones arranged in a row to one side. A copy of the ubiquitous *Hagakure* rested to one side next to the phones. There were five leather chairs bolted to the carpeted deck in a row in front of the admiral. A half-dozen wooden chairs were secured between bookcases, two in front of a corner table cluttered with communications gear. A yeoman first class sat there as expressionless as another piece of furniture. When extremely sensitive top secret matters were discussed, this man was usually dismissed.

Brent sat in the middle, directly in front of the admiral, while Yoshi, Dale, and Reginald Williams sat to either side. Relaxed by the embrace of the soft leather, Dale McIntyre sank back and crossed her legs, her calves and ankles showing like carved and polished ivory. The female presence was totally out of context, and to Brent she seemed to fill and light the room with a shimmering presence, the way a single exquisite bird can brighten a dim forest. It was disconcerting, and every man in the room except Fujita squirmed uncomfortably.

Remembrances of frantic evenings in the bedroom of her Manhattan apartment crowded back, and Brent was shocked by the strength of his sudden physical desire for her, his viscera reacting to her, clenching like a fist in his groin. He felt his heart barge against the cage of his ribs.

With an effort he concentrated on the picture of the emperor, studying the fine suit, silk tie, and benign expression. The turmoil began to settle. Then Fujita's voice broke in.

The old man began by addressing Reginald Williams. "You know all submarines of the Self-Defense Force have been sunk or scuttled. *Blackfin* constitutes our entire submarine force."

Before Williams could respond, there was a knock. Fujita nodded, and the yeoman opened the door. A middle-aged full lieutenant dressed in the uniform of the Maritime Self-Defense Force entered. A short, fat man scarcely taller than Admiral Fujita, he appeared so singularly squat and wide that one got the impression he was looking at a tall man who had been compressed by a prodigious blow to the top of his head. He literally bulged out against his uniform like a heated sausage bursting its skin. Slowly he waddled across the room with the swaying gait of a man troubled by the chaffing of thighs so large they rubbed against each other with each step. Answering Fujita's gesture like a toy pulled by its master, he finally halted at attention to one side of the desk. He had the expression of a man forced to face his firing squad without benefit of a blindfold. Brent remembered the face and toadlike body but could not recall the officer's name.

"You missed the meeting, Lieutenant Koga," the admiral said curtly to the newcomer.

Now Brent remembered. The fat Lieutenant Tadayoshi Koga had attended a staff meeting eight months earlier. Fujita's distaste for the entire Maritime Defense Force had been vented on the fat man.

"Sorry, Admiral" the lieutenant said in a reedy querulous voice. "There was a *Rengo Sekigun* demonstration—ah, I mean riot that blocked off the two roads leading to the yard."

Brent whispered into Reginald's ear, *"Rengo Sekigun* is

the Japanese Red Army." Williams nodded.

Fujita bellowed at the communications man. "Yeoman Nakamura. Call Captain Mitake Arai. Tell him to send a company of seaman guards outside our perimeter and to clear the streets of *Rengo Sekigun* rabble. If necessary, sweep the communist vermin from the streets with Nambus (machine guns)." Nakamura threw a switch and began speaking into a phone.

"Sir," Lieutenant Koga said, surprising everyone with a show of backbone. "We have a company of our own guards enroute, and the Tokyo police are on the scene. You can't be a law unto yourself, sir."

"Lieutenant! Do not try to tell me what I cannot do." Fujita waved at the picture of the emperor. "I have the backing of the Mikado—the supreme authority. The Tokyo Police and the Diet can be damned!" The narrow eyes stared unblinking at Lieutenant Koga. "You are aware of *Kokutai?*"

"Of course, sir. 'The emperor is Japan'."

"And Japan is *Yonaga*," Fujita countered quickly.

"But one must be judgmental, discriminating, Admiral."

Silently Fujita picked up a brush and quickly formed an ideogram. He held it up for all to see. "Do you know what this is?" he asked. Perplexed, Dale stared at Brent while Brent, Yoshi, and Koga studied the calligraphy. Brent was an expert on Japanese, but the character was foreign to him.

" 'Cowardice,' " Yoshi Matsuhara hazarded.

Koga's eyes studied the character and he squiggled his big bulk uncomfortably. "Yes. 'Cowardice,' and it's Chinese, Admiral," he said, obviously on guard.

Fujita's eyes drilled into Koga as his tiny hand held up the *Hagakure*. "It is written here in our sacred manual." He dropped the book and formed his fingers into a crooked steeple. "The Chinese character for 'cowardice' is made by adding the character for 'discrimination' to the character radical for 'mind.' He thumped the *Hagakure* with a clenched fist. "Now 'meaning' is 'discrimination,' and when a man attaches discrimination to his true mind, he becomes a coward."

Koga's lower lip trembled with distress. "Sir," he said. "I am not suggesting anyone fall into the swamp of cowardice—turn his back on his duty." He drew himself up. "I am a samurai, too." He gestured at the *Hagakure*. "I know the way of the samurai and the book . . ."

"Then if you know the way of the samurai, never suggest anything that could compromise honor, our devotion to the Son of Heaven."

"Of course, sir." Koga sighed and turned his thick crimson lips under. He glanced around at the other occupants of the room. Gruffly, Admiral Fujita introduced Lieutenant Tadayoshi Koga of the Maritime Self-Defense Force to the others. As each officer was introduced, the lieutenant moved his beady, ferret-like eyes in horizontal movements from face to face. However, the eyes changed their pattern when they reached Dale McIntyre. Here they lingered and swept vertically while a thick tongue ran over the pouting red lips. Finally, Reginald Williams was introduced, and Koga stared long and hard at the black face. His mind was obviously still lingering on the woman's body.

"You are the captain of *Blackface?*" he asked absentmindedly, totally unaware of his gaffe.

"*Blackfin! Blackfin!*" Williams retorted, his anger cracking like electricity. He began to rise. Brent pulled him back down.

The crimson of a fuchsia in full bloom spread across Koga's round face. Small beads of perspiration appeared miraculously on the brow. Everyone watched Koga curiously. He had leaped from one meat grinder into another. No one volunteered to help. He sputtered, "Ah . . .," gulped, and seemed to gag on his own embarrassment. "Sorry, Lieutenant Williams," he finally managed.

"An error, sir. Just a slip of the lip anyone could make." He raised both hands defensively, as if fending off an assassin, and then compounded the gaffe, "Ah, some of my best friends—ah, my maid is a Pakistani."

Williams breath exploded from deep in his lungs in an ominous rumble like a Kansas tornado. "I'm a Negro, not a Pakistani, and I don't wait on tables," he said through lips like the gash of a sharp blade. "And mind your *faux pas,* Lieutenant," Williams warned. "I won't tolerate a second."

"Of course. Of course," Koga said, obviously relieved to be released from the hook without further damage. Hastily he changed the topic, addressing the admiral. "Admiral Fujita," he said, pulling some documents from an inside pocket. "I have some good news for you direct from the office of Chief of Staff, Admiral Shuichiyo Higashiyama." Fujita hunched forward. Koga looked around at the others. "You know most of the Self-Defense Force was destroyed by an Arab carrier strike last year when *Yonaga* was making her attack on North Korea." Nods encouraged the lieutenant to continue. He spoke proudly. "Well, gentlemen and lady, we have a frigate and a destroyer back in commission." He glanced at a document. "The frigate is the *Ayase* of the *Chikugo* class, and the destroyer is the *Yamagiri* of the *Asagiri* class."

Fujita waved in irritation. "These are cast-iron toys loaded with useless rockets and missiles."

Koga came back quickly, "But sir, *Yamagiri* has a Melara 76-millimeter gun, which is fully automatic and can fire 85 rounds a minute. *Ayase* has two of these weapons, and both have two General Electric 20-millimeter *Phalanx* Mark Fifteen Gatlings with six barrels." The reedy voice began to take on a timbre of pride. "Why, the *Phalanx* has its own radar that can track not only attacking aircraft, even its own projectiles. These weapons can fire 3000 rounds a minute, every round is aimed by its own computer. Not one human being is involved."

While Koga spoke, Fujita pulled a pamphlet from his desk and opened it. Carefully he placed a pair of small steel-rimmed glasses with coke-bottle lenses on his nub of a nose. He thumped the pamphlet. "Yes, I know of these glamorous, 'smart' weapons," he scoffed, voice heavy with sarcasm. He glanced at the maritime officer, whose jaw sagged, and then returned to the booklet. "You forgot that," he read, "the *Phalanx* is a total weapon system consisting of six major assemblies." His eyes skimmed and he turned the page. "Supported by a high-speed radar-servo assembly and a digital computer, the fire control unit automatically makes its own target search, detects and declares target acquisition, tracks target, measures range, velocity, and angle, tracks its intercepting projectiles' velocity and angles."

"Correct, sir. Correct. It is a completely self-contained system."

Fujita removed his glasses, looked up and said to Koga, "I have interviewed officers who have used these new weapons, and I have studied them." Fujita patted the pamphlet and waved at his library. Then he hunched forward with both of his tiny hands flat on his desk. Blue veins were visible through the thin parchment-like skin. He caught Koga in the vise of his eyes. "Your weapons are fully automatic and fully unreliable." Koga winced as if he were experiencing physical pain. Brent actually felt sorry for the man.

"They are too full of your silicon transistors, computers, and glamorous circuits that are always breaking down," Fujita declared. Then he showed his vast naval knowledge. "The British lost ships in the war in the Falklands because of these highly sophisticated weapons that refused to function. They had rockets that would not fire, computers that would not compute. British officers began to cry and pray for old-fashioned machine guns that fired dumb bullets aimed by live men." He struck the teakwood with fingers that would not bend completely into a fist. "I read their reports. I have recorded an eyewitness account by one of my own flyers, Captain Willard-Smith, who fought there. They lost ships and hundreds of men who should not have been lost—sacrificed to your god of high technology who fell through his throne of paper." He thrust a finger at Koga. "Paper! Paper! It is so impressive on paper. But in fact, your ships are armed with unreliable junk that is always malfunctioning. My *Fletchers* can fire 125 rounds a minute of five-inch ordnance at five different targets. All weapons are hand loaded with semifixed ammunition. This American five-inch 38-caliber dual-purpose cannon is the finest naval gun of the twentieth century. And we have 25-millimeter, 20-millimeter and 40-millimeter machine guns, aimed by the eyes of samurais to a gunsight—the best fire control machines in the world." Silence filled the cabin as he drummed the desk, his volatile mind making another mercurial change in direction. "Radar. Your *Yamagiri* and *Ayase* have good radar." It was a statement, not a question.

"Yes, sir," Koga said, brightening and straightening. "Both ships are equipped with Furujo air and surface search, bands *G* and *H*. Excellent equipment, sir."

"I am quite aware of their electronics. We can use them as radar pickets. They are too vulnerable to use as escorts for *Yonaga*."

Commander Yoshi Matsuhara broke his silence. "You have approval from the Diet, Lieutenant Koga? After all, Japan is not officially at war with the Arabs, and the left-wingers are very strong."

Koga beamed. "Just this morning Minister for Defense Tsutomu Kawara not only got their permission for you to use *Yamagiri* and *Ayase,* but new financing for the National Parks Department was also voted."

Fujita glanced at Dale McIntyre. "You know *Yonaga* has been classified as a national park just as the antique battleship *Mikasa*. This is the only way we could receive support without violating the constitution."

"You mean no offensive weapons. Article Nine?"

"Correct, Ms. McIntyre."

Williams looked around. "Article Nine?"

Brent nodded. "Admiral Allen wrote it in 1947." He narrowed his eyes in deep thought before he spoke.

" 'Aspiring sincerely to an international peace based on justice and order, the Japanese people forever renounce war as a sovereign right of the nation and the threat and use of force as a means of settling international disputes.' "

"Very good," Fujita said. "That is the article verbatim." He gestured at Dale McIntyre. "You said you had not completed your report?"

"Yes, Admiral," the woman said rising.

Before Dale could begin, Lieutenant Koga said, "With your permission, Admiral, I will return to my duties."

"I want the complete specifications and the crew rosters of the *Ayase* and the *Yamagiri,* including the service records of their commanding officers."

"They will be on your desk this afternoon by special courier, Admiral."

"You are dismissed."

Koga bowed to the admiral and nodded at the others and then waddled through the door like a man fleeing an ambush.

As the door closed, Dale glanced at a sheet. "I have an update on the specs on the Libyan cruisers at Tomonuto. The first is the old British *London* the Arabs bought from Pakistan. They renamed her *Babur.* Seven thousand four hundred tons, length 570 feet, main battery six 5.2-inch, Vickers Mark Six dual-purpose rapid-fire guns in three twin mounts. The second cruiser is the *Umar Farooz,* the ex-British HMS *Llandaff* Kadafi bought from the Bangladesh Navy. Three hundred sixty feet long, main battery four 4.5-inch Vickers Mark Three dual-purpose quick-firing guns. Both vessels have been reengined with General Electric geared steam turbines and Foster-Wheeler boilers and have speeds that exceed 32 knots . . ."

Drumming the desk impatiently, Fujita interrupted. "We are aware of these specifications."

"I know, Admiral. I went over them with you the first time I briefed your staff. But they have been equipped with new radar and . . ." she glanced at Williams, "and sonar." Every man came erect with new attention. She glanced at her notes. "Both vessels have been equipped with the new Marconi Type Nine-Six-Five-M, single aerial air search and the Marconi Type Nine-Nine-Two-Q, A-band air search radars. They're very efficient up 250 miles."

"The sonar?" Williams asked anxiously.

"Graseby," she said. "The Graseby Type G-Seven-Five-Zero."

"That's the Royal Navy's latest—hottest," Brent said. "How did they ever got their hands on it?"

Dale's face twisted into a tight, sardonic grin. "Through their Indian friends, of course."

"On with it," Fujita said, waving a hand.

"Yes, sir. The new Graseby is quite sophisticated. It is capable of a 360-degree search and can track two submarines simultaneously. Also, it can track while maintaining independent Doppler search and passive search," she looked up, "and it even provides torpedo warning." She studied her notes for a short moment before continuing. "We have information that the Seven-Five-Oh has been interfaced with computer based ASW and tactical information systems to provide a source of range, bearing, and target Doppler data." Again, she looked at Williams, whose face was as grim as a pall bearer's. "It can operate in adverse reverberation conditions with ripple or omni-direction dual-frequency modulated and Doppler CW transmission modes. This information can be automati-

210

cally transmitted to her escorts."

Williams sank into his chair with a sigh. "Then their *Gearings* haven't been equipped with the Graseby?"

"Correct, Mister Williams."

Brent broke in. "I thought Russia and the United States have agreed at Geneva that this type of equipment was prohibited." He gestured at Williams. "Why *Blackfin* is still equipped with her World War II sonar and so are our *Fletchers*."

Dale sighed. "True. But no one can control the decisions of the Indian government."

Williams said to Dale, "Does the CIA anticipate that their *Gearings* will be equipped with the new sonar?"

Dale shook her head negatively. "Not to the knowledge of the CIA."

"And what about fire control radar?" Brent asked.

She shook her head. "None. Still prohibited. None of the Arab ships are equipped with it." An audible sigh of relief swept through the room as the officers looked at each other. Every commander wanted to use fire control radar on his enemy but feared facing it himself. To date, the Americans and Russians had managed to keep it out of the hands of the belligerents. Dale turned her lips under and stared down at the deck. "Now for the bad news," she said softly.

"Bad news!" Brent and Yoshi chorused. Even Fujita's aplomb was riffled by surprise.

She gestured at the yeoman. Fujita picked up her meaning. "Yeoman Nakamura," he said. "Stand guard in the passageway."

"Aye aye, sir." The yeoman bowed and left.

After the door closed, Dale looked hard at the other occupants. "This is not to leave this room. It's top secret and must remain so. That's why I didn't discuss this matter in front of the entire staff." The men nodded. She spoke in an uncharacteristically harsh timbre. "It's the poison gas."

211

There was a babble, and shocked looks were exchanged. The woman continued. "The Libyans are producing both mustard and nerve gas in a plant in Rabta."

"Rabta is near Tripoli?" Fujita interrupted.

"Correct, sir. About sixty miles south of Tripoli."

"But how could they do this?" Yoshi said. "The Arabs are too stupid to build and operate a plant without outside help."

"They had German help—the West German chemical company Imhausen-Chemie."

Fujita surprised everyone with his incisive prescience. "Kadafi must call it a pharmaceutical plant. Correct, Miss McIntyre?"

"Yes, sir. But it is guarded by a brigade of Kadafi's finest troops and is surrounded by heavy AA emplacements. You don't do that when you're manufacturing aspirin."

"What do you know of these gases?" Yoshi asked.

"They're producing both mustard and nerve gas."

"Mustard gas has been used, you know," Yoshi offered.

"During World War I, by the Germans," Fujita said.

"Correct, Admiral," Dale agreed. "It's extremely destructive to the skin and if breathed can sear the lungs and cause hemorrhaging. Nerve gas was actually developed by the Germans during World War II but never used. It kills by disabling the normal transmission of nerve impulses." She paused for a moment, apparently gathering herself for her next statement. "It can be made odorless and invisible, can kill by stealth." Everyone gasped.

"Quantities?" Brent said in quick voice.

The woman thought for a moment. "We estimate they have about fifty tons of mustard gas on hand and about thirty-five tons of nerve gas. At least enough for a thousand artillery shells or four hundred 500-pound bombs."

"Then they do not have enough to destroy Japan?"

212

Yoshi stated, almost to himself.

"Correct, Commander. However, they could inflict terrible casualties on the population of a large, congested city."

"And at sea these weapons are almost useless," Fujita concluded. Everyone nodded. Fujita pulled on the single hair dangling from his chin, and everyone knew he was deep in thought. He spoke to Brent, "Call Colonel Bernstein. All stations. He is to report to my cabin immediately." He gestured to the communications gear.

Brent walked to the table, picked up a microphone, threw a switch marked "All Stations," and spoke into a small microphone. The metallic sound of his voice could be heard echoing through the ship, calling, "Colonel Bernstein, report to Admiral Fujita's cabin immediately." Then he returned to his chair.

The admiral's eyes scrutinized every face. He said, "If the biggest threat is to a congested city, then Tel Aviv is at the greatest risk."

"Yes, sir," Dale said. "I was to meet with Colonel Bernstein in the American Embassy when this meeting closed." She ran a hand over a document on her lap. "I can assure you, all information we have has already been transmitted or hand delivered to Israeli Intelligence in Tel Aviv."

There was a knock, and Colonel Bernstein entered. Fujita gestured him to a chair. Dale told him of the poison gas.

The Israeli sighed. "Yes. It just came over in 'Blue Alpha.' I just finished decoding it."

Dale said to Bernstein, "I preferred not to discuss this matter in front of the entire staff."

"I understand."

Fujita said, "The threat is to your cities more than ours."

"I'm aware of this, sir."

Fujita creaked to his feet and moved to a chart of the

Mediterranean mounted on a bulkhead. He ran a finger over it. "From Israel to the plant at Rabta is about 2400 kilometers or 1500 miles, Colonel Bernstein."

"I know, sir. An air strike is out of the question."

Fujita made a small circle around Israel. "Yet you are ringed by Arab air bases that are within easy bomber range—even their Heinkel One-Elevens could deliver these hideous bombs to all of your major population centers."

The Israeli nodded grimly.

"What is to deter the Arabs?" Fujita asked.

The Israeli tugged on his beard. "We have a very strong deterrence."

"A strong deterrence?"

Bernstein sighed and looked around. "Top secret!" Everyone nodded. "Thermonuclear deterrence. The Arab leaders were informed yesterday that any attack by gas on our cities will lead to immediate retaliation."

There was a shocked silence.

"What kind of war is this?" Fujita asked. "Gas, atomic bombs, men pushing buttons and cities disappearing, entire populations gagging in their own blood. There is no honor, no glory in this."

The Israeli's brown eyes flared. "The superpowers have stood each other off for forty years with these threats. You would deny us the same? You would let the threat of blackmail by gas force us to surrender? Don't forget," he moved his eyes around the room, "don't forget, we Jews have an intimate acquaintance with the effects of gas. Six million of us learned by breathing Zyklon B. I was at Auschwitz when the lesson was driven home." He drove a fist into his palm. "Never again! Never again! I can guarantee you, if the Arabs unleash their gas, they will lose their major cities."

"A Mexican standoff," Reginald said.

"We can learn from the Mexicans," Bernstein said.

Fujita said, "I can understand the Israeli position,

214

Colonel Bernstein. But I cannot tolerate the existence of the poison-gas plant at Rabta. It poses a threat to Japan—and perhaps to the survival of civilization, if it precipitates a thermonuclear war." He tugged on a whisker. "We'll take it out." He turned to Dale. "You said the plant was sixty miles south of Tripoli?"

"Yes, Admiral."

The old man slammed a fist down on the teakwood. "No Israelis will be involved. We'll hit it from the Gulf of Sidra with Japanese aircraft only." He turned to Brent, "We did it in '84—destroyed their strips at Al Kararim and Misratah and sent Captain Fite into Tripoli Harbor to board the *Mayeda Maru*. We can do it again. We'll destroy the plant and Kadafi's air force and hit the harbor at Tripoli and destroy anything that floats."

Matsuhara shouted *"Banzai!"* But Brent remained silent. Instead, he said soberly, "There is the small matter of the Arab force at Tomonuto and their bases in the Marianas."

Fujita leaned against the chart. "We will sink their ships, invade their islands, and destroy them all. Then back to the Mediterranean and a strike on Rabta and Tripoli." More shouts of *"Banzai!"* This time Brent added his voice. Reginald and Dale stared at the young American. Bernstein glared at the chart.

There was a knock, and Yeoman Nakamura stuck his head into the room. "Admiral," he said, "the escort commander is here."

Fujita crooked a finger and Captain John "Slugger" Fite entered. Brent had not seen the escort commander for a year. When he had first met the husky Irishman, he had been impressed by the big laugh that could have filled the Metropolitan and the blue, mischievous eyes of a leprechaun. The captain had aged dramatically. What shocked Brent was the man's pallor. His face appeared drained, as though he had been bled from the jugular. It was the pallor of pain and exhaustion, and it was emphasized by dark eye sockets underlined with dark plum-colored smears, as though they were bruises. From the corners of his eyes, lines coursed downward over the once-smooth cheeks like cracks in a medieval painting. The iron-gray hair had streaks of snow brushed back from the temples and the leprechaun was gone, replaced by some wild creature of the forest, full of knowledge of burrows and barrows and arcane methods of eluding capture, yet still capable of surprising his enemy with murderous attacks. Although he was now thinner, he still hulked like a big stalking grizzly as he moved.

An Annapolis graduate and a thirty-year veteran of the navy, Captain Fite was a decorated destroyer commander of World War II. He was daring, fought with panache, and handled his destroyers with the dash of a calvary officer. He was fearless, but his command had taken heavy casualties: five ships sunk, two heavily damaged. Five of his commanders had died with most of their men. The faces of the dead captains were forever burned into Brent's mind: Warner and Ogren, who died horribly with their men making suicidal torpedo runs into the six-inch guns of a *Brooklyn*-class cruiser that had caught *Yonaga* in the Mediterranean; Fortino, Philbin, and Gilliland, who sacrificed themselves, their ships, and their crews to save *Yonaga* from two cruisers in the South China Sea.

Fite had been wounded. He walked with a limp, and his left arm was in a sling. In all the communications *Blackfin* had had with *DD-1* after the battle with *Tubaru*, Fite had described casualties and damage but never mentioned his own wounds. Brent had wondered after at least two five-inch hits to the bridge, how the escort commander had managed to escape injury. Obviously he had not.

"I did not expect your report until tomorrow, Captain Fite," Fujita said, his voice filled with concern. "You're wounded. You did not inform me."

"A couple scratches, Admiral—nothing serious. My

216

chief hospital corpsman sewed up my arm and put this stupid sling on it." He moved the arm gingerly. "It's not even broken."

"Your ship's doctor?"

"Dead."

"Your leg?"

"A few stitches. A little stiff."

"You should see Chief Hospital Orderly Eiichi Horikoshi. He is the best physician I have ever known."

"Thank you, sir. I'm in excellent health."

Brent looked at Reginald Williams, and Bernstein turned his head to Dale, who stared back. The ludicrous statement had not prompted even a snicker. Fite was no Koga—not the type of man who elicited chuckles at his own difficulties. Anyway, the big man was in obvious pain. Humor would have been obscene.

Fujita emphatically said to him, "You are ordered to see Chief Hospital Orderly Eiichi Horikoshi, Captain Fite."

Fite clenched his teeth and turned his lips under. "Very well, sir."

"At the end of this meeting."

"Yes, Admiral."

"Do you wish us to leave, Admiral?" Admiral Bernstein said, gesturing to those seated with him.

Fujita stared up at Fite, who smiled down at Bernstein. "Good to see you again, Colonel Bernstein," Fite said. "With the admiral's permission, I would like for you to remain." Fujita nodded his approval. Fite's blue eyes moved to Dale McIntyre, who smiled up at him. "You're the lady from the CIA—I've heard of you." His eyes ran over the woman and then moved to Yoshi, whom he greeted warmly, then to Brent, and he reached out and grasped Brent's hand. "Good to see you, Brent. Brent rose and responded with his own warm greeting and introduced Lieutenant Reginald Williams, who also rose and grasped the extended hand.

Fite turned to Admiral Fujita, "These boys saved my ass . . ." His cheeks turned florid, and he glanced at Dale. "Sorry, Ms. McIntyre." She waved the apology off with a smile.

Fujita said, "According to Mister Williams and Mister Ross, you saved their—ah, entire anatomy." Everyone chuckled.

The admiral gestured to the chair vacated by Lieutenant Tadayoshi Koga. Fite eased his big bulk carefully into the leather chair. His left leg would not bend, and he was forced to stick it out in front of him rigidly like a board. Fite continued, "No, Admiral. That *Gearing*—the *Tubaru*—had us in trouble." He gestured at Reginald and Brent. "They fished her—one of the most uncanny bits of shooting I have ever seen. And you were damaged, down by the head. Hell, I saw your bow planes rigged out. You were in trouble."

"You slowed her down for us, Captain," Reginald said. "She was an impossible target at 32 knots. You brought her down." He thumped Brent's shoulder. "And Brent is my attack officer. He made the run." There was warmth in the voice Brent had never heard before.

"Good work. Good work, Brent," Fite said. He turned to the admiral. "Admiral Fujita, you have my preliminary report."

Fujita adjusted his glasses and read from a document. "Number Five Gunhouse destroyed. Number Two stack holed. Eighteen five-inch hits to upper works . . ."

"Eighteen!" Brent and Reginald chorused in disbelief.

"Yes, gentlemen," Fujita said. He continued reading, "Six 20-millimeter and two 40-millimeter mounts destroyed, Number One Boiler Room took a hit, two boilers disabled. Hull holed between frames thirty-one and thirty-two at the waterline. Thirty-three dead, forty-three wounded." He looked at Fite's bandaged arm and stiff leg. "We will make that figure forty-four wounded." Fujita stared at Captain Fite silently. "Captain Fite," he said softly. *"DD-1* is out of commission permanently. It will take months . . ."

"Please, Sir. I have six DDs ready for sea. Two more *Fletchers* are in our reserve."

"Why, they are junk—used for spare parts!"

A note of desperation crept into Fite's voice, "But, sir. Put *DD-1* with one of the reserve cans, give me a drydock and three weeks, and I'll give you a first-class can."

"You need a rest."

"Respectfully, terrorism never rests. How can we, Admiral? Their task force is almost ready to sortie. Four weeks, maybe five. Everyone knows it. Ask any kid in the Ginza . . ."

Fujita thumped the desk. "You are wounded Captain."

"No, sir," the escort commander said, trying to sit erect. "Nothing more than two mosquito bites."

"With the jaws of tigers." Fujita tapped the desk and then turned to Dale. "The CIA is negotiating for more *Fletchers.*"

"True, sir," Dale acknowledged. "Two from the Philippines and another from Greece. We count forty-six in commission all over the world, and we're trying to buy more."

"Condition?"

"The Greek vessel is fair to good—the two in the Philippines are mint."

"Are the negotiations closed?"

"We can deliver the two from the Philippines to you within a month."

There was a murmur of excitement and approval. "Good. Good," Fujita said.

Fite expressed his greatest fear to Dale. "Are there any reports of the Arabs equipping their *Gearings* with fire-control radar?"

Dale shook her head. "No. That is one area where the United States and Russia are holding firm." Fite sighed audibly. "And no guidance systems for our Mark Forty-

Eight torpedoes or their Five-Three-Threes."

"Good. Good," Fite said.

Fujita spoke to Williams, "You estimate it will take at least four weeks to make *Blackfin* ready for sea?"

"Yes, sir. As we discussed in the briefing."

Again Brent saw a fleeting wave of confusion cross the admiral's face. Had he forgotten already? They had just discussed the matter an hour ago.

"Of course. Of course," the admiral said, hastily covering up his lapse.

Williams spoke, a troubled look twisting his face. "Admiral. There's a small matter of prisoners."

"We take them—a few." Bernstein, Brent and Fite exchanged fleeting smiles. Dale McIntyre caught the exchange, and her face clouded with confusion and suspicion.

"I saw men murdered in the water by my executive officer," Williams gestured at Brent. "By Captain Fite." His voice dropped, "And in Tokyo Bay, I was no better. I blew a terrorist's head off with a Thompson. He was helpless—in the water. I lost my head. I'm no better."

"No. You didn't lose your head, Lieutenant. You're learning," Fite said.

"Learning what?" Dale snapped, voice cracking ice, face reddening with the boil and surge of emotion. "The laws of the jungle—savagery. We did not know—the CIA never informed . . ."

Fujita stepped in. "You know of the *Mayeda Maru*. The garroting of over a thousand helpless Japanese civilians by Kadafi's murderers?"

"Yes," she said softly. "I know they're merciless. I killed one myself last year just outside the gate to the yard." She gestured at Brent. "He was there. It was self-defense. I had no choice. It wasn't an extermination."

Bernstein spoke up, "Don't ever tell a Jew anything about exterminations, Ms. McIntyre. Would you like to hear about Auschwitz?"

"This isn't Auschwitz."

"The whole word is Auschwitz," the Israeli retorted. "Didn't you know?"

She leaned toward the colonel. "I saw prisoner-of-war camps in Israel. You exchange prisoners. Don't give me that crap."

The Israeli's brown eyes became smoky lamps. "I will, Ms. McIntyre. Most Jews have never even seen an extermination camp. They don't know—they make their own mistakes. Our religion teaches humanity. That's our one weakness. 'Turn the other cheek,' the rabbis say. I ran out of cheeks in 1945." He drove a fist into an open palm. "You said the Arabs have gas. Do you think they would hesitate to use it if they didn't fear our bombs?" The rhetorical question hung in the air unanswered. "Vermin should be exterminated. That's the only way."

"Enough bickering," Fujita said, thumping the desk. His eyes bored into the woman. "Madam. The concept of surrender is unknown to the samurai. The greatest ignominy, the ultimate disgrace, is to be taken prisoner. We honor our foe when we kill him on the field."

The woman scoffed, "Some honor, Admiral."

The old eyes smoldered. He controlled his temper with an effort. "Regardless of the reasons, regardless of world opinion, the conduct of my forces is totally my responsibility. Let the world know it is my decision to eliminate the enemy whenever possible. They exercise the same prerogatives against my personnel—in the water, in parachutes."

Her wave encompassed everyone, "Then, when the helpless are killed, your men are obeying orders. The Nazis claimed the same thing at Nuremberg and were hanged for it."

Fujita stabbed a finger at the woman. "I am not interested in Nuremberg or the Far East Tribunal. Only the conduct of this war and the destruction of our enemies."

"Then it's total war?"

"You did not know?"

"I did not know. In fact, most of the world does not know." She glared at Colonel Bernstein, "Not even the Israelis—most of the Israelis."

"Is there any other kind of war?" the admiral asked.

"There is humanity."

Fujita laughed humorlessly. "Where? I have not encountered any in over a century."

"When my duties are completed, I will apply for a transfer."

"That is your decision, Madam." Fujita hunched his bent shoulders even more and brought the narrow eyes down to slits. "If you women want equality, you must be ready to fight and die with equality."

"I'm ready for it—have put my life on the line for it." Her eyes traveled over every occupant in the room. "But I'm not ready for murder—never will be."

"This is no place for a woman. War is man's business," Fujita said, matter-of-factly.

"You've said that before, Admiral. Now I know you're right." She rose.

Fujita brought up a hand. "I did not dismiss you." She stared down at the little man, eyes cold, frozen glass. The voice was vapor off dry ice. "I request permission to be excused."

"Were you escorted here?"

"No."

"You usually stay at the Imperial. The CIA keeps rooms there."

"Correct."

"It is dangerous and you know it. You took great risk coming here without guard." He looked at Brent. "Take two seamen guards and escort Miss McIntyre back to her quarters. Take a staff car."

Dale glared at Brent. "I'll take a cab. I can take care of myself." She patted her purse where Brent knew she carried her 7.65-millimeter Beretta. "I don't need him."

Brent knew exactly what the woman meant. She was not talking about guns or guards.

Fujita waved her off. "It's an order," he said. He spoke to Fite and Williams, "You two are to report immediately to sick bay. Yeoman Nakamura will show you there. Chief Hospital Orderly Eiichi Horikoshi will examine you and send me a report." Slowly he pushed himself to his feet. "This meeting is closed," he said. Everyone rose and moved silently toward the door.

Chapter Seven

When Brent and Dale crossed the accommodation ladder and left *Yonaga,* Dale was sullen and uncommunicative. They walked silently past the staggered concrete barriers like dragon's teeth installed after Kathryn Suzuki attempted to crash into the compound with a truck loaded with plastique. Walking toward the gate house between rows of giant warehouses and shops, they passed a half-dozen sandbagged machine gun emplacements. Obviously, word of *Blackfin*'s destruction of the carrier *Gefara* and the destroyer *Tubaru* had spread like a forest fire through *Yonaga*'s mysterious "ship's telegraph." Brent knew no official announcement had been made yet. Men saluted and shouted greetings to Brent: "Welcome back, sir." *"Banzai Blackfin"* "Good hunting, Mister Ross." "Great kill, Lieutenant." But all eyes were on Dale McIntyre's swaying hips and shapely calves as they passed.

"Great kill," Dale mimicked.

"There is no way you can understand," Brent said with resignation.

"I can understand this," she said. "Fujita deliberately set you up with me. He could have had me escorted by a hundred others."

"You object?"

She seemed not to hear. "He did it before—last year.

He made sure you took me back to my apartment."

Brent smiled. "You showed no lack of enthusiasm."

"He takes good care of his boy, doesn't he. After all," she said, her voice acid with sarcasm, "his boy's been to sea for six months. He must be horny—needs a good piece of ass. Why not score with the old broad again?"

Brent felt an amalgam of hurt and anger cut through the carapace and touch raw, quick nerves. His eyes flashed with cold blue light like the glinting of bayonets. His lips drew into a grim line, and the rims of his nostrils flared and turned pale. Grabbing her arm with one hand, he spun her around. A hundred eyes focused on the pair as they stood inches apart, glaring. "If you were a man, I'd punch your goddamned brains out."

"Why not? You fucked my brains out, you son-of-a-bitch." She ran her eyes over his angry face, taut arms, balled fists. "Go on," she taunted. "Hit me. Kill me. What's one more life, more or less?"

He grabbed her shoulders. "My God, have you forgotten how they tried to kill us out there?" He waved past the gate house at the parking lot where they had had to fight for their lives against a mob of Red Army hoodlums. "Have you forgotten the restaurant—the French restaurant where I lost Watertender Azuma Kurosu, a man who gave his life saving yours—ours from Sabbah killers?"

"No, I haven't forgotten. You killed three men that night. But it was a fair fight."

"A fair fight?" he said, incredulous. "They ambushed us."

"They weren't helpless in the water?"

He threw up his hands in despair and looked around. Most of the gun crews were standing and staring at them, and a half-dozen men at the gate were looking their way. "Come on," he said gruffly. "I've got to take you back." He gestured to the gate where a black Mercedes 300-SE sedan was parked. Two seaman guards

225

were standing next to it with slung Arisakas over their shoulders.

Side by side the pair walked hurriedly to the gate.

Dale McIntyre's apartment was on the thirtieth floor of the Imperial Hotel. Although the hotel was nearly a hundred years old, it was one of the most modern in Tokyo, with a swimming pool, recreation and exercise rooms, eight restaurants, and a shopping arcade. Brent saw Dale to her door while one of the seaman guards waited at the elevator door with his rifle at port arms. Passersby glimpsed the glowering seaman and hurried past fearfully. Everyone was accustomed to strange sights in Tokyo these days, but a helmeted seaman in green battle fatigues clutching a rifle in a corridor of the Imperial Hotel could jar anyone's composure.

Brent unlocked the door and stepped aside. Dale walked in and turned, holding the door open but barring entrance with her body. "Thank you," she said. "I'm quite safe now. You can leave."

She began to close the door. Brent held the door open with one hand. "It's more than the killing, isn't it, Dale?" he said, holding the glistening green eyes with the power of his stare.

"What do you mean?"

"The killing of survivors—of prisoners—could not have taken you by complete surprise. There must've been rumors, and the CIA has a way of finding things out." He rubbed his chin. "There's more to it—something personal between you and me."

"You flatter yourself."

He would not allow her to goad him. He continued in a calm voice, "What is it? Do you have another man? It can't be that. All this wouldn't be necessary if it were only another man. I could understand that. I've been at sea . . ."

226

"You've been at sea, so I had to find someone else to get laid. Is that it?" A film of moisture heightened the green of her eyes.

"It doesn't have to be that crude."

"You're wasting my time, Lieutenant."

"I'll be back, you know, Dale."

"The encryption box."

"Yes. 'Blue Alpha' is compromised. The Arab mainframes in Tripoli and Damascus have broken it by now. You know that."

"I know. I'll pick up the box and software at the American Embassy tomorrow. And you'll pick it up?"

"That's my job. You know that. I'm NIS—the only Naval Intelligence officer on board *Yonaga*. You hand the box to me personally and witness my signature."

"I assure you, Lieutenant, it's the only box you'll get in this apartment." She pushed his hand aside and slammed the door. He whirled and walked quickly to the elevator.

The apartment was dark, but Dale did not turn on the lights. There was adequate illumination streaming in through the big French windows from the garish signs glaring in the Ginza. She hurried, almost ran, to the bedroom and hurled herself down onto the bed. Pounding the pillow, she cried over and over, "My boy. My boy. I love you Brent. Oh God, I love you."

As Brent approached the door to Commander Yoshi Matsuhara's cabin, he was in a grim mood. The dark ride back from Dale's apartment over rain-slicked streets had been lonely and depressing. Visions of the woman and what they had meant to each other during those fiery nights in Manhattan stabbed at his heart. He knew she had been upset by the staff's casual attitude toward the killing of survivors, but he suspected there was far more to it than that. She seemed to suddenly and inexplicably hate him; or was she trying to hate, working at

227

it? And strangely, through her tirades, he had thought he'd detected a hint of the old soft warmth glowing behind the icy emerald of her eyes.

In New York they had talked of love, of a permanent thing, but her age had worked on her heart like an acid. He remembered the woeful look on her face one night as they lay side by side after hours of fierce lovemaking when she turned to him and said, "My darling, do you realize, when you're my age, I'll be fifty-three."

He had protested, claiming she was at the peak of her powers and would remain there for years. She had laughed and said, "You're insatiable, my beautiful boy. The last time we made love, I was so sore, the next morning I had trouble walking to the kitchen." They were both laughing when he pushed her onto her back. The memory brought a physical ache to his stomach as he reached up and knocked on the door of Yoshi's cabin.

Matsuhara had obviously anticipated his knock. When Brent entered the small cabin only two doors from his own in Flag Country, he saw a bottle of Haig & Haig and two glasses on the small table bolted to the bulkhead. Smiling, Yoshi said, " 'Welcome Brent-san. I have been expecting you." He gestured to the table and the bottle of scotch.

Sighing, Brent seated himself while Yoshi found his place opposite. "Straight up, no ice. That's how you like it," the flight commander said, pouring the amber liquid. He handed Brent a glass and held up his own. "To women," the Japanese said. "The most inscrutable, baffling creatures ever invented."

Brent stopped his glass inches from his lips. "You know, Yoshi-san?"

"I know, my friend." He held his glass high. "Drink!"

The men touched glasses and tossed off the drinks. Yoshi refilled the glasses. "She upset you?"

"Yes."

"You love her."

228

"I don't know." Brent took a sip of his drink. This time he swirled it and worked it around his teeth and gums, enjoying the sting and prickle and savoring the burnt charcoal flavor before swallowing it. "How can you know so much about Dale and me?"

Yoshi smiled. "Don't forget, Brent-san, I saw you with her when you first met—saw the glow on your face after you had been with her, know how you fought for her life that night in the Imperial's French restaurant. It was easy to see you were—ah, attached." He sipped his scotch. "Anyway, my friend, I know you better than any man I have ever known."

Brent took another drink. "Well, she doesn't glow for me any more."

Yoshi smiled. "She loves you, Brent-san."

The American choked and almost dropped his glass. "She hates me—called me a son-of-a-bitch," he sputtered.

The Japanese shook his head. "No, Brent-san: it was obvious to me. She deliberately antagonized the admiral, knew he disliked women and would bar her from the ship. I believe she wanted this and cleverly played on his prejudices. And she must have known more about the—ah, conduct of the war than she implied. After all, she is CIA." He stared at his friend silently for a moment. "And there is something else. There was heat in her eyes when she looked at you, but it wasn't hatred. She loves you. She is a woman with a problem, and the problem is herself."

Yoshi had confirmed some of Brent's own suspicions, but the woman had made a whirlwind of his mind. Certainly Dale knew more of the war than she had let on; but did she love him? No . . . he did not see that, feel that under the bristling, belligerent facade. Brent tried to sigh his confusion away but found it impossible. Instead he drained his glass and Yoshi recharged it. He could feel the warm incursions of the liquor spreading through his body, but the usual softening and relaxation of muscles refused to set in. All he could say was, "But why? Why?"

Yoshi smiled his slow smile that spread like a warm viscous, liquid over his broad features. "Sometimes, my friend, it is easier to fathom the depths of the Marianas Deep than the heart of a woman." He drew a thumb and two fingers down his cheeks until he clutched just the point of his chin. He spoke thoughtfully. "It could be her age, Brent-san. The years mount much faster, count much higher with women than with men."

Brent shook his head. "I can't believe that, Yoshi-san." He sipped his drink, tabled it, and tapped the glass with a single finger. "She brought it up in New York, but it never interfered."

"You've been at sea—had no other women—and she knows it. Jealousy is endemic with women, and I saw none in her anger. Mark me, under it all, I believe you'll find her age."

Brent chuckled as the liquor at last began to melt the ice that coated his mind and his quick sense of humor revived. "I'm afraid that under it all I'll find nothing at all, Yoshi-san."

"She loves you, Brent-san," Yoshi persisted.

Brent stared down at his glass and for a moment only the blower and the faint rumble of an auxiliary engine could be heard. He looked up at the concerned face across the table and smiled. "You're a good friend, Yoshi-san, the best I've ever had. When I saw your Zero-sen swoop in over *Blackfin,* I knew we'd make it." He was struck with a new thought. "Your Englishmen— they're a helluva pair of wingmen."

"The best. We need more good men like Colin Willard-Smith and Elwyn York." The flyer toyed with his drink, sloshing the liquid around the glass. "We have more good men coming to fill our empty cockpits."

"You have all the Japanese volunteers you need."

"True. But experienced pilots who hate terrorists are applying from France, America, Germany, Italy—even Greece and Turkey."

"That's good news, Yoshi. Can you use them?"

"Of course. Of course. It could mean a mix of aircraft, too, which I dislike. There's a problem with spare parts, and it's like mallards flying with teal—you never see it. But the Seafire fits in perfectly, and now we may have a few Grummans in our fighter group, too."

"The F-Six-F Hellcat?"

"Correct."

"One or two."

Yoshi smiled. "A squadron of twelve. The finest pilots in the United States Navy. All volunteers, of course, and employees of the Parks Department."

"How soon?"

"Maybe a month. They're completing their training at Pensacola." The Japanese chuckled to himself. "Kind of an AVG in reverse."

"AVG—American Volunteer Group. The Flying Tigers. They flew in China."

"I know. I fought them in 1940 and '41. Ironic, isn't it?"

Brent knew Yoshi Matsuhara had flown Zeros in China and had shot down three Chinese planes. Yoshi had never mentioned it to him before. It was a delicate subject, and both men had always avoided it. Brent felt himself relaxing, and his troubles did not seem so overwhelming anymore. After agreeing with a nod and, "Yes, very ironical," he breached a delicate subject. "You have a woman, Yoshi-san?"

The Japanese shook his head and took a deep drink.

"It's still Kimio Urshazawa?"

The air group commander turned his lip under and nodded. "I was responsible for her death that day in Ueno Park."

"That's a lot of crap."

Yoshi's brown eyes flashed a warning. "Don't talk to me that way!"

"The hell I won't. I was there too. I led us into the ambush. I remember, I was looking at some broad's butt instead of . . ."

"No! No! I was Kimio's lover, her protector—she took a burst of AK-Forty-Seven for me!" He emptied his glass with a single gulp and refilled it.

"I can't convince you."

"No, Brent-san."

"You're still *shinguari* (crazy to die)?"

"Don't you remember? The admiral refused my request to commit *seppuku*."

"And mine."

"Yes. What nonsense. An American requesting *seppuku*."

"I thought I was the American Samurai."

"You are."

"Then it's not nonsense."

Yoshi smiled his slow, warm smile. "No, Brent-san, maybe it's not."

Brent stabbed a finger straight overhead. "You seek your *shinigurai* up there."

"Is there a better place to die?"

"Rosencrance and Vatz will be happy to oblige you."

"No!" the pilot spat. "Never! I will kill them first. Then I can join my ancestors."

"I want that privilege," Brent said softly. He drummed the table with two thick fingers. Some of the things Dale had said to him long ago in Manhattan came back. "It's a crazy world, Yoshi-san."

"Some think we are crazy."

"Why . . . because we're samurai?"

"Not just that, Brent-san. Our way of life takes us from the Hondas, recorders, films—why, the Admiral even prohibits television."

"This is insanity?"

"Why of course," Yoshi retorted. "We won't be sane until we queue up for our cars, toasters, recorders, and televisions, and glue our eyes to that tube and let our brains melt."

"A touch of Camus."

"And Kafka."

Brent could see Yoshi's face brightening with anticipation. Similar to Fujita, he had been starved for books during *Yonaga*'s forty-two-year entrapment, and now he gorged himself on works on any topic and loved to discuss with Brent the ideas of the men he read. "They knew," Matsuhara asserted, his eyes brightening. "They both rebelled against the absurdity of existence, the lack of social justice, and the limitations of individual fulfillment." He pointed to a leather-covered volume resting on a tiny desk and showed his love for the books that jammed the bookcases in the room. "And Kafka, especially, viewed the world as a hostile, uncontrollable place."

"Well, he was rebelling against his father, who was tyrannical and irrational, but you're accurate," Brent noted. He added, "He also felt the ordinary man was helpless and at the mercy of powerful people who are as remote as the galaxies and entirely arbitrary and uncaring in their actions." He turned up both palms and shrugged. "That was his father again."

"Maybe, in a way, we all rebel against our fathers, Brent-san. But it is clear to me that Kafka found a universal truth, father or no father. And he was well aware of the people who give men like us employment. They have used us for millennia—made ours truly the oldest profession. Kafka described our world precisely and don't forget, in *The Trial,* he concludes that suicide is the only end to a man's life that really pleases God."

Brent chuckled. "A Jewish samurai."

"In a way. Just like us."

"Then we're the only sane ones."

"Obviously, Brent-san."

"Joseph Heller would disagree with you."

"The author of *Catch-22?*"

"Yes, Yoshi-san. He contended we were the mad ones—had to be crazy to do what we do."

"But we know he's wrong, Brent-san."

"Why, of course. He never met Kafka."

"Or Kadafi," the pilot countered. They both laughed and drank.

Yoshi tapped his nearly empty glass with a fingernail until it rang like a tiny chime. "Brent-san, the submarine captain, Lieutenant Reginald Williams, there is something septic between you. Do you dislike him?"

Again, Brent was taken aback by his friend's peculiar insights. He had hardly said a word to Williams in Matsuhara's presence and threw only a look or two his way during the staff meeting. Brent knuckled his forehead and answered, "I respect him."

"You did not answer my question. Is it his color?"

"Of course not, Yoshi-san. You know me too well even to suggest that." Brent described his early experiences with Williams, the arguments about football, the deep-rooted frustrations Williams felt about growing up in South Central Los Angeles, the death of one brother and jailing of another because of drug-related crime, the loss of his mother, his only parent, when he was an All-American linebacker at the University of Southern California.

Yoshi nodded and said, "Remember, I was born in Los Angeles and grew up in the west side with all races. I felt no hatred from the blacks or whites, although my father claimed *dōhō* (ethnic Japanese) and *nisei* (American born Japanese) were discriminated against. He was incensed by the Exclusion Acts of nineteen-twenty-four that barred the rest of his family from immigrating to the States. That's why he sent me back to Japan to complete high school and, he hoped, college." He drummed the

234

table top. "You functioned well as Lieutenant Williams' executive officer and his attack officer. He seemed quite proud of you, yet there was something in his eyes."

"Yes, unreadable."

"Brent-san," he waved, "when I found *Blackfin* out there and circled you, he wanted to shoot me down."

"You know?"

"Of course, I will say this for Williams, any pilot who wishes to survive knows enough not to casually fly over a warship—any warship." He drained his glass and refilled it and then poured more into Brent's depleted drink. "But you don't expect to see AA guns tracking you on a clear day when your markings are easy to see. You challenged him over this?"

"I was going to kill him."

Yoshi laughed, but he knew his friend was telling the truth. "That could be a major undertaking. He is a big, formidable man."

Brent took a drink. "As you said, it was a clear day and I had no trouble identifying you, and he still insisted we would take you under fire if you came within range."

"But I saw no real hatred between you. Some kind of barrier, true, but that was all."

Brent described Williams' horror at his killing of the Arabs in the water and Fite's massacre of the *Tubaru*'s survivors. "But he changed in Tokyo Bay," he added.

"When he shot that terrorist in the water," Yoshi observed.

"At that moment, he discovered he was no better than any of us—he was just as capable of the 'savagery' he accused Fite and me of showing."

"The same savage that lurks in the hearts of all men." The pilot sipped his drink thoughtfully. "The lessons of war are as numerous as the hairs on the leg of a three-year-old calf."

Brent found a familiar ring to the words. "The *Hagakure,*" he guessed.

"Correct, my young friend. And in the same chapter we are told, 'The samurai who does not use his sword will be forgotten by the gods and Buddha.'"

"Well, now, Lieutenant Reginald Williams has bared his sword and will not be forgotten by the gods, Buddha, Arabs or terrorists."

Yoshi held up his glass. "Let us drink to this strange man—a man who may become a samurai and not know it." He took a sip from his glass. The air group commander continued, "He is intelligent and well educated." Brent nodded his agreement. Yoshi continued, "Yet a man who has knowledge but lacks true wisdom is like a blind man carrying a lantern."

Brent chuckled. The aphorism was familiar. "You've been reading Bodhidharma," the young American noted.

The pilot pushed his glass from side to side until the scotch threatened to slosh over the lip of the glass. "You are acquainted with the father of Zen?"

Brent laughed. "I've been on this ship for over four years. You know I've been indoctrinated into Shintoism, Hinduism, Buddhism—even Islam." He took a drink and then spoke like a college professor. "Bodhidharma was an Indian monk who introduced Zen to China in the sixth century. Zen means 'meditation.' Enlightenment comes through meditation and intuition."

Yoshi smiled up at his friend and held up his hand with his thumb and forefinger forming a circle. "As you would say, my friend, 'Four-oh.' Very good, Brent-san. You've been studying."

Brent had been surprised by his friend's renewed interest in religion. After Kimio's murder, Matsuhara had abandoned all religions, claiming, "The gods abandoned us in Ueno Park, left only demons." Now he showed a sudden interest in Zen. But, to Brent, Buddhism was atheistic, anyway. The consistency was still there. "Thank you, Yoshi-san," he said. "I knew you had been a Buddhist, but I didn't know you had returned to it."

"Yes. Just recently I decided to return. It is austere, fits me. Bodhidharma was a purist, rejected ceremonies, scriptures, and the trappings of other Buddhist sects. Now I am a follower of Bodhidharma. And so is Admiral Fujita."

"I know," Brent said smiling. "He has spent hours lecturing me on it. He said it fits the tenets of bushido perfectly."

"True, and time well spent, Brent-san. Time well spent."

Brent held up his glass. "To Bodhidharma."

The friends touched glasses and drank.

Chapter Eight

The two prisoners captured by *Blackfin* were sched-
uled to be interrogated the next morning at a staff
meeting. The four men picked up by Captain John
"Slugger" Fite were kept in irons in *Yonaga*'s brig. In
addition to the Japanese members of the staff, Lieutenant Brent Ross and Colonel Irving Bernstein attended.
Lieutenant Reginald Williams and Captain John "Slugger" Fite nearly came to blows in the sick bay with
Chief Hospital Orderly Eiichi Horikoshi before the old
medic released them, but only after they promised to
return immediately after the meeting. They were the last
to arrive. Both ship captains had been relieved with the
news that their vessels were in drydock and their crews
sent ashore to the "Rest and Recreation" facility—a
large hotel-like complex within the enclosure where
there was an abundance of recreational activities; even
swimming, baseball, bowling, and tennis. Liquor and
women were to be found there, too.

Liberty was available in Tokyo. But the men could be
released only in groups of four and were escorted by
seaman guards. Every man carried a pistol, and the
Ginza was off limits. *Rengo Sekigun* lurked there, and
two members of *Yonaga*'s crew had been murdered in a
"house of pleasure" there the previous year. Most of the
men felt the facility at Yokosuka was far more attractive. Here they could have all the gambling, liquor, and
women they wanted. Brent had overheard an old chief
put it succinctly one day when talking to a group of
new men. "Why risk your life in Tokyo when you can
get everything you want here—cards, sake, and plenty

of women for 'pillowing.' "

Although everyone knew Admiral Fujita objected to the use of "pleasure girls,"—an old expression from the Greater East Asia War that the old Japanese insisted on using—he seemed not to notice whenever evidence of the presence of women should have been obvious. He also seemed unaware that someone had sneaked a television set into one of the small card rooms off the main hall. Brent was convinced the old man knew about all of it, but the shrewd admiral recognized the primeval needs of his men and that those needs could not be ignored without destructive effects on morale. The suicides of dozens of his men during the long entrapment in Sano-wan had driven that lesson home.

Looking around the table, Brent saw the entire staff, including Commander Yoshi Matsuhara and his two bomber group commanders, Commander Takuya Iwata and Lieutenant Jai Kai. Fujita had insisted that the three flyers delay their departure for Tokyo International Airport and Tsuchiura until after the meeting. Subordinates were dispatched in their place. The three aviators were obviously irritated and impatient. Fujita read their mood but refused to start the meeting promptly. Instead, he huddled with his scribe Commander Hakuseki Katsube and his executive officer Captain Mitake Arai. Finally the old man tapped the table and looked up. A half-dozen whispered conversations came to an abrupt halt.

"A few items of business before we interrogate the prisoners," the admiral said. He put on his glasses, which made an owl of him, and glanced at a document and then down the table to Lieutenant Reginald Williams. "Lieutenant," Fujita said. "My dockmaster has informed me he can have *Blackfin* ready for sea in three weeks or less."

"Three weeks or less," Williams repeated in awed tones. "I can't believe it."

The old man chuckled. "We Japanese are accustomed

to the unusual, but we can perform miracles when necessary." The requisite low chuckle commanded by the admiral's quip swept the room. The old Japanese eyed each other and nodded at the admiral's sharp wit.

Williams said, "Sir, my crew?"

"I told you we had already filled your roster with experienced replacements."

The big man fidgeted uneasily and glanced at the next chair where Brent sat. "My XO—Mister Ross—I would like to keep him."

The reply was instantaneous. "Sorry, Lieutenant. His orders have been changed."

"But I did not see them. I'm his commanding officer—they should've come through my hands. By whose authority . . ."

"By my authority, Mister Williams. I cut his orders personally."

Williams came half out of his chair before Brent could restrain him with a hand to the arm. "I object to that, sir," he said, unable to hide the anger in his voice. "*Blackfin* needs him. He's my XO. I told you he's the best attack officer I have ever seen. Those orders are arbitrary and . . ."

Fujita interrupted: "Command is arbitrary, Lieutenant. You should know that."

"You'll lower my efficiency, sir."

Fujita seemed suddenly conciliatory. "I know how you feel, Lieutenant. *Blackfin* has performed superbly—perhaps saved *Yonaga*. However, I must consider the fighting efficiency of the entire force—our task force, or battle group, as you Americans would say." He tapped the desk with his knuckles for emphasis. "Officially, Lieutenant Brent Ross has been assigned to *Yonaga* as my NIS liaison officer, and that is the responsibility he will fill. We no longer have Admiral Mark Allen or Commander Joseph Carrino." He stabbed a finger down the table. "You have a fine staff of junior officers. As an intelligent, experienced captain, you should be able to replace Lieutenant Ross with one of your own. They are all highly skilled submariners now, or they would be with their ancestors. And you, as captain, should be the attack officer. You are experienced and intelligent—should make a fine attack officer." Brent nodded concurrence.

Williams sagged in his chair and fingered the bandage that still wrapped his head. He looked at Brent Ross, and Brent saw something new in the black eyes. It was respect tempered for the first time by the warmth of friendship. "Sorry," the big man muttered. And then to Fujita with resignation, "Aye aye, Admiral. We will manage."

"Spoken like a samurai."

The old scribe Katsube took the statement as a cue and shouted *"Banzai!"* through a spray of spittle.

Fujita silenced him with a wave that almost hit Katsube's nose. At that moment, the door was opened by Young Lieutenant JG Asaichi Kubo, who self-consciously announced, "Rear Admiral Byron Whitehead is here, sir."

"Very well. Show him in." Every man in the room came to his feet, including Admiral Fujita, who struggled to rise by pushing on the table with both hands. Katsube did not fare as well, the old scribe lurching to the side and almost falling. Only a steadying hand and a boost from the executive officer saved him from pitching headlong onto the deck.

Carrying a small valise under his arm, Rear Admiral Byron "Deep Six" Whitehead entered. He appeared to Brent to be shorter and rounder than he last remembered. And he seemed much older, with the wrinkles and walk of a man at least seventy, although Brent knew the rear admiral was still short of his eighth decade by at least two years. Every aspect of the man was weighty. His head was big-nosed and gaunt-boned, with a heavy jaw and a broad forehead as massive as stone. He had a full shock of hair that was neatly brushed

241

back. Silvery white, and streaked with yellow, it reminded one of cornsilk. And indeed, with his weathered complexion, creased, baggy uniform, and tie slightly askew, his Midwestern genesis clung to him like lint.

He had the physique of a man who had been a fine athlete in his youth but had become soft and flaccid with years of duty in the confined quarters of ships, soft living, and overeating. Despite a tunic that was at least a full size too large, the beginning of a paunch was visible under his tans. There was a serious, almost apprehensive gleam in the rear admiral's gray eyes, and his attention was totally on Admiral Hiroshi Fujita. He seemed not to recognize Brent Ross when his eyes made a quick, nervous flick around the room.

The two admirals acknowledged each other and then Fujita introduced his staff, each Japanese bowing when presented. Finally, Fujita came to Brent, and Whitehead brightened and extended his hand. "Good to see you, Brent," he said, grasping the lieutenant's hand and speaking with a hint of a Midwestern inflection still in his voice. "Sorry about Admiral Mark Allen. He was one of the best."

"We lost a good man, sir," Brent said.

"Indeed we did."

Then Whitehead congratulated Lieutenant Reginald Williams for his fine work and then, following Admiral Fujita's gesture, moved to a chair next to the admiral. However, he did not seat himself. He looked down at Admiral Fujita and said, "I have a report, sir."

"You may give it now."

Whitehead drew some papers from his valise and spread them on the table. He placed a pair of old-fashioned horn-rimmed glasses on his nose. "I have some information so delicate we did not dare put on the air. Anyway, 'Blue-Alpha' has been chewed up by Arab mainframes and won't be replaced by 'Gamma Yellow' until 2400 Greenwich civil time today." He read for a moment and then looked up. "There has been a fire reported in Kadafi's poison gas plant at Rabta."

There were happy, excited whispers. Whitehead continued, "It has been reported that most of the plant was destroyed and Kadafi blames Western sabotage."

"How could you know this?" Fujita asked. "You have no spy satellites, no AWACS over North Africa."

Whitehead smiled enigmatically. "French sources— agents that have infiltrated from Chad."

"Are they reliable?"

The rear admiral nodded his head. "Usually."

"Usually!" Fujita said with a challenge in his voice. "We cannot risk everything on agents who may or may not be reliable! Kadafi may be using that report as a smoke screen, hiding his true production behind it. We will take it out."

"Take it out?"

"I will explain later, Admiral Whitehead. Please continue with your report."

The rear admiral pursed his lips and sighed. Everyone expected bad news. No one was mistaken. "Their *Essex*-class carrier *Al Kufra* was sighted off the western entrance to the Straits of Malacca this morning at 0530 hours by our nuclear sub, the USS *Los Angeles*. She was escorted by three *Gearings*. They were making for the entrance at thirty knots. They should make Tomonuto in a few days."

Fujita said, "Then they will have two carriers, two cruisers, and six escorts in the atoll."

"Yes, Admiral. That's what NIS expects." Whitehead adjusted his glasses and continued. "I'm afraid I have more bad news. The Arabs have large quantities of a new explosive. It's called Semtex, and it is odorless and colorless. It is manufactured in Czechoslovakia by the East Bohemian Chemical Company." He looked up and stared down the table. "It is so powerful that only seven ounces—two hundred grams—blew up a Pan American DC-6 over England last year with the loss of all eighty-two people aboard." And then, in a bitter aside, "Abu Nidal and his Fatah Revolutionary Council got credit for that one. Nidal was angry that English pilots were training for duty with *Yonaga*, so naturally he killed a planeload of innocent people—women, children. We must keep in mind, despite the open warfare the Arabs are waging against us, their terrorist networks are still very much alive and a mortal threat to strike and kill innocent people indiscriminately anywhere on earth. And Abu Nidal is their greatest threat."

Bernstein spoke with quiet passion in his voice. Again he showed the unbelievable efficiency of Israeli Intelligence which operated on a budget that would not keep the CIA in paper clips. "Abu Nidal is a nom de guerre. We have confirmed his true name is Sabri Khalil al-Banna. He was born in Jaffa fifty-two years ago. Learned his trade with Yasser Arafat and the PLO, but broke with Arafat when he felt Arafat was going soft on Jews." Laughter swept the room. Bernstein waited for the chuckles to subside and continued. "Nidal is a jackal, cares nothing about the innocents he kills, claims all that counts is the worldwide attention the massacres claim for his cause. He's based in Tripoli and is Kadafi's favorite, second only to Captain Kenneth Rosencrance."

Brent saw Yoshi Matsuhara stiffen and mutter, "Rosencrance, Rosencrance," as if the word was an obscenity almost too foul to mouth.

"We'll get him, Yoshi-san," Brent whispered. Yoshi stared blankly at the bulkhead.

Fujita said to Bernstein, "This Semtex, Colonel . . . how much does Kadafi have on hand?"

Bernstein returned to his notes. "We estimate Kadafi has at least a thousand tons of Semtex on hand."

There was a roar of anger and concern. Fujita raised his hands. "Can it be adapted to bombs and torpedoes?"

"Yes, sir. They're working on that problem now."

244

"But they do not have it ready yet. It is plastic and unstable," Fujita suggested.

Whitehead nodded, took off his glasses, and rubbed the bridge of his nose wearily. "That is our understanding, Admiral Fujita." He replaced the glasses and glanced at another document. "There is a report from our agents in both Kuwait and Bahrain that the hundred-thousand-ton tanker *Jabal Nafusa* is loading highest-test gasoline at the Iranian port of Bushehr—it's on the Persian Gulf. We expect her to get underway for Tomonuto and perhaps the Marianas Islands in perhaps a week."

Fujita came to his feet and began to turn toward the chart, stopped, and questioned Whitehead. "Why send aviation fuel all the way from the Persian Gulf when they can ship it from the Balikpapan in the NEI—ah, I mean Indonesia. It's much closer."

Whitehead said, "Because the Arabs have installed the new Daimber Benz *Valkryie* engine in all of their fighters and a few of their bombers. It requires a specially refined high-test fuel that the refineries at Balikpapan cannot process." He tapped the desk with a big set of knuckles. "Remember, two years ago Arab cruisers shelled those same refineries the first time they sortied into the Celebes Sea."

"We sank them in the South China Sea," Fujita said.

"Banzai!" the Japanese shouted.

Fujita stepped to a chart, picked up a pointer, and spoke to Whitehead without turning his attention away from the map. "What is the SOA (speed of advance) of tanker *Jabal Nafusa?*"

"Twelve to thirteen knots, sir, and at least two *Gearings* are in port with her. We assume they will be her escorts."

Fujita placed the tip of the pointer on the Persian Gulf and then traced a line south and east, muttering to himself while every eye was focused on the journey of the rubber tip. He stopped at Tomonuto. "If they take the shortest route, twelve thousand kilometers—about seventy-five hundred miles—at twelve; thirteen knots, about thirty days of steaming." He whirled, face hinting at one of his rare smiles. "Good! Good, gentlemen. The gods favor us. We have at least five weeks, perhaps six." He spoke to Whitehead, "The CIA agent, Dale McIntyre, reported three of their *Gearings* were in the yards in Surabaya."

"McIntyre—Dale McIntyre," Byron Whitehead said, eyes narrow, voice low and tense. Brent felt sudden tension tighten his muscles, and he hunched forward. Did Whitehead know Dale? Why the cryptic look on the rear admiral's face almost as if he had been transfixed by shock? He must know her. Suddenly, it seemed obvious as Whitehead continued, "She was here—on board *Yonaga?*"

Fujita waved fretfully as if he were chasing an irritating fly away from his nose. "Yes. She was. But never again." He tapped the desk as if he were driving the woman's memory out of the room. "The destroyers at Surabaya. Their status is critical to our strategy," he said impatiently.

The American rear admiral shuffled through his papers, selected one, examined it, and looked up. "They should be ready for sea in five weeks."

Fujita tightened his tiny jaw in a grim line. "So, the entire force should be ready for sea in six weeks." He tapped the desk. "How critical is the Arab logistics situation?"

Whitehead stared at his documents. "As of yesterday, they had an oiler and three depot ships anchored at Tomonuto."

"Along with carrier *Ramli al Kabir,* two cruisers and three *Gearings*. Miss Mc . . . I mean the CIA . . . reported this, and we are aware of their presence, anyway."

"They have plenty of fuel for a major engagement, both diesel oil and aviation gasoline," Whitehead said.

246

There was an apprehensive groan. "However, we know their stores of gasoline are low and their ability to sustain their air strikes is questionable. It is absolutely essential to their operations that tanker *Jabal Nafusa* arrive at Tomonuto with her cargo within six weeks."

Fujita tapped the table with the pointer. "Everything is converging. Their tactical window opens in six weeks. We must sink the tanker and"—he stabbed the pointer at Williams—"this is a job for our submarine force."

Commander Reginald Williams straightened, and it appeared the man's face actually brightened. He came to his feet, pointed a finger at the chart and said to the admiral, "If my boat is ready for sea in three weeks we can patrol in the Celebes Sea at the north exit of the Makassar Straits. Be waiting when she exits and pick her off like a cherry bomb."

There were shouts of *"Banzai!"* and this time Brent joined in.

Fujita pondered the statement for a long moment, his eyes fixed on the chart. "Good idea, Mister Williams. However, they are not stupid. A good commander would avoid a narrow passage where a submarine attack was possible—even likely."

"But if he's an Arab he won't know how to think," Williams said.

Whitehead spoke up. "The skipper of the tanker is an American. His name is Gary Kuhn. He's one of the best. Ex-United States Navy, and very experienced." Williams, Brent, and Fite looked at each other. Brent felt both anger and humiliation and saw the same in Fite's and Williams' eyes. It seemed money in large enough amounts could buy anything, anyone. He cursed under his breath as Whitehead's voice droned on. "Kuhn is a World War II skipper, and you can be assured he won't give you any more opportunity than geography will allow. I would expect him to take the South China Sea route. It's longer but safer."

Fujita jabbed the chart and stared at Williams.

"Here, at Tomonuto. You can be on station there in four weeks. The longer South China Sea route will give you even more time. The *Jabal Nafusa* with her deep draft must use the southern entrance, and you can welcome her there with your Mark Forty-Eights."

Brent said to Whitehead, "It's heavily patrolled, Admiral. They'll have one can anchored and listening in the entrance while another runs a 'ping line' maybe a mile at sea. It's a tough attack problem. He'll be up against two cans at the entrance, two more escorts, and both passive and active sonar."

"True, Mister Ross. But whoever said war was easy?" A chuckle swept the room.

Whitehead continued, "And remember, we have nuclear subs patrolling off the Persian Gulf, in the Indian Ocean, the Celebes Sea and the South China Sea. They will report any movements of Arab ships — all shipping, for that matter." Everyone nodded.

Williams rubbed his hands together and licked his lips. "It's going to be tough, but we'll nail that mother . . ." he muttered under his breath. Brent smiled and Admiral Fujita's eyes gleamed. It was obvious the old sailor approved of Lieutenant Reginald Williams.

Commander Takuya Iwata, the commanding officer of the dive bombers, heaved his big bulk out of his chair and came to his feet. A sneer twisted the young officer's face, and he stared balefully at Reginald Williams. "If our submarine commander feels this assignment is tough, my dive bombers can not only sink the enemy tanker, but destroy all of the enemy units at Tomonuto." He turned to Admiral Fujita, playing the scornful, fearless samurai to the hilt just as his hero, Yukio Mishima, might have played the role. "Just launch us two hundred kilometers out, Admiral, and you," he pointed rudely at Williams, "and you will not need the USS *Blackface* . . ."

"*Blackfin!*" Williams roared, leaping to his feet. Bernstein, Matsuhara, Fite, and Whitehead shouted an-

248

grily at Iwata, who ignored them imperiously.

Brent was right behind Williams, realizing Lieutenant Tadayoshi Koga's "Blackface" faux pas must have been whispered around the ship and enjoyed by Iwata and his friends. Now it had been thrown at Williams again.

"Iwata!" Brent shouted. "That was unconscionable." Through the corner of his eye Brent saw Admiral Fujita lean back against the bulkhead with the usual cabalistic look of an observer who was almost disinterested. Would he let this clash run its course too? This time there could be violence.

Fujita made his decision instantly, and his voice slashed through the heated exchange. "Enough!" he shouted. "All of you seat yourselves." Grumbling, the seething rivals dropped slowly into their chairs. "I have said this before," the old admiral said. "We must kill our enemies before we kill each other." He glared at Iwata. "This is the second time Lieutenant Williams has been exposed to this slur. The first time was an obvious blunder. But I am not convinced you suffered a slip of the lip, Commander Iwata." He pounded the table with two clenched fists. "Any repetition—any racial affront that comes to my attention will be dealt with harshly." The knuckles of the two tiny fists met in front of him in a series of collisions. "I will summarily dismiss from this command any officer who offends Lieutenant Williams on the basis of race. If you are to fight and argue, find your fields of combat elsewhere—like gentlemen and samurai."

Williams was still staring at Iwata. "Respectfully, Admiral," he said in a hard monotone. "I feel quite capable of defending my dignity and my honor and reserve the right, when the enemy is defeated, to settle any insults to my honor on a personal, man-to-man basis."

"Hear! Hear!" Brent Ross, Bernstein, Fite, and Whitehead agreed.

Fujita said to Williams. "Your words are those of a samurai. I always honor such requests because the defense of one's honor is a basic tenet of bushido."

"I am at your service," Iwata growled.

"Right now!" Williams countered, pushing on his arm rests.

"No!" Fujita said sharply. "When we have smashed the Arab *jihad* (holy war), and only then." He turned to Colonel Bernstein in an obvious attempt to change the subject and allow time for the fires to cool. "Israel's defenses have stabilized, Colonel?" He seated himself.

Understanding the admiral's motives, the Israeli took the floor and moved quickly to a chart of the Middle East covered with a clear plastic overlay. He spoke to the staff, "Thanks to *Yonaga*'s intervention and the four 12-inch guns of monitor *Mikasa,* our front with the Arabs has been stable." He picked up a red pen and marked the plastic overlay. "This is our David Ben-Gurion Line, a continuous three-deep line of concrete blockhouses with interlocking fields of fire. It compares with the old German Hindenburg Line of the Great War because the Arabs are still thinking in terms of those old offensive tactics." The red felt tip pricked the chart on the Mediterranean coast at Gaza, moved east to Al Khalil where *Yonaga*'s bombers had smashed an Arab tank attack four years before, north along the Jordanian frontier to the Syrian border and the Golan Heights, turning west toward the coast when the tip reddened Al Khushniyah. Then a line south of Lebanon that finally reached the coast at Haifa. The Israeli turned to the staff, "Thanks to Kadafi's preoccupation with *Yonaga,* he has committed most of his energy, ships, and aircraft to the Western Pacific. In fact, the Israeli Air Force still holds control of the air over the Ben-Gurion Line."

Lieutenant Joji Kai, the commanding officer of the torpedo bombers, spoke for the first time. "But there are over two-hundred million Arabs and only four million Israelis."

"True, Lieutenant. But a man named Adolph Hitler

250

taught us how to fight." He pointed at the chart. "The Arabs have lost over a quarter of a million men and most of their armor in foolish frontal assaults on our positions."

"Then you feel confident?" Kai asked.

The Israeli shook his head. "Confidence is a luxury no Israeli can afford. It is better to say we are determined—can make the price so high, the Arabs will think many times over before trying to make their *jihad* good against us."

"This is the first time the Arabs have been united in anything since the eleventh century," Kai said.

Fujita laughed. "Yes. True. They need a *Mahdi . . .*"

"*Mahdi?*"

Bernstein picked up the conversation, "Yes. A *Mahdi* is the expected messiah of Muslim tradition—a spiritual leader."

"And Kadafi is trying to assume this leadership?"

"Of course, Lieutenant Kai. He is playing the messianic role to the hilt."

Kai continued, "But Arab feuds run deep, *Mahdi* or not."

Bernstein's laugh was ironic and completely devoid of humor. "The Jordanians hate the Syrians, who hate the Iraqis, who hate the Egyptians, who hate the Lebanese, and they all hate the Iranians, who aren't Arabs anyway . . . they're Persians. And the hates are interchangeable and reciprocal and so ancient no one really remembers why they exist. It's just an Arab way of life, they enjoy killing each other."

"But they've put these feuds aside."

The Israeli nodded grimly. "Now they can hate the Jews and the Japanese with the Americans a close third." Whitehead, Fite, and Brent Ross chuckled. Williams remained silent, glaring at Iwata.

Fujita tapped the table impatiently and addressed himself to Rear Admiral Whitehead. "We have reports that there are six Super Constellations based on Tinian.

These LRAs have been converted to bombers and pose a mortal threat to *Yonaga*. Does NIS have any more information on these aircraft? Our PBYs, PBMs, and observers on Aguijan report no supply vessels putting into Saipan's Tanapag Harbor since *Blackfin* sank *Gefara*."

The American admiral nodded. "Of course they wouldn't dare send in supply vessels without air cover. Their ME 109s have a range of only about six hundred miles. I think they fear squadrons of your *Fletchers* are patrolling in the southwest Pacific between Tomonuto and the Marianas—especially since Captain Fite engaged their *Tubaru* just west of the Marianas."

"But still, they have their Super Constellations."

"True, Admiral . . . but as you said, only six of them, and they can't maintain them in complete readiness for bombing missions and maintain patrols in all sectors at the same time." He moved his eyes to Williams. "And there is something else. They have suffered heavily to your *Blackfin*. Four more of *Blackfin*'s sisters have been put into commission, and we have planted the rumor three of these boats have been sold to the Parks Department and are now in the Pacific." The men looked at each other and laughed in delight. "They wouldn't dare send in unescorted transports." He stabbed a finger at the chart of the Middle East. "Look at tanker *Jabal Nafusa*. They won't send her without two *Gearings*."

"But they are supplying their forces on Saipan and Tinian? They did this by submarine last year."

"And they're doing it now, Admiral." The American admiral pulled a new document from his valise. "The Russians sold Kadafi ten old diesel-electric *Zulus* two years ago."

"Do you have the specs of these submarines, Admiral Whitehead. We have new members on our staff."

Whitehead waved a sheet. "Yes, sir. First you must realize, Kadafi insisted on all-Arab crews for his submarine fleet . . . sort of an underwater *jihad*. This was a disaster. The crews were completely unmechanical and most of them couldn't even read the manuals. Four submarines were lost by accident. In fact, one even submerged without closing its main induction valve. It's in shallow water just off Tripoli still. The other three disappeared without a trace while on training missions. Now he has brought in some old German U-boat officers and the six remaining boats are still operational."

"The *Zulu* is basically an old German World War II design," Fujita said.

"Yes, sir. The Russians built twenty-six of them in the early fifties and then stopped the program when they decided to go nuclear." Whitehead studied his documents. "Two hundred ninety five feet long, twenty four foot beam, three Type 37D diesels, 6000 horsepower, three electric motors, three shafts. Speed sixteen on the surface, twelve submerged, ten torpedoes or thirty-six mines. Range 20,000 miles at eight knots surfaced." He looked up. "Our latest reports indicate these boats are all in use as supply boats for the garrisons on Saipan and Tinian. They have done an excellent job, bringing in fuel, ammunition, more troops, and even some 105-millimeter artillery." An anxious rumble filled the room.

Fujita tugged at the single white hair hanging from his chin and Brent knew the old sailor was deep in thought. "But still, Admiral Whitehead," he said. "Submarine supply is tenuous, and six *Zulus* cannot transport large units, big guns, and heavy armor."

"True."

"Then let them fortify their old blockhouses, dig their holes, and emplace their artillery." He looked around the room. "We will sink their ships, let the garrisons wither on the vine, and then wipe them out at a time of our choosing."

"Banzai!" boomed through the room.

Fujita flung a single palm in the air like a Nazi saluting Hitler, and the shouting stopped. "It is time to in-

253

terrogate the prisoners." He turned to the communications rating. "Yeoman Nakamura," he said to the rating who had huddled over his equipment unnoticed like a piece of furniture. "Show the German in."

The big German was pushed into the room by two seaman guards who prodded him to the end of the table where he stood, glaring the length of the long oak slab at Admiral Fujita. The hate in his eyes filled the room like a toxic wind. "You are Conrad Schachter," Fujita stated.

The German drew himself up, "I am *Hauptmann* Conrad Schachter, *Sechste Bombardement Geschwader*," he announced, mustering all of the dignity available to a prisoner who had just been manhandled into a room full of enemies.

"Speak English," Fujita commanded. "The language of this ship is English."

"Captain Conrad Schachter, Sixth Bombardment Squadron," the German translated.

"Your base?"

The German spat back with unbelievable arrogance, "Valhalla!"

Fujita nodded and one of the guards punched the German in the stomach with so much force, his fist vanished into the fat and the German doubled over, gagging with pain and spraying mucus and spittle. Whitehead and Williams looked at Brent in shock. Brent, Bernstein, and Fite smiled. The Japanese chuckled with amusement.

Gasping like the victim of a strangler, Schachter straightened slowly, finally managing, "The Geneva Conventions?"

Uproarious laughter filled the room. Fujita said, "Japan never subscribed to the Geneva Conventions. Did Germany?"

Bernstein raised a hand and his sleeve dropped, flashing the blue numbers tattooed on his forearm. The German's eyes caught the numbers and burned with new venom despite the pain. Fujita acknowledged Bernstein. The Israeli consulted some notes before speaking. "You are the former *Leutnant* (Second Lieutenant) Conrad Schachter of the *Luftwaffe?*"

Breathing in short gasps, the German drew himself back up. His face was flushed, and perspiration beaded his forehead. It was obvious the man was not a coward. "How can you know that, *Juden?*"

Every eye was riveted on the pair. Fujita seemed mesmerized by the face-to-face encounter of two participants in the greatest tragedy of the century — perhaps of all time. Brent knew this time Fujita would sit back and let the unending hatred of the two old enemies run its course like lava coursing from Mount Miyake.

"We keep archives on all of our friends of the Holocaust. I ran you through our computers this morning," Bernstein said, tapping a document. "You were born in Munich in 1929, the son of a party official, Fredrick Schachter, who was appointed Bürgermeister of Bad Waldeck by Hitler himself. You joined the Hitler Youth at age eleven, were cited for 'Devotion to der Fuehrer and the Third Reich' by the head of the movement, Baldur von Schirach, at age fourteen, and you were the youngest pilot to ever enter flight training at age fifteen."

"Someday, we will finish it — *Endlösung* (final solution) *Juden scheisse.*" Schachter gestured at the tattoo, "You were our guest."

" 'The Auschwitz Finishing School' from '43 to '45. I graduated with honors. In fact, I was the class — you roasted the rest." For the first time, bitterness crept into his voice. "All my neighbors from the Warsaw ghetto, my father, mother, brother, sister — they were all part of your *Endlosung*. Did their bit by breathing your Zyklon B."

"How did we miss you, *untermenschen nille* (subhuman prick)."

The German's gall was amazing. Perhaps he already

255

knew he was a dead man and was goaded by the inevitability of death to speak out with his most fetid hatreds and prejudices. Everyone stared at the pair, jerking their eyes back and forth like spectators at a tennis match.

"I was a former dental student. Pulled dental gold for you in a small room just between Gas Chamber Number Two and the main crematorium." The Jew's brown eyes bored into the German. "Actually did a little work on my own father," he said matter-of-factly. Brent was astonished by Bernstein's control.

Still managing to muster arrogance, the German looked around at the hard, implacable faces, finally stopping on Reginald Williams. *"Ein Neger,"* he said, thick lips twisted with disdain. *"Ein Neger und ein Juden scheisse."* He shook his head in disbelief and spoke with incredible gall, "A room full of *untermenschen schwein."* He stared hard at Reginald Williams, "Tell me," he asked casually, lips pouting in mock civility, "Have you lost your foreskin too, *Neger?"*

Iwata giggled at Williams' obvious umbrage. Brent grabbed the big black instinctively before he could leave his chair. "I'll cut your *nille* off—if you *have* any balls, Nazi prick," Williams spat. "You aren't dealing with helpless women and children here."

Bernstein glanced at his document and interrupted. "You were only fifteen when you joined the *Luftwaffe?"*

Schachter drew himself up and spoke with haughty pride. "I was the youngest pilot ever to fly for the Third Reich." He looked around. Every eye was focused on him. He was obviously enjoying holding center stage. He continued, waving a hand with a theatrical flair, "I flew with General Adolph Galland's ME-262 unit, the *Jagdverband* 44 in nineteen forty-five."

"The Messerschmitt 262," Fite said thoughtfully. "It was a jet—the first operational jet."

"I shot down two of your B-17s. I only wish I could

have killed more of you Yankee *schwein.*" Brent, Reginald, and John Fite all growled angrily. The German laughed.

Fujita slapped the table as the last of his patience drained away. He had obviously tired of the sport, and the German had become unbearable even to him. "Captain, Schachter, we knew you flew from Tinian," he said. "We also know there are less than thirty fighters left to you in the Marianas and less than a dozen JU-87s. You have six Lockheed Super Constellations." The admiral rubbed his tiny knuckles together. "What I want to know is how many reinforcements are you expecting? When will they arrive? How many troops occupy Saipan and Tinian? How much artillery do you have and the calibers?"

The German stared at the admiral for a long, silent moment. The pudgy face was expressionless. Then a slow smile rolled through the fat cheeks and twisted the sensuous lips like ripe sausage. "Would you like to know how many latrines we have built, too?"

Fujita threw up his hands in a rare show of anger. Both guards struck the German simultaneously, one punched to the stomach, the other to a kidney. Schachter shrieked with pain and staggered against the table. Two more blows drove him to the deck. Fujita waved and the moaning captain was dragged from the room.

Bernstein said to the admiral. "You will behead him?"

"Why, of course," Fujita answered as if the question was completely academic. And then wryly, "Do you object, Colonel Bernstein?"

The Israeli's answer shocked everyone. "Yes."

"Yes!"

"That's too good for him."

"What would you suggest?"

"Leave him to me, Admiral."

Fujita smiled. "I will consider your request, Colonel." He rubbed his chin thoughtfully. "But keep in mind,

Colonel, obviously, what happened over forty years ago cannot be changed. I can understand your desire for vengeance—vengeance is sacred to a samurai. But you can only kill Captain Schachter once, not six million times." He toyed with the single white hair dangling from his chin. "I can remember back in '84 on our mission to the Mediterranean, I honored your request to fight another German prisoner, ah, ah . . ."

"Captain Werner Schlieben," Brent offered. "He was captain of the Libyan freighter *Zilah* we sank in Tokyo Bay when she tried to ram us. They fought with *wakizashis* in the 'Shrine of Infinite Salvation.' "

"Yes. Yes," Fujita acknowledged. "It was Captain Schlieben, and you killed him."

"How can I forget?" the Israeli said.

"And you dispatched him with great ingenuity and skill, Colonel," Fujita continued. "But after it was all over, you said you could never avenge the Holocaust, that all it could ever be was a lesson."

"I remember."

"Then you would repeat this exercise in futility? You could lose your life, you know."

"Everything you say is true, Admiral. But, yes, I would like to fight him—kill him with these." He held up his thin yet strong hands. "Please consider my request."

"Of course, Colonel. But keep in mind, you may be too valuable to risk." He turned to Yeoman Nakamura, "Bring in the Arab."

Sergeant Haj Abu al Sahdi was pushed into the room by two more guards. The haughty arrogance that had fired from Schacter's eyes was missing in the small Arab's black eyes, but defiance was there, and revulsion glowed when he spotted the Israeli. Then the hate came. Bernstein bristled in the glare.

Fujita asked for his name, rank, duties. Quickly the Arab answered, readily admitting his squadron had flown from Saipan's Isley Field. Then the same questions that had been put to Schachter about supply and reinforcements.

Palming his prayer beads and muttering some of the ninety-nine names for Allah, the short dark man stared at Fujita. "Submarines—sometimes submarines. The ships have not come for a long time." The Arab moved his eyes back to Bernstein and hate danced there like mad fireflies. He shouted at the Israeli, *Itbakh al Yahud!*"

The Japanese looked at each other in confusion. Bernstein explained, "He just yelled 'Death to the Jews'!" He actually yawned. "It's old hat. The Fedayeen—Arab commandos—use it all the time."

Every Japanese in the room had been aware of the Holocaust for decades, the timeless hatred and persecution of the Jews all over the world. Notwithstanding, Jews were scarce in Japan, and most of the Japanese in the room had never met a Jew until Colonel Irving Bernstein had reported aboard as a liaison officer with Israeli Intelligence. However, none was prepared for the intensity of hatred directed by both Captain Conrad Schachter and Sergeant Haj Abu al Sahdi at the Israeli. Both the German and the Arab had good reason to detest the Japanese, yet the full intensity of their abhorrence focused on the Jew. Bernstein was unbelievably cool in his response, as if he were dealing with an everyday problem that had endured to the point of ennui.

" 'Haj'." Bernstein remarked casually. "That's an honorific. You've been to Mecca, Sergeant Abu al Sahdi? You've honored Muhammad's Fifth Pillar of Wisdom?"

The Arab drew himself up proudly, "I earned the title Haj ten years ago when I walked from my village of Bir Nakhella to Mecca. I prayed at the Al Aksa Mosque and the Dome of the Rock, *Yahud.*" He waved a fist, "Perish Judea!"

Fujita interrupted, "Captain Conrad Schachter was your squadron leader?"

The Arab tugged on a corner of his huge drooping mustache. "That pile of donkey's dung led us to destruction."

"He was the only German?"

"Yes, Admiral."

"You dislike Germans?"

"Only Schachter." He stabbed a finger at Bernstein. "I like most Germans. They help us kill *Yahud*."

Bernstein spoke with completely unruffled aplomb. "I know your village of Bir Nakhella. It's typical—a miserable place twenty kilometers southwest of Jerusalem."

Fujita sank back, eyes focused on the pair. By his relaxed demeanor, yet an intense concentration betrayed by his eyes, Brent knew the old man intended to allow the string of acrimony to play itself out.

"You grew up in Bir Nakhella?"

"Yes, *Yahud*."

There was irony in Bernstein's chuckle. "Then you never saw a green lawn, toys, flowers that were not wild, streets not covered with donkey and camel's shit, a library, a museum, a cinema, a swimming pool, a toilet, medical clinic, a machine shop, milking machines for your cows, tractors, reapers, electric lights, a painting. You lived like the rest of your brethren like Bedouin dogs—just as you have for centuries and then blame the Jews for your own stupidity and sloth."

"May a thousand scorpions feast on your mother's cunt, *Yahud*." Bernstein amazed everyone with his unflappability, his face as stoic as a temple icon. The Arab drew himself up with new bravado, his great mustache bristling as if it had been suddenly waxed. He raced on, "I am not a Bedouin dog, I am not a stupid *fellah*. I am a Hashemite of the same clan of Muhammad. My ancestors came from Arabia, from the Hejaz. We were the keepers of the holy places of Mecca. I never saw those things in my village because you drove my father—my family from our lands when you conquered Jerusalem in 1948. You drove us to Bir

Nakhella when you stole Jerusalem, our national capital of the Palestinians."

"Nonsense!"

Haj Abu al Sahdi ignored the Israeli and waved a fist and shouted an ancient Roman oath adopted by the Fedayeen, "Perish Judea! Down with the enemies of God and humanity. Allah Akbar! (God is great!)" The fist became a dagger which he stabbed at Bernstein. "Your Torah is filled with scandals and debauchery that reveal your true nature of filth. You falsify God's message. You claim Abraham was a Jew, when in truth he was a Moslem. You deny Jesus, while in fact he was sent to earth by the Moslems and saved by Allah and became a prophet for Allah. You lied about Abraham, falsified the Bible, and murdered all the prophets. You are scum that do not have a legitimate nation. Your Israel is a depravity that is a total contradiction to Allah's 'abode of Islam.' Muhammad has put a curse on you forever." He waved a single finger back and forth like a scolding schoolmaster and looked around the room to make certain his audience was attentive. "Read the Koran and you will find proof that Islam is superior. Its truth guarantees its triumph over all of you—all infidels." His hand swept over the room grandly, like a mullah dispensing blessings. "In the name of Allah, the merciful, the compassionate, Islam will triumph over all religions and all peoples. Only Allah teaches the lesson of renewed purity and purpose." The Japanese and Americans looked at each other in amazement. None had expected this Arab to be so confident, so articulate and unafraid.

Bernstein rocked with laughter, his face a dictionary of amusement. He seemed to be enjoying the sport of debating the Arab. Every man in the room watched in fascination. "We Israelis have a saying," he said, grinning at al Sahdi. " 'One quiet word with a wise man is better than a year of pleading with a fool.' " The Arab growled but Bernstein continued, "You grew up in Bir

261

Nakhella because in May of 1948 five Arab states launched a military assault designed to destroy us. Arab armies drove you out of your homes — a half-million of you who were actually prisoners of King Abdullah of Jordan and his Arab Legion. Now you have grown to two million. You've been living off the UN and the Israelis while your leaders — your muktars (village leaders) and effendi (men of property) — steal from you. Now you want to steal the lands the *kibbutzim* have restored — harvest the fertile fields we have created out of the ruin left by centuries of overgrazing by your goats and neglect by your lazy men who send their women out into the fields to do the work." He thumped the table for emphasis. "Never! Never! *Never* will you steal our lands from us."

"Canaan is an Arab land. Joshua stole it for the *Yahud*." al Sahdi countered.

"Nonsense. Even in the Middle Ages, when you were at your zenith of power, Arabs identified with Mecca, Baghdad, Cairo, and Cordova. Not Jerusalem, or, as you say, Canaan. Why, during four hundred years of Turkish rule, there wasn't a single attempt by the Arabs to liberate Jerusalem." He leaned forward. "The truth is, there is *no* Arab memory of a religious or generic relationship with Jerusalem. Your claim is hypocritical and false."

"Enough!" Fujita said suddenly. He addressed the guards, his words cutting the Arab like razors, "Take this dog back to his kennel!"

Sergeant Haj Abin al Sahdi roared with anger, "Your mother's milk was camel's piss, old *fellah!*"

Fujita's narrow eyes widened and he said softly, "Your tongue is preparing itself for amputation, Arab dog." Abu al Sahdi did not flinch.

Brent expected to see the Arab beaten, and the guards stood alertly waiting for a signal from the admiral. It never came. Instead, Fujita stared at Haj Abu al Sahdi silently while the Arab's black eyes moved to

Bernstein like metal to a magnet. Perhaps the old man admired the prisoner's courage. Certainly he had spoken out from his beliefs without hesitation or equivocation—a performance no one had expected from an Arab. Watching the Jew and the Arab stare at each other, Brent felt a palpable force of hate filling the room like a pestilential cloud. There was no hope. It would never end.

Fujita waved three fingers, and the guards dragged the prisoner from the room. His shouts of *"Allah Akbar!"* could be heard from the passageway.

After the meeting, the officers dispersed hurriedly, Reginald Williams and John Fite to the sick bay; Yoshi Matsuhara, Takuya Iwata, and Joji Kai to Tokyo International Airport where new cadres of pilots awaited them; the executive officer Mitake Arai and the scribe Hakuseki Katsube into Admiral Fujita's office; the chief engineer Tatsuya Yoshida to the engine room; and Gunnery Officer Nobomitsu Atsumi to the dock where some new 25-millimeter gun barrels were being unloaded. Brent was anxious to inspect the CIC (Combat Information Center) and his communications equipment. But he was stopped in the passageway just outside Flag Plot by Rear Admiral Byron Whitehead.

"Got a minute, Brent?" the rear admiral asked. "Got to talk to you." He gestured to the door to his cabin, which had been Admiral Mark Allen's. The request was polite but firm, and there was command in the voice. The lieutenant followed him into the cabin.

Designed to be the quarters of a flag officer, the cabin was much larger than Brent's. In addition to a wide bunk complete with reading light and nightstand, there was a leather chair in one corner, a desk and typewriter in another. A head complete with a shower, sink, and full-length mirror was entered through a door in the corner of the aft bulkhead. A large table with

263

four chairs occupied the center of the room. Small staff conferences could be held here. Whitehead opened the room's two scuttles, allowing sunlight and fresh air to stream into the room. The cacophony of yard noises also poured in. He gestured to the table. Brent seated himself, and Whitehead sank into a chair opposite him. "Like a drink?" he asked, gesturing to a small cabinet bolted to the bulkhead.

"No, thank you, sir. Still too early."

"For me, too." Quickly, the rear admiral congratulated Brent for his fine work and spoke of his close friendship with the lieutenant's father, Ted "Trigger" Ross. Then he had a few words of praise for Admiral Mark Allen. "I'm the only one of the triumvirate left," the old officer sighed. "As you know, we served in Japan together during MacArthur's reign—ah, tenure. We all worked on Samuel E. Morison's *History of US Naval Operations in World War Two* together—did most of the research while Morison put his name on all fifteen volumes. In a way, it was the culmination of our careers."

"You retired in '81?"

"Yes, Brent. I came out of retirement in '87, when the oil crisis almost paralyzed the world. The chief of staff claimed they were desperate for NIS personnel." He shrugged. "I told him I was an old war-horse who knew very little about modern computer generated codes and ciphers—the entire communications network. They gave me a quick course and here I am—ship's company." He drummed the table, and only the sounds of blowers and the usual yard noise could be heard. The man was troubled, on the edge of a unsettling subject. Brent held his silence.

"This is off the record—something personal, Brent, and there is no military expedient that would compel you to discuss this with even a rear admiral."

Brent studied the troubled face—a face he had known since his childhood and that had been as dear to him as Mark Allen's and even, at times, his father's. "Try me, sir."

"You—ah, you were pretty well acquainted with a woman—the CIA agent Dale McIntyre?"

Brent was taken by surprise but managed to nod casually. "We were very close—especially in New York."

The old man shook his head, his shock of white hair tumbling over his brow. He pushed it aside irritably and said, "We know."

"We, sir?"

"I'm afraid so, Brent."

"We were under surveillance by NIS?"

Whitehead freed his eyes from Brent's and stared at the bulkhead at a copy of the famous painting of heavy cruiser USS *Los Angeles* crunching through a huge sea in a burst of spray. "The FBI and CIA, too."

Brent felt heat begin to rise from his neck, and his cheeks felt hot. "That's quite a crowd. Did they bug her apartment? Maybe they had cameras recording—ah, recording everything."

"Please, Brent. There's no need for sarcasm." He hunched forward. "Both of you were involved in operations of the most sensitive nature—most of it top secret. Kenneth Rosencrance, Wolfgang Vatz and their lackeys were in New York specifically to meet with you and Admiral Mark Allen."

"I'll never forget the riot at the UN, sir."

"Naturally, you were being watched. There was always the chance some of you could have been kidnapped—held hostage, tortured, or just murdered in the streets."

"I never saw anyone."

Whitehead smiled. "We're good at our work."

"This doesn't make sense, Admiral. Why do you even bring this up? Dale was a good, loyal agent. She never discussed matters of a sensitive nature with me—with anyone. We—ah, we had a personal relationship."

"I know. But Dale McIntyre has personal problems, and it appears she is on the verge of some kind of

265

breakdown. I was informed about her conduct on board this ship yesterday and I understand the CIA is recalling her immediately and she will be placed on permanent R and R."

"I don't understand. What are you driving at, sir?"

"You know she was divorced?"

"Of course—years ago."

"And you know about her son?"

"Her son?"

"You didn't know?"

Brent shook his head but held his silence.

The old rear admiral sighed and sagged back. "Edward James McIntyre was born when Dale was nineteen. He was raised by his grandparents in Philadelphia while Dale pursued a career with the CIA."

"His father?"

Whitehead shook his head. "Not interested. Too busy chasing young broads. Dale sent monthly checks for Eddie's support but did not see him very often. Anyway, he was brilliant, enrolled in Cornell when he was only seventeen." He rubbed his forehead as if he was troubled by a persistent headache. "Anyway, he fell in with the wrong crowd—drank and then switched to the heavy stuff."

"Cocaine?"

"Cocaine, heroin—the whole bit."

"Christ." Brent shook his head. "Poor Dale."

"Yes, poor Dale. Last month he OD'd. They found him wrapped in a blanket and dumped on the side of a road like a piece of garbage."

"My God."

The old man tapped the table with a pudgy finger. "Dale can't handle it. I think she feels overwhelming guilt. She can't be trusted. She's breaking down, Brent."

A new thought entered Brent's mind. "You have a great interest in her—know a lot, Admiral."

Whitehead's smile was somber. "I should. I'm her uncle."

Chapter Nine

When Brent knocked on Dale's door it was late afternoon. He had been accompanied to the Imperial Hotel by three seamen guards. All were armed with Arisaka rifles, Otsu pistols that matched the one Brent carried in a shoulder holster, and knives. In addition, each man was in full battle kit: steel helmet, cartridge boxes hanging from duty belts and canvas leggings wrapped around the green trousers of their Number Two battle fatigues. They were authentically fierce men and looked the part. One remained with the staff car and driver, another took a post at the elevator door on Dale's floor, and the third walked with Brent to the woman's apartment. Frightened guests gawked and hurried past.

When Dale opened the door, Brent could see she was upset. She had a drink in her hand and waved him in with, "Enter, my boy. I have the encryption box for you." The voice was sharp, but the viperish hostility of the previous day was gone.

Silently, Brent walked to the plump sofa and seated himself, his knees crowded by the expensive marble table before it. He glanced out of the huge picture windows at the grand yet gaudy vista of Tokyo: Nihombashi and the Ginza to the southwest, with jam-packed stores and shops; the Imperial Palace to the west, with its elysian grounds and spectacular lighted fountain; the Azubu residential section to the east, crammed with tiny, flimsy houses that could fall on their inhabitants during an earthquake and not hurt anyone; and to the northeast a part of the Shinjuku, with its thicket of skyscrapers that loomed like impersonal slabs of mundanity topped with neon signs glaring obscenely. Back-dropping it all was the harbor with its rows of gantries, warehouses, and dozens of pregnant freighters tied to the docks.

Clutching her drink, Dale stood on the other side of the marble table and stared at him silently. She was wearing a green satin lounging outfit of matching blouse and slacks. The fit was tight, her breasts clearly delineated, perfect hips and buttocks accented by the clinging material. Her spectacular hair was down, flowing in soft waves like a river of gold, framing her face and caressing her shoulders. But she looked haggard, her eyes swollen; and new lines had sprung to life at the corners of her eyes and mouth. She was the picture of a troubled woman.

Brent wasted no time. "I heard about your son."

Dale's eyes widened as if she had been touched by an electric prod. "How? How?"

"Rear Admiral Byron Whitehead."

"My uncle. I didn't know."

"He's replaced Admiral Mark Allen. He came on board this morning. He's ship's company."

She turned her lips under and then emptied her glass. "Care for a drink?"

Brent nodded his assent. She moved to a small bar that separated the living room from the kitchen and returned with two drinks. "Haig & Haig straight up, with a twist of lemon," she said, handing the lieutenant his glass. This time she sat on the sofa.

"Good memory."

"You gave me a lot of practice." She sipped her drink and then said bitterly, "My uncle has a big mouth."

"You never told me about your son."

268

She chuckled humorlessly. "He was only a few years younger than you."

"Was that important?"

A film of moisture brightened the green of her eyes to the intensity of polished emeralds. "I was an old broad shacking up with a young boy only a few years older than my own son. You don't think that's important?"

"Don't say that."

She seemed not to hear. "My poor son Eddie, whom I neglected, let down, killed." She tore her eyes away and began to sob into her fist.

Brent put an arm around her narrow shoulders. "Not true. Just plain not true, Dale. What happened to him has happened to thousands."

She took several deep breaths and managed to bring herself back under control. She stared up at him, and the timbre of her voice was low, came from deep within her. "I hate war, I hate killing. But when *Yonaga* finishes with the Arabs, it should go after the drug producers of Central and South America. They're murdering a whole generation of our best and most promising. That's where you'll find the real war."

"Yes. Yes, you're right."

She reached up and traced a single finger across his forehead and down his cheek to the thick cords of his neck. "Poor, sweet Brent. I was so cruel—so crude yesterday."

"I understand."

"No, you don't. I despise Admiral Fujita and all he stands for."

The words brought shock to the young lieutenant's face. "You can't mean that."

"Oh, but I do. He's an incurable male chauvinist who holds women in contempt."

Brent shook his head vehemently. "He respected you."

It was Dale's turn to shake her head. "He respected what I knew. He realized he needed the cooperation of the CIA and I was the CIA."

"You deliberately antagonized him?"

She drank and tabled her drink. "I didn't diabolically plan it, if that's what you mean. But yes, I have wanted to bait him, to tell him off since the first time I met him. And then when Eddie died, something seemed to snap. Something seemed to say to me, 'What is this all about? Why take crap from anyone'?"

"To understand the admiral, you must understand his whole generation. He's a nineteenth-century man."

She laughed and then answered bitterly, "His generation—they're callously machismo and as abusive of their women as the Arabs they hate so much. Hypocrites! Hypocrites!"

"They don't cut off women's clitorises and make them work in the fields while they loaf."

She blanched. "That's from the Middle Ages."

"The Arabs have never left the Middle Ages. It's still practiced—they make female eunuchs of some of their women, still."

"I can't believe it."

"And they'd enslave us all to their great god oil."

She took one of his big hands in both of hers. "The hell with the Arabs, Brent. I was terrible to you yesterday, even called you an SOB." She raised his hand and kissed his palm. "Dear boy, I was trying to end it. I was awfully clumsy. I must've come on like Bette Davis in one of those pot-boilers from the thirties—the Late, Late Show in living color." Her lips tightened at the memory, and she drank. "When I buried Eddie, the grave seemed to take you too. He was so much like you."

"You told me you loved me."

She smiled for the first time. "At certain moments, I couldn't help it. You know how to drive a woman out of her mind."

"You're very passionate."

"I know, and I reveled in my young lover—told myself

270

I was young again. Did you know what you did for my ego—the ego of an old broad on the verge of menopause?"

"Don't be ridiculous. You're not an old . . ."

"Yes I am, and it had to end." She dropped his hand and looked away. "We must face it, dear Brent. I'm too old—too old for you, Brent. It was really over before it started."

"You're a young girl."

She laughed. "I know what you mean. But, no, it wouldn't work. Eventually, I would become the old companion of a young man. It would kill me to see you eyeing younger women."

Brent sighed in frustration at her intransigence but knew further arguments were useless. "All right," he said with resignation. "I'll not trouble you in the future." He took a big drink.

She began to cry and he held her close. "It's been decided for us, anyway, Brent," she managed, choking back her sobs.

"What do you mean?"

She dabbed at her eyes with a linen handkerchief and regained control. "I'll leave tomorrow morning. They claim I need R and R. My replacement is already here—Horace Mayfield."

"Don't know him."

"He's a good man; Fujita should approve. After all, Mayfield does have balls." She emptied her glass, picked his up and recharged them both. When she returned, she sat very close to him. She sipped her drink and stared at him over the glass. Her eyes probed deep, as if she were trying to read the book of his soul. He squirmed uncomfortably and took a large drink.

"What drives you, Brent?"

"What do you mean?"

She waved at the harbor, and her quick change in tack took him by surprise. "Out there. The fighting, the kill-

271

ing. With all those other young boys hunting for the Arabs—hunting for death, not life." She kissed his cheek. "Is that your white whale, Brent? Is death such a sorceress she can lure you beautiful young boys away from everything—families, loved ones, children?"

Brent knew to speak of duty would be nonsense. He could only say, "I truly don't know. All I can say is, it must be done and I am here to try to do it."

"That's what men have been saying as long was there have been men and their stupid wars to fight." She paused, seemed to grope for her thought. "Peace has never been the destiny of man," she said and took a drink.

Brent emptied half his glass. "You sound like Oliver Wendell Holmes."

"He knew what he was talking about."

"He didn't know that it is the future that commands today."

She snickered. "I don't agree. You can't see the future, Brent. But try. You can't find regrets there—only in the past."

"We will all find regrets there if we don't stop Kadafi and the rest of those madmen."

It was her turn to sigh at her companion's obstinance. "Useless, isn't it, Brent?"

He emptied his glass. "I'm afraid so." He rose. "The encryption box?"

Quickly she vanished into her bedroom and then reappeared carrying a small black plastic case. Handing him the case she said, " 'Gamma Yellow' hard wired into the box and your software."

He crammed the box into an inside pocket, signed a receipt she handed to him, and walked to the door. She moved close to him, lifted her face, and circled his neck with her arms. "Dear boy. Dear boy. If only . . ."

He placed a single finger on her lips, silencing her. "Don't say it, Dale. I'll see you again."

"Yes, of course, Darling. I'll see you again."

They both knew they were lying. They held each other tight and kissed with a final urgency known only to lovers at their final parting.

He stepped into the hall, the guard snapped to attention and then followed the young lieutenant to the elevator. He heard the door close softly behind him.

Chapter Ten

The next morning before breakfast, Lieutenant Brent Ross was summoned to Admiral Fujita's cabin. The old sailor was alone and seated in his usual place behind the teakwood desk. He waved Brent to a chair.

Brent stirred with a familiar uneasiness. Seated before Admiral Hiroshi Fujita, the young American felt an abstruse presence permeate the room as if the old man had aged to the point where his physicality was a shadow of life and his essence an inexorable force that could penetrate one's mind, read thoughts, and even predict and perhaps control a man's reactions. It was an eerie, disquieting feeling, and Brent felt foolish at his discomfort. But it was there whenever he was alone with the ancient mariner, and he suspected others had reacted in the same way.

"It is good to have you back on board, Brent-san," the admiral said.

"It is good to be back, Admiral."

Brent expected a subtle reference to "the woman," perhaps some sage observations on the place of women in general. He knew the old man was aware of his close attachment to Dale McIntyre and probably even knew of their torrid affair in New York—he seemed to have eyes and ears everywhere. And something else suddenly jarred the young man: he was certain Fujita knew Dale's explosion in his cabin had been planned, contrived, and executed by a clever, scheming mind. Fujita did not surprise him.

Arching the remnants of a single white eyebrow, the old man said wryly, "Sometimes it is easier to defeat an enemy task force than to cope with the vagaries of the female mind, Brent-san."

Brent smiled at the sly humor. "I know too well, sir. That lesson has been driven home several times."

The admiral tapped the desk and the humor was gone. "Do you feel that any personal problems could interfere with the executions of your duties?"

"Of course not, sir."

Brent was shocked by the bluntness of the Admiral's next words. "I could transfer you—you could be given duty closer to the woman."

The young man came erect, and the line of his jaw hardened. "My duty is here, sir. And I resent the implication that my duty could suffer because of a personal issue."

"You are a man of great strength, Brent-san." He fingered his chin and toyed with the single hair. "We can learn from the Hindus, Brent-san."

"The Hindus?"

The old man stared at the overhead and spoke slowly. "According to the Laws of Manu, the man who guards his speech, his mind, and his body with regard to all living things—the man who bridles his anger and lust shall receive fulfillment and total liberation shall be his." He drummed the desk with his tiny fingers. "Wise words, indeed, gems for the ears of the samurai."

Brent stared at the irascible little man for a moment. He was not surprised by Fujita's reference to the Laws of Manu. They were as old as Jesus and had had a powerful influence on Asian thinking. The foundation for Indian law, they were an immense body of precepts drawn from

275

religion, custom, ethics, and law. It ranged from the origin of the cosmos to the penalties for crime and the rules governing a wife's duties to her husband. All Eastern religions borrowed, exchanged, and sometimes merged beliefs and tenets in their evolutions, yet all converged on a basic philosophy: all things were somehow one. This concept of "the river of life" imbued the Laws of Manu. This was a remarkable contrast to Brent's Christian world of natural law, with its passion for making distinctions based neatly on corresponding macrocosms and microcosms.

Since serving on *Yonaga,* the young American had learned to accept and live with the conflicts and contradictions neatly pigeon-holed in his mind side by side. This ability to live with contradictions was typical of the Asian mind, and the greater the number of contradictions, the stronger the man.

"I can control—I can bridle my emotions, Admiral," he said. "You must be aware of that by now. Must I remind you of my length of service in *Yonaga?*"

"It is settled between you and the woman?"

"It's over."

The old man nodded and there was a contented look on his face. Something else was occupying his mind and he changed direction in his usual fleeting fashion. "Commander Takuya Iwata has requested you serve as a radioman-gunner in one of his Aichi 3DAs. He has heard of your prowess with a Nambu, your kills."

"I would prefer to serve the devil, however, I will accept whatever assignment that will profit *Yonaga* most."

The scabrous flesh cracked with a web of lines that would have conveyed an expression of pleasure on a younger face. "You have the eyes of an eagle, the brain of a scholar, and the heart of a samurai, Brent-san. You have always served me well—as a junior officer on the bridge during combat, as a gunner, even as the executive officer of the old fleet boat *Blackfin*." He tapped the teakwood as his quick mind changed direction. "I know there is bad blood between Commander Iwata and Lieutenant Williams and a challenge to Lieutenant Williams is a challenge to you."

"Iwata is a bigot."

The old man sighed. "He is a good officer. However, you heard my warning to him, I will transfer him if he ever insults Lieutenant Williams again."

Brent smiled. "There may not be enough left of him to transfer."

"Iwata is a samurai, a follower of Mishima, and very patriotic and courageous. He would tell a lion his breath smells bad."

"He could become a quick meal, too."

The old man patted the copy of the *Hagakure* resting on his desk and quoted a familiar passage, " 'If a warrior carries loyalty and filial piety on one shoulder and courage and devotion on the other and carries these burdens twenty-four hours a day until his shoulders wear out, he will be a samurai.' " He stared into Brent's eyes, "Commander Iwata has these qualities, and he was personally recommended by Emperor Akihito."

So that was it. Emperor Akihito, one hundred twenty-fifth in a direct line of descent from the sun goddess Amaterasu-O-Mi-Ka-mi, the only authority Admiral Fujita honored as he had Akihito's father Hirohito, grandfather Yoshihito, and great grandfather Meiji before him. Iwata was on solid footing indeed. Brent turned his lips under and pondered for a moment, his mind on a recent conversation with Yoshi Matsuhara. "Respectfully, sir. According to Bodhidharma, in this world the soul in conjunction with the body performs three kinds of acts — good, indifferent, and evil. Commander Iwata has proved to me he is capable of the second and third. Only the crucible of battle will prove if he is capable of the first."

"You are very wise for one so young, and I am happy to see you have been studying Zen."

Staring at the stern, wrinkled face with its incongruous black eyes, Brent was struck with the respect and genuine affection that glowed there just as incongruously. It gave Brent a queer twinge, almost of conscience, to see the evident pleasure which Fujita experienced at the sight of him. It was odd to know that he was held in such high esteem by this bridge to the past, fearless fighter and legend in his own time. Maybe Yoshi Matsuhara was right. Maybe Brent reminded the old man of his long-incinerated son, Kazuo. But there was more to it than that. Brent had proved himself in battle time and again. This was the most important thing to this relic of the nineteenth century—this walking, breathing personification of the Code of Bushido.

Fujita's voice interrupted his thoughts. "You must remember, my young friend, a samurai is loyal to his *daimyo* but does his utmost to control his own destiny—his time to live, his time to die."

"Of course, sir." Brent tapped his armrest with a set of massive knuckles. He moved back to a troubling thought. "You'll assign me to one of the bombers?" He stabbed a finger at the sky. "Find my place to live or die up there? Yoshi said a man is closer to the gods up there and it's the best place to die."

"Once, after you held yourself responsible for the death of Watertender Azuma Kurosu, you asked my permission to commit *seppuku*. Is that still in your heart?"

"No, sir. But every samurai," he gestured at the *Hagakure*, "knows when there is a choice of either dying or not dying, it is better to die." He raised the fist and shook it. "And as you told me once, sir, before I took off for my mission to Tel Aviv, the very first time I flew as a gunner, 'If you are to die, die facing the enemy.' "

278

The old man reached up and ran a hand over his forehead thoughtfully. "You have learned the laws of bushido well, Brent-san. As usual, you speak with great logic."

"Do I fly?"

"You love to fly, Brent-san." It was a statement, not a question.

"Yes."

The old man tapped the teakwood. "Admiral Whitehead can handle my NIS liaison, and your enlisted personnel are very efficient. I may assign you to an aircraft if we are short of good gunners." He chuckled. "Lieutenant Joji Kai has requested you for the rear cockpit of one of his Nakajima B-5-Ns, too."

Brent reacted to the sudden good humor on the old man's face. "I'm as popular as a homecoming queen." Fujita's laugh surprised him. "You know that one, sir?"

"Of course. Remember, I attended the University of Southern California as a young officer. I knew of those traditions, even watched some students build a great bonfire in a field in West Los Angeles." He shrugged. "I believe the fire was to bolster their spirits, or perhaps, call on their gods to aid them in an athletic contest with some other nearby college."

Brent roared with laughter. "Why do you laugh, Brent-san?"

The young lieutenant stabbed a finger at the admiral. "You and Williams have the same alma mater."

"You mean we are schoolmates?"

"Yes. In a way," Brent said, bringing himself under control. "You're alumni of the same school."

"He is a good captain. That may explain it," Fujita said, expressing himself in one of his rare moments of humor. They both laughed.

A hasty knock interrupted them. Yoshi Matsuhara entered. His face was flushed, and he was obviously in a

279

state of high excitement. Fujita waved him to a chair, but the air group commander stood behind it with both hands on the backrest. Fujita said, "I assumed you were on your way to Tokyo International Airport by now."

"Sir," the pilot said. "I just got word that a new Sakae Forty-Three engine has arrived. Nakajima calls it the *Taifu* (Typhoon.) I have already ordered my crew chief to stand by to install it. With your permission, I will test-fly it within a week." He looked at the American. "Brent-san, this is a 3200-horsepower engine."

"We discussed this new engine before, Yoshi-san," Fujita said. "Must I continue to remind you your fighter was originally designed for a 950-horsepower power plant?"

"But, sir, you know it has been reinforced for the new Model 42 engine."

"Yes, and only 2000-horsepower, Yoshi-san. The monster you describe is 1200-horsepower greater."

"We will do extensive remodeling, sir. As I assured you, we already have plans to further reinforce the engine mounts, and the main wing spar with a new aluminum-titanium alloy beam, rig new control lines and strengthen the control surfaces—even the aileron hinges and wing fillets. The parts were fabricated by Mitsubishi months ago and are in storage at Tokyo International Airport."

Fujita tugged at his single whisker. "How did Nakajima manage to cram so much horsepower into this new engine?"

"The *Taifu* is modeled after the Wright Cyclone R-3350 and has water-methanol injection . . ."

Fujita halted him with a raised hand and again showed his amazing knowledge of the minutest detail of World War II. "That is the engine that powered the Boeing B-29, the Super Fortress. You did not tell me of this before."

Brent and Yoshi exchanged a startled look. "I did not know, sir," Matsuhara said. "I was just informed that Boeing engineers were hired by Nakajima to build it."

The old man drummed the table. "It had two banks of cylinders, eighteen in all. How in the world can you expect to install this monster in the nose of a Zero-sen?"

"Two banks of nine cylinders and they are small and compact. The engine only weighs a hundred kilograms . . ." He looked at Brent, "Two-hundred-twenty-pounds more than my Sakae 42."

Brent was astonished. "How did they cut down in the weight, Yoshi-san?"

"Extensive use of titanium and magnesium. Magnesium is one-third lighter than aluminum."

"It will be nose-heavy," Fujita observed.

"No, sir. We will counterbalance with a heavier fuselage, stronger arresting hook and cable. We will install larger, heavier longerons and formers and replace the wooden stringers with aluminum alloy." His eyes fairly danced with excitement. "And we have new, larger fuselage fuel tanks which will increase my range and with the heavier construction will perfectly compensate for the heavier nose."

"This is a major rebuilding that you intend to complete in only a week?"

"Yes, sir."

"You will need more time."

"We have it. At the most, it will take ten days—perhaps, two weeks."

Fujita turned his thin lips under. He was still not convinced. His narrow eyes were filled with misgivings, and he showed more of his incredible knowledge with his next statement. "I have read that the Cyclone R-3350 had a stubborn tendency to overheat and burst into flames. The engine is too compact, is air cooled, and the air does not circulate and cool well enough. Do you know that in 1943, Boeing's chief test pilot and ten of its flight engineers test-flew a prototype, and they were all killed when the magnesium in an engine ignited and burned completely through a wing spar?"

Yoshi showed his knowledge. "But that was a prototype, sir. The engines were remodeled, and the magnesium crankcases were replaced with those of molded aluminum alloy. And, Admiral, a new turbo fan has been installed to suck in air and cool the engine."

"Does it work?"

"I will test it and let you know, sir."

The old man shook his head. "The torque, Yoshi-san. It must be monstrous. It could kill you."

"We will retrim the aircraft, Admiral, and I will fly with one hand on my trimming wheel." He leaned forward over the chair. "Do I have your permission, sir?"

"You have faith in this engine—the *Tajfu?*"

"Of course, Admiral. I will have the greatest fighter in the sky."

"Or the quickest death."

"My karma is strong, sir." He pointed at the *Hagakure* and mouthed one of the the admiral's favorite passages, " 'The way of the samurai is one of righteous impetuousness, and it is best to dash in headlong with your sword unsheathed. Anything less, and the gods and Buddha will turn their backs,' " His eyes moved to Brent and then back to the admiral and he said, "I will have the greatest sword in the heavens—a sword that can slash through Rosencrance and Vatz in one stroke."

The old man sighed. "Your first test could be your *seppuku*, Yoshi-san."

The aviator waved a hand upward. "Up there, Admiral. Could there be a better way, sir?"

The old man sank back, and his watery eyes wandered over the two men who were dearest to him. "No," he conceded simply. "There is no better way."

There was a knock and Yeoman Nakamura entered. "There is a CIA gentleman to see you, Admiral. His name is Horace Mayfield."

"Show him in."

Brent and Yoshi Matsuhara stood as Horace Mayfield entered. A short man, Horace Mayfield had a sunken chest and walked with slumped shoulders, as if he had been beaten across the back with a board. He was at least twice the age of Brent Ross—a man of about fifty with gray in his brown hair and once-fine features marred by years of heavy drinking. In fact, the evidence was worn like a badge for everyone to see, the little red and purple veins in his nose and cheeks standing out in vivid contrast to his pallor. "I'm Horace Mayfield, CIA," he said in a reedy whiskey-addled voice that bordered on falsetto. Brent found the timbre grating, as if someone were scratching his fingernail across a chalkboard. After placing a briefcase on the floor, Mayfield handed his orders to the admiral, who remained seated.

The admiral introduced Yoshi and Brent. Mayfield eyed Brent from head to toe with a stare that measured. He smiled for the first time, glossy and urbane, and said, "You're the 'American Samurai'?"

Yoshi chuckled. "Our young friend is learning—he's one of the best." Brent smiled at the aviator and nodded his head. Matsuhara had said quite enough. The three men seated themselves while Fujita adjusted his glasses and glanced at the orders. "Permanent liaison," the admiral observed.

"Correct, sir."

The admiral turned to Yoshi Matsuhara, "You can return to your new *Taifu,* if you wish, Commander Matsuhara."

"Thank you, sir. I would like to remain for a few minutes. I have some questions for Mister Mayfield." He gestured to a corner where a table held the communications equipment. "With your permission, I will phone my crew chief, Chief Teruhiko Yoshitomi, and tell him to commence the installation of the new engine immediately." Fujita nodded, and the aviator stepped to the corner, talked into a phone for a few short sentences, and returned.

"You have a report?" Fujita inquired.

Mayfield cleared his throat, removed some documents from his briefcase, and then told them of the Arab forces at Tomonuto, the tanker, *Jabal Nafusa*, loading at Bushehr in the Persian Gulf. He concluded, "Their new carrier, the converted *Essex, Al Kufra*, should make Tomonuto in three days or less."

"Her air groups?"

"Over a hundred aircraft—fighters and bombers."

"ME-109s, JU-87s, and North American AT-6s. Ms. McIntyre reported thirty-six fighters, thirty-three dive bombers and thirty-two torpedo bombers."

"That is correct, Commander Matsuhara. That is our intelligence." The CIA man's hazel eyes wandered over the three other men in the room. Brent noticed the eyes were bloodshot and rheumy like those of a man twenty-years older. Mayfield continued, "Your squadron of Grumman F-6-Fs will arrive within four days. The freighter carrying the fighters and their pilots left Honolulu yesterday."

Yoshi clapped his hands together so hard the slap sounded like the report of a small pistol. "Thank you, Amaterasu," he shouted. Everyone chuckled.

Mayfield continued. "In addition to the American pilots, we have several volunteers." He scanned a report. "Two Frenchmen, a German, a Greek, and a Turk." He looked up at Admiral Fujita. "Good men all who hate terrorism and will fight it anywhere, anytime." Everyone nodded and pleasure was on every face. "Here are their names and résumés of their service records." He handed

284

the admiral the report. Fujita scanned the zeroxed copies. Mayfield gestured at the documents. "I know the language of *Yonaga* is English and these men are all highly proficient in English and experienced fighter pilots." He shifted his eyes to Yoshi Matsuhara. "At least a hundred pilots are in training in the United States and England. But it's a problem to find aircraft suitable for your operations. Has the Seafire been satisfactory?"

"Yes. It is an excellent fighter." The commander rubbed his knuckles together. "I have heard of the Grumman FX-1000. Is it available? Can I test-fly one?"

The CIA man sank back with a sigh. "You know Curtis Wright has developed a new 4500-horsepower engine?" Brent heard Yoshi gasp. Fujita shook his head. Mayfield continued. "They call it the Super-Cyclone. But they're in deep ah . . . deep trouble with it. Too much magnesium. It has a nasty habit of bursting into flames at high rpms. They've lost two test pilots."

Fujita stared hard at Matsuhara, who squirmed and looked at Brent. Fujita said to Mayfield, "Has the program come to a halt?"

The CIA man shook his head. "Negative. Two hundred air frames are completed, and Curtis Wright figures they'll have the problem whipped in a month or two. The navy is converting thirteen carriers to operate the new aircraft."

"Bombers?" Matsuhara asked.

"General Dynamics, Northrop, and Douglas are all involved in building new torpedo and dive bombers. Douglas is the prime contractor, and both aircraft will carry the Douglas name. The dive bomber is called the Douglas 'Snipe,' while the torpedo bomber is called the Douglas 'Shark.' The Snipe is modeled after the old Curtis SB-2C, and the Shark after the Grumman TBF. By the end of this year we hope to have at least two carrier battle groups consisting of three carriers each and escorts at sea."

Matsuhara came half out of his chair. "You can give us some help—take back the Mediterranean from the terrorists?"

Mayfield looked down at the deck. "That could lead to something we all wish to avoid."

"You mean Russian intervention," Fujita said. "A possible nuclear war."

"I'm afraid so, Admiral," Mayfield conceded. "We have managed to maintain a balance of terror for over forty years with our nuclear warheads." He looked around at the skeptical faces. "You must keep in mind, the Russians are keeping apace with us with their own building program. They are building their own new air force around new models of their old Yakavlev Yak-9-U fighter and Ilyushin-2, Stormovik, and Tupolev bombers."

"Stormovik," Fujita said to himself. "The so-called 'Flying Tank.'"

"That's right, Admiral," Mayfield said with a surprised look. "Its vital machinery was actually encased in steel plate."

"An outstanding attack bomber—two 37-millimeter guns, three machine guns, and bombs. Would make an excellent torpedo bomber. Will the Arabs be supplied with these new aircraft?"

"No, Admiral. We have agreed to withhold our new aircraft from our allies . . ."

"You're talking about us," Brent injected.

"Correct, Mister Ross." The voice climbed an octave higher. "And the Russians have promised to do the same with the Arabs. The new Stormovik and Yak fighters will be withheld—used only by their own air force." He tugged at an ear. "You see, in a very strange way, *glasnost* is working. We have made progress at Geneva."

Yoshi slapped his armrest. "And my boys are making

286

progress to their graves."

"That's unfair," Mayfield shot back. "We're sending you all the help we can, short of war. And I will serve with you, take the same risks with you. I will not be 'doing nothing.' "

"We do not need another dead CIA man. We need another carrier, escorts, better aircraft, pilots, fuel." Matsuhara's face twisted into a mask of sarcasm. "Otherwise, we have everything we need."

The veins in the CIA man's nose bulged. He waved at Brent. "You have our men, we send you our entire Alaskan oil production and we maintain a continuous surveillance for you with our nuclear subs."

"That's not enough." The pilot stabbed a finger at Mayfield. "And your death in *Yonaga* would mean nothing, redeem nothing. Death is a constant companion here. The CIA man Frank Dempster had most of his head blown off in the South China Sea, and his death served us nothing except to make a mess of the flag bridge."

Mayfield stared hard at the air group commander. His voice dropped an octave. "Next year, if we can sneak the deal through without those idiots in Congress finding out—next year, we will send you a *Midway*-class carrier—the *Coral Sea*. She's being retired and will be stricken from the lists."

All three officers shouted, *"Banzai!"*

Mayfield stared at Brent in surprise. "It's not a sure thing," he added hastily.

"But you're working on it?" Brent said.

"Yes. We intend to sell it to Taiwan for junk. We have a friendly government there. It would be easy to tow it to Japan."

Fujita said to Mayfield. "But, unfortunately, we operate in the present, not the future or the promises of the future. My force will put to sea within five weeks. You said you will sail with us?"

"Yes, sir." He waved at the documents on the admiral's desk. "You have my orders."

"I would not hold you to them, Mister Mayfield. We may all die. As Commander Matsuhara has already told you, one CIA man has already died in action on *Yonaga*. Mister Dempster was at my side when shrapnel from a 500-kilogram bomb took off most of his head."

The little man set his jaw. "I prefer to sail with you."

Fujita smiled. "Very well." He turned to Brent Ross. "Lieutenant, perhaps Mister Mayfield would like a short tour of our CIC."

"Thank you, sir," Mayfield said.

As the three men rose and turned toward the door they were stopped by Fujita's voice. "Yoshi-san. Be wary of your *Taifu*. They have great power. They can kill, Yoshi-san."

"I know, sir."

As the three men filed toward the door, the phone rang. Brent and Mayfield were halted by Fujita's voice, while Yoshi Matsuhara hurried down the passageway. After a short conversation, Fujita replaced the receiver and said to Brent with an amused smile, "Captain Fite and Lieutenant Reginald Williams have been dismissed from—ah, I mean, they have discharged themselves from sick bay. Mister Williams requests that you meet him in the pilot house. He is waiting there for you now."

"Aye aye, sir." Brent and Mayfield left the room.

Lieutenant Reginald Williams was waiting eagerly for Brent just at the forward end of the passageway. His head was still bandaged, but his eyes were bright and alert. After a quick introduction to Horace Mayfield, Reginald said, "Got full clearance, Brent. *Blackfin*'s in Dry Dock Two with Fite's battered can. Fite's already over there. I wanted to see you before I left." He extended a hand, and his grasp was firm and friendly.

"How about a short tour first, Reggie? Take less than thirty minutes—CIC, hangar deck, and if time permits, the flight deck."

Williams pondered for a moment. "Good idea. I'd like a look at your communications equipment."

Brent led. First the trio passed through the chart house, where a pair of quartermasters were hand correcting charts of the Marianas and the Western Carolines. The men came to attention. Then they entered the radio room—"radio shack" to the men—where old tube sets and modern transistorized receivers sat side by side on the same shelves. "At ease. As you were, men," Brent said repeatedly as enlisted men came to their feet.

But there was applause, bows, and shouts of "Good kills! *Banzai!*" as Brent was recognized instantly and then the black captain of the lethal *Blackfin*. Brent noticed that all the looks thrown Reginald's way were filled with respect, some with awe. Horace Mayfield looked around, drinking it all in and smiling at the warm camaraderie evident on every face.

Brent stopped in front of a bank of receivers and transmitters and spoke to a young cryptologic technician first class who was standing with his earphones pushed to the back of his head as if he expected a conversation with Brent Ross. "New encryption box installed, Hashimoto?" Brent asked.

"Yes, Mister Ross. 'Gamma Yellow' is operable as per your orders."

"Good. Good. Return to your watch." He clapped the technician on the shoulder, and the young Japanese pulled his earphones back over his ears and seated himself.

Following Brent, the trio entered the pilot house. It was a wide compartment with a low overhead. The

289

woodwork was oak, the decks scrubbed teakwood. The entire room was surrounded by six-inch molded armor plate, pierced by a dozen scuttles, glistening with polished brass. The glass was five inches thick and made of layers of armored glass. Under the portholes was the huge wheel served with varnished line, the gyro-repeater, half-hooded with a polished brass cover a magnetic compass which was compared with the repeater hourly when underway, speed across the bottom indicator, speed through the water indicator, four engine rev-counters, and four engine-room telegraphs. On each side, doors led to the wings of the bridge which were swept back elegantly and covered to protect the men stationed here in the cruelest weather.

Two ratings were busy polishing brass. They came to attention, and Brent waved them back to their work. "Jesus Christ," Williams said, looking around. "It's as big as Grauman's Chinese."

Brent laughed and gestured to the rear of the room to a chart table, drafting machine, parallel rules, dividers, and pencils in their usual slots beneath the table. "The navigation area. Admiral Fujita still believes in navigating in the old-fashioned way—estimated position, chronometer and sextant, elevations on stars and planets, sunlines."

"Shades of Christopher Columbus," Mayfield said. "No LORAN."

Brent waved at more equipment, "Radar repeater, RDF (radio direction finder,) radios for ship-to-ship communications. He stabbed a finger at a single radio set apart from the others. "FM-10 and Channel 16."

Mayfield nodded. "International voice radio."

"Right." Brent led his two companions aft through a door into the CIC—a world of dim blue-red light. It was a long narrow room, jammed with electronics equipment and plotting boards. Six men, all of whom were seated and studying scopes or typing into processors, came to their feet, and more warm greetings and congratulations were shouted. In the weird light their skin appeared gray-green, teeth yellow, lips the color of currants, and their veins stood out as dim purplish lines. Brent smiled and waved the men back to their posts. "As you were. As you were."

Working their way toward the back of the compartment, Mayfield looked around in awe. "ECM, radar—the latest stuff. I thought you said the admiral believed in the old-fashioned methods, Mister Ross. He's sure using antique navigation methods."

Brent laughed. "Not when it comes to radar, counter measures, and support measures." He waved. "The enemy has this stuff, too, remember." He stopped in front of a large console where a young American with the scholarly look of a graduate student stood with a wide smile on his face. "Congratulations, Mister Ross," he said warmly.

Brent introduced Electronics Technician Martin Reed to Williams and Mayfield. Reed seated himself while the visitors arranged themselves in a semicircle about the console. "ESM," Mayfield said.

"Correct, sir," Reed said, gesturing at rows of dimly lighted switches above the green scope and more switches and buttons on the overhead. He patted the machine as if he were fondling a mistress. "A real beauty, the best Raytheon has built. It's the SLQ-38. Just got it and I'm checking it out now." He looked up at Williams and Mayfield. "It has both port and starboard antenna assemblies giving us 360-degree azimuth coverage in all bands and instantaneous frequency measurement."

"IFM," Williams said.

"Yes, sir. This little baby can identify electronic transmissions with its own digital processor within thirty-two milliseconds. Can give us the transmitting vessel's name, specs, and captain's name."

"Christ!" Mayfield muttered. "Can it tell you if he's constipated?" Everyone laughed. The CIA man was not finished. "How can this little genie do all of that?"

"By analyzing pulse repetition, type of scan, scan period, and frequency, and then accessing its own 80K threat library, Mister Mayfield." He tapped the scope. "We read out bearings and ranges here on our CRT."

"I'll be damned."

Mayfield looked around and then said to Brent, "You have your radar in full operation in the harbor?"

Brent nodded. "There's a lot of clutter in our surface search, true, but the admiral insists it be manned on all watches. Radar did pick up an attempt to ram us by the freighter *Zilah* out there in the harbor." He pointed to a pair of green scopes. "Air search is efficient here—anywhere." He gestured to the door. "You've got to see the hangar deck. The only thing bigger is the Grand Canyon." Chuckling, the two men followed Brent.

The trio exited the elevator on the cavernous hangar deck. Banks of overhead floodlights bathed the massive area with a glare like high noon. Only a dozen dive bombers were on the deck. Mechanics were swarming over them, installing the new Sakae Forty-Two engine, testing controls, and working in the cockpits. There were shouts, the glare of a welder's torch at the far end, gunfire-like bursts of pneumatic tools, and the sounds of steel-wheeled bowsers being pulled over the steel deck. Heads turned and there were curious stares. Williams stopped in his tracks, staring the length of the vast, 1000-foot compartment, "Jesus, man," he said. "You could damned near stick the Coliseum in here."

Brent gestured to galleries lining the compartment amidships, high above the deck. "Gallery deck. Pilot's ready rooms, briefing rooms, crew chiefs' quarters." He pointed to rows of empty racks bolted to the bulkheads.

"Ready racks for bombs and torpedoes." He pointed down. "They're stored in their magazines below. When we get underway, those racks will be full."

Mayfield stabbed a finger forward to a corner where a large plywood structure had been built. It was very plain and unpainted. Brent answered the unvoiced question, "That's the Shrine of Infinite Salvation. It's a combined Shinto and Hindu shrine. The cremated remains of our honored dead are kept there, if they have no families to claim them. It's often the case with our older crewmen." He pointed to the single doorway crowned by a gilded board. "That's a *torii*, and those flowers painted on both sides are sixteen-petaled chrysanthemums that represent the emperor."

"Religious ceremonies are held there," Mayfield offered.

Brent nodded. "All kinds of special ceremonies." He turned his lower lip under and popped his lips. "I suspect in a day or two you'll both be ordered to attend a special ceremony the admiral is planning."

"For what? I don't . . ." Before Williams could complete his question, he was interrupted by a shout.

"Well," the voice rang out sarcastically. "Our American samurai and his black friend have condescended to pay us a visit."

The men whirled. Brent was surprised to see Commander Takuya Iwata standing in front of a dive bomber that was having a new engine installed. He was dressed in the same green overalls worn by aircrewmen, and he had a large screwdriver in his hand.

Williams bristled. "I don't like your big mouth, man." He gestured at the tool. "Shut it or I'll cram that screwdriver up your ass."

All work stopped, and at least thirty men dropped their tools and followed Iwata as he advanced on the newcomers. He stopped a short distance from Brent Ross and said to Williams, "I have nothing to say to you. Admiral Fujita has prohibited any—ah, exchange between us."

"Don't let that stop you. If you have some hard-on for me . . ." Williams waved at a huge open space between planes. "Let's settle it now. Rank, military codes be damned." He reached for the two gold bars on the collar of his tans. "I can take these off."

Brent stopped Williams. He had seen Japanese display exaggerated bravado many times before; the samurai, eager to prove his mettle to others and to himself, choosing the strongest, the most formidable foe as a testing ground. Brent would never forget how Lieutenant Nobutake Konoye and Commander Shusaku Endo had both challenged him like medieval knights daring an opponent to enter the lists. But these lists could be fatal. Still, it was an archaic drive, a relic of feudal times and the power of bushido that still drove men like Iwata to his own personal "High Noon." Besides, it had been obvious, the man disliked blacks and loathed Brent. The young lieutenant felt a familiar heat begin to brew and seethe deep down inside. "Look, Commander Iwata," he said. "Admiral Fujita said nothing about you and me." He smiled, a flat, hard grimace of a man accustomed to physical violence and on the verge of indulging in more. "If for some reason you feel compelled to prove your manhood," he gestured, "be my guest."

"I can fight my own battles," Williams spat angrily.

"It's not you," Brent said. "It's not your battle."

Iwata agreed. "I do not like you, 'American Samurai.' Your courage is all in your mouth." He waved the long glistening shaft of the screwdriver back and forth in front of Brent. "Someday I will make rope of your guts and choke you with it."

There were shouts of excitement, and the men crowded closer. Brent stared at the stainless steel shaft like a man measuring a cobra. "I thought samurai fought fairly, sought no unfair advantage. Are you afraid of me, oh mighty samurai?

Iwata laughed and stepped closer.

"Drop that screwdriver or give me one," Brent warned, muscles tightening, eyes narrowing, anger clutching and squeezing his guts. He felt his dislike for Commander Takuya Iwata suddenly ripen into hatred, a tangible thing that sat heavily at the base of his throat, tingling in his fingertips and charging his legs and arms with new strength.

Williams shouted at Iwata, "No screwdriver, you bastard." He began to reach for a large pipe wrench on the deck near his feet. "If you don't drop it, I'll beat your brains out with this."

Iwata laughed. "I need nothing but my fists." Casually he flung the heavy screwdriver to the side, and it clattered across the deck. The burly bomber commander squatted low, weight balanced on the balls of his feet, hands low before him and balled into fists. "I will fight you American style. Crudely, with fists." His grin bared sharp yellow teeth. He gestured at the screwdriver, "I would not wish to kill Admiral Fujita's favorite."

"Gee whiz, thanks," Brent mocked. "I was awfully worried. Almost lost sphincter control."

Williams laughed and stood with his arms akimbo. The wrench remained on the deck. Mayfield stared at Brent and Iwata in disbelief. All the others crowded in close for the treat.

Iwata's gleaming eyes wandered over every man. "There is no rank here. Not until this is finished. We are all equal." The men squealed with delight and anticipation of the grand show of watching two officers batter each other.

Mayfield's shocked voice echoed in the cavern. "I can't believe this! You can't be serious. Both of you, stop!

295

This can't be happening." Mayfield's words bounced off the steel bulkheads and the ears of every man with equal effect. Not one man even moved his eyes. The CIA man could only stare with wide eyes and open mouth.

Williams stared silently with the look of a man who had been to this place many times and understood the mad drives that pushed the two antagonists inexorably toward each other and the violence that was now inevitable. Both had crossed the point of no return long ago.

Iwata took two quick paces toward Brent. Brent expected a swing, a barroom approach, but was taken by surprise when the dive bomber commander drove off to the side and kicked left-legged for his genitals.

With lightning-like reflexes, Brent rolled to the side, but he had time only to cross over his leg to protect his crotch. The kick caught him in the upper thigh.

"American style, you son-of-a-bitch," Williams roared, leaping forward. Four burly mechanics grabbed him.

"Back, Reggie," Brent shouted. "I can handle this asshole." But an explosion of white pain had shot up into his groin and numbed his leg all the way to his knee. The momentum of the kick had carried the Japanese to Brent's left side. Driving off his good leg, the American brought up a huge fist in a curving right upper-cut that had all of his 220 pounds behind it. The fist caught Iwata on the side of the head. Gasping at the power of the blow, the commander reeled backward into a group of mechanics. They pushed him back toward his adversary. He took his stance, knees bent, this time balled fists held higher.

This time the barroom brawler Brent expected came on. Big fists lashed out in a barrage, and Brent retreated, ignoring the pain in his leg and taking the blows on his arms or allowing the fists to slide off his shoulders. One big fist glanced off his shoulder, impacting the side of his head. It felt as though someone had slammed a door behind Brent's eyes and his vision narrowed suddenly, rockets flashing across his retinas. Another blow caught him on the jaw, and suddenly his mouth was filled with the salty, metallic taste of blood. A stream of blood shot out of the side of his mouth. Still he gave ground, ducking, weaving, waiting.

Iwata misread his retreating opponent. Scenting victory and shouting triumphantly, Iwata charged like a corrida bull smelling blood. It was a mistake. He was momentarily careless and gave Brent the opening he had been waiting for. Coming off his heels, Brent caught the big Japanese with a three-punch combination that smashed into the man's face. Blood, spittle, enamel, and mucus sprayed. The bomber commander stopped like he had hit a stone wall. His mouth looked as though he had chewed a mouthful of black cherries, the jagged stumps of broken teeth bright red.

Iwata tried to kick, but all he accomplished was to open his body to terrible punishment. At least four punches crashed into his ribs and solar plexus. Staggering back, he gasped like the victim of an executioner's garotte, blood streaming down his chin and onto his overalls. However, his fists were up. He would not quit.

Williams yelled, "Kill the son-of-a-bitch!"

Mayfield screamed, "Stop! Stop!"

But Brent had caught the scent of blood. An unbridled rage seized him with startling ferocity as though a beast had pounced on his back and was goading him with its claws. The beast growled but he recognized his own voice. Civilization had vanished, replaced by a bestial drive to destroy, obliterate his enemy.

Iwata was superbly conditioned, recovered fast. He came on with remarkable tenacity, jabbing, punching, punishing Brent to the body, and further cutting Brent's mouth. A fist caught him high on the cheekbone; the crack of it seemed to explode in the dome of his skull.

He gave ground, feeling a tickling warmth on his lower lip and blood pooled in his mouth. He spat it out like a stream of cherry juice. Another wild blow caught him on the jaw, jerking his head so that his teeth clashed. Pain shot down his neck and Brent could feel his tongue bleeding where it had smashed against his teeth. All attempts at finesse and clever boxing had long gone by the boards. He drove into the barrage, counterpunching straight on with short powerful jabs. Suddenly changing pace and shifting his balance to his right, he looped a left from the balls of his feet, feeling the solid shock of the aviator's jawbone under his fist. Then a shift back and a right bludgeoned Iwata's face squarely, the gristle in the flat nose giving way with a pop that could be heard by everyone. Iwata staggered back, and Brent caught him with a another ferocious punch to the point of his jaw.

The Japanese staggered, knees giving like reeds overweight with rain, trying feebly to shake the blackness from his head and the blood from his eyes. His fists were still bunched but too heavy to lift above his waist. His chest heaved for air, he swayed, trying to catch his balance, but only managing to stagger. He grabbed Brent and then stumbled over the screwdriver. Both men tumbled to the deck, locked in a close embrace like two maddened lovers. They rolled, punched, spat into each other's faces. The men followed them, cheering, screaming feverishly. Brent locked one of Iwata's arms onto the deck with his body and then began to punch him with a single fist. Every punch was good, thudding into the pilot's eyes, the already flattened nose, mouth, jaw. Blood, spittle, mucus, and bits of broken teeth sprayed.

"Stop! Stop!" rang in the distance. This time Williams' voice joined Mayfield's.

Nothing could stop Brent. The beast hungered for the jugular—the kill. He grunted, growled, spat incoherently, blood and saliva streaming down his chin. Finally a dozen strong hands grabbed him, pulled him off, and dragged him to his feet.

Iwata remained on his back, bleeding from the mouth, nose, and both ears. His eyes were swollen shut and puffed up as if someone had inflated them, lips like swollen red sausages.

"Let me finish it, god damn it," Brent screamed, bloody froth running off his chin.

"Jesus man! Jesus," Williams said. "No more. No more. Enough!"

Mayfield could only repeat, "My God. My God. Animals. Animals . . ."

Brent tried to lunge back at his opponent, but strong hands pulled him away and led him to the elevator.

The killing lust had not completely faded as Brent stood before the admiral's desk, flanked by Mayfield and Williams. The old sailor was busy talking on the phone. Finally, he cradled it and looked up. "Commander Takuya Iwata is in the sick bay. Chief Hospital Eiichi Horikoshi reports the commander sustained a broken nose, cracked cheekbone, numerous cuts and contusions to the mouth, ears, hands, ears, and possibly three broken ribs." The old man shrugged. "When will this end, Lieutenant Ross?"

"That's unfair," Williams said, sharply, his anger overwhelming his respect for rank. "Iwata goaded Brent—forced him into a fight. Kicked him."

"That's right," Mayfield agreed. "I saw it, too, Admiral."

Fujita silenced the pair with two raised palms. "That is not the point. I am not interested in placing blame." Mayfield and Williams looked at each other in wonder. The admiral continued, "Mister Mayfield, you are dismissed—you have much to learn of *Yonaga's* communications department." He moved his eyes to Reginald Williams. "I know you are anxious to return to your boat. Both of you are dismissed to your duties."

"But, sir . . ."

"I said you are dismissed, Mister Williams!"

"Aye, aye, sir." Williams patted Brent on the back and followed Mayfield out of the door.

Admiral Fujita indicated a chair and Brent sank into it slowly, sore muscles stiffening and objecting to the new position. As he sank back, the aches diminished. The old man gestured, "You look as if you need some of Chief Horikoshi's ministrations."

Brent rubbed his sore jaw with a delicate touch. "No, sir. A few bruises." He patted his chin. "A few cuts inside my mouth. Nothing serious, sir."

"I am not angry because of the fight."

"I know that, Admiral."

"But you lost control of yourself again. It has happened before. You killed a man and blinded another in an alley in Tokyo when you first reported. You were with that Israeli woman—ah . . ."

"Sarah Aranson, sir. Terrorists. They ambushed us."

"You did the same thing in Hawaii."

"Another assassin, sir."

"I know. But that is not the point." He knotted the little knobby fists and tapped his knuckles together. "It is your temper—you lose control . . ."

"Become an animal?"

"Precisely." The little fists stopped their warfare and dropped to the table. "I knew your father well."

"I know."

"You have the same lack of control your father had."

"We've discussed this before, sir."

"I know," Fujita said, waving a hand impatiently. "But your father's temper and rage turned against him—led

300

him to his destruction. A terrible waste."

"A good samurai is ready for death, delivers it to himself with his own hand if disgrace or defeat is imminent."

"It is not necessary to quote the *Hagakure* to me." The black eyes flashed. "You are a valued assistant, and so is Commander Iwata. This madness that seizes you can lead to your destruction." He waved. "Or the loss of a valuable officer. You wanted to kill Commander Iwata."

"True, sir." He looked at the bulkhead above the little admiral's head. "But he was no longer Commander Iwata." He sighed. "They all become the same. They all become animals, creatures to be obliterated. Plagues, pestilence . . ." He looked straight into the admiral's eyes. "Can't you understand, sir?

The old man tugged on his chin and stared back with an unwavering stare. "In battle this killing frenzy can be an asset. But when it cannot be controlled, when it is turned on a valued member of my staff, I cannot understand or condone."

"You wish my resignation?"

"No. I want control." He leaned forward. "You are one of the most valued members of my staff. You know I do not object to clashes even between members of my crew. But you must choose the correct place and time."

"Respectfully, Sir. I did not choose the time or place this time. Commander Iwata made the decision. He insulted me, approached me, degraded my honor." He pounded his armrest. "This is unacceptable to a samurai."

"True. You know I would never disagree with that. But this time, you should have tried, should have reported the incident to me."

"I'm sorry, Sir. I find that prospect repugnant."

Brent expected the old man to bridle with anger. Instead, he sat back almost in resignation. "Then this is my decision—if there is a repetition, I will transfer both of

301

you. After we deal with the Arabs, you can kill each other and I will be happy to witness the proceedings."

Brent ran his tongue over his sore lips. "I understand, Sir."

The old man tapped the desk thoughtfully. "Do you remember when we discussed the Laws of Manu this morning?"

"Why, of course." The American smiled. " 'The man who bridles his lust and his anger shall achieve fulfillment. Total liberation is his.' "

The old man smiled and nodded his head like a pleased schoolmaster. "Correct, Brent-san. Your mind is like one of those new recording devices."

Brent chuckled for the first time. "Thank you, Admiral. But I flunked the course."

"This 'flunk'?"

"Sorry, sir. I meant 'failed.' "

The old man shrugged his shoulders in a noncommittal gesture. "But your quote is correct, Brent-san. Manu also taught that that which proceeds from a man's soul shall shape his soul, that which proceeds from his speech shall shape his speech, and deeds that proceed from his body shall shape his body."

"Then there is no hope for Brent Ross."

"On the contrary, Brent-san. You shape yourself very well into these laws."

"Except for the last."

"Yes. The last."

Brent sighed and stared at the stern old face. "Then I shall carefully monitor the deeds that proceed from my body, Admiral."

The old man nodded and his eyes stared back into Brent's like beams from the sun. "I know you will, Brent-san."

Chapter Eleven

The following weeks were filled with frantic activity. At the end of the first week Captain John "Slugger" Fite was overjoyed when two completely rebuilt *Fletchers* arrived from the Philippines. Now he had eight first-class destroyers and the men to man them. Immediately new crews were assigned and rigorous training procedures began. The frigate *Ayase* and destroyer *Yamagiri* steamed out of the bay to take their stations as radar pickets: *Ayase* to a patrol three hundred miles southeast of Iwo Jima, *Yamagiri* taking station four hundred miles almost directly east of Tokyo Bay. Reports and sightings by the two pickets and a dozen land-based stations were fed into *Yonaga*'s computers continuously. However, no enemy planes were detected by any of the searches except for *Ayase*. The frigate reported numerous long-range contacts with unidentified aircraft apparently operating out of Saipan and Tinian. These appeared to be search aircraft maintaining well-defined patrol areas. Only one visual sighting was made: a high-flying DC-6 far to the west. Maritime Defense Force PBMs and PBYs maintained continuous patrols but avoided overflying the Marianas, where they would be easy meat for enemy fighters.

Word of Brent's fight with Commander Takuya Iwata had spread throughout the ship with the speed of a brushfire. Crewmen bowed deeper, saluted with more panache, and even smiled when the American passed. Iwata's injuries were painful, but he insisted that he be dismissed from the sick bay within two days despite three cracked ribs. He reported immediately to the airfield where his dive bomber squadrons were training. Brent did not miss the arrogant commander.

The first days of the second week found Commander Yoshi Matsuhara happily welcoming the twelve American Grumman F6F Hellcats and their pilots. Also, two new Seafires were delivered to Tokyo International Airport. Because of the rigorous training procedures, the American pilots were billeted at the airport. However, Brent did meet the squadron commander, Commander Conrad Crellin, who reported aboard during a Communications Department meeting with Admiral Fujita. Very young for a commander, Crellin, a thin fair man, was soft-spoken and had the demeanor one would expect from an engineer or scientist, not the leader of a fighter squadron. The two Frenchmen, the German, and the Greek also reported aboard. The Turkish pilot had been murdered by Sabbah in New York City. The four foreign pilots were billeted at the airport with most of the other aviators and Brent did not have an opportunity to become acquainted with them.

On Thursday of the second week, the American submarine *Dallas* reported the entire Arab task force of carriers *Al Kufra* and *Ramli al Kabir,* cruisers *Babur* and *Umar Farooz,* and six escorts were anchored at Tomonuto. Then, *Dallas* was pulled from her station by the United States Navy and sent to the Mediterranean. Fujita's anger was unbounded. In a fit of rage, he called all the demons in hell down upon the "brass heads" in the Pentagon.

The repairs on the damaged *Gearings* at Surabaya were reported as nearing completion on two of the damaged destroyers. The third was still in dry dock, having new hull plates welded into place. Most ominously, the great 100,000-ton tanker *Jabal Nafusa* had departed Bushehr with two escorts and was reported already in the Gulf of Oman on a southeasterly heading. Repairs on *Blackfin* were rushed and Brent saw very little of Lieutenant Reginald Williams. If *Blackfin* were to make a successful attack on the tanker off Tomonuto, she would be forced to get underway within a week.

New 25-millimeter and five-inch gun barrels arrived and Gunnery Officer Nobomitsu Atsumi personally supervised the replacements. Radar was calibrated, directors checked and rechecked, and gun crews drilled by tracking *Yonaga*'s own aircraft as they flew overhead.

Every day formations of Aichi D3A dive bombers, Nakajima B5N torpedo bombers, and Mitsubishi Zero-sens streamed over Tokyo Bay in tight formations. Daily the number grew as Mitsubishi, Nakajima, and Aichi hurried the delivery of replacement aircraft. The day twelve magnificent Grumman F6F Hellcats roared overhead, a great throaty cheer came from crewmen waving from *Yonaga*'s weather decks. Others rushed up from below to catch a glimpse of the graceful American fighters making a low pass around the bay. Brent thought he would burst with pride.

Often Brent thrilled when he saw the Mitsubishi with the red cowling and green hood flash over with the two Seafires close aboard its elevators. He knew his friend Yoshi Matsuhara and the two Englishmen were up there. It gave him a feeling of pride and confidence. Yoshi's plane had changed. The cowling was longer and a trifle wider than before. Then, Brent realized Yoshi was flying with the new Sakae 43 *Taifu* 3200-horsepower engine. He saw nothing dramatically different in the performance of the fighter until one day the "three" swooped low over *Yonaga* and then Yoshi pulled up sharply into a vertical climb. There was a roar like thunder reverberating in a canyon and the Zero shot straight up like a space shuttle launch Brent had seen as a youth at Cape Canaveral. The Mitsubishi outstripped the Seafires as if they had suddenly been turned to lead. It was a breathtaking exhibition of power; but it looked dangerous, as if the aircraft had really been pushed beyond its design limitations. However, the Zero disappeared into a cloud still in one piece.

Brent renewed his friendship with Rear Admiral Byron Whitehead and found the man's company pleasant and stimulating. Whitehead's mind was clear and incisive, and he picked up new information and procedures very quickly. He had heard of Brent's fight with Iwata and cautioned him about his temper. In fact, he made the same comment Brent had heard from Admiral Fujita: "Just like your father, Brent. You've got to keep it under control."

"I know, sir. I know," Brent had answered.

The CIA man Horace Mayfield spent most of his time ashore either at the American Embassy or with Colonel Bernstein at the Israeli Embassy and, Brent guessed, in bars. Brent enjoyed Bernstein's company, but did not miss Mayfield. Mayfield had eyed him suspiciously—almost fearfully—since the fight in the hangar deck. Brent knew the man regarded him as a volatile hothead who could explode at any instant.

At the end of the third week, Admiral Fujita called for a "special ceremony." All officers not on duty were requested to appear in the Shrine of Infinite Salvation with white gloves and swords. Brent had expected the special ceremony weeks earlier and had been wondering at the delay.

At 1000 hours, Brent stood rigid with perhaps eighty other officers in the close quarters of the shrine. His big hands were sheathed in white gloves, the fabled Konoye sword hung at his side. The large number of officers standing in ranks made the large space seem smaller. Although it was a place of worship, there were no pews, chairs, or even benches. Everyone stood. Admiral Fujita and his senior officers occupied a space close to a raised platform in the center of the room. It was covered with a white satin-like material.

Against the far bulkhead, which was the starboard side of the ship, was an altar with a large golden "Buddha from Three Thousand Worlds" which had been a gift from the temple at Kanagawa, a carved rosewood talisman of the "Eight Myriads of Deities," and a golden *tora* (tiger), the animal exalted by the Japanese because it wanders far, makes its kill, and always returns home. The altar was cluttered with a variety of other talismans and icons of minor gods sacred to the Japanese.

Stretching to both sides of the altar, long shelves held white boxes covered with ideograms. Here rested the ashes of *Yonaga*'s honored dead and the real reason for the existence of the shrine.

Reginald Williams, Byron Whitehead, and Horace Mayfield arrived late. Williams was anxious because his boat was to put to sea the next day, Whitehead and Mayfield breathless after rushing ashore in the early hours to the American Embassy and returning just in time for the ceremony. Brent had kept his suspicions to himself, and no one was certain what was about to transpire except Fujita and his executive officer, Captain Mitake Arai. But the formal dress was a tipoff to Brent; he expected the worst or, in the Japanese mind, the best. He suspected blood would be spilled.

Byron Whitehead took a place on one side of Brent, and Mayfield stood on the other with Williams at his side. Captain Colin Willard-Smith and Pilot Officer Elwyn York crowded into a place next to Reginald Williams. Willard-Smith considered the submarine commander his saviour and always sought him out.

Then the Israeli, Colonel Irving Bernstein, entered. He was strangely garbed. A linen *yarmulke* capped his head, and his arms were wrapped with strange thongs and a fringed prayer shawl hung to his waist. He was holding an open Book of Psalms and was muttering to himself without glancing at the book. He took a place directly behind Brent. Brent, Mayfield, Williams, the Englishmen, and Whitehead all turned and looked at the Jew curiously. He seemed not to see them, obsessed by his chant, which became audible to all, "O Israel, the Lord our God, the Lord is One. And thou shalt love the Lord thy God with all thy heart . . ."

He stopped, as if suddenly aware of the stares, and closed the prayer book. He indicated the wrapped thongs. "These cords are called phylacteries, and I have wound them so that they form the letter *Shin* of the word *shaddai*—ancient Hebrew for God."

"But the shawl, the skullcap—and you were praying," Williams noted.

The Jew's eyes peered unblinking into the black man's eyes. "I am here to pray for the dead."

Williams waved at the white boxes. "Honor them?"

Bernstein shook his head. "No. You shall see . . ."

Before he could explain, Fujita's voice filled the enclosure and all noises of work in the hangar deck ceased as if by an invisible command. "We are here," the admiral said, "to perform a final honor for our defeated enemies."

Now Brent knew, and Bernstein resumed his prayers.

The admiral gestured to the door, and an ensign opened it. Captain Conrad Schachter was pulled into the room by a pair of young, strong seaman guards. He was dressed in white, and his hands were bound behind him. The German's beady eyes quickly surveyed the scene, finally fixing on the platform. He stopped, his great weight holding even the guards back, and his usual blustering bravado was suddenly transfixed by fear. *"Nein! Nein!"*

"What the hell's going on?" Williams whispered.

"I say, what's what?" Willard-Smith asked, softly.

Before Brent could answer, a gesture from Fujita made the purpose of the ceremony clear. Two seamen placed a large block on the edge of the platform while a third placed a basket on the deck directly beneath it. Commander Takuya Iwata stepped from the ranks and mounted the platform. He pulled his sword from its scabbard with the ring like a struck chime.

"Nein Gott. Nein!" The German was dragged forward.

"No!" Whitehead said. "You can't."

"I'll be buggered," Elwyn York muttered. "They're gunna cut off 'is blinkin' 'ead." He turned to the admiral. "Bully for you!"

Mayfield and Whitehead clamored at the admiral. "This is barbaric! You can't do this. There are international laws."

Fujita raised his hands. "Please do not try to impose your Christian-Judaic probities upon me and my command. They are fit for women playing children's games, but not for the samurai. *"Banzai!"* rang through the huge hangar deck. Fujita stared at the group of foreigners. "If any of you lacks the stomach to witness the application of a just act of war, please leave."

Mayfield made a start toward the door, stopped, and returned to his place. "I remain only to witness this savagery and then make a report of it to my superiors."

Fujita waved a hand as if he were warding off an annoying insect. "Follow your own conscience, Mr. Mayfield. I care not if you report this action to your president — your supreme being."

Sobbing, Schachter was dragged to the platform. Two more seaman guards were required to pull the big man up the three stairs.

"Is there anything you wish to say before you exit this existence?" Fujita asked.

The pilot looked around the room, finally fixing his eyes on Colonel Irving Bernstein, who was staring up at the overhead and chanting. *"Juden!"* Schachter shouted. "You pray for me?"

Bernstein's brown eyes found the platform. "I pray for the soul of man."

"You get your revenge, *Juden?"*

Bernstein ran his hands over the prayer book. "You have served Baal and Moloch. The Law of Moses says you must pay with your immortal soul. I will pray to God for you."

The German suddenly drew himself up as if his hatred for the Jew had uncovered another tiny wellspring of courage. "This *Gott,"* he shouted. "This *Gott* of yours does not exist. Where was he when the Jews of Poland dug their own graves? Where was he when we used the skulls of Jewish children in soccer matches? Where was he at Auschwitz? Treblinka? Buchenwald? If he did exist, he kept silent. He is as much a murderer as all of us — as Adolph Hitler." He sneered. "So you are the 'chosen.' Ha! Chosen for what?"

Bernstein stuffed the Book of Psalms into his pocket. Piety dropped from his face like a wax mask in a fire. "Chosen to outlive you, Nazi pig."

"Nein! Gott! Gott!" Schachter shouted as the guards pulled him to the block. Then his head was pulled down and a line looped over his neck and secured to the deck while his feet were shackled. Another line was pulled around his shoulders and tied down hard. Fujita nodded. Iwata raised the big two-handed killing blade and held it poised high over his right shoulder in the classic pose of the samurai about to strike. A silence as heavy as thick oil poured through the room. Not even a breath could be

310

heard, not even the usual ship sounds of engines and blowers.

Bernstein sighed and resumed praying softly to himself. The German began to scream and howl at the top of his lungs, the sounds reverberating through the compartment with all the horror of gutted creation. The great sword flashed in a silver semicircle, humming as its great speed parted the air like a missile. There was the sound of steel cleaving meat. The screaming stopped, and Schachter's head dropped neatly into the basket. There were the usual involuntary jerks of arms and legs and then he was still, his severed jugulars hosing streams of blood onto the deck. Quickly, the body and head were removed and four seamen with swabs cleaned up the blood. Iwata wiped his blade clean and stood in a corner of the platform, gripping his side.

"My God. My God," Mayfield said. "What are we witnessing?"

"Not a bit sporting, but fit," Willard-Smith commented.

"Served the bugger right," York said, grinning.

Whitehead turned to Brent. "You knew this was going to happen."

"Yes."

"Why didn't you try to stop it?"

Brent stared at the rear admiral long and hard. "Why? The son-of-a-bitch had it coming."

Whitehead looked at Mayfield. "I can't believe this." The CIA man nodded agreement.

There was a commotion at the door, and the Arab Sergeant Haj Abn al Sahdi was dragged in. His hands, too, were bound behind him, and he was dressed in white. He saw the platform, the blood, the man with the sword, and began to shout "No! No!" He twisted, planting his feet in futile efforts to resist the power of the two seaman guards pulling him to the platform. Once on the platform, the two guards held the whimpering Arab erect.

"A last statement before you join Allah?" Fujita asked.

"A rug."

Fujita motioned and a rating unrolled a small tatami mat on the platform.

"That is not a rug," the Arab said, with sudden composure that shocked everyone.

"It will do."

"Which way is Mecca, Effendi?"

Fujita pointed to the east. Abu al Sahdi dropped to his knees and prostrated himself. He prayed in a loud voice: "Allah Akbar! Glory to Allah, full of grace and mercy. He created all, including man. To man he gave a special place in His creation. He honored man . . ."

"Enough!" Fujita shouted. "We do not have the time to hear you recite all one hundred fourteen suras (chapters) of the Koran—all ninety-nine names for Allah. One verse is enough." He waved at the guards, "Proceed with your duties." The guards pulled the Arab to the block.

"Go fuck a dead camel!" the doomed man yelled at the entire assemblage in a final show of defiance. Then he saw Bernstein, who was again praying. The Arab began to scream as he was pushed down and lashed to the block. "The Japanese and the Jews are the enemies of Allah and humanity. You are scum—all of you! Israel and Japan will be destroyed!" He began to blubber incoherently as his head was secured.

Fujita gestured at Iwata, who was leaning on his sword with one hand and holding his ribs with the other. Now Brent knew why the ceremony had been delayed. Iwata's ribs had been too sore for earlier executions and, apparently, Fujita had promised him the honor of being the executioner.

Iwata spoke to the admiral with a pained look on his face. "Admiral," he said grimacing and holding his side.

312

"My ribs. The swing damaged something."

"Do you wish a replacement?" Scores of eager eyes turned to the admiral.

Iwata breathed haltingly and in obvious pain. "Yes, sir. I deeply regret this request. I am remiss . . ."

"Nonsense. You have performed a most strenuous and demanding duty." He looked around at the eager faces.

Before the admiral could speak, Iwata said, "May I suggest my own replacement?" The admiral looked up questioningly. Iwata moved his eyes to Brent Ross. Brent felt his spine become as rigid as steel, his stomach churn. He knew what was coming.

A sneer twisted the bomber commander's face into an ugly mask. "Let the man who damaged my ribs replace me." He gestured at the prostrate Abu al Sahdi, who was blubbering in a kind of madness of fear. He had soiled himself, a common occurrence with those about to be executed. The Arab began to howl like a mortally injured animal caught in a steel trap.

"Gag him!" Fujita shouted. A seaman guard stuffed a rag into the Arab's mouth and bound it behind his head.

Iwata pointed at Brent Ross. "Let the 'American samurai' dispatch this filth," he taunted.

"I say," Willard-Smith said.

"No!" Mayfield and Whitehead chorused.

"I refuse," Brent said.

"Has your courage escaped you?" Iwata waved. "Like a wisp of smoke in a gale?"

"I need not prove my courage or any other quality to you, Commander." Then Brent did his own taunting, "That was done on the hangar deck."

"Lieutenant Ross," Fujita said. "You have been offered an honor."

"I know, sir. I performed this honorable duty with this sword years ago on Lieutenant Konoye." He patted the Konoye sword.

313

"You were a fine *kaishaku* (second and decapitator) at Lieutenant Konoye's seppuku. You earned the sword with great honor. You have great strength, can perform this duty with the one final stroke better than any man in this shrine."

"This is insane," Whitehead exclaimed.

Brent spoke to Admiral Fujita, "Is this an order?"

"No. A request."

Brent sighed, fingering the hilt of the sword. He had beheaded two men; Lieutenant Nobutake Konoye in this room in 1985, and Lieutenant Yoshiro Takii, his frightfully burned pilot, at Takii's request in the sick bay three years later. He had accepted the Konoye sword by right of *kaishaku* but refused the Takii killing blade. In the eyes of the Japanese, his performance in both cases had been incredible, the one swift stroke more powerful than any of them had ever seen. In fact, his blow to Takii's neck had slashed all the way through the mattress of the burned pilot's hospital bed and into the wooden frame itself.

"Don't do it, Brent," Whitehead said.

"Chop the bloody bastard, guv'nor," Elwyn York said. "If you ain't, give me the bloody shiv. I'll do 'im good."

"That's contemptible," Mayfield said.

"Up your arse with two hot stuffs, your nibs," the Cockney scoffed.

Brent looked around. Fujita, Arai, Katsube, Iwata, Yoshida, Atsumi, Kai, Matsuhara—all stared at him expectantly. All the other officers, too, had turned toward him. He felt a strange upwelling of pleasure in the warmth of respect, even admiration, in every eye. He belonged here, was part of *Yonaga,* part of the bushido tradition and belonged to these samurai irrevocably. He could not disappoint them and perhaps cast dishonor upon himself by refusing a task that, despite Fujita's opinion, was onerous and would leave him drained and depressed for days. He stepped forward.

"Banzai! Tenno heiko banzai!" bounded from the bulkheads, to the walls, to the overhead, and reverberated the length of the hangar deck.

Slowly, like a man in a trance, Brent mounted the stairs and stopped next to the doomed man. Abu al Sahdi had vomited into his gag and was choking on his own vomit. His face was purple, and the veins in his forehead and neck bulged as if they were ready to burst through the skin. "Remove the gag." Fujita ordered. "He will be dead before we kill him."

A seaman guard pulled the binding from the Arab's mouth. Commander Takuya Iwata did not leave the platform. Instead he sheathed his sword and took a position in a far corner. There was an expectant, satisfied expression on his face.

Brent took a position to the left side of the doomed man. The Arab was muttering, a garbled string of sobs, oaths, and prayers run-in together in a blend of incoherence. Through the blubbering, Brent could discern, "Allah Akbar," over and over again.

Gripping the silver-fitted *tang,* he pulled the three-foot sword from its jeweled scabbard. Strangely, the sword rang from its home with little effort from the young American, fairly leaping out of its lair as if it were eager to fulfill its destiny. Crafted in the fifteenth century by the master swordsmith Yasumitsu, it was fashioned of layered and tempered metal, folded and drawn eleven times, finely wrought as a polished diamond, and as sharp and spare as a Kano Eitoku painting. Slowly, Brent raised the blade over his right shoulder. He gripped down tight on the *tang* with both hands.

The silence of death filled the room. Only the Arab's sobs and mutterings could be heard. It seemed to Brent the whole world was holding its breath. He stared down at Abu al Sahdi's neck. It was very dark from the sun or

315

dirt. Perhaps both. Three vertebrae stood out like little knobs of wood. His aiming point was between two of them.

He felt an involuntary charge of strength flow into his muscles, and his mouth was suddenly filled with saliva. With all his strength he whipped the blade up and down in a vicious arc. The blade cut the air with a soughing sound, the kind of sound a woman might make in the height of sexual pleasure. The impact hardly slowed the blade and the fine steel slashed through flesh and bone almost as cleanly as slashing thin slivers of bamboo.

The blubbering stopped and the severed head dropped neatly into the basket. But the blood spurted, pooling immediately on the deck. The Arab's body twitched and jerked a few times and then fell still.

Breathing hard, Brent came erect, bloody sword at his side. *"Banzai! Banzai!"* rolled through the room like peals of thunder. A guard handed Brent a towel, and the lieutenant wiped the blade clean.

Iwata stepped very close and spoke into his ear. "You will be my gunner, Mister Ross."

Brent stared into the flat, immobile face. Hostility still lived there, but something new had come to life in the depths of the black eyes. Brent caught a glimmer of respect. The young American nodded, sheathed the sword, and left the platform.

Chapter Twelve

The day *Yonaga* and her escorts stood out of Tokyo
Bay was blustery and ominous. With Captain Fite's *DD-
1* leading, two destroyers to port, two to starboard and
two more scouting far ahead, the task force slowly exited
Uraga Straits into the rising Pacific swell. Fortresses of
dark clouds banked the entire northeastern horizon in
solid phalanxes of dark grays, outriders of line squalls
advancing in a row ahead of the thunderheads, dense
dun-colored curtains of rain slanting beneath them. A
storm was moving down from the north and the sea was
restless, the scend of the rollers charging unimpeded
across the limitless wasteland. Overhead, thin clouds the
color of sow's bellies scurried before the wind like frightened sheep. The early morning sun had fought a losing
battle with the clouds, its rays streaming feebly overhead,
only able to tint some of the thin clouds with weak
shades of pink and scarlet like dried blood.

Standing on the flag bridge with Admiral Fujita, the
executive officer, Commander Mitake Arai, who was also
the navigator, Rear Admiral Whitehead, the talker Seaman Naoyuki, and a half-dozen lookouts, Brent Ross
gripped the windscreen as the great carrier finally cleared
the channel and began to feel the power of the North
Pacific swell. Admiral Fujita spoke to his talker, Seaman
Naoyuki, "Secure the special sea detail, set the starboard

steaming watch, Condition Two of readiness."

Naoyuki spoke into his headpiece, and the commands could be heard carrying through every speaker on the ship. Half of the ship's armament would be manned. Brent could see green-clad and helmeted gunners tumbling into their tubs and manning their weapons in the galleries that lined both sides of the ship and the foretop above his head. There were shouts, the sound of steel on steel as breeches received their rounds and sixteen five-inch guns and thirty-one triple mounts were cranked skyward. No doubt the Arabs knew the force was standing out. Moving Yonaga was like moving Fujisan: it was impossible to conceal, and everyone knew spying eyes lined the shore. Fujita would take no chances.

"Starboard steaming watch set, the ship is at Condition Two of readiness, sir" Naoyuki reported.

"Very well."

Captain Mitake Arai hunched over a small covered chart table while a short, middle-aged quartermaster, Quartermaster First Class Kinichi Kunitomi, stared through the gunsight of a bearing circle mounted on a gyro repeater. Quickly, he took tangents on points of land. "Nojima Zaki two-seven-zero, Irō Zaki zero-five-five, south tangent Ō Shima one-one-zero," the quartermaster announced.

"Very well. Very well," Arai repeated, parallel rules clattering, pencil moving over the chart. He turned to Admiral Fujita, "Suggest we change course to two-one-zero, sir."

"Very well." The old man turned to Talker Naoyuki. "Signal bridge make the hoist, 'Execute to follow, course two-one-zero, speed sixteen.' " The talker spoke into his mouthpiece, and in a few seconds flags and pennants were ironed out flat in the strong wind at the halyards.

Brent chuckled to himself. Not one bearing had been verified by radar. Fujita and Arai knew the channel so

318

well, had made the transit so often, and were so confident of their old piloting procedures, neither man called on radar unless there was heavy fog. And Fujita was observing radio silence. Not one transmission would be made until the enemy was engaged.

They all heard the call from the foretop before the talker reported it. "All escorts answer!"

"Execute!" Fujita shouted at the talker. *Yonaga*'s flags and pennants were whipped down. After the signal bridge reported, "All escorts have executed hoists," Fujita said into a voice tube, "Right standard rudder. Steady up on two-one-zero, speed sixteen."

The command was repeated by the men in the pilot house, and the ship swung to the right. Brent could feel the tempo of the engines pick up through the soles of his shoes, and the roll and pitch changed as the big swells began to take her on the port bow. "Steady on two-one-zero, sir. Speed sixteen, eighty-three revolutions, sir."

"Very well."

Now the bow of the great carrier was pointed into the open sea. The force of the seas grew, and *Yonaga* lifted her bows grudgingly, the seas passing in smooth and weighty majesty beneath the ship's hull. The wind was from the north and it brought the Arctic cold with it, whipping the breath from the lips of every man in banners of white vapor. Brent flexed his fingers and gripped the windscreen tighter. The steel felt cold even through the leather of his gloves.

The young American raised his glasses and focused on a destroyer five hundred yards off their starboard side. The seas through which the 84,000-ton *Yonaga* shouldered her way disdainfully were like the Rocky Mountains to the 2,100-ton destroyer. The narrow-hulled ship, heavy with guns, rolled and pitched violently, taking the swells on her port shoulder in explosive bursts of white spray, digging her nose into the seas, water tumbling across her forecastle and sweeping her from stem to stern. Sometimes she would drop sickeningly into a deep trough with only her upper works visible. Brent would hold his breath as new cliffs of black water bore down on her and smile as the tough little warship threw her head back and swooped up the slope to meet the crest in another explosion like the impact of a torpedo. Then the drop and the whole procedure would be repeated.

Brent lowered his glasses and glanced at Byron Whitehead through the corner of his eye. In the four weeks since the beheadings, the rear admiral had found little to say to him except for official consultations concerning the decoding and encoding of messages. In fact, a message received the day before had sent the entire force to sea. *Blackfin,* on station off Tomonuto, had sent a special CISRA encoded transmission—CISRA was a acronym for a special code developed by the CIA and Israeli Intelligence. It was used only for messages pertaining to *Yonaga* and forces under the control of Admiral Fujita. It had been sent in a millisecond burst and Williams had taken a grave risk in even making such a short transmission. But the news warranted the risk: the entire Arab task force had put to sea including the three *Gearings* that had been repaired at Surabaya. Two carriers, two cruisers, and seven escorts had sortied from the atoll on a northwesterly heading, apparently intending to fly in reinforcements to their depleted squadrons in the Marianas. Or perhaps it was a plain and simple challenge to *Yonaga* to come out and fight, settle the issue once and for all. In any event, Fujita received the news with undisguised relish. He had his escorts, his air groups were up to full strength, and he was spoiling for a fight. Now the feint on the Marianas to "draw out the swine" was not necessary.

After the islands of Ō Shima, Nii Shima and Mikura Jima were cleared to starboard, course was changed to one-three-five. In a briefing, Fujita had explained this course would take the force into the vast void of the Pacific six hundred fifty kilometers to the west of the Marianas Islands. Here, in this enormous empty arena, Fujita hoped to find his enemy and destroy him. The fact that he was outnumbered and outgunned never mitigated his decision. The enemy was expected here, he would find him and engage. It would be a fight to the death—the way of the samurai.

By noon the storm had moved to the east, the sea calmed, and the sun finally broke through the dissipating clouds. The dark blue outline of the Japanese land mass had long since vanished beneath the horizon. Suddenly the talker put his hands to his earphones, listened intently for a moment and then turned to the admiral. "Radar reports large formations of aircraft bearing three-five-zero true, range 310 kilometers. IFF reports friendly emanations, sir."

"Very well. Our air groups."

An hour later the first specks were spotted off the starboard quarter and a deep rumble could be heard.

Fujita shouted at Naoyuki, "Signal bridge, make the hoist, 'Stand by to receive aircraft.' Flight deck, stand by to handle aircraft."

In a few minutes, a deep rumble could be heard approaching from the north. Raising his glasses, Brent could see over a hundred aircraft approaching like migrating geese. Handlers, wearing their colorful clothing, rushed to their stations on the flight deck and the fearsome steel-mesh barricade was cranked out of its slot in the middle of the flight deck. Any aircraft that missed all five arresting cables would be caught and probably crushed by the barrier.

Fujita glanced at the ensign whipping at the gaff, ordered a new course hoisted and after every ship had answered his hoist with its own, he shouted, "Execute!"

Every hoist was dropped simultaneously and the old man shouted into the voice tube, "Left standard rudder. Steady up on zero-eight-zero, speed twenty-four."

The ship came about with every escort holding station in the turn like a ballerina and her consorts. "Steady on zero-eight-zero, sir. Speed twenty-four, one-hundred-twenty-eight revolutions," came from the tube.

"Very well." Fujita nodded with satisfaction. Their bows were in the wind, and the motion of the deck was at a minimum. For the first time, he turned to Rear Admiral Whitehead. "We are ready to receive aircraft, Admiral Whitehead."

"Very efficient, sir." He glanced at his watch. "But it's late, sir. Can you take aboard all those aircraft before dark?"

Fujita glanced around anxiously at the sun that was well into its descent in the west. "We must, so we will."

The roar of aircraft engines became thunder that caused the windscreen to tremble under Brent's hands, the first squadrons of bombers passing low and to the starboard side of the ship. They began to orbit counter-clockwise. The white fighters hung high in the sky. They would land last. "Two block 'Pennant Six'!" Fujita shouted. Within seconds, the black and white pennant was whipping from the halyard. Slowly a destroyer dropped back and began to trail the carrier on its life-guard station. The landing control officer took his post just abaft the island. Dressed in yellow overalls, he held two yellow fan-like wands. He raised them and gestured toward himself.

Then the first B5N approached, Fowler flaps down, prop at full pitch, hook extended. Brent liked the B5N. He had flown scores of missions as the rear gunner with the old, long-dead Lieutenant Yoshiro Takii. Takii had described the aircraft to him in great detail. He had been very proud of his bomber, which he had named *Tora*.

Designed to a 1935 specification of the Imperial Navy, the B5N had been known as "Kate" to the Allies. With a 50-foot wingspan, thirty-three feet in length and carrying a three-man crew in a long greenhouse, it was a big aircraft with clean aerodynamic form. It had been ahead of its time, a low-winged monoplane of all-metal construction with great integral strength and endurance. It had a variable-pitch propeller, retractable carrier-stressed landing gear, integral tankage, stressed-skin construction, and mechanically folding wings. At its inception, it had no peer. It devastated "Battleship Row" at Pearl Harbor, and during the first year of the war in the Pacific, it destroyed or damaged more Allied vessels than any other single Japanese weapon. Among its victims were the carriers *Lexington, Wasp, Hornet,* and *Yorktown.*

Brent leaned over the windscreen and watched as the control officer dropped the fans to his knees and flattened them. The pilot cut his throttle and the Nakajima caught the first cable and flopped down on the deck like a big stuffed goose. Quickly the barrier was lowered and the big mottled blue-green bomber was pushed to the forward elevator and struck below. Plane after plane landed, the pilots showing superb skill in handling their aircraft. The last Nakajima was piloted by the torpedo bomber commander Lieutenant Joji Kai. Kai's bomber was identified by a yellow cowling and a wide yellow stripe painted around the fuselage just forward of the tail. A trifle clumsy in his approach, Kai was caught by a shear of wind that bounced him upward and brought him down well forward. He caught the third cable and bounced to a screeching stop. There was no damage. Then the first Aichi D3A approached the stern.

Brent smiled to himself as he watched the first dive bomber smartly catch the first cable. Although the Japanese would deny it vehemently, Admiral Allen had told him years ago the D3A was a copy of the old German

Heinkel He 50, which was first flown in 1931. A two-seat biplane of sturdy construction, a dozen advance models of the Heinkel were exported to Japan in the early thirties. The He 50, not the JU 87, as most Americans believed, became the prototype for the Aichi D3A. Much smaller than the Nakajima with only a 37-foot wingspan, it was a graceful aircraft with a big cowling enclosing its new Sakae 42 engine, spatted wheels and the trapeze beneath its fuselage for a 250-kilogram bomb. The spatted wheels and large dive brakes were reminiscent of the JU 87 and probably led to the myth. Similar to the Nakajima, every dive bomber was painted mottled blue-green on top and sky blue on the underside. The most effective Japanese bomber of the the Second World War, it sank more Allied fighting ships than any other Axis aircraft.

The landings were uneventful until an Aichi overshot. Frantically the control officer tried to wave it off. The pilot gunned his engine, but its dangling hook caught the last cable. Slammed down with great force, it skewed to the left, bounced five or six times, and blew out both tires, and its landing gear collapsed. Luckily, there was no serious damage, but clearing the damaged bomber claimed valuable time. Every man on the bridge fretted anxiously. Finally, the damaged dive bomber was pulled clear. The last to land was Commander Takuya Iwata. His aircraft was distinguished by a bright red cowling and a red stripe painted around the fuselage. His gunner's seat was empty. Following Iwata, the fighters began to land.

The light Zeros were whipped to a halt quickly, while the heavier Seafires and F6Fs stretched their cables like giant rubber bands. A stubby, low-winged aircraft with a high canopy, the big Hellcat impressed everyone. Built as a response to the Zero that had dominated the Pacific skies in the early part of the war, the Grumman Hellcat could outperform the Mitsubishi in every way except for maneuverability. It was faster, had armor protection for its pilot and fuel tanks, and carried a terrific wallop in its six fifty-caliber Browning machine guns mounted just outside the break line. Each weapon was supplied with a 400-round ammunition box. Its secret was in its great power: the Pratt & Whitney R-2800, double Wasp, 18-cylinder two-row radial engine with water injection. Originally designed to produce 2100 horsepower, the engine had been upgraded to 2800. The Hellcats now landing on *Yonaga*'s deck were actually four tons heavier than Matsuhara's modified Zeros.

The superb Hellcat fighter had claimed over 5000 kills during the war — more than any other Allied fighter. In fact, during the Battle of the Philippine Sea, 402 Japanese aircraft were destroyed while six Hellcats were brought down by the Japanese fleet. This massacre would forever be known as the "Marianas Turkey Shoot." The Americans exulted on it while the Japanese tried to put it out of their minds. Watching the blue fighters land, the older Japanese eyed the Hellcat with an amalgam of resentment and pleasure — resentment over the terrible losses inflicted by the Grumman, pleasure at finally having this vicious nemesis fighting on their side.

The last aircraft to land was that of Commander Yoshi Matsuhara. As usual, he caught the first cable and made a perfect three-point landing. He approached in fading light, the dying sun bisected by the line of the horizon. Everyone breathed easier. Forty-seven Aichi D3As, forty-five Nakajima B5Ns, and forty-two Zero-sens, two Seafires, and twelve Hellcats, had been taken aboard with only one minor casualty.

Brent had never met the two Frenchmen, the German, and the Greek pilots who had spent most of their time at Tokyo International Airport and Tsuchuira. However, they were all fighter pilots, and because each Japanese pilot wore a *hachimachi* head band — a white band around the helmet with brushed ideograms which testified to the man's determination to die for the Emperor—he was able to pick out the foreigners. It pleased him to see the four flyers land their Zeros with verve and confidence. But more important to Brent was the fact the battle group was taking on a more international flavor. Good men from all over the world had had enough of terrorists and terrorism. Now more and more of them were willing to put their lives on the line to stop it.

"Good pilots. Good pilots. Terrific deck force," Whitehead said, obviously impressed.

Beaming, Fujita shouted commands and the task force came back to its base course of one-three-five. Captain Arai and Quartermaster Kunitomi went below to the navigation bridge. Here they would break out sextant and stop watch. They would be taking the evening sights in a few minutes.

Fujita said to Brent, "Commander Iwata landed with his second cockpit empty, Mister Ross."

"I noticed, sir. I appreciate your permission allowing me to stand out at my old special sea detail post." He tapped the windscreen with gloved knuckles. "I feel I belong here."

The old man cracked a small smile. "I am pleased you have that loyalty to *Yonaga,* Mister Ross. However, Commander Iwata is saving that cockpit for you. You have trained well with him, Mister Ross. He has been lavish in his praise of your gunnery skills."

"Thank you, sir," Brent said, allowing his glasses to drop to his waist.

"It is good that this bad thing between you has been put to rest," the old man said, staring through his glasses.

"Yes, sir," Brent answered simply. He raised his binoculars and stared into the gathering darkness. However, it had not been "put to rest," and Fujita should have

326

known this. Perhaps the old man had been just fishing. True, he was Iwata's gunner, but not suddenly the man's friend. This could never be, not with Iwata. Brent had beaten him senseless before a large number of the crew. In Iwata's samurai's mentality, vengeance was still there to be claimed. Brent admired the man's flying skills, but always regarded him with a wary eye.

"Sir," Rear Admiral Whitehead said suddenly. "Our nuclear sub *Phoenix* sighted tanker *Jabal Nafus* three days ago in the Celebes Sea."

"I know, Admiral Whitehead," Fujita said. "They made much better time than we expected."

"*Blackfin* should have made contact by now," Whitehead said.

The old admiral dropped his glasses and looked up at the American rear admiral. "True. *Blackfin* should have made contact."

Brent wondered about *Blackfin,* Williams and the crew that had become so dear to him. Had they spotted the tanker? Sunk her? A specially encoded message had been constructed for just this eventuality and it had not been transmitted. Maybe they had been sunk themselves. Perhaps they were all dead, been spotted after their transmission, and depth-charged into their grave. He sighed and drummed the windscreen uneasily.

With her engines throttled down to a burbling rumble, submarine *Blackfin* cruised slowly through the calm sea. Overhead, the stars shown brilliantly in the blackness of a cloudless, moonless sky that showed not the faintest hint of the impending dawn. A fatigued Lieutenant Reginald Williams leaned against the windscreen and raised his binoculars. They were only eight miles off the southern entrance of Tomonuto Atoll, where ESM had picked up both S- and J-band emanations from a *Gearing*-class destroyer anchored in the middle of the entrance. Her active sonar was secured, but Williams knew she was sitting with her sonarmen listening with their earphones clamped to their heads. Even with the four big Fairbanks-Morse engines idling at a speed only great enough to maintain steerageway, there was always a chance *Blackfin* could be detected. He had learned on his first patrol off Tomonuto that the RAM (radar absorbent material) with which *Blackfin* had been sprayed made the boat hard to detect. In fact, with her two main ballast tanks partially flooded, the boat was low in the water, offering even a more difficult silhouette for a return.

He was pleased with his crew. Fifteen highly experienced men, nine Japanese and six Americans, had replaced their dead and wounded. A new officer, a young lieutenant junior grade named Shohei Imamura, had reported aboard to fill the void left by the transfer of Brent Ross. Williams had elevated Lieutenant JG Charlie Cadenbach to executive officer and assistant attack officer while Imamura took over navigation duties. Williams sighed. He missed Brent. True, they had had their differences, but the lieutenant was brilliant, a courageous officer who was almost worshipped by the men. He had been sickened when he watched Brent behead the Arab. But, strangely, afterward, it *did* seem just, and Brent had performed his duty with cold efficiency. And, indeed, he knew the Arab had been the 'American Samurai's' third beheading.

They had intercepted a message from the SSN *Phoenix* three days before. Tanker *Jabal Nafusa* and two escorts had been sighted in the Celebes Sea. He had expected to sight the convoy the previous afternoon, but they had seen nothing, and ESM had not detected the enemy. He had shut down all electronic equipment except for ESM—their WLR-8. However, only the destroyer's radar and the occasional radar searches from distant inter-island steamers "waterfalled" across its scope.

He quickly surveyed the bridge crew to assure himself everyone was alert. It was easy to become bored and inattentive on these long watches cloaked in the darkness of night. He glanced at the helmsman, Quartermaster Second Class Harold Sturgis, who gripped the wheel and stared into the only lighted instrument on the bridge: the dim red glow of the gyro repeater mounted between the helmsman and the wheel. To his right, Reginald watched as the man at the annunciators, Seaman First Class Tatsunori Hara, raised his binoculars and searched over the bow. A glance up and over his shoulder assured the captain that the two men standing on their platform on the periscope shears were alert and scanning their sectors. Two extra lookouts, one on each side of the bridge, leaned into their glasses. But all was quiet, only the throaty bark of the diesels firing through the spray and the sluicing sound of water washing over the low main deck and pouring through the drains, ports and scuppers could be heard.

"Bridge!" came up from the speaker. It was the voice of Crog Romero.

"Bridge aye."

"Captain, ESM's got something," Romero said. "Three powerhouse radars. My threat library only has one and it's the *Jabal Nafusa*. No identification for the other two."

Williams felt his heart suddenly pound against his chest just as it had the two times just before he played in the Rose Bowl. His tongue as suddenly thick and his throat was a desert. "Very well," he managed with a calmness he did not feel. "Range and bearing."

"Range ninety-miles, bearing two-two-five true, sir."

"Very well. Can you give me a reading on their SOA (speed of advance)?"

"Maybe, ten, eleven knots, sir."

"Very well."

Reginald made a quick calculation. The convoy should arrive in the middle of the afternoon—maybe 1500 hours. He glanced at the eastern horizon, where a hint of a rosy glow reminded him dawn was only minutes away. He cursed. They had no choice but to submerge. But their battery was fully charged and they still had enough fuel for another week at sea before returning to Japan. He spoke into the speaker, "Plot."

Shohei Imamura's voice came back, "Plot aye."

"Depth under keel?"

"One-hundred-forty-fathoms, sir."

"Give me a course for the center of the channel."

"Zero-three-two, Captain."

"Depth four miles off the entrance?"

"The hundred fathom line passes through that point, sir."

"Very well." Williams was pleased. He should be able to submerge and bring the boat within four miles of the entrance without being detected by the Arab's World War II sonar. However, if the enemy had cheated, equipped his DDs with newer equipment, they could all be dead men. He had no choice. Only in that position would he have the best possible chance for a shot at *Jabal Nafusa*. He spoke softly to Sturgis, "Right standard rudder, steady up on zero-three-two."

Sturgis repeated the command and brought the wheel over. "Steady on zero-three-two," he said.

"Very well." Williams took a deep breath and then shouted, "Lookouts below, clear the bridge, stand by to pull the plug!" He could hear the commands repeated through the open hatch to the conning tower.

Quickly, the two lookouts dropped from the shears and vanished down the hatch with the port and starboard lookouts, followed by Hara and Sturgis. One last look around and then Reginald Williams shouted, "Dive!

330

Dive!" and dropped down through the hatch. Hitting the alarm button with one hand, he pulled the wooden handle and jerked the hatch cover shut with a clang. Then he whirled the wheel until the hatch was dogged watertight. The old auto horn sound of the diving alarm—"Oogah! Oogah!"—resounded throughout the boat. Immediately, operators in the diving station in the control room threw levers and popping sounds were heard as the vents of the main ballast tanks clanged open. With a thump that shook the conning tower, the cover of the main induction valve slammed closed, the throb of the diesels stopped and the soft hum of electric motors could be heard.

He dropped into the conning tower and took a position behind the two periscopes, the wide-angled night periscope and the narrow attack periscope. Quartermaster Sturgis had taken his station at the forward end of the compartment, where he grasped the helm and glanced at the mass of instruments in front of him and above him: speed indicator, pitometer, compass repeater, depth gauge, water pressure gauge, engine room controls, rev counter, rudder angle indicator. To Sturis's left, Yeoman Randolph "Randy" Davidson, the talker, already had his headset on and was staring at his telephone board.

On the starboard side, Crog Romero settled onto a stool in front of the old Mark Four sonar, adjusted his earphones, and stared at his scope. The instrument was set on "passive" and would remain so until ordered to "active" by the captain. Next to him, Petty Officer Tadashi Takiguchi stared at his radar scope, which was blank. The TDC (Torpedo Data Computer) was unmanned.

"Blow negative!" Williams heard diving ófficer Ensign Herbert Battle shout at his men. The boat inclined downward and then lurched and listed to port. Before

Williams could say a word, Battle's angry shout at the two men manning the big wheels that controlled the bow and stern planes came up through the hatch, "Mind your trim, God damn it!" Immediately the boat righted itself.

"Green board," a man in the control room shouted up the hatch.

"Green air!" another man shouted. "Pressure in the boat.

"Very well," Williams said, pleased that the "Christmas Tree" showed all green lights indicating all hull openings were closed. The shout of pressure in the boat brought a slight pain to his ears as the air pressure was increased to test for leaks. He shouted down the hatch, "Secure the air and take her down to sixty-four feet." Sixty-four feet would give him two-and-one-half feet of periscope length above the surface.

"Take her down to sixty-four feet," Battle repeated. Williams heard the venting of air as more water poured into the main ballast tanks and trim tanks. He felt the downward bow angle increase. There were slapping and bubbling sounds as the sea crept up the bridge, black water covering the tiny eye ports. Williams felt the familiar ache in his eardrums increase as pressure built up, the boat sinking into the depths. The usual thought that ran through every submariner's mind on submerging plagued Williams: *Will this be my last dive? Will I ever see the surface, the blue sky, breathe sweet air again?* He shrugged off the gloom and tried to enjoy the awesome quietness that filled the boat. Despite the fans and ventilating system, the heat set in immediately. And the familiar odor endemic with old fleet boats was there: unwashed bodies and the faint aroma of diesel oil.

"Passing forty-five feet, sir" Herbert Battle shouted up the hatch.

"Very well."

"Fifty feet," Battle reported. And then to the crew at

the diving station, "Blow negative to the mark and level off."

The sound of incoming water ceased and Williams felt the incline lessen. "Leveling, Captain."

"Very well."

"Passing sixty feet, Captain."

"Very well." Williams said to Sturgis. "Steady on zero-three-two."

"Aye aye, sir. She's steady on zero-three-two."

"All ahead one-third."

Sturgis moved the knobbed handles of the annunciators and the whine of motors dropped. "All ahead one-third."

Williams pulled a microphone down from the overhead. "Now hear this," he said. "We will post the maneuvering watch and remain at our stations until we are four miles off the entrance. Then the port watch will take over while we wait for that motherf . . ." He caught himself. "While we wait for *Jabal Nafusa* to come to us. Remember, that can's on watch in the entrance. We'll observe silent running and steam in within four miles of the entrance and lay-to at sixty-four feet until sonar picks up cavitations. Then we'll clobber the sons-of-bitches!"

A cheer resounded throughout the boat.

Chapter Thirteen

By 0930 hours it started. Radar picket *Ayase* reported that she was under attack by a dozen Junkers 87, Stuka dive bombers, and five high-flying Douglas DC-6s. Then, suddenly, her radios fell silent. Everyone expected Fujita to send fighters to her aid. However, the old man did nothing for the beleaguered picket. Instead, he doubled the number of BSNs scouting the four quadrants surrounding the task force, assigning two to each sector. At 1000 hours, Scout Number Two sent a partial transmission reporting two carriers and escorts at latitude twenty-one-degrees-thirty minutes, longitude one-six-one . . ." and then the scout's radio fell silent, too.

Within minutes of the reception of the scout's message, an enemy DC-6 flying at nearly 30,000 feet sighted the task force. The six Zeros of the CAP shot her down quickly, but everyone knew the damage had been done. The enemy knew where they were, too. They were within a few hours of a bloody showdown.

Brent was in Flag Plot, seated between Commander Conrad Crellin and Commander Yoshi Matsuhara when the Admiral briefed his staff and air group commanders. First he pointed at the chart, indicating the enemy's position. "We are here," he said. "At latitude twenty-seven, longitude one-six-one. We will steam south until we are within three-hundred kilometers of the enemy and then launch our aircraft. Launch time in one hour." A dozen wristwatches were checked as if choreographed. The small black eyes were fiery with a new excitement as the old man surveyed the eager faces in front of him. "Remember," he said. "The fate of the Mikado and Japan is in your hands—of the entire free world. Kill the swine!" There was a cheer, and cries of *"Banzai!"* filled the room.

The old man clapped twice and everyone stood. "Amaterasu-O-Mi-Kami," he said, bowing toward the shrine. "Show us the way to destroy the enemies of the Mikado—the enemies of all free men." He looked up and stared at his men. His hand found the *Hagakure*. "Remember, our sacred book tells us, 'If one's sword is broken, he will strike with his hands. If his hands are cut off he will press the enemy down with his shoulders. If his shoulders are cut away, he will bite through ten or fifteen enemy necks with his teeth.'"

A great roar erupted, and every man waved a fist in the air. Fujita raised his hands. "Brief your groups and be prepared to take off within an hour." He gestured at Captain Mitake Arai. "Just before take off, my air operations officer will provide you with your point-option data." He surveyed the eager faces grimly. "Send the fingernail and hair clippings of your men to my cabin. I will see to it personally they are sent to next of kin. You are dismissed."

"Tenno heika banzai!" resounded in the room and then the men crowded into the doorway. Conrad Crellin pulled Brent aside and whispered in his ear, "Fingernails and hair clippings?"

"If a samurai is lost in battle, his fingernail and hair clippings are sent to his family," Brent explained. "That way, they will have something to cremate. It helps the man's spirit enter the Yasakuni Shrine, where he can join all the dead heroes of the ages." Crellin nodded,

335

smiled and walked out of the room.

Stepping into the passageway, Iwata stopped Brent Ross with a hand on his arm. "Are you ready, gunner?"

Brent smiled. "I'm always ready."

Typical of the samurai mentality, it was an all-or-nothing strike. Forty-five Aichi D3As, 42 Nakajima B5Ns took off from *Yonaga*. They were followed by twenty-seven Zeros, twelve F6F Hellcats, and the two Seafires. Fifteen Zeros remained with *Yonaga* as CAP.

As soon as Iwata cleared the carrier's deck, Brent swung his big bulk around to the rear of the dive bomber, the ball-bearing mounted gunner's seat moving as smoothly as a glider. Iwata's voice filled his earphones, "Load and lock."

"Load and lock," Brent repeated. After unsnapping the upper strap of his safety harness, the lieutenant released the Nambu's well lock and pulled the Type 96, 7.7-millimeter machine gun from its compartment, releasing its locking mechanism. Leaning back with his feet firmly planted on the footrest, he swung the beautifully balanced 24-pound weapon in an azimuth from beam to beam and then from the vertical to the horizontal and finally, he pushed up on the twin pistol grips until the muzzle pointed down beneath the tail. Not quite satisfied with the feel the machine gun, he moved it from side to side in quick, jerky motions before nodding to himself with satisfaction.

He reset the lock, released the spring-loaded breech plate lock, and raised the top cover. The armorers had pulled the belt through the receiver, but, for safety, had not seated a round in the firing chamber. The belt was perfectly aligned and each projectile had been carefully lubricated. There was the usual mix of color-coded rounds: alternately red and blue for anti-personnel and armor-piercing with every fifth round tipped yellow for tracer.

He snapped the cover shut and grabbed the wooden cocking handle. He pulled it back hard and released it. Ringing metallically, the spring pulled the handle back and the bolt snapped into place, driving a round into the firing chamber. As was his habit, he partially opened the breech plate and peeked into the firing mechanism. A round was seated and it all looked ready. Sighing, the gunner sank back and raised his weapon by gripping the double pistol grips and pushing down. He locked the weapon into place and opened his microphone, "Weapon loaded and locked, Commander."

"Very well. Keep a weather eye out for enemy fighters, Mister Ross."

Brent chuckled. That last command had been completely unnecessary. He began his habitual scan, short, jerky movements that depended more on peripheral vision to detect specks than the direct, piercing stare which often could be fooled or just miss something that could be caught by the corner of one's eye.

The first aircraft airborne, Iwata circled the bomber counterclockwise and gained altitude as the echelons of "threes" formed up behind him. Superstitious about the number "three," the Japanese preferred to fly in three, threes of threes. Consequently, Iwata's first twenty-seven bombers climbed to 8,000 feet and then headed to the south and west. They were followed by 18 more D3As.

Iwata flew at a slow speed as the Nakajima torpedo bombers took off followed by the fighters. It was a huge train of aircraft, and time was required to assemble the disparate units into a cohesive whole. But fuel was priceless, and none of it would be wasted circling the carrier. Instead, the bombers proceeded toward their target at a slow speed into a brilliant eggshell blue sky, unmarred by a single cloud. It was a day brimming with life, but Brent knew it would soon be filled with death.

Finally, almost an hour after taking off, Brent could

look down from 8,000 feet and see the swarm of mottled-green B5Ns lumbering 2,000 feet below with their 1,760 pound torpedoes slung beneath their fuselages. Then, high above at twenty-four-thousand-feet, he stared at the fighters. All were painted white with black cowlings except for Yoshi Matsuhara's which led and was identified as the air group commander with its red cowling and green hood. Raising his binoculars, Brent felt a thrill of joy and confidence as he studied Yoshi's Zero and the two Seafires which had black bands painted around the tapered noses of their Rolls Royce engines.

For nearly an hour the great armada droned southward without sighting anything. Brent had turned on his radio and switched to all six frequencies, but only a blank carrier wave rustled and hissed in his earphones. He left the set tuned into the fighter frequency because the high-flying fighter pilots should spot the enemy first. He was not disappointed.

Yoshi Matsuhara broke radio silence and Brent knew the curtain was going up. "Edo group, this is Edo leader. Many fighters at one o'clock high," he reported, using the English and American system of reporting. He called on his flight leaders, each commanding three sections of Zeros. "Edo, Shogo and Musashi flights engage. Beer Bottle flight remain in top cover."

Brent brought up his glasses and studied the sky high to the south. He saw swarms of gnats descending toward them. Yoshi was intercepting with twenty-five Zeros and his two Seafires. "Beer Bottle" was Commander Conrad Crellin. He was to maintain top cover with his Hellcats while Matsuhara led the interception. It appeared he would be greatly outnumbered.

Then Brent heard Iwata's excited voice in the intercom calling his dive bombers. "Yosano flight, this is Yosano leader. Many ships to the south!"

Brent stood up and raised his glasses. It was the enemy's battle group, unmistakably. He could see the entire force of 11 ships on the horizon just above the leading edge of their starboard wing. Two carriers in a column, two cruisers flanking the carriers and the entire group surrounded by seven escorts. Moving at flank speed, the enemy ships churned white curving wakes in the beautiful turquoise sea. He glanced to the east. JU 87s and AT 6s with fighters, streaming far to the east and headed north toward *Yonaga*. The enemy had launched his attack, but late. His aircraft did not have the great range of the Japanese, and he had been forced to wait and close the range. A terrible disadvantage. But he had the advantage of numbers.

Brent heard Lieutenant Joji Kai's voice shouting orders to his torpedo bombers. "Kami flight, this is Kami leader. Sections one through seven, take the lead carrier, sections eight through fourteen, take the second. *Banzai!*" The torpedo bombers began to lose altitude and split into two groups.

Then Iwata split his Aichi D3As between the two targets and Brent felt the pulse of the Sakae engine pick up. He unlocked the Nambu and swung it up over the tail. High above he could see trouble. Now he could count about fifty enemy fighters racing in to challenge Yoshi's twenty-seven. Brent muttered a short prayer.

Yoshi peered through his new 90-millimeter anti-glare armorglass windscreen and felt his stomach suddenly contort and sicken. At least fifty ME 109s flying in pairs were diving on him. And racing in from what seemed the entire southern hemisphere of his compass, another twenty to twenty-five fighters were already closing in on the bombers. He needed every available fighter—now! He spoke into his microphone, "Beer Bottle leader, this is Edo leader. Screen the bombers. Engage! Engage!"

Crellin's voice came back. "This is Beer Bottle leader. Thanks for the invitation. I hate being a wallflower. On our way."

Glancing upward, Yoshi saw the twelve great fighters peel off into split-esses and follow their leader in screaming dives, plummeting toward the carriers and the Japanese torpedo and dive bombers that were closing in fast on their targets. The Hellcats could offer some immediate protection, but they could not stop all of the fighters. At least the odds would be better. But he had abandoned his top cover. He had no reserves. The enemy had given him no choice.

He had punched his throttle to the next to last stop. The new Sakae 43 was red-lined at 3100 rpms, and the cylinder head temperature showed a maximum of 290 degrees. He dared not jam the throttle into overboost for more than a minute or two. Once when climbing hard over *Yonaga* over Tokyo Bay, the temperature had suddenly shot up to 280 degrees. But even at the next to last stop, he was pulling away from York and Willard-Smith. He throttled back slightly.

He stared through his range finder. The enemy filled the first ring. His heart jumped, eyes widened. A blood-red Messerschmitt led with a black and white zebra-patterned fighter close aboard. Rosencrance and Vatz. He felt hot hate rise like a poisonous gorge that clogged his throat and thickened his tongue. He spoke into his microphone. "All sections hold on the first pass and then individual combat." The red ME filled his second ring.

The MEs had the advantage of altitude and speed. But in a head-on pass, the advantage went only to the better shots and the lucky ones. Rosencrance saw him and ruddered over to bring his spinner nose-to-nose with the Zero. The renegade American had some hate of his

340

own to satisfy, and he was not deficient in courage.

Both men opened fire at three hundred meters. Then the sky was laced with intertwining threads of tracers. A Zero exploded, another dropped off trailing smoke. A wing flew off a ME, and another flipped over onto its back and screamed for the sea, a dead pilot at the controls. Two more ME dropped off trailing smoke and glycol.

Yoshi snarled with pleasure as he saw small fire motes blink on the leading edge of the red fighter's wing and bits of aluminum whip into the wind. He was scoring. Shells and bullets snapped past, and he felt a slight jar as slugs hit his right wing. At the last instant, both Yoshi and Rosencrance dropped right and left wings and passed each other like two stunt flyers at an air show. The ME brushed by so close, the Japanese felt his fighter bounce in the backwash. Neither had been seriously damaged.

As Yoshi pulled the stick back into the pit of his stomach, his earphones were filled with the usual frantic shouts of men fighting for their lives and the lives of their comrades in aerial combat: "Kuruna! There's one on your tail!"

"See him. Give me some help!"

"Break left—break left!"

Matsuhara's one German pilot, Heinrich Stuffermann, was in trouble early. He heard the Greek, Nicholas Antonopolis, shout out, "Stauffermann! Above you. Dive! Dive!"

But Stauffermann must have been too slow. Out of the corner of his eye, Yoshi saw a great yellow-red flash as the tanks of a Zero exploded. A good man gone in a blink.

Everywhere the sky was filled with twisting, turning planes and tracers sizzling through the sky, leaving white trails of burned phosphorous. Perhaps a dozen funeral pyres already hung in the still air like black grave markers. Four or five white parachutes descended slowly. The battle had degenerated, as all dogfights do, into a big, brawling battle that filled hundreds of square kilometers of sky. The air group commander had no time to look and wonder. In a dogfight a man survived more by instinct than by careful reason. By the time a man deliberated all the ramifications of a maneuver, he could be killed several times over.

At the top of his loop, Yoshi jammed the stick to the right and balancing delicately with rudder, half-rolled into the final maneuver of an Immelmann. Anticipating the Zero's quickness, Rosencrance had not tried to match it. Instead, he chandelled far to the south, curving up into a graceful turn of his own. Yoshi cursed. The American was far out of range. Then a shout in his earphones sent icewater coursing through his veins. It was Elwyn York. "Edo Leader, two of them buggers are on your arse!"

A drumming on his control surfaces turned his head. Two MEs were closing in fast from both quarters. He put Rosencrance out of his mind. His life was on the line, and he could lose it in the next second. He jammed the throttle into overboost and the fighter leaped like a startled rabbit. The needle of the cylinder head temperature began to move. But the MEs had the advantage of great diving speed and were well within range. Then two Seafires closed in behind the Messerschmitts to complete the murderous ensemble. The MEs were firing, the Englishmen were firing, and Yoshi Matsuhara was twisting and diving for his life.

A shout from the Cockney, "Scragged the whoreson!"

Then Willard-Smith's triumphant cry, "One more of the bastards on his way to Mecca, or wherever the bloody cutthroats go."

Both MEs were burning and twisting toward the sea.

There was no time to rejoice. Rosencrance with Vatz by his side was making another run with two more black MEs following closely. The two Seafires closed in close aboard Yoshi, and the seven aircraft stormed toward each other.

The sky was raining fighters. Brent swung the machine gun and crouched down low in his wicker seat as a black ME 109 screamed down on his tail. Already ten or eleven torpedo bombers had been blasted from the sky as if the enemy were sharpening his eye with target practice. And the enemy ships had opened up with a storm of five-inch, 38-caliber AA fire. Hundreds of black smudges blossomed in the sky like the flowers of death, menacing friend and foe alike. Two Aichis just to the right and behind were shot from the sky in the ME's first pass. The third vanished as a five-inch shell detonated its 250-kilogram bomb. Everywhere the fighters were diving and climbing, shooting down bombers like hungry lions tearing at the carcass of a downed wildebeest.

Brent's heart pounded so hard he could feel it pulse in his neck. The black fighter grew in his ring sight. Flame leaped from its wings and cowling. Tracers rained past. The black plane finally filled all three rings. Zero deflection. He pressed the trigger. He felt the weapon jerk and vibrate in his hands and saw his tracers punch straight on into the enemy's spinner, some ricocheting off the hood and armorglass windscreen. Immediately the Daimler Benz left a trail of smoke as its oil tank was shot out and hot oil sprayed the engine. Brent was waving his fist and shouting, "Burn, you son-of-a-bitch!" as the stricken fighter plunged toward the sea.

"Good shooting!" Iwata said into his earphones.

But the entire bomber force was facing disaster. At least half of the big planes had been shot out of the sky in less than three minutes. Then the F6F Hellcats arrived, hurtling down from twenty-four thousand feet like vengeful blue javelins. On their first pass, four MEs were shot to pieces. Then most of the pressure was off the Aichis and the Nakajimas, the Arab fighters turning to fight the big, powerful American Hellcats. But the Americans were outnumbered by at least two to one.

Brent switched to the fighter frequency. "Crellin, this is Fife. Give me some help."

"Break right, Fife!"

"God damn it. What the fuck's wrong with your radio, Crellin? You're coming in like shit!"

"Shaw. At two o'clock. Two of 'em."

"See 'em, Yates. Take the one on the right."

"Crellin, this is Spevak. For Chrissakes, there are three on your ass. Dive! Dive! Nothing can dive with us!"

"Crellin's burning."

"Oh, shit."

Brent watched as a black trail of smoke arced off into the sea far below. There was no parachute. Here the gallant young American Conrad Crellin would rest for eternity with thousands of other young men. And he had scarcely known him, spoken to him, and now he was gone forever, not even fingernail and hair clippings to send home.

The dogfight moved off far to the south, but not all of the MEs were occupied by the Hellcats. Brent caught a glimpse of something coming up hard from below. "Bank, Iwata!" he shouted into the intercom. "Bank left!"

The pilot put the stick over hard to the left and the big plane dropped its wing. Standing up on his toes, Brent pushed the pistol grips up and stared down into the flaming jaws of death. A ME 109 was standing on its tail and firing into their blind spot.

Brent pressed the trigger and saw his tracers smash

into the fuselage and march forward. There were hard thumping sounds as the enemy's tracers raked the fuselage. Chunks of aluminum flew off into the slipstream. Then the ME fell off and streaked toward the sea.

Iwata righted the dive bomber and said, "Well done, gunner." And then, "Stand by. We will begin our run in a few seconds." The voice was very calm.

Brent took a quick look to the south. At least ten more enemy Messerschmitts had been shot down, but only eight F6Fs were still in the sky. And two of these were trailing smoke and had turned for home. He looked down and he thought he would vomit. He could only count twelve B5N torpedo bombers. Lieutenant Joji Kai still led, but large patches of skin had been blasted from his wing, his canopy was shattered, and it appeared his two crewmen were either dead or badly injured. Yet the big plane still bore on toward *Al Kufra* with its unmistakable silhouette of the *Essex*-class carrier—high island structure with pyramiding five-inch gun houses both fore and aft.

The entire Arab battle force was firing now with their 40-millimeter and 20-millimeter batteries. The two cruisers and the seven *Gearings* had bunched in close to the carriers to concentrate their fire support. With hundreds of guns firing, each ship rippled with leaping flashes, billowing clouds of brown smoke trailing in its wake. Thousands of tracers stormed to meet the torpedo planes, shorts ripping the water in front of the Nakajimas as they lumbered in, hundreds of spent 40-millimeter shells self-destructing in small black puffs astern of the bombers. Six MEs of the CAP attacked in desperate attempts to destroy the survivors. One Nakajima was hit, lost a wing, and tumbled across the surface, disintegrating as if it were bouncing across concrete. Another exploded, and two more plunged into the sea in enormous splashes. The eight survivors drove on with fatal

345

determination. Seven finally launched their torpedoes.

Immediately the two carriers turned hard to starboard in an attempt to thread through the seven wakes. The big planes turned away . . . but not Kai's bomber. The Nakajima with the yellow cowling and the yellow stripe charged in on the *Al Kufra*. It seemed impossible that *Al Kufra*'s gunners could miss. And some did not. The windscreen disappeared in a blizzard of broken Plexiglas and aluminum peeled from hits on the wings and fuselage like the skin of a snake. But somehow the B5N remained airborne and closed in on the wildly turning carrier, which appeared to be evading all three torpedoes streaking toward her.

Kai released his torpedo at only a hundred meters. He could not miss. Brent waited to see the big plane pull up and turn. But Kai had a long memory — a long, hateful memory of a time off Okinawa when he missed this same ship. Worse, he had been constantly reminded for over four decades by humiliating taunts aimed at the kamikaze pilot who had returned. But the gods had been kind. He would not miss the second time.

"My God, he's going to ram," Brent shouted.

The Nakajima hit *Al Kufra* squarely on the bridge. There was a huge, roiling red fireball that mushroomed skyward, followed by a stem of black smoke. Chunks of the bomber and flaming gasoline rained down on the flight deck. Then the torpedo hit amidships, sending a great column of water cascading into the sky. Immediately flames engulfed most of her bridge and superstructure, but the carrier did not slow.

Then it was *Ramli al Kabir*'s turn. She fairly leaped from the sea as two torpedoes caught her on the starboard side. Billowing huge clouds of smoke and steam from two gaping holes, she slowed and turned. Immediately began to list. She had been gravely wounded.

Brent felt the Aichi vibrate and slow as Iwata set the

variable pitch propeller to full coarse pitch, and then there were two thumps as the air brakes dropped below the outer wings.

"Grab your handgrips, gunner," Iwata said. "Here we go—*banzai!*"

Followed by the other dive bombers, which had split into two groups, the Aichi dropped off into its dive. The line of the horizon rose, the sky disappeared, and Brent's vision was filled with the sea and enemy ships. Iwata had selected the staggering *Ramli al Kabir* for his section. Quickly the D3A steepened its dive. Commander Iwata kept glancing at the red lines on his side windows, which were designed to help him set up the correct dive angle, until the plane finally fell into the ideal 85-degree dive angle.

Turning his head, Brent could count only five more dive bombers behind them while six more swerved off to attack *Al Kufra*. Only 12 left out of 45. Brent screamed in anguish and pounded the padded combing. Then, looking down, he could see only the great rectangular flight deck growing in his vision. The big carrier had almost stopped and was turning sharply to starboard, smoke and steam pouring out of her entire starboard side from amidships aft. But her rows of flaming AA guns were concentrated on Brent Ross—Brent Ross alone. Hordes of white streaks hailed upward, climbing slowly and then whipping past as if they had suddenly accelerated. Sheer horror gripped his guts with a frozen hand. The Aichi bounced and staggered as proximity fuses detonated five-inch shells, but the plane's great speed left most of the shrapnel behind. And the Arabs' six remaining fighters of the CAP were busy chasing the surviving torpedo bombers. At least they would be free of fighters, thanks to the sacrifice of the torpedo bombers. Then a macabre thought swirled into the turmoil of his mind: *Midway. This was Midway again.*

Midway in reverse. He laughed wildly into the howling slipstream.

Brent could see Iwata hunched forward, staring through his sight, but Brent knew the bomb release was still a matter of pilot judgment. The bomber was vibrating, bounced around by AA bursts, and yawing slightly from the force of the wind drag off the big airfoils of the air brakes. Now they were close to drop altitude and the rectangular target had become the entire world. Finally, with the huge deck looming only two thousand feet below, Brent felt a bump and he knew Iwata had released all of their bombs: a single 250-kilogram bomb and two 30-kilogram bombs.

Immediately the pilot pulled back hard on the stick, and the carrier dropped beneath their wings. Brent felt himself pushed down hard in his seat, and his stomach was driven into his groin. The prop went to fine pitch, and the dive brakes retracted with two thumps and for a moment the world whirled around his head. Flattening in the dive, the pilot horsed the stick to the left and kicked rudder, turning the nose of the aircraft to the north. Shaking the dizziness from his head, Brent could see the horizon and the blue sky stretching overhead. Passing between two of the *Gearings,* Iwata actually lost more altitude until the bomber skimmed the water, not giving a lurking enemy fighter a shot from below. A few surprised gunners on the outboard AA batteries of the destroyers fired, but the rounds were wide.

Staring over the tail, Brent saw an awesome sight. All their bombs hit the *Ramli al Kabir* squarely amidships on the flight deck. A Vesuvian eruption of flames, plate, and shattered aircraft shot into the sky. Two of the five bombers following were shot down, but the other three scored with two more hits and a near miss. The entire flight deck burst open like an overripe melon as the tungsten-uranium-tipped AP bombs penetrated to the hangar deck, gouts of flame and black smoke leaping into the deep blue sky. The great carrier was dying— dying with theatrical pyrotechnics as her own fuel and ammunition stores immolated her. She slowed even more and listed to starboard while enormous luminescent balls of red and yellow flames ballooned skyward from stem to stern, heavy, greasy black smoke billowing into the sky and spreading like a black shroud across the sea.

Waving his fist over his head, Brent shouted *"Banzai! Banzai!"* He was joined by Iwata, who watched the cataclysm in his rearview mirror and pivoted his head around eagerly.

But *Al Kufra* fared much better. Three of the six D3As diving on her were shot to pieces. Only one of the survivors managed to hit her. But the one hit was devastating, a 250-kilogram bomb penetrating the aft elevator and blowing the entire lift high into the sky, complete with the hydraulic pump and shaft. Trailing clouds of smoke and listing slightly, the big *Essex* carrier turned to the south.

Flying so low, their prop wash left ripples in the sea, the Aichi headed north toward *Yonaga* and home. Now the entire southern horizon was smeared with the black pall pouring from the dying carrier. Only six more D3As trailed them. The price had been enormous. Many of the best had died this beautiful day. Brent looked high into the sky. Yoshi Matsuhara was up there somewhere. Or was he dead already? He saw vapor trails. Fighters. Still fighting it out. Brent said a silent prayer for his friend.

When still well out of range, the four enemy fighters split, the two black MEs banking to Yoshi's port side, Rosencrance and Vatz pulling up to starboard. The commander shouted into his microphone, "Edo Two and

Three, take the two black fighters, I have the others."

Now the red fighter and the zebra-striped aircraft were climbing at full throttle. They were much faster than Yoshi had expected. In fact, all the enemy Messerschmitts had shown great speed. They must have upgraded the new Daimler Benz *Valkyrie* and Rosencrance was using his greater power to claim the fighter pilot's most valuable commodity—altitude.

Yoshi felt his lips peel back and he grinned, exposing his straight white teeth like a death's head. "Get a taste of this engine," he said, jamming the throttle to the fire wall and pulling the stick back.

The engine roared with the full fury of all 3200 horsepower. With the stick back, the Japanese pilot felt himself pushed back and then down into his seat as if an invisible giant had both hands on his chest and was pounding with all his power. The horizon dropped precipitously, his windshield filling with the glare of the perfect sky. He was climbing almost vertically at an incredible 340 knots and with his speed slowing only slightly. Light pressure on the stick rotated the fighter so that the MEs were visible to his left side. He centered his controls and watched the startled enemy drop off beneath him, losing speed, mushing into stalls. Yoshi laughed like a madman, pulled the stick back, and whipped into a tight, wing-bending loop.

The two MEs had dropped off into dives and were at least two kilometers ahead of him, trying to streak away from this unreal Zero. Glancing at his engine temperature, Yoshi was satisfied he was still in a safe range. He screamed after the enemy like a vengeful demon from hell, airspeed indicator zooming past 450 knots and climbing toward the last calibration at 540. Cleverly, the the MEs split, Vatz rolling up and away, clawing for altitude, Rosencrance continuing his dive, which should have put distance between him and the Zero. But not this time.

The enemy was thinking. If Yoshi got a shot at Rosencrance, Vatz would have his opportunity for a shot at the Zero. Yoshi ignored Vatz and brought his range finder to the blood-red machine. His cylinder head temperature began to creep upward. He looked around. York and Willard-Smith were brawling with the two black Messerschmitts far out on the northeastern horizon. In fact, in the strange, almost eerie way of dogfights, most of the fighters had vanished. The fighter frequency was ominously silent. Either most of his pilots were dead, or the fight had moved so far over the horizon, he could not pick up the transmissions. He punched the instrument panel.

He heard York shout, "Got the bugger."

Then Willard-Smith's horrifying reply, "And he got me."

"Hang on. Be there in two shakes, guv'nor."

The red ME filled all three rings. Yoshi could see Rosencrance's startled white face staring back at him. With a good killing angle of one-quarter deflection and slightly above, he pressed the red button. The fighter bucked and vibrated, 20-millimeter and 7.7-millimeter shells and bullets hosing down on the ME. But Rosencrance had jinked savagely to the left, causing most of the burst to miss. The Japanese pilot cursed. Then a little left rudder brought the stream back to the enemy's right wing. Small blooms of red marked the hits. Yoshi screamed with joy. Abruptly the Zero began to vibrate and a hammer was pounding his fuselage. Joy turned to horror. Vatz! Slashing in with his own great diving speed, making an incredible full deflection shot from the right as the Zero bolted past. And the rounds crept forward.

Yoshi had no choice. It was turn or die. He was fighting two of the best fighter pilots in the world. One slip and he was a dead man. He kicked left rudder and jammed the stick to the left and down, increasing his dive and banking away from Rosencrance's tail. At the same time, Rosencrance turned sharply to the right with Vatz covering him close behind. Yoshi plunged down to the left and began to pull back on the stick. A glance at his instruments changed his mind. The cylinder head temperature was crowding 280, and the tachometer was at the red line. His speed indicator showed an impossible 540 knots. There was a good chance he would break up if he pulled out at this speed. Most certainly he would lose consciousness, and control of his bladder and his bowels.

He eased the throttle until the needle dropped below 500 and pulled back on the stick. The cowling came up, the horizon dropped, and so did Yoshi's guts. He would be punished by six or seven g's. With the airspeed indicator now below 500, the fighter began to flatten its dive. Then the vibrations began. The wings shook so much, he thought they would tear themselves free. They were actually flapping, as if the aircraft had suddenly become a bird and was trying to fly on its own. But the sturdy new wing spars held. Yoshi felt all the effects of a high-speed pullout, only this time much greater than he had ever known before; dizziness, loss of peripheral vision to the point he thought he was staring down a tunnel, pain in his groin, sharp, stabbing pains in his neck and spine as his head became lead, urine staining his flight suit, and tears streaming down his cheeks. He squeezed down hard to keep his bowels in check. But this time something new was added. He wiped his upper lip with his glove and came away with blood. A nosebleed. He ignored it, the salty liquid trickling down to his upper lip, where he dabbed at it with the tip of his tongue. Then a shroud covered the sun and he was in a world of blackness. Groggily, he shook his head to clear it. The Zero was bounding up and down like a wild stallion with a first-time rider and threatening to stall. Blinking like a man who had been drugged, he gripped the stick, worked the rudder pedals clumsily, finally regaining control. He looked around and tried to focus his eyes. It took him priceless seconds to find his enemy.

They were far to the south, pouncing on a crippled Seafire while another Seafire engaged them both in desperation. A black ME 109 was spinning into the sea. But Willard-Smith was hit, streaming brown-white smoke and diving while Elwyn York slashed into the two attackers, firing. Yoshi ignored his instruments and punched the throttle to the last stop again and whipped the fighter into a turn until the Sakae 43 was pointed at the fight. The Cockney was giving a good account of himself, brilliantly turning, rolling, and diving, never giving his enemies a good shot. Finally, York turned, got off a quick burst at Vatz that hit the German's engine and then fell off into a high-speed stall.

Yoshi screamed, "No!" as Rosencrance knifed in, firing a long burst that raked the Seafire, blowing off the air scoop and an exhaust manifold fairing strip. Shells punched into the engine, severing gas lines and spraying the hot Rolls Royce with petrol. Immediately, flames streamed and the fighter dropped off into its last dive. Rosencrance banked sharply, and smelling blood, raced after the burning British fighter.

"Bail out, Elwyn!" he heard Willard-Smith scream into his earphones. But the warning came too late or York was already wounded or dead. The red Messerschmitt's next burst hit the cockpit squarely, Plexiglas and bits of combing, aluminum bracing, and shattered instruments streaming into the slipstream. The Seafire dropped off into a vertical dive with its burning engine still at full throttle and streaked toward the sea, twisting slowly in its plunge.

Sobbing and punching his instrument panel, Yoshi ruddered his range finder to the red Messerschmitt. Vatz was limping off to the south, streaming coolant and a white haze of smoke. Yoshi glanced at his instruments. His engine temperature was out of hand. But death filled his mind; nothing else mattered. He was above Rosencrance and was in a shallow dive that brought his airspeed to over 470 knots. Not designed for this high speed, his airfoils were overwhelmed by the turbulence, and his airframe began to vibrate. His range finder was jumping. He throttled back. The vibrations diminished. Rosencrance was turning. But Yoshi had the American killer in his sights. Directly astern and at 150 meters, he pressed the red button and held it down.

A ferocious maelstrom of explosions raged along the ME's wing and then smashed into the Daimler Benz. The cowling fasteners were blown loose and the cowling and hood peeled away, caromed off the windscreen, and flew off into the slipstream. Two 20-millimeter shells blew out the entire supercharger assembly, the heavy compressor unit flying loose and taking the left horizontal tailplane with it. Flame sprang to life with the intensity of a blowtorch. Black smoke ribboned back from the fighter's engine. Yoshi cried out with joy, his face covered with saliva, tears, mucus, and blood streaming from his still bleeding nose.

The red machine rolled onto its back, and a black figure plummeted from the cockpit. Then, like a beautiful blossoming lily, the parachute opened. Yoshi looked around. With the exception of Willard-Smith's smoking Seafire, which was disappearing over the northern horizon, the sky was empty. He owned the sky and had one small matter to settle with the American who oscillated slowly beneath his white umbrella far below.

Yoshi laughed hysterically. He remembered how Rosencrance had murdered the young Lieutenant Todoa

Shigamitsu in his chute. Now the wheel had come full circle, as it always does, and priceless revenge was in his grasp. "Just you and I, renegade dog," he whispered to himself.

He throttled back to only 200 knots and pushed over into a leisurely dive. Eagerly he ran his thumb over the red button. He would savor every second of this delicious moment. Rosencrance saw him coming and knew exactly what the Japanese intended. He freed his pistol and raised it. Yoshi laughed and brought the figure precisely into focus where his cross hairs intersected. At a hundred meters, he squeezed the trigger. There was a hiss of compressed air. He screamed with agony and fury. He was out of ammunition. Rosencrance was laughing and firing. Yoshi banked away.

For a long moment the Japanese pilot had an urge to ram the figure, and then a glance to the north showed a limping Willard-Smith dropping toward the sea. One last look at the American who was drifting down into the sea where a slow death awaited him and the air group commander banked after the Seafire. He put Rosencrance out of his mind and glanced at the clipboard strapped to his knee to check *Yonaga*'s point option data. He was steering 010, which should have put him on a course of interception. Obviously, Willard-Smith had checked his own data.

His groups had lost terribly. Truly, it was a victory, but it was Pyrrhic. Crellin and perhaps half of his pilots dead. York gone. Maybe most of his Zero pilots had joined their ancestors; he could only guess. The bomber groups had almost ceased to exist. Brent Ross was probably dead. He pounded the combing, cried out in agony from deep in his heart. He lifted his head to the heavens and screamed the question men who go to war have cried for millennia, "Why? Why are the gods so cruel — so hungry for young blood?" But the heavens stared back silently . . . there were no answers there, never had been. Now Yoshi knew there were no answers anywhere.

The commander edged the throttle forward a notch and gained rapidly on the Seafire. The British fighter was holding its altitude at a thousand meters and the smoke had diminished. Apparently, the automatic extinguishers had been able to control the fire, at least for a time. He heard Willard-Smith's voice, "Welcome to the soirée, old boy. Good to have some company."

Yoshi edged above the wounded fighter and spoke into his microphone, "I will give you an umbrella." He did not mention the fact that he was out of ammunition.

"Thanks awfully, old man."

Yoshi shook his head, not believing the Englishman's unflappable decorum. Their losses had been hideous, including the Britisher's best friend, yet the man spoke as if he had just left a soccer match. Good men. Such good men from all over the world. He glanced at his watch. Maybe *Yonaga* was under attack at this moment. Maybe she had already been sunk. Certainly the enemy attack force should have made their runs. And what of *Blackfin?* If Williams failed and the Arabs reinforced the air groups in the Marianas by submarine, their terrible sacrifices could have been made for nothing. He prayed for *Yonaga* and then for *Blackfin.*

Chapter Fourteen

Jammed with the entire attack team, the conning tower was almost unbearably hot and stuffy. Now, to the ubiquitous smell of diesel oil and unwashed bodies, was added the insidious aroma of fear. The crew had been at battle stations since sonar had first picked up cavitations eight miles to the south and west thirty minutes earlier. The sounds were unmistakable: the two pairs of small high-speed screws of destroyers and the ponderous flailing of the single huge bronze screw of a tanker.

Reginald Williams leaned back against the bulkhead and stared past the oiled tubes of the two periscopes at his assistant attack officer, Charlie Cadenbach, who fidgeted nervously with the plastic "Is-Was" which hung around his neck. An antique instrument dating back to the twenties, the "Is-Was" looked much like a circular slide rule with two concentric discs. It was calibrated so that the assistant attack officer could keep a continuous reading on the target's course and speed relative to the submarine. In the old submarine navy, Cadenbach would have been called the "yes-man" because his duties included keeping the attack officer current on the developing attack problem, and the readiness condition of the boat and the torpedo battery, and in general, supplying the captain with anything else he wished to know. Staring at the heavy layers of perspiration beading Caden-

357

bach's forehead, the nervously twitching jaw, Williams was glad he had Ensign Hasse on the TDC, Crog Romero on the Mark IV sonar, Harold Sturgis at the helm and engine room controls, Randy Davidson on the telephone board, and Goroku Kumanao manning the SPS-10 radar console. They were all good men.

Short of breath, Reginald inhaled deeply, but relief was impossible. With sixty-seven men breathing in oxygen and exhaling carbon dioxide, the livability of the submarine's atmosphere decreased by the minute. *Worse than Los Angeles smog in July* ran through his mind. All of the old fleet boats carried carbon dioxide absorbent, hermetically sealed in metal canisters and oxygen was stored in bottles. However, these were used only in emergencies. Reginald sighed with resignation. It was time for his first observation. His discomfort was suddenly forgotten.

Randy Davidson turned to him. "Technician Matthew Dante wants to know if you want an ESM confirmation, Captain."

"Negative. We know who they are and I'm going to get my first observation now." He turned to the TDC. "Stand by your cranks, Mister Hasse."

"Aye aye, sir. TDC standing by." The young ensign threw four switches and the little room was filled with the sounds of electric motors coming up to speed. "TDC ready for input, sir."

"Very well." The captain shouted down the hatch, "Diving Station!"

Ensign Herbert Battle's voice came back, "Diving Station aye!"

"Depth?"

"Sixty-seven feet."

"Bring her up flat to sixty-four feet." This would give Williams two-and-one-half feet of periscope above the surface.

"Bring her up flat to sixty-four feet," the diving officer shouted, repeating the command and ordering his planesmen at the same time. The change in depth was almost imperceptible.

"Sixty-four feet, sir," Battle reported.

"Very well. Up 'scope!"

Cadenbach punched the "pickle" control, and the hoist motor clacked open. Accompanied by the sounds of spinning sheaves and the squeak of steel cables, the periscope slid up from its well like a long-dormant reptile. Wet and oily, the shining steel barrel almost appeared motionless, only the movement of the hoist cables indicating the instrument was rising. Suddenly the periscope yoke appeared, bolted to the ends of the hoist cables. Then the base of the periscope appeared with the eyepiece, range dials, and two handles folded up at its sides. Stooping, Reginald Williams snapped down the handles and rose with the instrument, eyes glued to the rubber-lined eyepiece. Immediately he swung the lens to the west.

"What was that last bearing, Crog?"

"Two-six-zero true, zero-eight-zero relative, sir."

"God damn it. Where in hell are they?" Williams shouted, working the lens over the reported bearing.

Crog turned his crank and studied his scope, hand over his single earphone. "They should be there, sir. My sonar has them loud and clear."

"Right!" Williams shouted with undisguised joy. "They were in a squall. We've got 'em. A big mother—the *Jabal Nafusa,* all right, and two cans leading—maybe six-hundred yards off each bow." And then to Cadenbach, "Check me on this, XO. Length one-thousand fifty, beam one-ten, draft fifty-one, height of mast one-five-zero."

Cadenbach studied a chart attached to the bulkhead behind the captain's head. "Correct, sir. Except height of

359

mast one-six-zero."

"One-six-zero." Williams made the adjustment by turning a knob on his range finder slightly. "Stand by for first observation," he said. He squinted, moving the periscope with slight motions of the handles. "Bearing, mark!"

Cadenbach studied the spot where the vertical cross hair on the periscope barrel matched the bearing circle etched on the overhead around it. "Zero-seven-zero."

Hasse turned a crank on the TDC. Cadenbach adjusted the "Is-Was."

Williams fingered the knob of the range finder until the split image of the tanker became a coherent whole. "Range, mark!"

"Seven-seven-seven-zero."

Hasse turned another crank. Cadenbach fumbled with the "Is-Was."

"Angle on the bow starboard fifteen." The target was fifteen degrees from heading directly at the submarine—a terrible firing problem. Ninety degrees was ideal. "Down 'scope!" The barrel slid down. "Give her a course of zero-four-zero."

Williams turned to Crog. "We've made a lot of noise. What's that can doing in the entrance?"

The soundman cranked the sound head around, listened for a moment. "Still just running his auxiliary engine, sir. His steam is up—I can hear it hissing, but no shafts or screws are turning."

"Very well." The captain spoke to the entire attack team. "We're too far east of *Jabal Nafusa*'s track. I expected her to approach from one-eight-zero. We'll have to steam west to get close enough for a decent shot, and the angle on her bow is terrible." He spoke to Sturgis, "All ahead two-thirds, come right to two-seven-zero."

Sturgis repeated the commands, pushed the annunciators forward, and brought the helm over. There was the sound of electric motors and the boat surged forward. "Steady on two-seven-zero, speed six, sir."

"Very well. Sonar, the can in the entrance?"

"No change, sir."

"The tanker?"

"Holding her course at zero-four-zero."

"Very well." Williams shouted down the hatch, "Plot, depth under keel?"

"Forty fathoms, sir," Imamura answered.

"Forty? What happened to the hundred-fathom line?"

"We're inside it, Captain, and the chart shows eighty fathoms. But these charts are inaccurate. My fathometer reads forty."

"Damn!" Williams punched the tube. And then down the hatch again, "Imamura, I want to know when we've covered one mile."

The speed of the response took everyone by surprise. "Seven more minutes." Obviously, the navigator had already plotted the entire problem on his plotting sheets and was anticipating the captain's attack scheme.

The seven minutes were interminable. A new, frightening sound crept into the boat. It was the "pinging" sound of the enemy's destroyers' sound gear searching from beam to beam. *Blackfin's* RAM — US Navy designation "Deflecton Four" — was highly efficient against radar, but it did not give much protection against powerful, well-manned sound gear. As the sounds grew louder, no one could look into another man's eyes. "Are they ranging us?"

"Negative, Captain," Romero said.

Finally, Williams shouted "All stop!" Sturgis pulled the annunciators all the way back to the last stop, and silence filled the boat. The atmosphere was so heavy, it felt liquid. Williams spoke to Sturgis, "Let me know when you lose steerageway." And then down the hatch, "Mister Battle, let me know if you have trouble holding her at sixty-four feet."

"Aye aye, sir."

"Up 'scope. Stand by for second observation." The tube slid up and Williams peered into the lens. "Bearing mark!"

"Two-seven-five."

"Range mark!"

"Four-two-zero-zero."

"Angle on the bow four-five starboard. Down 'scope."

Hasse cranked his handles furiously. He glanced at his dials and turned to the captain. "Initial range four-one-zero-zero, speed eight, distance to track three-one-zero-zero."

Williams nodded. They were only three thousand one-hundred yards from the *Jabal Nafusa*'s projected track. And with her bows pointed dead center into the atoll's entrance, there was very little chance she would change course. "Hot damn!" he shouted, slamming a big fist into his sweaty palm.

He turned to Crog. "The cans?"

"No change, sir."

"Very well. All ahead one-third." He wanted to fire from within two thousand yards, but with such an enormous target, he could fire at a longer range.

Again, silence for a few minutes. Then Williams shouted the fateful words at Randy Davidson. "Flood tubes one through six." And then to Cadenbach, "Up 'scope. This will be a shooting observation!"

He pulled down the handles and rose eagerly with the eyepiece of the attack periscope glued to his eye. A quick look at the escorts. The closest was crossing their bows only about two thousand yards ahead. The other was far off the tanker's port bow at least three miles distant. He turned the lens to the tanker. He felt a near sexual thrill as the enormous target plodded into his view. This would be like shooting a pregnant cow. "Bearing mark!"

"Three-one-zero."

"Range mark!"

"Two-four-five-zero."

"Angle on the bow zero-six-zero. Down 'scope. Open outer doors tubes one through six." He turned to Hasse. "TDC?"

"Range three-six-five-zero, speed eight, distance to track two-two-zero-zero."

Williams said to Hasse, "Set depth of fish for twenty-feet, speed fast, we'll give him six fish on a ninety track or as close to it as we can."

"Twenty-feet, speed forty-six-knots, ninety track, six-fish spread," Hasse echoed. The spread would aim one torpedo at the bow, four spaced evenly amidships, and one at the stern. With such a huge target, they should score at least three hits—unless a destroyer detected them.

The captain spoke to Crog, "Turn on the speaker."

The soundman flipped a switch, and a small speaker immediately filled the tiny room with the sounds of pinging and the cavitations of small screws and the one big "chunk chunk" of the single huge screw of the *Jabal Nafusa*. Both destroyers were conducting standard beam-to-beam searches. They were still undetected.

Everyone stared at Hasse. Now the success or failure of their attack, their very lives, depended on this young man and his machine. The ensign's eyes were glued on the TDC, waiting for the red glow of the "F" indicating a solution to appear on the grid face of the elliptical distance-to-track indicator.

"Sir," came up from the control room. "The bottom's shoaled to twenty fathoms."

"You're sure?"

"Yes, sir."

"Shit!" They had only one hundred twenty feet of water under them. They would catch hell if they sank the tanker. But there would be no hesitation. The training, the lives of every man on board had been directed and dedicated to this one, supreme moment. This was why *Blackfin* existed. They were part of her, part of her destiny, and they could be part of her death.

Hasse's voice electrified every man in the attack team. "I have a solution light. You can fire anytime, Captain."

"Shoot!" the captain shouted, snapping the periscope handles up as a signal for the periscope to be lowered.

Cadenbach reached up to the firing panel, where six windows glowed red. He turned the switch of Number One torpedo tube to on.

"Fire!" Hasse shouted.

Cadenbach pushed the firing key with the palm of his hand. Compressed air blasted, jolting the boat, and the whine of the 3500-pound torpedo leaving the boat could be heard clearly on the sonar loudspeaker.

"One fired electrically," Davidson reported.

Hasse made an adjustment to the angle solver with his right hand while staring at a stopwatch held in his left hand. Six seconds later he shouted, "Fire two!"

Cadenbach palmed the firing key and the boat shook again. Four more times the command was given until all of the forward tubes had been fired. The sounds of the torpedoes' tiny high-speed propellers hummed through the speaker like a swarm of departing mosquitoes.

Williams stared at Hasse. "Torpedo run?"

"Two-one-zero-zero."

"About a minute and twenty seconds," Williams said to himself. Then more commands: "Left full rudder, all ahead emergency. Steady up on one-eight-zero." They needed the open sea, where they would have more water under their keel.

"All fish running hot, straight and normal," Crog reported. Then he shouted in alarm, "Sir! The can in the entrance is getting under way, and the closest of the other two is turning hard this way."

"Up 'scope!" At nine knots, water splashed up and over the periscope head, running down the lens. But Reginald felt a stab of horror as he saw one destroyer turning away from the tanker and accelerating to flank speed toward him while the other in the entrance was digging her stern into the sea, coming up to speed.

At that instant, a flash like a nuclear detonation filled the lens. Then another and another as the *Jabal Nafusa* was blown to pieces by torpedoes and her own explosive cargo. Great booming sounds filled the boat, and the hull plates vibrated like a tuning fork. Cheers filled the boat. It was impossible to tell how many torpedoes hit, and it was unnecessary. Tank after tank exploded, burning high-test gasoline spreading in vast pools around the burning ship. Burning crewmen could be seen jumping into the hellfire around them. No one would ever escape the holocaust.

"Down 'scope!" Williams knew he should send the coded message reporting the successful attack, but with two destroyers bearing down on him, there was no time. He shouted down the hatch, "Emergency! Take her down to one hundred feet and rig for depth charge." There was a *whoosh* of released air up the hatch from the control room as the diving team flooded the "Down Express" negative tank with hundreds of tons of water. Williams could hear the sounds of slamming watertight doors and bulkhead ventilating valves throughout the submarine. Crawling slowly, the bubble of the inclinometer, which was mounted beneath the depth gauge, moved until it showed a down angle of 15 degrees.

The speaker was transmitting a cacophony of sounds, most deadly: the "ping" of sonar gear dopplering up as the two destroyers closed in; the whirling, thrashing sounds of the *Gearings'* speeding propellers; the hissing of steam and the whine of high-speed turbines; the wrenching, screeching sounds of tortured metal as bulkheads gave way in the sinking tanker.

"Depth under keel?"

"Forty fathoms, sir."

"Good! Take her down to two hundred feet."

The sounds of the destroyers filled the boat. They were going to cross at right angles above *Blackfin;* one, perhaps, a half-mile before the other, so that the second would be well clear of the depth charges of the first. The first set of propeller beats suddenly dropped in frequency. Crog glanced overhead. " 'Down Doppler.' He's passed overhead," he reported. Then he stiffened and hunched forward. "Depth charges in the water," he said calmly, sliding the earphone from his ear.

"Turn off the speaker!"

Every man looked up as one set of screws faded and the other grew. They were going to be caught in a hailstorm of six-hundred-pound charges. Then the click of a hydrostatic detonator collapsing in the hollow core of a depth charge could be heard clearly. A stupefying blast shattered the depths, and every man grabbed his ears. Dust rose, and bits of cork packing rained. There was a hissing, swishing sound of thousands of bubbles as if someone were sweeping down the the hull with a stiff-bristled broom. Then three clicks and three more charges exploded almost simultaneously. The boat swayed and rolled, hull plates bending and groaning with the strain. Men held their heads, rocked, and made deep, frightened sounds. It was like being inside an empty oil drum and having a giant trying to beat his way through with a sledge hammer.

Another blast, much closer than the others, struck *Blackfin* like a battering ram. Jarred and whipped by the concussion, the boat lurched thirty degrees to port. There were shouts of panic and confusion. Cadenbach was thrown to the deck. The CRT of the radar set burst, showering Goroku Kumanao with razor-sharp slivers of glass. He screamed, grabbed his face, and fell on top of Cadenbach, blood streaming through his fingers.

Williams shouted down the hatch, "Take her down to the bottom."

"It's coral."

"I don't give a shit. Take her down."

Williams turned to Randy Davidson, "Get a medical orderly up here!"

"My lines are dead."

At that moment, the second set of screws passed over. Everyone looked up, as if searching for his executioner. Four more tremendous blasts hammered down the stern and forced the bow up. Two more explosions beneath the bow flung the boat up almost vertically. Bedlam. Screams of pain and horror as every man in the conning tower was hurled into the aft convex end. Williams tried to hang onto the periscope shaft, but his hands slipped on the oiled surface. He fell on top of Crog and Hasse just as the lights went out.

"Emergency lights!" he shouted.

One man in the heap managed to reach the switch of the waterproof emergency lights. A feeble red glow filled the compartment. Then something horrible struck the bow, rolled, and clattered down the deck. A charge was actually rolling down the deck plates toward the bridge. It slid along the side of the bridge, and every man held his breath. A cataclysmic burst hit just between the conning tower and the pressure hull. Bodies were hurled up and then back down again. Water jetted in like a Niagara, the small compartment almost blown from the pressure hull. Davidson and Sturgis crashed down on top of Williams. The big black thrashed, tried to scream. But he could only gag as his lungs filled with water.

Two more charges blew the cover from the main induction valve and hundreds of tons of water poured through ruptured plates, driving *Blackfin* into the black depths. Those who were killed immediately were fortunate, the survivors of the explosions writhing and drowning in their own blood as the pressure soared in the flooding compartments and the air superheated, roasting lungs.

Stern first, the boat hit the coral bottom, settled slowly, and then rolled over onto her starboard side on the coral bed. Bubbles of air and gouts of oil streamed upward. But all was silent, as silent as a tomb.

Just after a PBM reported one enemy carrier sunk and another damaged, *Yonaga* made contact with the enemy air groups. The cheering and shouts of *"Banzai!"* ceased abruptly.

"Radar reports many enemy aircraft closing from the south and southeast. Range one hundred kilometers," Seaman Naoyuki reported to Admiral Fujita, who had been on the flag bridge the entire day.

"Very well," Admiral Fujita said, raising his binoculars. Flanking the admiral, with their helmets pulled down and strapped, Rear Admiral Whitehead and Colonel Bernstein stared through their own glasses.

A shout from a lookout on the foretop, "Many aircraft bearing zero-three-zero, elevation angle twenty."

Whitehead shifted his search and found them. A flock of insects winging toward them. He had been sunk five times. Would this be his sixth? This couldn't be happening. How in the world did he ever get himself into this crazy situation? An American rear admiral on the bridge of a Japanese carrier fighting Arabs. Like all men committed to combat, he felt helpless, the victim of other men's decisions made in faraway places. Faceless men, perhaps on the whim of injured pride or vanity, had unleashed the forces that drew him inexorably to a face-to-face showdown with death. He had never been able to adjust to that feeling.

Fujita shouted into the voice tube: "Break radio silence. CAP intercept raid approaching from the south. Flagship to escorts: assume AA stations. New course zero-nine-zero, speed thirty-two."

For a long moment there was silence as dozens of pairs of binoculars studied the southern horizon. Now Whitehead could see the unmistakable form of the JU 87s: gull-winged, spatted wheels, and he could even see the huge bombs slung beneath their fuselages. And old North American AT-6 "Texan" advanced trainers could be seen: Pratt and Whitney radial engine, high "greenhouse" canopy for the two man crew, retracted landing gear. They flew low on the water with torpedoes hanging from their crutches. And above the bombers, a screen of ME 109 fighters.

"All escorts answer," came up the tube.

"Very well. All ahead flank, left full rudder, steady up on zero-nine-zero."

Whitehead felt the plates beneath his feet vibrate with new intensity as the four great engines strained to deliver all of their power to the drive shafts. The carrier heeled and turned to the east, uncovering her entire starboard AA battery to the approaching aircraft. All seven destroyers raced in, taking stations within five hundred meters of *Yonaga:* Fite leading, three *Fletchers* to starboard and three to port.

Whitehead caught a flash of white high in the sky as twelve Zeros of the CAP raced in to intercept—the remaining three were struck below for one defect or another. The first Stuka spiraled down in flames, followed by four AT-6s. Then the Messerschmitts poured down and the dogfight forced the CAP to abandon the attack on the bombers.

Whitehead turned to Admiral Fujita. "I count only twelve enemy fighters, Admiral. They must have left most of them with their carriers."

"One squadron. Foolish." He turned to the talker, "All guns that bear, stand by to open fire." The command was unnecessary. Hundreds of barrels were cranked up, and trainers and pointer were already tracking the approaching aircraft.

The dogfight tumbled across the sky and veered off to the west. The enemy must have kept his best pilots with his carriers. The single squadron of fighters trying to protect the bombers seemed poorly led, and the pilots were definitely second rate. Within minutes the superb Zero pilots shot down half the fighters with only the loss of one of their own. The surviving MEs fled to the south. But the distraction had freed the bombers for their runs.

Whitehead counted twenty-two torpedo bombers and thirty-three Stukas. He said to Admiral Fujita, "They must've overloaded their air groups with fighters. Two fleet carriers should be able to launch more bombers than this." He waved to the south.

Fujita's smirk was filled with irony. "If we do not stop them, this may be quite enough, Admiral Whitehead."

Naoyuki turned to Admiral Fujita, "Fire control reports enemy in range, sir."

"Batteries one and three, engage the dive bombers. Batteries five and seven, engage torpedo bombers. Main battery, commence firing. Commence! Commence!"

Thunder boomed and lightning flashed as sixteen 5-inch guns fired as one. Every man on the bridge grabbed his ears as the cannons blasted out a steady barrage of twenty rounds per gun per minute. Whitehead almost gagged on the sharp smell of cordite, brown smoke billowing up and enveloping the bridge before being whipped away by the stiff breeze. Six of the torpedo bombers were plucked from the sky, crashing into the water, skipping, tumbling, disintegrating. And the Zeros whirled, five of them racing in after the "Texans" while the remaining six shot upward after the dive bombers, their 2000-horsepower Sakae 42 engines giving them incredible climbing power.

Four destroyers had opened fire with their five-inch guns. The slow AT-6s dropped down close to the water. Now the *Fletchers* were firing with their automatic weapons. The torpedo bombers were excellent targets. Slow, lumbering. Ignoring their own AA fire, five Zeros raced in behind the torpedo bombers while the old trainers charged into the jaws of flaming hell. Two more exploded, the Zeros savagely tore in on the tails of the aircraft which had formed a ragged line, converging on the carrier. The rear gunners fired back at their tormentors with single 7.7-millimeter guns. They were hopelessly outgunned. Cannon shells and machine gun bullets sent three more of the North Americans crashing into the sea. But the survivors passed over the line of escorts and bore on toward *Yonaga*. These men were made of much sterner stuff than the inept fighter pilots. Whitehead counted ten survivors.

Fujita stabbed a finger upward where the Stukas were wheeling in preparation to dive. The sound of their engines deepened as pilots set their propellers at full coarse, their hinged dive brakes were down, and they had formed a single line. "Well-coordinated attack," he said. But the Stukas were also taking heavy casualties. They seemed to be floundering in a sea of ugly, blackbooming flowers. Half of them had been shot down and the Zeros zoomed up under their fuselages where they were blind and shot down five more in their first pass. But the fighters and the AA would never stop them all and every man in the fleet knew it.

Whitehead felt an old familiar fear clutch at his

throat. He had known this strange, tingling coldness many years before. He had survived the horror of those five ghastly sinkings. Now, perhaps, he had tempted fate once too often. He stared at the torpedo bombers—only six were in the air now. They were close, splashes leaping up all around, tracers streaking by, Zeros still in pursuit. But they formed their line, came on as a single unit, and at only 800 meters, dropped their torpedoes. One plunged into the sea behind its weapon.

"Right full rudder!" Fujita screamed.

The great carrier turned sharply, heeling to port. The first three torpedoes passed ahead, another with a defective gyro leaped from the sea like a great fish and turned away crazily. But the last two did not miss.

Yonaga fairly leaped and boomed with agony as a tremendous one-two punch of high explosives caught her amidships on the starboard side. Fujita came off his feet, binoculars flying up over his head with the force of the blasts which came so quickly that they seemed to blend into each other. Wrapping one arm around a stanchion, Whitehead grabbed the little admiral and held him steady. The bearing ring flew off the gyro repeater and sailed out over the flight deck, and the tiny chart table broke its deck bolts and crashed down onto the deck, drafting machine, parallel rules, pencils and dividers flying.

Two AT-6s crashed into the sea, one veered off *Yonaga*'s bow where Fite shot it down, another zoomed off toward the carrier's stern, and the last actually flew over the ship. Looking up, Whitehead felt he could almost touch the oil-streaked bottom of the fuselage: The roar of the 600-horsepower radial engine barked down at him, and he could see flames shooting out of the exhaust ports of the collector rings. Twenty-five-millimeter guns in the foretop ripped off the cowling, shot off the greenhouse, and the plane skidded across the sky, its starboard elevator blown away. Then its wing folded up at the root, flew free, spilling hydraulic fluid like blood, and the big plane barely cleared *Yonaga*'s stack as it tumbled wildly into the sea, sending up a column of blue water and white spray. The wreck floated for a few seconds and then the weight of the big Pratt and Whitney engine dragged it under like an anchor.

Whitehead felt the deck move under his feet. They were listing. "Are you going to reduce speed?" he shouted into Fujita's ear.

The little admiral stabbed a finger upward at the Stukas, which were peeling off. "We cannot."

Showing unbelievable calm, the old man shouted down the tube, "Left full rudder and circle left until I change the order."

"F6Fs!" Bernstein shouted.

"Impossible!" Whitehead said. But they were there, six of the magnificent fighters. They joined the Zeros and tore into the Stukas.

"I can't believe this," Bernstein cried.

But Whitehead understood. "They're returning from our attack—they have great range and carry four hundred rounds of ammunition for each gun. That's forty seconds of fire power." He waved. "Obviously, they have some left for the dive bombers."

The Mitsubishis and the Grummans ripped into the Stukas like hawks after pigeons. At once, five of the Arab aircraft spun, tumbled, and burned, streaking for the sea and vanishing in geysers of water. But three were diving on *Yonaga,* and then two more winged over into dives despite the fighters. The big Jumo engines shrieked, the aircraft grew, *Yonaga* circled, AA guns fired, tracers webbed the sky.

Whitehead stood hypnotized. His fingers were suddenly numb, and his binoculars dropped to his waist. He had experienced every kind of engagement, every kind of attack. Nothing was as horrifying as a dive bomber screaming down on you. *No place to hide,* he said to himself as he had many times decades before. He choked back the fear, set a brave, hard-jawed expression on his face and raised his binoculars. No one, absolutely no one would know how scared he really was.

The first plane was so low he could clearly see the pilot's goggled face peering through his sight. He released his single 500-kilogram bomb and pulled up directly into the six streams of 50-caliber slugs fired by a pursuing Hellcat. The great slugs ripped the bomber and blew off the pilot's head. The big plane twisted across the sky like a mallard blasted by buckshot and gyrated into the sea, smoking and shedding aluminum skin in sheets.

The big black bomb shrieked down. Convinced as all men were who had ever been under dive-bombing attack, Whitehead knew that bomb was plunging down directly on him. He gritted his teeth until his jaws ached, gripped his binoculars so tight the bones of his knuckles showed through the skin like snow-white knobs. His bladder was suddenly dangerously full. The bomb struck just off the starboard bow, jolting the ship with the power of the near-miss. Blue water and spray drenched some of the gun crews.

Two more Stukas howled down, bombs swinging free beneath their propellers by their crutches. The first missed, too, shooting a tower of water 200 feet in the air just off the port beam. The second did not miss. There was a booming sound like a rifle shot in an empty boiler, ripping tortured metal. The great ship shook and trembled, and two 5-inch guns and four or five 25-millimeter mounts exploded skyward from the bow along with a dozen bodies. A bomb had hit directly in a gallery on the starboard bow. Flames and acrid smoke poured over the bridge.

"Flood Number One and Number Three magazines!" Fujita shouted at Naoyuki. "And I want a damage report." He looked around at the sky. A few enemy planes were fleeing toward the south with F6Fs and Zeros in pursuit. There was no threat. He shouted down the tube, "Rudder amidships, let her swing to one-eight-zero and steady up. All ahead standard. Relay the changes to the escorts by bridge-to-bridge."

Immediately the pulse of the engines slowed and the great carrier swung to her left until the course was finally found and she was held steady on a southerly heading. A new, ominous whistling sound could be heard throughout the ship: the sound of escaping air. The high-pitched sound came from pipes, leaky gaskets around watertight doors, ventilation ducts and electric cables passing through bulkheads. To the experienced seaman, these were serious danger signals: air was being vented by the pressure of water entering the ship from the torpedo hits.

Fujita shouted anxiously at Naoyuki, "Tell the chief engineer I am waiting for a damage report!" He punched the windscreen with a tiny fist. "Expedite! Expedite!"

"Sir," Naoyuki said. "Chief Engineer Yoshida suggests you reduce speed. There is serious flooding on the starboard side."

"Sacred Buddha. *Yonaga* should take two torpedoes like mosquito bites." He shouted down the tube, "All ahead slow."

Bernstein said to Fujita, "Those were unusually powerful warheads, Admiral. They must be using Semtex."

Before Fujita could answer, Naoyuki said, "Chief Engineer Yoshida reports two hits on the starboard side between frames one-one-eight and one-zero-nine. Both hydraulic machinery rooms on the starboard side are flooded, and there is water in the starboard compressor

375

room. The starboard ready oil tank is ruptured, and we have some water in Number Two damage-control station. At least one H beam has been driven through the bulkhead between Number Three and Number One boiler rooms. The boiler rooms are flooding, and there are leaks in the outboard bulkheads of Number Three fire room. He is shoring the fireroom bulkheads, and it appears the flooding can be contained in the machinery rooms and the boiler rooms. But there is saltwater in the freshwater lines in Engine Room Three. Casualties are heavy. Every man on watch in Number Three boiler room was killed, and most of those in Number One boiler room are casualties."

Fujita was grim. The list had increased to about seven degrees. He shouted at Naoyuki, "Tell the chief engineer to counterflood with fuel tanks two and four. They are empty. And he is to pump from the bilges in the Number Three engine room to the bilges in a port engine room until we are on an even keel. We can not have this list when our air groups land."

"Returning aircraft!" was shouted from the foretop.

"Our air groups." Every man on the bridge raised his glasses.

"There are so few," Whitehead whispered.

Bernstein spoke grimly. "Eleven Zeros, seven Aichis, and five Nakajimas."

"Can't be—can't be," Whitehead groaned.

The returning aircraft joined the CAP, and all of the aircraft began to circle *Yonaga* counterclockwise. Red flares indicating casualties were fired from four bombers.

"Sir," Naoyuki said "the chief engineer reports all bulkheads holding, bilge pumps are reducing the flooding in Number Three fire room."

Fujita nodded, then muttered, "Very well." The frightening sound of escaping air had ceased, and the list had decreased. Everyone relaxed.

A backfire high overhead turned every head up. All of the aircraft were low on fuel.

The old admiral glanced at the ensign. The wind was from the northeast. He shouted orders down the tube, and the carrier swung into the wind. "Two block Pennant Two. Stand by to receive aircraft," he said to the talker.

The first Nakajima with a huge hole in her wing and with a dead gunner approached the stern, hook extended.

An hour later, *Yonaga* had recovered her decimated air groups and cut a new course for Tokyo Bay. Shipping ten thousand tons of water by flooding and counterflooding, she steamed four feet lower in the water. Still, with over one thousand watertight compartments and a superb damage-control party working like madmen, she could make twelve knots safely. Her seven escorts hovered close, like concerned courtiers tending their wounded queen.

A quick, limited staff meeting was held in Flag Plot. Chief Engineer Lieutenant Tatsuya Yoshida did not attend; he was busy in the bowels of the ship. The damage had been controlled, and the flooding was being gradually reduced. Along with the rest of the staff, Commander Yoshi Matsuhara, Captain Colin Willard-Smith, Lieutenant Brent Ross and Commander Takuya Iwata were all there. The flyers had shed their heavy, fur-lined jackets and helmets, but were still in their flight clothes. All were filthy, exhaust and gunpowder streaking their faces and outlining the shape of their goggles as if they had been spray-painted.

Numbed by shock, Brent had to force himself to concentrate on the voices that droned on, itemizing the casualities, cloaking the horrors of their losses in the camouflage of cold, impersonal statistics. Their air groups had been virtually wiped out. A few more stragglers had managed to find the carrier, but the tally of returning air groups was appalling; thirteen Zeros, one Seafire, six Hellcats, eight dive bombers, and seven torpedo bombers, a total of 28 survivors out of a proud fleet of 138 warplanes that had departed. And *Yonaga* was gravely injured, but not in danger of sinking. One hundred twenty-four of her crewmen were known dead, and 173 were wounded.

But the enemy's losses had been catastrophic. The carrier *Ramli al Kabir* had been sunk and *Al Kufra* seriously damaged. Most of the enemy's aircraft had been destroyed.

"*Blackfin? Blackfin?*" Admiral Brent said, leaning over the table anxiously.

The old man's face was grim. "There have been reports by some of our native observers of an enormous explosion just off the southern entrance of Tomonuto. And we have further verification by intercepted plain language transmission from enemy destroyers which indicated rescue operations were underway and a great vessel must have been sunk."

Brent pounded the table with a closed fist. "Then the old linebacker scored." He turned to Matsuhara. "I knew he had it in him." The expression on Fujita's face squelched his levity. "They're okay?"

Fujita shook his head. "*Blackfin* did not transmit the prearranged signal. It has been five hours since the reports."

"Maybe his radios are out."

Fujita shook his head. "No. The transmissions from the Arab destroyers indicated a submarine definitely sunk with all hands. They claim they have picked up wreckage and two bodies."

"Oh, no. No! Not all those guys."

"Many good men have joined their ancestors this day, Mister Ross."

Brent stared down at the table as the meeting was dismissed. However, the admiral held the flyers. After the last officer left, the little admiral said to the aviators in a rare generous mood, "You did a splendid job. With a carrier sunk, another badly damaged, air groups destroyed, and his fuel supply destroyed, the enemy has been dealt a crippling blow."

"Admiral," Matsuhara said. "We met too many fighters over the enemy task force. I believe some of his fighters must have come from the Marianas."

The old man nodded agreement.

Iwata spoke up. "But we engaged the enemy at least five hundred kilometers from the Marianas—too far for Messerschmitts."

"True, Commander," the admiral said. "But with his new Daimler Benz *Valkyrie* engine, he should be able to increase his tankage and even use drop tanks." He gestured at the air group commander. "I believe Commander Matsuhara is right."

"We must clean out that nest of vermin, Admiral," Matsuhara said. *"Yonaga*—Japan will never be safe until we take those islands."

"True, Commander. And do not forget the poison gas plant at Rabta. There is much work to do."

The phone rang, and the admiral put the receiver to his ear. He smiled and replaced the instrument. He looked at Captain Colin Willard-Smith. "Air-sea rescue has been busy over the scene of your engagement. Thus far twenty-nine airmen have been recovered." He held Willard-Smith with his eyes. "One of our PBYs picked up a very angry Cockney."

The Englishman came half out of his chair, mouth agape, eyes wide. "Why, that tough little bugger! I knew

379

they couldn't kill him." His voice shook and he sat heavily, his cold British aplomb finally pierced. Brent grabbed one of his arms and Yoshi Matsuhara the other. They shook him and laughed with delight. Willard-Smith stared down at the table not daring to look up. Someone might see the moisture that had pooled in his eyes.

Fujita spoke gently, almost tenderly, "I congratulate you on a job well done. You need rest." He stood slowly and clapped twice. Everyone rose and faced the paulownia shrine. "Oh Amaterasu," the old man said. "We thank you for your aid, your guidance, and ask you to lead the spirits of our heroic dead through the gates of the Yasakuni Shrine or into the heaven they seek." He placed his hand on the *Hagakure* and quoted it, "It is a cleansing act to give one's life for the Mikado. For a man who will cut off his life for the sake of righteousness, there is no need to exhort, to implore divine intervention. All the gods of heaven will protect him."

He looked at his men for a long silent moment. "You are dismissed."

The men filed through the doorway. Iwata stopped Brent in the passageway just outside the door. Yoshi stood close by. "You did a good job, Mister Ross," the bomber commander said.

"Thank you, Commander."

"We've had our differences."

"True," Brent answered. Brent was fatigued, and his senses had been deadened by the loss of so many close friends, yet he felt his back stiffen. He expected the usual samurai enduring spirit of vengeance and remembrance of past humiliations to surface even in this atmosphere of terrible loss and costly victory. Williams' death, the loss of the entire crew of *Blackfin* and the slaughter of over a hundred pilots and air crewmen

380

weighed heavily, as if a great burden had been placed on his shoulders and was crushing him down with its weight. He was ready to lash out violently at anyone or anything. He was taken by surprise. Iwata silently extended his hand.

For a long moment, Brent stood motionless with his arms at his sides like deadwood and stared at the hand. Then, slowly, he raised his and grasped the big palm. Iwata stared unblinking into his eyes, dropped his hand, whirled, and walked down the passageway. Brent felt Yoshi's hand on his back.

"Come on, American Samurai. I've got a bottle of Chivas Regal in my cabin."

Silently, Brent followed the pilot through the door of the cabin. Yoshi pulled the bottle and two glass tumblers from a cabinet and collapsed in a chair opposite the American. He filled the tumblers. The men touched glasses and Yoshi said, "To our dead."

The glasses were drained and quickly recharged. It took another drink before Brent felt the slow relaxation of muscles begin. Sipping his third drink, he stared across the table at his friend. "We lost too many good men today, Yoshi-san," he said.

The Japanese took a big swallow, poured more scotch into both glasses. He spoke softly but with conviction. "Evil triumphs when good men do nothing. When madmen run loose, Brent-san, good men must fight."

"And give up their lives?"

"You saw, Brent-san."

"Our losses will be replaced?"

"Why, of course. You know that, Brent-san. They always are."

"They died horribly—especially those on *Blackfin*. And Kai finally kept his date with *Bon Homme Richard*."

"They died with glory—every one of them."

"With glory? *Blackfin?*" The American stabbed finer downward. "Like rats! Rats! You call that glorious?"

"Yes." Yoshi studied his friend intently, searching for some words that could console—might restore the lieutenant's spirits. A sudden thought widened his eyes and brought the trace of a grin to his face. "You have read Lord Tennyson?"

"A little."

Yoshi swirled the amber liquid with tiny circular motions. "Tennyson said, 'The path of duty is the way to glory.' "

Brent looked hard into the black eyes staring back at him across the table. He emptied his glass and slammed it down on the table. "You know something, Yoshi-san?

"What?"

"Alfred Lord Tennyson was full of shit."

THE FINEST IN SUSPENSE!

THE URSA ULTIMATUM (2310, $3.95)
by Terry Baxter

In the dead of night, twelve nuclear warheads are smuggled north across the Mexican border to be detonated simultaneously in major cities throughout the U.S. And only a small-town desert lawman stands between a face-less Russian superspy and World War Three!

THE LAST ASSASSIN (1989, $3.95)
by Daniel Easterman

From New York City to the Middle East, the devastating flames of revolution and terrorism sweep across a world gone mad . . . as the most terrifying conspiracy in the history of mankind is born!

FLOWERS FROM BERLIN (2060, $4.50)
by Noel Hynd

With the Earth on the brink of World War Two, the Third Reich's deadliest professional killer is dispatched on the most heinous assignment of his murderous career: the assassination of Franklin Delano Roosevelt!

THE BIG NEEDLE (2776, $3.50)
by Ken Follett

All across Europe, innocent people are being terrorized, homes are destroyed, and dead bodies have become an unnervingly common sight. And the horrors will continue until the most powerful organization on Earth finds Chadwell Carstairs — and kills him!

Available wherever paperbacks are sold, or order direct from the Publisher. Send cover price plus 50¢ per copy for mailing and handling to Zebra Books, Dept. 3213, 475 Park Avenue South, New York, N.Y. 10016. Residents of New York, New Jersey and Pennsylvania must include sales tax. DO NOT SEND CASH.

THRILLERS BY WILLIAM W. JOHNSTONE

THE DEVIL'S CAT   (2091, $3.95)

The town was alive with all kinds of cats. Black, white, fat, scrawny. They lived in the streets, in backyards, in the swamps of Becancour. Sam, Nydia, and Little Sam had never seen so many cats. The cats' eyes were glowing slits as they watched the newcomers. The town was ripe with evil. It seemed to waft in from the swamps with the hot, fetid breeze and breed in the minds of Becancour's citizens. Soon Sam, Nydia, and Little Sam would battle the forces of darkness. Standing alone against the ultimate predator—The Devil's Cat.

THE DEVIL'S HEART   (2110, $3.95)

Now it was summer again in Whitfield. The town was peaceful, quiet, and unprepared for the atrocities to come. Eternal life, everlasting youth, an orgy that would span time—that was what the Lord of Darkness was promising the coven members in return for their pledge of love. The few who had fought against his hideous powers before, believed it could never happen again. Then the hot wind began to blow—as black as evil as The Devil's Heart.

THE DEVIL'S TOUCH   (2111, $3.95)

Once the carnage begins, there's no time for anything but terror. Hollow-eyed, hungry corpses rise from unearthly tombs to gorge themselves on living flesh and spawn a new generation of restless Undead. The demons of Hell cavort with Satan's unholy disciples in blood-soaked rituals and fevered orgies. The Balons have faced the red, glowing eyes of the Master before, and they know what must be done. But there can be no salvation for those marked by The Devil's Touch.

Available wherever paperbacks are sold, or order direct from the Publisher. Send cover price plus 50¢ per copy for mailing and handling to Zebra Books, Dept. 3213, 475 Park Avenue South, New York, N.Y. 10016. Residents of New York, New Jersey and Pennsylvania must include sales tax. DO NOT SEND CASH.